LAGNIAPPE

Lagniappe
The Destiny, Arkansas, Series
Book One

K.D. McLemore

First edition October 2025

Book Cover and Design copyright © 2025 Randi Gammons

Library of Congress Control Number Data 2025918294
K.D. McLemore
Lagniappe / McLemore K.D.
[Black and White – Fiction / Mystery & Detective General, Fiction / Thrillers / General, Fiction / Crime
Thema: Crime and / or Mystery Fiction, Thriller / Suspense Fiction

ISBN 979-8-9987001-8-7 (paperback)
ISBN 979-8-9987001-9-4 (eBook)

Published by CS Publishing
Marshall, TX 75670
www.countryspunk.com

Dedication

To my wife, Carolyn, who gave up the time for me to write.

Table of Contents

CHAPTER ONE
ALWAYS FAITHFUL

Since Brock Beckett witnessed his sister plunge into oblivion from the World Trade Center South Tower on 9/11, he hasn't taught high school literature in 20 years. Beckett wheeled his Jeep Cherokee into the Destiny Public Schools campus parking lot. He sat there for a long moment considering his options; this was, after all, only an interview. Was he prepared for a new life in the middle of nowhere in Arkansas?

"Who am I kidding?"

Beckett jammed the stick shift into reverse to back away from the parking space; then, he noticed her. She couldn't have been more than 16, but she was gorgeous. More importantly, she was the living image of someone Beckett knew in a different lifetime. Auburn-haired with an auricular face, she was lithe, leggy and lean with taut musculature, yet with an innocent grace. Beckett killed the engine and sat silently. He watched her anxiously gaze from the school entrance into the rain. Finally, he decided she wasn't waiting for someone.

Beckett pushed open the passenger door and honked the Jeep's horn. The girl jerked about with a start and immediately stared warily at the vehicle with its passenger door ajar. Beckett tapped the horn again. This time, the girl waited to see someone else appear but, finding no-one, she turned back toward the Jeep, cocked her full mane of auburn hair to one side and with a questioning regard pointed a finger at herself.

"Come on," Beckett shouted encouragingly. "I'll drive you."

"I don't know you from Adam," the girl said. "You might be a pervert."

Beckett swallowed hard. "No… but I might be your father," he replied.

The girl quailed, the remark awakening something profound in her expression. "Why am I supposed to call you Daddy?" she asked caustically. "My father is the mayor of this town."

Beckett climbed out of the Jeep and lumbered toward the school entrance. The girl backed away as he approached, and she reached for the front door handle to retreat inside the building.

"Your mother and I named you Cecelia Beckett when you were born at Little Creek, Virginia," Beckett replied. "I was in the Marine Corps when you were born; that was two years before your mother died, and you disappeared. I didn't know you were alive until two years ago, when I found out you have a new family, Cissy Nelson."

Beckett shook away the rain from his salt and pepper hair as he ducked beneath the entry awning. He stood there silently, his boyish features and steel blue eyes belying Cissy's impact on a visibly shaken 6-foot 5-inch, 190-pound man. Beckett sighed wearily and smiled weakly as he offered Cissy his hand.

"I'm Brock Beckett… your birth father," he said quietly.

Cissy did not reciprocate, and she kept her distance. "Wait, how do you know my mother died?" she asked defensively.

"I was told by The Pentagon that your mother, Jolene, died. But I found out the truth about you when I finally got back to the States after we pulled out of Afghanistan," Beckett said.

"How did my mother die?" Cissy shot back.

"You were never told; am I right?" Beckett said matter-of-factly. "You don't know anything other than she died and another family adopted you. The truth is Jolene was killed in a car crash after she recovered from cancer, and your adoptive parents weren't told anything."

"You're scaring me," Cissy murmured. "Please leave."

"I can't," Beckett said. "I'm supposed to interview for a teaching job in ten minutes."

"Like, seriously?"

"Seriously," Beckett said. He reached into his pocket and produced his Jeep keys. "Do you have a driver's license?"

"Why?" Cissy asked skeptically. "You wanna make sure you got the right girl? Everybody in Destiny knows me…"

"No, I'm certain enough of your identity," Beckett said. "But, if you can legally drive, take my keys and drive yourself home. Then, meet me at that little café down the street at about four-thirty. Bring whoever you want with you; your adoptive dad… even the cops. I can prove I'm your father. I want the opportunity."

"What if I don't bring back your Jeep?" Cissy teased as he pressed the keys into her hand.

"Call it collateral against the truth," Beckett whispered.

She took his measure again; his eyes were sad, but honest. "Oookay," Cissy replied. "The Blue Bird Café at four-thirty. And I can bring the whole football team if I want?"

"Sure," Beckett said. "If everything goes well, I expect to teach them American and English literature on Monday."

Cissy giggled and tossed Beckett his keys. "Nope, not happening," she murmured with a breathlessness that reminded Beckett of her mother.

"Lord, you're so much like Jolene," he whispered.

The rain abated, and Cissy quickly brushed past Beckett, then, she stopping short turned back with a long, studied gaze, as though she was deciding something… important. Cissy offered Beckett a small, shy smile; then, she turned and hurried across the street toward the Destiny City Hall building.

Beckett sighed. "Probably going to report the pervert to the cops."

The interview with Destiny School Superintendent Raymond Bittle was typical to a point. That was when Beckett decided whether he genuinely wanted the job and wanted any opportunity to know the girl he was convinced was his daughter. He gutted it up.

"No, sir, I haven't taught in almost twenty years because I've been in the military," Beckett explained. "Deep… in the military."

Bittle, a smallish, slender man with a professorial look, was impressed and slightly unnerved. "Can you elaborate on that, Mister Beckett?" he asked.

"Very little," Beckett replied. "Let's just say while I was teaching, I was motivated by the events of Nine-eleven and the loss of a loved one. I've traveled to many places on and off the map, and I haven't been back in the classroom."

"Uhm, classified, I take it?" Bittle asked.

Beckett smiled engagingly. "I'd have to kill you."

Bittle laughed which surprised Beckett. He was beginning to like the little guy.

"I'll level with you, Mister Bittle," he said. "There are two reasons I want this job: One, I want to settle down in someplace small, out of the way, and comfortable. And, two, I met a young girl a few minutes ago; red-head, named Cissy, whom I believe to be my daughter."

Bittle was agog. "Cissy Nelson is your daughter?"

"That is my belief," Beckett said. "And, if it's true, I want to get to know her. I'm not here to make trouble, mind you, but it compels me to do whatever is necessary to get this job. So, don't expect any theatrics from me about it."

Bittle smiled. "Commendable of you, Mister Beckett. I assure you that Mayor Nelson and his wife won't give up custody without a fight."

"Not intending to put up a fight or seek custody," Beckett replied. "I simply want to tell Cissy my story, learn her story, and teach junior and senior American and English literature."

"You strike me as being benignly clever… like Jett Rink," Bittle said.

"There was nothing benign about Edna Ferber's antagonist in *Giant*," Beckett said with a grin. "Jett stalked Leslie Benedict as surely as he intended to be a thorn in Bick Benedict's side when he staked his claim in the middle of Reata after Bick's sister died. Jett Rink forced Bick Benedict to face the reality of change.

"Have you seen the King Ranch, Mister Bittle?" Beckett asked. "It goes on forever across a giant swath of South Texas. Captain Richard King built the ranch, but oil brought it into the Twentieth Century. Bick Benedict owned the grass and the ground of Reata, but Jett Rink changed its soul, once he acquired the mineral rights. I'm not making a claim against the soul of Destiny, Arkansas, or to the custody of my daughter."

Bittle chuckled, stood and offered Beckett his hand. "Fair enough, Mister Beckett," he said. "The contract is yours, pending the school board's approval. But mind you, Mayor Nelson sits on the school board. His family is well-respected in Ouachita County."

"Roger that, sir," Beckett said as they shook hands.

Moments later, Beckett pushed through the double doors at the main entrance and into a rain-cleansed daylight. He glanced at his Jeep in the parking lot, then peered down the street bisecting the small business district and spotted the faded but discernable blue bird on the sign outside The Blue Bird Café. Beckett decided to walk to his meeting with Cissy Nelson. She refused the offer of his Jeep, so would she come to meet him again? Common sense argued against it but Jolene often defied common sense.

Beckett took stock of the milieu along Center Street in front of the campus, the Snappy Mart convenience store across the street, the town hall and volunteer fire department beyond on Nelson Street, the Veterans' Memorial Park and the Friday afternoon bustle at the South Arkansas Bank.

"The small-town basics," Beckett mused as he walked the street and turned into the Blue Bird Café.

The animated buzz that met Beckett as he stepped inside the café reminded him of a military "mess" hall. The cozy, hometown intimacy of the eatery impressed Beckett with a sense of belonging he had not comprehended in years, the scurrying waitresses, and snippets of kitchen noises beyond the swinging doors at the rear as plates were delivered to a meeting of the Destiny Lions Club.

"Chicken fried steak, gravy with fries?"

"Over here…"

"Double jalapeno burger with fries?"

"Lion Fred, at the end," a chorus replied.

Coverall-clad farmers jawed about cattle prices over coffee, and the occasional traveling salesman hunched over an order book while munching on "breakfast served all day" bacon and eggs. Cissy sat alone in a wall booth beyond the cash register queue at the café entrance. She waved Beckett to the booth. Two Lions gave Beckett a long, wary stare which he noted as he approached Cissy.

"Where is your… dad?" he asked, a bit befuddled. "The… whole football team?"

Cissy pouted. "Not glad I showed up?" she chided, patting the empty seat beside her. "Isn't it what you wanted? Besides, everybody in the place knows me, but they don't know you."

Beckett shook his head. "No. Not this," he said. "I'll… wait by the door while you call your dad."

"Not necessary," a low growl replied from the next booth.

A stout, square-jawed man with close-cropped sandy hair, a slightly ruddy complexion, and work-worn hands stepped from the booth into the light. His demeanor belied a temperament not given to foolishness.

"Brock Beckett, Mister Nelson," Beckett said, offering his hand.

Nelson took Beckett's hand warily and gave it a hard, firm squeeze as he shook it. "Lloyd Nelson," he said, not releasing Beckett's hand. "Cissy told me you claim to be her father."

"Yes, sir, that's true," Beckett said.

"You told *my* daughter you can prove she is *your* child?" Nelson asked with a sharpened skepticism as he sat down opposite Cissy.

"Roger that," Beckett said.

He pulled an empty chair to the side of the booth, settled himself, and ordered a cup of coffee as a waitress glided by. Beckett turned back to address Nelson directly.

"She has a half-moon strawberry mark on the right side of her lower back," Beckett said matter-of-factly. He looked at Cissy, and her eyes grew wide.

Beckett smiled. He pulled a worn photograph from his wallet and handed it to Nelson.

"She has her mother's hair and eyes," Beckett said. "And she has a tiny scar just beneath her lower lip where her tooth bit through when she fell and hit her chin against the dining table at age two… the last time I saw her."

Cissy self-consciously brushed a finger against the small mark. "I never knew," she whispered.

Beckett smiled. "I nicknamed you Little Red for obvious reasons…"

"Where have you been?" Nelson demanded; Beckett accepted his condescension.

"You served?" Beckett asked, pointing to a USMC tattoo on Nelson's arm. "Semper fi; bring 'em…"

"Back alive," Nelson added. "I was a gunnery sergeant in Iraq. Where did you serve?"

"Captain in Afghanistan; mostly, Seal Team Eighteen," Beckett said.

"No such animal," Nelson snorted. "That's reserves…"

"Double duty since Trump," Beckett shot back. "And you?"

"Geronimo…"

Beckett smiled. "Bin Laden's codename…" Nelson nodded. "Do tell," he said.

"You and your wife were planning to adopt a child after you got out," Beckett offered. "Suddenly, all the red tape disappeared, and Cissy was 'placed' with you directly on a recommendation by the brass…"

Nelson's gaze narrowed into Beckett's eyes. "How high?"

"General staff," Beckett said.

"What are you guys talking about?" a perplexed Cissy asked as the waitress brought Beckett's coffee.

"Nothing you need to understand now, Honey," Nelson said. "Let's just say I think I know why you don't remember this man."

He handed Cissy the photograph. She gasped. The woman in the photo was lying in a hospital bed; she had no hair. But she had sparkling hazel doe's eyes, and she hugged a little red-haired girl at her bedside, who had a bright smile, a missing tooth, and a stitched lip.

"She was… dying… wasn't she?" Cissy whispered.

"We thought so at the time," Beckett said. "You were all I had left, and later, I was determined to know what happened to you."

"You didn't just happen to show up here," Nelson said with an inquisitional tone.

Beckett sipped his coffee. "I've been looking quietly for two years," he said. "The teaching thing here… call it karma."

"Did you get the job?" Cissy asked, a shyly mischievous smile telegraphing her curiosity.

"Yes," Beckett said, glancing at Nelson. "I got the job… pending the school board's approval."

"Cool…" Cissy turned to Nelson. "What do we tell Mom?"

"Your mother doesn't need to know anything, not just yet," he said. "But neither your mother nor I will allow Mister Beckett, here, to take you away from us…"

"That's not my purpose," Beckett said. "I want the opportunity to know you, Cissy… and start over. For all that anyone knows, your dad and I are simply old Marine buddies."

Cissy glared at Beckett for a moment. "Why didn't you find me sooner? What happened?"

Beckett sighed. "Your dad understands when I say I can't tell you the details," he said. "I was misled for fourteen years, through most of your life. I was told you were killed in a car accident."

Cissy turned to Nelson, a questioning regard in her expression demanded an answer.

"Your mother and I weren't told anything about your family, Hon," he said. "We were only told… you needed a new family."

"You and Mom didn't know who I was or where I was born?" Cissy asked, incredulously.

"No, Hon," Nelson said. "Honestly, we didn't care. You needed a family, and we wanted a child."

A tear coursed along Cissy's cheek, and she pursed her lips into a tight little smile. She studied both men for a long moment, then she turned to Beckett.

"You said… *semper* something," she said softly. "What does it mean?"

"Semper fidelis," Beckett said. "The Marine Corps motto. It's Latin for 'always faithful'."

Cissy smiled weakly. "I like that," she whispered. "Always faithful."

Cissy rested her hand lightly against Beckett's shoulder. He felt her tremble, and Beckett did his best not to cry.

CHAPTER TWO

I'D HATE TO KILL YOU

Esther Franklin, a retired Black schoolteacher, was surprised when the redoubtable widow answered her doorbell that Friday afternoon and she saw Brock Beckett standing on her front porch. "May I help you, young man?" she asked in a tone that bespoke her years in the classroom.

"I understand you have an apartment for rent," Beckett posed.

"Uhm, yes…" Mrs. Franklin struggled with the moment until she comprehended Beckett's information on the point. "I normally rent to single ladies of color who teach at the school."

"Obviously, I don't qualify, except that I am single and a teacher," Beckett replied. "I start Monday as the high school American and English literature teacher."

He handed the woman a letter signed by Superintendent Bittle. Mrs. Franklin pulled her reading glasses from the pocket of her house apron and settled them against the bridge of her nose without bothering to open them.

"Yes; well, all right, then," she muttered. She handed the letter to Beckett, stepped back, and opened the door. "Come on in, young man."

"Thank you, ma'am; I'm Brock Beckett," he said, offering her his hand. She shook it loosely.

"Esther Franklin," she replied. "Folks hereabouts call me Miss Esther because I taught school here for thirty years; that's why

I deal with schoolteachers. Now, it's not typical for me to rent to you because you are a young man; noticing that you are not a man of color, but that is not the point. No, sir; the fact is that you are not a young woman. But, since you come with the recommendation of Mister Bittle, I am disposed to make an exception."

"I'd very much appreciate it," Beckett replied. "I'm prepared to offer more than you're asking for the apartment if that will help."

"My arrangement with the school district is quite satisfactory," Miss Esther noted. "But I appreciate your generosity. Some of the district's teachers live in Camden but, there are times when a young lady of color needs housing, and Mister Bittle sends her to me. So, if you are comfortable with the arrangement, we will look at the apartment."

"No problem, ma'am," Beckett said.

"Miss Esther," she said.

"Miss Esther..." Beckett smiled, and she returned his gesture.

Esther Franklin's story and a half home was the only one of its kind south of Center Street. Nestled in the middle of a spacious quarter-block immediately south of the municipal building and fire station, the upper half-story commanded a view of Center Street in both directions.

"This house was originally a brothel," Miss Esther explained as she and Beckett walked through the house to the rear kitchen door, onto the screened rear porch, and outside to the apartment staircase. "It was built by Mister Theodore Chesterton, the lumberman, as a place for his sawmill hands to spend their pay. I taught U.S. and Arkansas history in Destiny for thirty years, and I found that fact intriguing when my husband and I bought the house. He passed away some years back. I run a clean house, Mister Beckett; there will be no hanky-panky, loud parties or carrying on."

Beckett chuckled. "I love your sense of irony, Miss Esther," he quipped.

She smiled as she turned the key in the apartment door lock. "Well, who knows; perhaps, you will write a great American novel in this house," she replied.

The apartment was well-suited for Beckett. The layout was comfortably open, with a spacious sitting area to the left of the entrance and dining/kitchen area to the right. Both of which had been carved from four smaller rooms. One window opened to the kitchen's north and one window to the south in the sitting area. Two large bedrooms were on either side of a shared bathroom that opened into the front room.

"You can shut off the bedroom you choose not to use," Miss Esther explained. "The bathroom is original to the house, and it is where the special feature to the apartment is located."

"Excuse me?" Beckett muttered.

The old woman chuckled. She opened the door to the bathroom and pointed toward a closet.

"My husband added that enclosure," she said. "It's built around the escape hatch in the floor. During election years, the county sheriff conducted raids to get the Baptist vote. The metal pole down to the basement is still in working condition. And, the cellar door opens from the inside only."

Beckett laughed. "I'll take it, Miss Esther," he said.

Unpacking the Jeep required little time; Beckett traveled light. He was accustomed to carrying a single duffel bag and an ordnance case. Not much had changed. The duffel bag contained civilian clothing rather than desert drabs, and the ordnance case was smaller than regulation, but no less lethal. He stowed his gear in the north end bedroom of the apartment, its westward and northern windows affording the best scans for approaches in the middle of the night or predawn hours. He secured the windows in the unused bedroom; then, he wired a sensor to the apartment entrance that signaled his cell phone when the door was opened.

After stowing his gear, Beckett showered, shaved and changed clothes for an evening he imagined for two years. The introduction to his daughter Cissy left him anxious to know more and an invitation to the Nelson home was offered. Beckett liked Lloyd Nelson beyond his service as a Marine and SEAL. He seemed to be a common-sense man who taught Cissy the same common sense. Her refusal that afternoon of Beckett's Jeep told him as much.

The rain abated, but the day remained gray. Still, as Beckett climbed into the Cherokee for the short drive to the Nelson residence, he ignored the chill of a newly arrived cold front and the somberness it settled upon Destiny. He wheeled the Jeep out of the drive at Miss Esther's and coasted to the end of the block on Nelson Street, making a momentary assessment of the Destiny City Hall and Volunteer Fire Department complex on the right.

The building was a single story with clean lines set against a small manicured lawn at its entrance, and more modern than the remainder of the business district. It looked like a federal grant project. Beckett appreciated the distinction. The fire station adjoining the municipal building was more modular in its appearance, with a wainscot of pale brick along the two sides open to the street. The two large bays that comprised the bulk of the building housed a sleek-looking fire engine with a small rear-mounted expanding ladder unit, and a modern-looking box ambulance.

Beckett was impressed by Lloyd Nelson's role as the guiding force for improvements that gave Destiny a semblance of modernity. He liked the idea of such foresight in charge of Cissy's parenting for 14 years; it was a settling influence after the uncertainty in his life.

He swung the Jeep left from Nelson Street onto Center Street and scarcely had time to shift gears before turning right onto North Cross Street. The Lloyd Nelson residence was not the "historic" home that loomed in the distance between the Briggs and Chesterton estates, despite the Nelson name on the mailbox. Beckett swung the Jeep right off North Cross Street about a block beyond that home and onto Cherry Tree Lane, a bit perplexed. He drove on for a block past several Fifties and Sixties era ranch style and split-level homes to approach a cul-de-sac where a modest, comfortable-looking split-level Tudor style sat nestled beyond a few lodge pole pine trees and a semi-circular concrete driveway.

Cissy met him at the front door almost as soon as he rang the bell. "Hi," she chirped shyly, as she greeted him. "I'm so glad you came."

Beckett looked down into her deep hazel eyes and smiled. "Thanks," he replied. "It means a lot to hear you say that, Cissy."

Lloyd Nelson ambled into the foyer wearing a "Kiss the Cook" barbecue apron and a grin. "Glad you could come," he remarked. "I've just brought the steaks in from the grill. Want a beer?"

Beckett shook his head. "No thanks," he said quietly as Nelson returned to the kitchen. "Still keeping vigil."

Nelson stopped short. "What did you say?" he asked.

Beckett smiled. "Still keeping vigil," he repeated.

"That's… what … I thought you said," his host murmured. He turned to Cissy. "Hon, you and your mom get the steaks and potatoes plated for me. I'm gonna visit with Mister Beckett for a minute before we eat."

The girl smiled and gave Beckett's hand a loving squeeze. "Don't keep him too long," she said, and she hurried away.

Nelson crossed his arms against his chest. "Why are you still keeping vigil?" he asked warily.

"Old habits," Beckett retorted.

"I don't buy it," the other man replied. "You don't say something like that without a reason."

"I'm not here for anybody," Beckett replied. "I'm here to escape that, but you and I know it doesn't… just… go away."

"How long have you been out?" Nelson asked.

"Two years," Beckett said.

"How did you get out?"

"Nasty," Beckett said quietly. "Real nasty, but clean."

"CIA? NSA? DOD?" Nelson posed.

Beckett shook his head. "State?" the other man asked cautiously.

Beckett said nothing. He raised an eyebrow. Nelson settled back against the wall in apparent shock. "Holy mother," he muttered.

"That's just between you, me, and God," Beckett said. "That said, it's obvious I don't need to do anything about Cissy, except be here. And enjoy watching her be your daughter."

"Roger that," Nelson replied. He slapped his palm against Beckett's shoulder and gave it an assuring squeeze as the two men walked into the dining room together.

The Mesquite grilled steaks and sea salt-rubbed baked potatoes reminded Beckett of an America he hadn't experienced in almost 20 years. He reveled in the moment, the Nelson family laughter, and their home's warmth.

"I noticed your family has been in Destiny generationally," Beckett posed over coffee and a delightful pecan pie.

"You mean the big house by the river?" Cissy posed. "That was great-grandpa Nelson's house. My uncle Freemon lives there now. It's nice, for an old house; but, I like our house much better."

Beckett smiled. "Good to hear," he said. "It seems you've had a firmly grounded life."

"My brother is something of a renegade," Nelson offered. "He owns the Hot Spot on the other side of town; it's a dance hall and 'bring your own bottle' place. I don't have anything to do with it. But, as mayor, I can't put my brother out of business. Freemon knows where I draw the line."

"Lloyd works hard as the mayor of Destiny," Nelson's wife, Grace, interjected. "We're very proud of him; he's done wonderful things for the town and the schools. He is president of the school board, too."

"We raise cattle and pine timber, too," Cissy added. "Maybe we can go to the ranch on Saturday and show you around?"

She glanced hopefully at Nelson, who smiled and nodded, and Cissy brightened. "She'll pester me until we show you," he said. "So, if you're free Saturday afternoon…?"

"That would be great," Beckett replied. "I'd like to get out into the country a bit; sounds fine."

"Cool," Cissy chirped.

"Cissy tells me you're teaching at the high school this semester," Grace offered.

"He's going to be my junior American literature teacher," Cissy explained.

"Oh, and what will you cover this semester, Mister Beckett?" her mother asked.

Grace struck Beckett as a transplant to Destiny, much like himself. She was a statuesque woman with a sense of style that bore a patrician mark and an understated manner typical of the confidence of inherited money. Beckett surmised what attracted her to Nelson and Destiny, Arkansas, must have been remarkable.

"This year's study involves a contrast in styles and approach to much the same general subject matter," he offered. "First, we'll take up *Gone with the Wind*, and, then, we will read *Giant* and contrast the development of America from the Civil War through World War II via the romanticism of wealth in both eras."

Grace's eyes brightened. "How delightful," she said.

"Something for everyone," Beckett quipped. "War and manhood for the boys and family and romance for the girls."

"Deliciously non-woke," Grace murmured.

"On the contrary," Beckett replied. "Scarlet O'Hara is a prototypical feminist, despite her failings over Rhett Butler, all the way down to her declaration in the ruined garden at Tara that, whether she borrow, steal or kill, she would never know hunger, again. Leslie Benedict is the prototypical progressive bringing the Twentieth Century to Reata's rough and tumble conscience by providing better living conditions for its Hispanic ranch hands and their families."

"How wonderfully astute of you, Mister Beckett," Grace effused. She turned to Cissy and smiled knowingly. "How I wish I were in your class this semester, sweetheart."

"Mom," Cissy moaned, rolling her eyes.

The next day's outing to the Nelson ranch was met with slightly better weather though a chill in the air portended the winter to come. Nelson wore a light jacket, Cissy was bundled in a sweater and jacket, but Beckett wore only a long-sleeved shirt.

"Aren't you freezing?" Cissy wondered as the trio stepped from Nelson's extended cab pickup truck into the bluster of a gusty afternoon.

"Cold is a state of mind," Beckett replied. "You left your house with warmth embedded in your thinking. Consequently, all you feel is the chill. But, if you live at fifty-two degrees, it's not difficult to deal with thirty degrees, whereas living at seventy-two degrees or more makes compensating against the difference much more improbable for your mind."

"Seriously?" Cissy posed mockingly.

Beckett shrugged and grinned.

"Believe it, Hon," Nelson interjected. "Seal… uh, some soldiers are trained to ignore the cold, the heat; whatever the weather might be, they embrace it so they don't fight the weather and the enemy."

He smiled and slapped his palm against Beckett's shoulder. "Trust me, baby, Mister Beckett…" Nelson paused for a long moment and composed himself. "Your father ... knows what he's talking about."

Cissy smiled and sniffed through a chuckle. "It just hit me," she murmured. "I've got two dads."

Beckett addressed himself to her, his hands on her shoulders. His eyes adored her.

"Listen to me, Cissy," he began. "Yes, you have two men in your life to whom you mean the most in life: one is your birth father, who wants desperately to know you better and see you remain happy and whole. The other is your adoptive father, who reared you for fourteen years to be the intelligent, compassionate, loving daughter you are to him and your adoptive mother. Everything about Lloyd and Grace, and their character, is bound up in you. You are their lives.

"So, yes, you have two dads; but, only one, Lloyd Nelson, is your 'Dad' in the sense of your life every day revolving around him," Beckett added, offering air quotes. "He has kissed your hurts, helped you learn, taught you right from wrong. He is your 'Dad.' Me, I'm your father, and while I'd like to be more of a 'dad' to you. Well, for the most part that has passed. So, I'm asking you to accept me as who I am now."

Cissy reached up to him, and he bent as she hugged him. "I… get it," she whispered.

"Thanks, Hon," Beckett replied.

They rolled out three ATVs from a shed by the ranch office and veterinary barn and headed into the timberline along a feeding trail for the cattle, Lloyd in the lead, followed by Cissy and Beckett in the rear. He shook away a sense of déjà vu in the experience. Beckett recalled riding a well-muffled ATV through the darkness along narrow mountain passages into the valleys on the Afghanistan-Iran border, tracking one radical element or another, and the tricked-out dirt bikes he rode through the narrow alleyways of Damascus.

Beckett was pulled back to the present by the meager sunlight woven through the pine canopy and streaked across Cissy's figure in intermittent shards as she rode the trail in front of him. He smiled and goosed his ATV alongside hers.

"Nice ride," he called out. He waved a hand about. "How many acres?"

"Six hundred more or less," she replied. "About half timber."

"Wow," he replied. "It's awesome."

"Yeah, I love it," Cissy said. "Wait 'til we get to the back pasture; it's amazing. Our land is on the north side of the Ouachita River, behind Uncle Freemon's place outside of Destiny."

The timberline began to thin and suddenly gave way to an expanse beyond a small meadow of winter clover, where Nelson slowed his ATV to a stop.

"That clover," he said, "is sown for the deer; it keeps them ranging through this pasture and bottles them against the river so we can manage the herd and keep them away from the cattle pastures back up on the other side of the timber nearer the road."

"It's gorgeous," Beckett remarked.

"We use these pastures for cattle, breeding the heifers back away from the river and we keep the bulls on the opposite side," Nelson added. "We let the mamas and babies pasture here through the middle, then round up, and pen them back near the timberline."

"How many head of cattle do you manage here?" Beckett asked.

"Anywhere from three hundred to four hundred, depending on whether we use the front-end pastures," Nelson replied. "We like to keep about three hundred which allows us to employ our ranch hands year-round; and good hands are hard to come by."

"Where do you find your ranch hands?" Beckett posed.

"Don't worry, Captain; they're all legal folks," Nelson replied. "Most of them grew up in Ouachita County."

Nelson gestured for Cissy to ride ahead. "Go on to the cabin and get it opened," he said. "Beckett and I will be along in just a minute."

"Don't lollygag," Cissy retorted. "I want us to go fishing before we leave."

Nelson laughed as Cissy roared away. "That girl loves it out here," he said. "She wants the family to live here, and I told her that, one day, when she is old enough, she can live here if she wants."

He swept the horizon with his hand. "All of this will be hers one day, Beckett," Nelson added. He turned and studied Beckett sternly. "Whether you ever came along or not, it's hers. Nobody else's."

"I get it, Lloyd," Beckett replied. "I respect it. And I'm glad you feel that way. Frankly, I don't need all this to be comfortable."

"Good," Nelson shot back. "I'm glad we understand each other." He grinned. "I'd hate to kill you."

Beckett considered Nelson's ability to follow through, but only for a moment; he understood his host's capacity to kill as a former SEAL. He pondered whether Nelson still had the skills. But Beckett took comfort in knowing Cissy would always be safe if he could not get past Nelson.

"Yeah, I think you would… hate to kill me," Beckett said with a laugh. "I know you'd damn sure die trying if anyone ever hurt Cissy, and I thank you for that."

Nelson offered Beckett his hand. "Just so we understand each other, Captain," Nelson said as they clasped their hands in what, for Beckett, was a satisfyingly bruising handshake.

CHAPTER THREE
WHY DID YOU GIVE ME UP?

Dinner for Saturday evening was fresh bass grilled over an open pit with a tossed garden salad, prepared by Cissy. She met Beckett and Nelson at the rear of the log and stone cabin holding a stringer of three respectable-sized spotted bass.

"I got tired of waiting, so I caught dinner for us," she explained.

"Is there anything she doesn't do?" Beckett remarked.

Nelson shook his head. "I could drop her in the middle of nowhere… and she would find her way home," he said. "She cooks like a champ, hunts like an Amazon, makes great grades in school, and doesn't have an enemy. I couldn't be prouder."

Beckett watched as Cissy fileted the bass, her fingers moving deftly along the spine of each fish as she wielded the knife. The fresh lemon, butter, salt and pepper baste she used as she slowly grilled the fish over a bed of embers opposite the comfortably warm fire in the outdoor pit left each filet moist and tender. Although the meal was simple, it was a complex mixture of flavors that left Beckett momentarily marveling as he looked at his plate.

"I don't know how many times I've caught fish in a mountain stream, some not particularly edible, sometimes I ate them raw," Beckett offered quietly. "This fish is marvelous."

"Thank you, I do the cooking when we come to the cabin," Cissy replied brightly, and wrinkled her nose. "Raw fish... 'ew.' Why?"

Nelson chuckled. "Let's say Mister Beckett wasn't always in friendly territory to have a fire burning at night," he explained.

Cissy seemed perplexed by the point, but Beckett evaded it.

"How did you catch these fish?" he asked. "We couldn't have been more than thirty minutes behind you."

"I've tried to get her to tell me," Nelson said. "I've watched her fish on the river." He shrugged. "It's a gift."

Beckett laughed. "Well, I haven't had anything like this since... ever," he said.

They all laughed; it felt good to all of them. The day cleared as it waned, and the western sky glowed with brilliant red and orange hues. A quiet settled around the fire pit.

"Red sky at night, sailor's delight," Cissy murmured. "It'll be a nice day tomorrow."

She took a pit poker to spread the banked embers at the cooking end of the pit as Nelson gathered the plates and the sparse leftovers from the meal. "She cooks, and I wash up," he said. "You two enjoy; I'll be a few minutes."

Cissy jabbed the poker against the wood on the fringes of the fire until it blossomed into small flames. "He wants to give us some time together," she said. "It's because I want to ask you a question."

The rippling river's flow against the rocks along the banks on either side drifted up into the night beside them. It was a soothing sound against the counterpoint of tree frogs in the willows planted along the shoreline. Cissy fidgeted on one of the pine tree stumps which served as fire pit furniture.

"I've thought about it since I met you at the café yesterday," she began. "It kept me awake all night because, as I listed all the possibilities in my head, I really, truly didn't want to believe you just walked out on my mother and me. But there it was. I didn't like it, but I had to consider it."

Cissy straightened herself to her full sitting stature and looked into Beckett's eyes. She searched for his soul as she asked, "Why did you give me up?"

Beckett did not flinch. "I had no choice," he replied. "You were taken away from me when your mother died. I was thousands of miles away for reasons I can't tell you; yet, I had no idea what happened… until it was too late."

His jaw tightened. "I didn't give you up," Beckett said. "I would never give you up. I fought like hell to learn the truth for two years and wanted to get you back, but other people made that decision. I was told you and your mother were dead, and I was given no choice but to accept it. I never believed it."

Beckett caressed Cissy's cheek with a fingertip. "I was tied to something I could not change," he said. "Because, for me to break away then would leave thousands of people at the mercy of a monster and, perhaps, plunge the world into a war which would kill millions."

Cissy gasped. Her mind raced against the possibilities and drew her to one question.

"Did you… kill someone… important?" she whispered.

This time, Beckett's eyes searched her soul. "Yes," he said dispassionately.

Cissy pulled away, but Beckett grasped her arm and guided her gently back to her seat. "You," he said firmly, "are the only person on God's green Earth I've told. And I'm entrusting our lives to your hands by telling you."

"No pressure there," Cissy muttered wide-eyed and trembling.

Beckett drew Cissy into a tentative embrace. "I shouldn't have told you," he said ruefully. "I'm sorry…"

"Yes… You should have told me," Cissy insisted. "It's the only thing that makes sense. I wouldn't have believed anything less… less… weird, wild, way out there; because you're too… 'sin disimulo' for it not to be the truth."

"Sin disimulo?"

"It's what the ranch hands call someone who is undisguised," she said, gazing at Beckett with a small smile. "That's why I almost took your Jeep. It was just too weird not to be true. You're such a gallant knight."

"How did you become so… sarcastically insightful?" Beckett asked, returning her smile.

Cissy shrugged. "I guess it's in the genes," she replied. She hung her head. "So, tell me… where is my mother buried?"

"I was told she is in a little cemetery outside of her hometown of Sulphur Springs, Texas," he said. "You were supposed to be there, too."

"Is there actually… a grave…for me?

"Yes," Beckett said. Cissy shivered and he pulled her closer.

Tears pooled onto Cissy's cheeks. "Could we go sometime?" she asked.

Beckett offered Cissy his shirt sleeve to dry her eyes. "I'd like that very much," he said. "Perhaps, after your adoptive mother figures out who I am."

"That won't take long," Cissy retorted. "She was juicing you last night at supper with all that post-DEI stuff."

Beckett smiled. "I figured as much," he said.

"She's a sharp lady," Cissy replied.

"What about your dad?" Beckett asked. "No offense, mind you, but how did he rate an awesome lady like your mother?"

"He's a lot like you," Cissy giggled.

"Sin disimulo?"

"Right," she said. "Mom liked that. She calls him her 'knight in country armor.'" Cissy offered air quotes. "She's from Maryland."

"Almost out of *Giant*," Beckett quipped.

"Seriously?"

"Read the book," he said.

"Aww, c'mon," Cissy pleaded. Beckett shook his head. Cissy relented. "So, I'll read the book."

"What book?" Nelson asked as he appeared at the deck steps with cups of coffee.

"*Giant*, by Edna Ferber," Beckett answered.

"Yeah, you and Grace were talking about that last night at supper," Nelson said. "Sounds like an interesting story."

"Oh, seriously, Dad…?"

Cissy became instantly conscious how the term of endearment redounded; and the thought momentarily befuddled her. "I'm still having trouble getting my head around the two dads thing."

Nelson and Beckett laughed.

The chill of the night around the fire pit, and the long evening of conversation left everyone sufficiently relaxed to retire sleepily.

Cissy fought the urge, but she consistently drifted away. Nelson scooped her into his arms and carried her inside the cabin. Beckett remained outside. He settled himself onto the deck and stared upward at the stars strewn across the plush velvet of the night sky. He remembered the stars at night over the mountains of the Kandahar Valley, millions of them on pitch black nights when nothing but death moved across the moonscape of the Middle East. Beckett recalled the nights of the muffled helicopters and the long ATV rides; when the barking of dogs was suddenly quieted in the ISIS-controlled villages, giving way to the lethal whisper of two or three automatic weapons, all carried out beneath the diamond-encrusted canopy of the heavens.

Beckett lay on the deck, stretched out comfortably, until he found a peaceful sleep, one he had not known in almost 20 years. Deep into the night, Beckett realized he was not alone. He warily opened one eye. The night was darker now, with the glow from the fire pit reduced to the amber of its embers. Beckett became aware of a small form beside him curled beneath a blanket against the chill of the night. He recognized the shock of auburn hair pressed against his shoulder. He smiled and turned onto his side, folding Cissy beneath his arm. She gave a small, soft whimper, then quietened.

Beckett gazed upward, again. The stars of the Middle East once shone for the man who commanded them from a palace in Damascus, and his master in Moscow, Beckett mused. But these stars belonged to Beckett and Cissy.

CHAPTER FOUR
Is He Always Like That?

Sunday morning dawned brilliantly across the deep pine stands along the Ouachita River, the first shafts of light warming Beckett's face as he lay beside Cissy on the cabin deck. Her weather forecast was correct, he thought, rehearsing the old rhyme again in his mind: "Red sky at night; sailor's delight. Red sky at morning; sailor take warning." He glanced at the horizon; it was almost an ocean blue as the sun began to command the day.

Cissy soon roused, shivered, and stretched. She smiled at Beckett. "Morning," she whispered. "How about some breakfast?"

He smiled. "Can I help?" he posed. She shook her head and waved him off.

"I do the cooking at the cabin," she reminded him. "I enjoy it."

Nelson joined them shortly and, before long, hot coffee, crisp bacon, biscuits, and pan-fried eggs were offered up and consumed with gusto. Cissy cleared the breakfast plates and washed up while Nelson secured the remainder of the cabin site.

"Nobody will be out here until tomorrow," he said. "We don't work Sundays."

Beckett smiled weakly and nodded. He considered the point; Sunday was simply another day. Killing on Sunday, however, was atypical for him; there was no military injunction against it, but Sunday was the day after the Muslim holy day, so there was usually plenty of local activity. It was a good day to hunker down and stay out of sight. Saturday, however, was always the best day for operations. The activity was limited to religious services and target environments to and from them were often rich.

The return ATV ride to the ranch office was pleasant as the chill of the night wore away to offer an almost Spring-like morning. Birds were noisy in the pine stands, and the intermittent lowing of cattle gathered around stocked hay rings for their early feeding provided the only counterpoint to the putter of the ATV engines along the return trail. Ten minutes later, Nelson's extended cab pickup truck pulled into the semi-circular driveway in front of the split-level Tudor residence at the end of the cul-de-sac on Cherry Tree Lane.

"Hope you enjoyed the outing," Nelson said, offering Beckett his hand.

He shook his host's hand heartily. "Best evening and night's sleep I've had in years," Beckett said.

Cissy shook her head skeptically as she approached the two men. "I don't understand how you can say that about sleeping on the deck without anything," she groused.

Beckett smiled and let his fingers half-heartedly slip through the silky crush of her auburn hair. "I've slept on far worse, but never with such comforting acceptance as last night. Thank you."

Cissy smiled up at him. "Yeah, it was kinda cool," she whispered.

Beckett kissed the crown of her head and offered his hand to Nelson, again. "She's a gem," he said. He turned back to Cissy and grinned. "Of course, come Monday, I'm just Mister Beckett… understood?"

She frowned. "Okay," she replied. He offered her a high five which she slapped on her tiptoes and Beckett climbed into his Jeep.

"See you, Monday," he said.

"Yes, sir, Mister Beckett," Cissy called out as he pulled away.

The notion of a church bell never entered Beckett's mind as he slowly drove back across Destiny toward Miss Esther's apartment house, but there it was, tolling in the distance and growing clearer as he approached the house on Nelson Street. He parked the

Jeep behind the residence and climbed the stairway to the apartment turning back to a panoramic view of the heart of Destiny along Center Street to determine where the sound originated. The two-storied Destiny Masonic Lodge No. 61, F. & A.M., was the tallest building in the business district at the west end of Center Street, the three-storied Destiny Public Schools building was the tallest at the east end directly across from the Snappy Mart and Destiny Municipal Building and Volunteer Fire Department at the intersection with Nelson Street. Nelson's Dollar and More Store stood adjacent to the Masonic Hall, with the Center Street Grocery next in line and the U. S. Post Office at the intersection on South Cross Street. The Blue Bird Café occupied the east side of the intersection with the vacant Dolly's Antiques and Notions beside it.

Fairway Lumber Co. fronted Center Street opposite the Masonic Hall with the Cut and Curl beauty and barber shop next door and the Briggs Building, including the Briggs Law Firm, Briggs Insurance, and Briggs Pharmacy, filling the remainder of the block on the north side of the street. The South Arkansas Bank, the newest building in town, commanded the corner in both directions across North Cross Street, with the sadly maintained Destiny Veterans' Memorial Park spread between the bank and the high school campus at the Destiny Public Schools complex.

Beyond the school complex lay the north residential district of modest circa 1940s to 1960s homes of post-World War II growth. The "historic homes" of Destiny were prominent along the North Cross Street frontage of a stretch parallel to the Ouachita River, marking the northwest limits of Destiny at the boundary of the Poison Springs Wildlife Management Area. There the Briggs, Nelson, and Chesterton names dominated, the newest manse being the home of Edmond Alford Briggs, great-great-grandson of Destiny's founder, and son of James Alford "Mister Jimmy" Briggs, senior partner of the Briggs Law Firm and chairman of South Arkansas Bank. But no church bells rang from the north side of Destiny.

The south side of Destiny between South Cross and Nelson streets was dotted with plainer residences, mostly well-kept albeit humble. The remainder of the predominately Black south side was more ramshackle as both streets became simple, oil-topped lanes beyond Nelson Street. Miss Esther's residence lay along a section of the Ouachita River as it ran southward past the former Black school campus, now the Destiny Services Resource Center, The Hot Spot, dance hall and "bring your own bottle" club owned by Freemon Nelson, and the Ouachita County Fairgrounds at the outskirts of town.

Beckett listened for a long moment. The sound was new to him. Beckett was frequently awakened in the early days in Afghanistan by the blare of the call to prayers played over loudspeakers, until he became accustomed to the distinct singsong. This was different; the crisp, clear peal was a tonal beacon emanating from the south side of town against the still of the morning. Beckett decided to investigate.

The only discernable stretch of concrete sidewalk on the south side of town lay along Nelson Street. Beckett stood for a moment in front of the house discerning the direction of the chime. The sound emanated from somewhere beyond Nelson Street about two or three blocks away. Beckett strode off in the direction of the initial toll's burst. The sound became more resonant as Beckett made his way, until he spotted the source some two blocks west of Nelson Street. The paved street devolved into an oil-topped lane bounded on either side by modest homes with small, marginally maintained lawns, older detached single-car garages, and the occasional carport. The neighborhood was generally devoid of trees except an expansive oak shading much of the lawn and a bell cupola atop a brick-based sign in front of the Ebeneezer Baptist Church.

Beckett was dressed in the same shirt and khaki pants he wore to the Nelson ranch. He turned to leave, when an elderly Black man stepped from behind the bell cupola, smiled and motioned for Beckett to approach.

"Good mornin', brother," the old man said brightly. "And, welcome."

Beckett recalled being pinned to the dirt by crossfire, but he never felt as vulnerable as in the moment when the elderly Black man extended his hand. He politely grasped the old man's hand and was greeted with a firm, resolute grip.

"Good morning," Beckett muttered. "I was just listening to your bell."

"The call to God's house," the old man offered. "It's for all who will hear it."

"Really, quite nice," Beckett replied in embarrassment. "Uhm, well, I won't keep you, sir."

"Come on in, young man," the old man said quietly. "I was a stranger and you took me in…"

"I, really, I'm not suitably dressed for your services," Beckett said.

"Consider the lilies of the field, how they are dressed; for Solomon in all his glory was not like them, and, yet, they wither," the old man recited. "Are you not worth much more? Do not worry what you shall wear…"

"I'm not a member of your denomination," Beckett said.

"But, go out into the highways and the hedges and call them that they may come to my feast," the old man replied.

An ancient-sounding piano stirred from within the building and the mismatched voices of a mostly female choir rose alongside it in an old spiritual, followed in the chorus by the congregation. The sound quieted Beckett for a moment.

"I is Deacon Lester James," the old Black man said. "I rings the bell on Sunday worship. Why don't y'all come on in and be with us in service this mornin'?"

"If you don't mind, Mister James, I'd prefer to stand out here and listen," Beckett said.

"Ask, and it shall be given you; seek, and you shall find; knock, and it shall be opened to you," the aged Deacon said. The old man smiled, made his way to the door and went inside the building, careful to leave the door ajar.

Beckett quietly admired the simple wood framed clapboard building with its carefully maintained white painted sides, almost stately black shutters, and gently majestic steeple crown. He pondered how long the building stood, a generational symbol of denominational loyalty, not unlike the minaret-topped mosques of Afghanistan. Beckett considered the conundrum: One building, filled with mostly elderly Black congregants singing of their deliverance not so many generations before, a symbol, however humble, of a freedom which, in the other building thousands of miles away, was reviled with equal fervor by much younger congregants eager to conquer infidels and produce their own deliverance.

"How odd," Beckett whispered.

Beckett remained outside throughout the service, listening carefully to the Scripture readings, the almost sing-song cadence of a robust male voice intent in prayer, and the stern-sounding admonition of a sermon interrupted frequently with affirmations of "That's right," and "Amen." Beckett was almost compelled to step through the open door during the quiet of prayer, when a sudden "thap" sounded against the intermittently creaking wooden floor.

"Them red wasps up in the ceiling is wakin' up from the mornin' sun," Deacon James called out to the congregation's laughter.

Beckett captured the image in his mind, laughed aloud; and quickly quieted himself. But, there it lay, as he pictured the tall, slender Black deacon, his head bowed in prayer, spying the unsuspecting insect as it buzzed about and alighted on the floor. He considered the old man's stealth, impressed by the idea of his weathered black hand reaching toward the song book rack on the back of the pew in front of him, and carefully sliding a hymnal from its place. Beckett considered how the old man leveled his gaze over the still unsuspecting red wasp, hefting the song book in his hand much like a sniper takes the measure of his mark before making a single, calculated movement to release death.

"Thap," Beckett whispered. "Dead meat."

The stir of feet and the conviviality of casual conversation pulled Beckett back from his reverie as the minister, a stout Black man of six feet or so, with a full graying head of hair and a square-jawed face opened the front door and positioned himself in the threshold to shake hands with each of the congregants. Beckett quickly stepped away and started to walk across the graveled parking area.

"'S'cuse me, brother," a voiced called from behind him.

Beckett closed his eyes in frustration at being discovered. He shook his head and thought how many times he simply walked away from a crowded open-air market in Damascus, leaving a body on the ground, and no-one noticed. Beckett remembered the many hours he lay in wait on a rooftop, then melted into the milieu after sending a single bullet through a window in a Middle Eastern building. He turned and faced the old Black deacon with an embarrassed smile.

"I was just leaving," Beckett said.

"Naw, naw, brother," James admonished. "Pastor Bellchase would like you to come to the fellowship dinner. We is eatin' back here behind the building today, what with the weather bein' so nice and all."

The old man rested an aged and work-wearied hand lightly against Beckett's shoulder and pointed to a group of tables at the far side of the property, within the shade of the monumental oak. Beckett turned to see women dressed in Sunday finest with cloth-wrapped casseroles and aluminum foil-wrapped cake plates in hand trouping toward the tables. Children ran and wove their way in and out among the adult congregants. Within moments, a table nearest the door was filled with plates and pots of food that had been warming during the service. The air was pungent with aromas of savory pit barbecue, honey-sweet baked beans, home-style pot roasts with mounds of new potatoes… and fried chicken which took Beckett back to his childhood.

"All things are ready, come to the feast," Deacon James said.

Beckett stood beside the serving table shaking the hand of the church pastor and realized he was the only white person in the crowd. He smiled politely as he took notice of four or five boys, all wearing Destiny High School letterman jackets, and decided to make the best of his circumstances.

"Glad to meet you, Pastor Bellchase," he said. "I'm Brock Beckett, the new high school literature teacher."

"I know," the minister replied. He pointed to a woman standing with a group setting out paper plates, cups and dinnerware. "Miss Esther explained that to me when Deacon James said you were outside."

Beckett smiled as Miss Esther recognized him and waved. He returned her gesture and sat down as two plates laden with food for Bellchase and the special guest were served.

"It's good to see you this mornin', Mister Beckett," she said brightly.

"Good to see you, ma… Miss Esther," he replied.

Beckett struggled to recall when he tasted food as close to his past. He ate with a savor he had not known in years as he experienced the simple pleasures of food which was not raw, natively exotic or military.

"Is this the only church in Destiny?" Beckett asked off-handedly.

"No, there is the Briggs church, First Baptist, and the Chesterton church, Saint John Episcopal, on the north side of town," Miss Esther said. "But, this is the only Black church in town."

"Excuse me, the Briggs and Chesterton churches?" Beckett asked.

Miss Esther smiled knowingly. "The white churches," she said quietly.

"Seriously?"

"I suppose you are not a church-going man, Mister Beckett?" Bellchase asked.

Beckett wiped his lips with a paper napkin. "Not... for a while," he said.

"That is a shame; for, it seems, a man to whom we entrust the secular education of our children should have some church home," Bellchase retorted.

"You can be assured of my credentials," Beckett said.

The minister shook his head. "It's not your credentials of which I speak, but your commitment," he said with a wry smile.

"How so?" Beckett asked, plainly taken aback.

"As I understand it, our young people are to study two novels in the American literature class: *Gone with the Wind* and *Giant,*" Bellchase said. "That seems somewhat... skewed... to me."

Beckett smiled and took the measure of the Black minister. "I would teach *Roots*, but Alex Haley, like James A. Michener's *Texas*, is too long-winded for a one-semester class."

"So, you teach the Black experience through the lens of Margaret Mitchell's controversial short story, instead?" Bellchase asked.

"Mitchell took some skin off the Civil War South," Beckett said. "She offered questions... and, answers, no one else would broach. Hollywood came along and denuded her finer points about slavery to make the character Mammy a Step 'n Fetch It. She is likable, capable, but still a slave. In Mitchell's novel, Mammy is more independent than Scarlett in her attitude about herself. Mammy makes it clear to Scarlett she is no slave because Mammy is indispensable to the O'Hara family. Scarlett is the one who is bound to the glories of the past now swept away. Mammy remains with Scarlett only to be certain Miss Ellen's daughter survives.

"The truest to the book Black character from the film was Big Sam. Jonas Wilkerson may be the overseer at Tara but Big Sam is the motivator in the fields," Beckett said. "Certainly, Wilkerson was never as successful at that task. He wasn't trusted to know the dignity of the difference when slave or not, a man can genuinely lay down his labor at the end of the day and say he has done a good job. It wasn't a white man who came to Scarlett's aid in the shantytown assault. It was Big Sam, a decent human being.

"Mitchell, like Harper Lee's *To Kill a Mockingbird,* took stereotypes and used them to ask some larger questions at a time when no-one else cared," Beckett said. "Why were all the virile, young white sons of slave owners so willing to ride to war… even, the laconic Ashley Wilkes? They were stupid, ignorant of the cost of war versus a nobility with which they imbued it. That much in the film is true to the book. Mitchell's theme wasn't a romantic saga. Her point was more cultural, the Black experience of the era as the accelerant to the flame which almost consumed the nation. The movie created caricatures rather than characters; and, except for its visual scope, the book is better, as they say. So, yes, one can somewhat understand that era of the Black experience through Margaret Mitchell's lens, because she refused to allow it to be clouded."

Beckett was suddenly aware he was lecturing, but he was unrepentant. It felt good to express what he had said, and he sensed why as he considered his reasons for going to war. Beckett wrestled with the question whether he was as stupid as the white sons of slave owners, or whether he served from a purpose which brought about genuine change and personal absolution? It had thrown his life into chaos… until now, until Cissy.

The buzz of conversation overtook the moment, bringing Beckett back into the exchange, but the minister moved on, apparently satisfied with his guest's exposition on Margaret Mitchell. Beckett sipped his iced tea as Bellchase shifted rhetorical gears.

"So, we understand you do not have a church home, Mister Beckett; which turns us to the question of why?" the clergyman posed.

Beckett put his glass of iced tea aside, wiped his lips with a paper napkin, and rose from the table. "I appreciate your hospitality, Pastor Bellchase. And I appreciate your interest; but let's suffice to say God and I haven't been in formal communication for some time."

"Make not long prayers in the streets as the hypocrites do… for they do to be seen of men, …and they has they reward," Deacon James said between bites of corn on the cob.

"Indeed, Mister Beckett," Bellchase said. "Has God not communed with you in the Scriptures to know Jesus?"

Beckett offered Bellchase his hand. "I appreciate your thoughts; honestly, I do. But, I'm a man who acts with considered deliberation… and, rarely, from the moment."

"Go your way for now, and when I have a convenient season, I will call on you," Deacon James said.

Beckett smiled. "Is he always like that?" he whispered.

Bellchase leaned in close to Beckett and with a small, wry smile and a wink said, "It may not be King James, but the man's heart is in it."

The false Spring of the morning began to give way to the fickle nature of Arkansas autumn as Beckett returned to Miss Esther's and the apartment. He decided the chill of a new cold front would not spoil the surprising encounter at the Ebeneezer Baptist Church. There was a certain determinism in the Baptist minister which both intrigued and put off Beckett. He was reminded of a young couple, married less than a year, who, with the same kind of determinism became church missionaries in Israel.

"They graduated with teaching degrees from a denominational university," General Pierpont Maxwell explained. "They tutored the children of diplomats in English and they're like a lot of other civilians involved in this or that sort of 'Christian' endeavor around Jerusalem and Tel-Aviv. And they've disappeared. Find them and bring them home, Captain. Alive…"

Five days later, Beckett was close on their trail as the couple was moved to an ISIS safe house on the outskirts of Damascus, Syria. There, from his nest on the rooftop of an abandoned automotive garage, Beckett watched and listened inside the livestock stall of a house via classified technology. The young husband was forced to witness the repeated rape of his wife, and she was forced to see her husband brutally sodomized. Each was violated, a gun held to their head by one jihadi as another raped them. And, throughout the degradation they were repeatedly commanded, "Renounce your Jesus and we will let you die quickly."

The initial bravery of the couple was short-lived, but Beckett wasn't there to critique their conviction; he was sent to prevent them from becoming ISIS propaganda. He watched as the two attempted to pray aloud or quote The Bible and were repeatedly slapped into stunned silence.

Finally, the young man and his wife were dressed in orange jogging pants and tee shirts; and, with their hands bound behind them, they were forced to their knees. A video camera was brought in and connected to a live internet feed on a computer. The ISIS unit commander stood behind them, a serrated-blade knife in his hand. He excoriated the couple as infidels, and said they were worthy only of death. He grasped a handful of the young woman's long hair and pulled it toward him, forcing her head backward to expose her throat. The commander rested the blade of the knife against her skin, pricking it ever-so-lightly with the pinpoint of the tip to produce a tiny bubble of blood which collapsed into a small, crimson trickle across the young woman's neck. She winced with a tense, demure gasp.

Beckett drew a deep breath and held it as he sighted the first shot; it killed the cameraman instantly. The next shot killed the man guarding the young husband; and, the third shot killed the unit commander. The knife fell away from his hand as his body was thrown backward by the impact of the bullet that shattered his skull. All of it was captured on the live ISIS internet feed, also recorded by Beckett and immediately transmitted to… somewhere.

A gust of wind blown across Beckett's face brought him back to Sunday morning in Destiny, Arkansas. Beckett stood silently on the sidewalk in front of Miss Esther's house. He felt a tear settle onto his cheek, perhaps from a dust speck swept by the wind into his eye.

CHAPTER FIVE
I'VE STAYED ALIVE BY BEING UNREMARKABLE

The advantage to teaching in Destiny for Beckett was the small class sizes and the high school enrollment was only 300 or so, resulting in junior and senior level American and English literature classes of 15 to 20 students each. The class size was fortunate, given the reception Beckett's choice of *Gone with the Wind* received.

"Ain't readin' no lame slave story 'bout no rich slut white chick and her sugar daddy," Devonte Washington, star football running back and man about campus, said.

There was a low rumble of Black male voices in agreement mixed against some general recognition of the challenge, which Cissy seemed to regard with disappointment. Beckett smiled.

"Chill the wannabe gang slang, Mister Washington," he said. "It appears to me you've at least read the Cliff Notes, if not the book, given your accurate, if not colorful, review of the principal characters."

Washington rolled his eyes and others in the klatch of athletes in the class egged him on. "So what if I did?" he shot back. "Don't mean I liked it; don't mean you not throwin' shade on Black folks in Destiny…"

"Ooooooo, bam."

"Oouch."

"That's right."

"Yeah, this Margaret Mitchell was makin' fun of Black folks," Wade Fairway, white quarterback and son of Fairway Lumber Co. owner Boyd Fairway, said.

"About as much as she was makin' fun of white folks," Cissy said indignantly. "Scarlett being all, Oh, Ashley, sweet Ashley. The little wimp."

Beckett folded his arms across his chest. "Booyah," he said. "Did all of you read the book over the summer?"

The class erupted into laughter. Beckett raised his hands in a mock surrender.

"Shoot," Washington said. "Folks got all jiggy with that book when the school board put it on the reading list. I meaaaan…"

"Yeah, so, we, like figured we gotta see what all the ruckus was about," Fairway said.

"We couldn't let a book divide us," Cissy said.

"I…am…impressed," Beckett admitted.

"Seriously, Mister B, did Margaret Mitchell think she was gonna stir up some real stink with Black folks?" Washington asked.

"That's a fantastic question, Mister Washington. Why weren't Black folks rioting in the streets?"

"Cause they couldn't back then," James Robert Bellchase, son of Pastor Bellchase, said from the back of the room. "Doctor Martin Luther King hadn't come yet."

"Thank you, Mister Bellchase," Beckett said with a clap of his hands. "The Civil Rights Movement of the Sixties started to sweep away the barriers Black folks encountered; but wasn't slavery… the Civil War itself… part of America's history? How can you just sweep that away?"

"You can't," Cissy insisted. "You have to deal with it."

"Exactly," Fairway said.

"That's right."

"Preach."

"So, Margaret Mitchell was kinda remindin' America it was gonna have to deal with the whole Civil War and slavery thing eventually?" Washington asked.

"Perhaps, Mister Washington, that was the unintended consequence of her book," Beckett said. "Consider this, ladies and gentlemen. The book was published in Nineteen-thirty-six."

Cissy and others began to take notes as Beckett launched into his point. He was animated and seemed to enjoy the repartee. Cissy smiled as she saw her father's passion as a teacher. She started to raise her hand when Washington appeared to unload a sense of outrage about the book. Then, Beckett stunned Cissy as he took the outrage and converted it into an explanation.

"By Nineteen-thirty-seven, the book was a bestseller; it won the Pulitzer Prize for fiction…"

"Got that right; it's bogus," Bellchase quipped.

"But is it, Mister Bellchase?" Beckett asked. *"Gone with the Wind* became an enormously popular movie by Nineteen-thirty-nine. And, what happened? Hattie McDaniel, who portrayed Mammy in the movie, became the first Black actor to win an Academy Award. Think about that a moment. A Black woman was named *Best Supporting Actress* by white Hollywood in nineteen-thirty-nine. Somebody in America understood what Margaret Mitchell had done."

They went on, back and forth, through the class period, until the bell rang. "Okay, people, that's a wrap for today," Beckett said.

"Oh, no," Washington said with a mischievous smile. "Ain't gettin' off that easy, Mister B. We're comin' back on it tomorrow."

"Wouldn't expect anything less, Mister Washington," Beckett said.

The mood as the class broke up was congenial and normal. Beckett was satisfied. He erased the white board in preparation for his senior English literature class, as Cissy made her way quickly to the front of the room.

"Hey," she chirped.

"Hey, yourself. So, what do you think?"

She smiled. "You did good," she said. "All the football guys like to argue, and they argue about everything. But they're about as tight a crew as you can get. It was cool the way you picked up on the attitude everybody had about the book. This town is… mostly settled about the race thing."

"White and Black churches?" Beckett posed.

"Mostly settled is not perfect," Cissy said with a shrug. "Don't push your luck… Mister Beckett."

She smiled and turned away to hurry to her next class, leaving Beckett taken aback by his daughter's insight. But the morning left him invigorated. His senior English literature class wasn't as engaged, but as the lunch bell rang, Beckett was satisfied they hadn't fallen asleep.

He flipped off the classroom light switch and ambled into the hallway, still taking in the lay of Destiny High School as he made his way to the cafetorium for lunch. Upper-level classes were literally on the upper two floors of the building as it faced Center Street. Freshmen classes, high school offices, the cafetorium and a single-story science annex were all at ground level of the long, rectangular red-brick building. A newer district offices building sat in the middle of the block on the east end of the high school complex, with the junior high school building immediately to the north, and the primary-elementary school building across a bus lane that extended from Center Street north through the campus to the Freemon Nelson Athletics Complex parking lot.

Beckett's impression of the high school building was one of distinctive longevity, old but solid. He suspected somewhere in town there was someone, perhaps Freemon Nelson, who would like to demolish the place and build shiny metal and glass erector set buildings with no character. Beckett chuckled as he walked into the cafetorium and waited in the teacher's lunch line. Obviously more alumni of Destiny High School who studied in the red brick Federal style building were not ready to expunge it from Destiny.

Beckett took his lunch tray and settled himself at one of the faculty dining tables nearest the cafetorium stage. He remembered the institutional ambiance of a mess hall; where, on a Friday night, he might eat a good steak and baked potato, the equal of anything offered at most franchise restaurants. Base mess halls were contracted services that were gourmet compared to the field-rationed MRE, or Meal Ready to Eat. Beckett chuckled. As bad as MREs might have been, there were times he would have killed to have one. Beckett understood why a man can stomach snake meat only so long. He glanced down at the two ground beef patties and mashed potatoes covered with brown gravy, the green beans, lettuce and tomato salad, and fruit cup on the tray in front of him. Beckett smiled and dug in.

"Seriously?" a deliciously feminine voice asked from beside him. "You enjoy that?"

Beckett looked up from his tray to see two large sapphire eyes surrounded by an astonishing "cougar" body. She was breathtaking, in the sense of a mature sensual creature, unlike any woman Beckett encountered.

"Good Lord," he murmured.

She smiled. "I get that a lot."

"Uhm, uh…"

"And, that," she quipped.

Loretta's eyes consummated her intent with Beckett. "You are… refreshing," she whispered with a small, tense, gasp.

Beckett offered his hand. "Brock, uhm, Brock Be…Beckett," he muttered.

"Loretta Chesterton," she replied, clasping her hand over his and nestling it onto her fashionably ripped denim pant leg as she cuddled beside Beckett. Loretta shook back her midnight black hair and smiled as she discretely guided Beckett's hand across the curvature of her outer thigh. The woman's name echoed through Beckett's mind, but he could have cared less. He was captivated. Was it that she could have been a brunette Jolene 30 years older; or was Beckett simply kidding himself? She was every bit of 40, or 42…and she was gorgeous.

"Chesterton?" Beckett finally asked. "As in…?"

"My great-great-grandfather got filthy rich from this town," Loretta sighed. "And, I get to play schoolmarm to its little darlings. I often find it so entirely tedious, but of course, that was what great-great-granddaddy put into the will. A Chesterton woman has to live here and teach school here, or the whole estate goes to the Episcopal Diocese of Arkansas."

"Oh," Beckett said. "You are… uhm, not married?"

She leaned in and whispered into his ear. "Aren't you lucky?" Loretta purred.

Across the cafetorium, Cissy scowled at the way Loretta acted toward her father. Cissy stewed in her lack of options until Loretta's hand covered Beckett's and both disappeared from view. Cissy shook her head and stood. *"I gotta go rescue the boy."*

Cissy hurried across the cafetorium toward the tray return window on the far side of the faculty tables. She feigned a small surprise at seeing Beckett and waved.

"Hi, Mister Beckett," she called out, looking directly toward him, ignoring the other faculty table in her path.

Beckett turned toward the sound of her voice at the instant Cissy crashed into the other table, sending her tray arcing away from her towards Loretta. Beckett's hand shot upward and grasped the tray, stopping the projectile in mid-flight without disturbing its contents. The moment was seized upon by the denizens of the cafetorium. Applause broke out from the faculty table and students at the tray return window responded.

"Woo, woo, woo."

"Awe…some."

"Way to go, Mister Beckett."

"You see that? Dude… his hand was like… bam… there."

The coincidence of the moment was captured on a cellphone video recorded by two students. The video went viral locally minutes later… with appropriate sound effects. And Cissy's gambit failed completely.

"Why, Mister Beckett; you're my hero," Loretta exclaimed with a gentility that might have rivaled Scarlett O'Hara.

The end of the school day brought Cissy to Beckett's classroom with an apology. "I messed up," she said. "But, it was for a reason."

Beckett smiled as he stowed papers into his briefcase. "No harm; no foul," he replied. Then, he sat back in his chair and listened.

"Loretta Chesterton is… ewww," Cissy said. "Lord knows how many affairs she's had with other teachers. Men… and, maybe, women. But nobody is going to suggest she be fired, not these days. You know, because of all the, uhm… woke garbage. She could seduce the superintendent in the middle of Center Street at noon and not get fired, mostly because she's a Chesterton."

"Whoa, there," Beckett replied. "What makes you such an authority, young lady?"

Cissy stood her ground. "It's common knowledge, for cryin' out loud, Dad," she said. "She's teaching only because it keeps her in the family money. Why else would she teach art appreciation as a required class to seniors in Destiny, Arkansas?"

Beckett zipped his briefcase. "Hon, I appreciate your concern. Really, I do," he said quietly. "But you can't protect me from life, crazy or whatever. I've stayed alive by being unremarkable. I'm exceptionally good at it. But what happened in the cafetorium today can't happen again."

"Yeah, that was a pretty smooth move you had," Cissy said with a hint of pride.

He stood and slipped his hand beneath her chin. Cissy smiled at him, and he reciprocated.

"I love you, sweetheart," Beckett said. "And, if I need to pull any smooth moves for someone, I'd rather it be for you… when it genuinely counts."

"Yes, sir," Cissy replied sheepishly.

But, as his daughter turned and left the room, Beckett was secretly impressed. "Standing up for her old man," he said with a satisfied chuckle. And the thought left him grateful for the moment.

CHAPTER SIX
GOTCHA

The end of the day brought Beckett back to Miss Esther's house in a good humor. Ordinarily, he might have put aside the incident in the cafetorium as a silly sense of jealousy on Cissy's part, had it not been for a disturbing message on his cell phone: "Intruder alert." Beckett slowed his gait as he walked into the driveway on Nelson Street. There were no lights showing in Miss Esther's first floor residence. She was unlikely to be in the apartment. But the security minicam Beckett installed above the apartment door was activated. Someone was inside Beckett's apartment.

"Somebody is curious."

Beckett knew someone with proper training might defeat his minicam system. And, while he was inclined to discount this incident, he remained… cautious. He quickly scanned the street beyond the house, but there were no out-of-place vehicles parked anywhere. He took up a post at his parked Jeep near the large magnolia bush at the rear corner of the house beside the apartment staircase. There were no vehicles in the garage. So, he decided to wait and use the bush as cover.

Commanding a view directly up the staircase, Beckett watched without results for a few minutes. He considered how many times he breached a residence or apartment to learn how the occupant lived. It was simple reconnaissance, the most efficient means of understanding an adversary. Beckett glanced at his watch. The time of day was wrong, and the intruder was overstaying reasonable time limitations.

"Stupid or dangerous; neither is good."

Beckett quietly opened the driver's door of his Jeep, reached beneath the steering wheel dash, tripped a small lever, and the digital radio panel fell forward with a "click." He withdrew from the void a loaded Ruger automatic pistol. A nagging curiosity prevented Beckett from chambering a round in the gun. He decided to consult the apartment minicam and the image on his cellphone screen made him chuckle.

Loretta Chesterton sat comfortably curled upon the sofa in the front room, wearing a semi-sheer black baby doll negligee, and sipping a glass of what appeared to be champagne. Beckett shook his head in amazement.

"Of course, Loretta would have a key. The woman is incorrigible."

Loretta was gorgeous and the night the two might spend together could certainly be memorable. But Beckett was accustomed to choosing his relationships. It was a precaution which kept him alive. Beckett remembered Cissy's simple assessment: "Ewww…" For now, that was good enough.

The important question for Beckett was how long Loretta intended to stay before she became bored or impatient, and left? Beckett wasn't inclined to find out. He returned to the Jeep, holstered the Ruger and quietly closed the driver's door. He checked his watch again: 6 p.m.

"Give her an hour." Beckett crossed the street and headed for the Blue Bird Café.

Monday night at the Blue Bird Café was "domino time" for Destiny Police Chief Harley Randle, Ouachita County Sheriff's Deputy Jimmy Dale Means, retired county Judge Campbell Meecham, Fairway Lumber owner Boyd Fairway and, anyone they might coincidentally invite to sit in on the game. Dominoes is a game of many variations which Beckett played for hours at military base camps. Partners dominoes required an even set of players. With Means out for the evening working a traffic accident, Beckett became a likely fourth, once the introductions were completed and the hamburgers and French fries were ordered.

"My son actually put his cellphone down long enough to read the assignment from *Gone with the Wind*," Fairway remarked as he shuffled the dominoes. "How did you make that happen?"

"It wasn't me, Mister Fairway…"

"Boyd," the other man said.

Beckett smiled. "It wasn't me, Boyd," Beckett said munching on a French fry. "Every student in class came prepared to discuss the book. You folks have done a fantastic job in challenging your children to learn outside of their comfort zone."

"It created a stir when the book wound up on the reading list," Fairway said. "But, you're right; it challenged their comfort zone… for the most part."

Beckett looked at his dominoes. He was weak in fives. "Not much help here, partner," he said. "What do you mean by 'for the most part' about the reading assignment?"

"Well, the Black Baptist preacher's son, the Bellchase kid, got to talking about it among the Black kids; went to the school board and asked for an explanation," Fairway said. "It seems he is most comfortable getting other people out of their comfort zone."

"Yeah, James Robert has his own mind about things," Beckett said. "I didn't know that when I applied for the job."

"You can say that, again," Randle, the Black police chief, remarked. "The coaches say he is hard to work with in practice, but the kid gets it done on Friday night. He's breathin' on a hundred career quarterback sacks this season, but the kid has the attitude."

"It's not the Bellchase boy's fault. Freemon Nelson got him lathered up," Meecham, the retired county judge said. "He keeps the Black community simmering so they think he is their liberal, white advocate. Freemon doesn't do anything for anyone unless there is something at the other end for him."

"Spoken like a man who ran without Freemon's endorsement," Fairway said.

The others laughed, but Beckett sensed an unsettling grain of truth in the statement. He hadn't met Cissy's "uncle," but Beckett was certain of the man's reputation from Lloyd Nelson's remarks.

"I'll have to thank Mister Nelson for his contribution to the discourse, as I'm sure he has read the book," Beckett said drolly.

"Oh, Lord, no," Fairway said. "Freemon and books never got along. He barely graduated from high school. But he did watch the movie on late-night TV."

Meecham grunted. "Yes, but its most memorable scene for Freemon was Rhett Butler carrying Scarlett upstairs to bed her."

Beckett chuckled. "In which case, he'd have liked the book better," he said with a knowing smile. His hosts howled with laughter.

The dominoes night broke up about 8 p.m., later than usual. Randle's excursus on the prospects for the football season generated a new debate which discarded the rule of time altogether. Beckett sat back and listened. He hadn't given the sport of football a serious thought in years, much less the importance of high school football as practiced in Arkansas. He marveled at the near reverence of the police chief's tone, and the dedicated rhetoric of a man as seemingly intelligent as Meecham, over a game which resembled the rough and tumble of boys contesting over a battered soccer ball in an unremarkable village deep in the Afghan mountains.

Beckett gave the boys of that village a soccer ball as a sign of respect for their way of life. The boys scuffed about, kicking and chasing the ball in a semi-continuous game on the dusty outskirts of the village almost every day.

"The soccer ball is a symbol of unity among them," the village elder said. "It is passed from family to family for keeping after each day's play of the game, but the game never ends. That would create a division: a winner and a loser."

"Perhaps the soccer ball will arbitrate between whatever their ancient cultural differences might be, and they might grow one day closer to manhood without becoming radicalized to those biases," Beckett said.

The village elder smiled. "The American with the rifle is a man of… peace."

The soccer ball was the first thing ISIS insurgents destroyed when they overwhelmed the village and pressed its young men into service after murdering their parents. ISIS spotters watched the village, and the soccer game, for some time before the raid. Beckett learned of the carnage from the few surviving men too old to fight and women too old to bear children when he returned.

ISIS spotters were part of mercenary units that raided villages; conscripted boys into combat service and used them as bombing martyrs. And, provided fresh girls to ISIS men for diversion and forced marriage. Beckett relied upon the raiders being stupid in their tactics, brutal in their methods, and not committed to genuine jihad. Beckett tracked the raiding party through the mountains, following a trail of candy bar and chewing gum wrappers. He fell back during the day, trailing the contingent by four or five miles through the mountain passes until they reached a base camp, where the boys were separated into holding pens and the girls taken into tents.

The girls' pleas, cries of pain, and shame began almost immediately, and lasted into the night. The corresponding righteous indignation of the boys in the holding pens was met with blunt force. There was little Beckett could do alone against a base camp force except call in a drone strike. He waited until the early morning hours, when the girls were handed into the tutelage of the other women, and separated prior to the morning prayers.

The entire ISIS unit assembled in the center of the encampment and knelt facing toward Mecca for prayers. Beckett laid in the coordinates on his cell phone for the drone strike and waited for confirmation of the mission. Waiting was the most frustrating part of the endeavor. Beckett could not succeed in freeing anyone until he had cover within the chaos of the drone strike.

Beckett was lucky; his target was too tempting for operations command. "You have a go, Texas; ETA is fifteen minutes. Good hunting," the voice in his earbud commlink said.

Beckett settled into his sniper's nest. He intended to pick off the outliers immediately after the flash of the drone attack. He sighted the three outlier posts in order and quickly completed the necessary calculations. Then, he waited, again.

Beckett compared drones to buzzards. They circle high above their prey, which presents the problem of shadows. Beckett saw the streak of a shadow against the cliffs along the far side of the mountain encampment, he targeted the first outlier, drew a deep breath, and held it. Beckett rested his finger against the trigger of his rifle. The drone's first blast came almost immediately, as did

Beckett's first shot. The far outlier fell backward from his position. Beckett took out the man on the other side of the camp nearest the center of the compound next. The ignition flash and concussion from the drone's Hellfire missile made it the most difficult shot. Beckett scrambled down along the hillside from his nest ready to make the third shot. But the boys in the holding pen, emboldened by the drone strike, took down the third man.

Beckett held his cover, taking out potential threats to the developing holding pen escape. Automatic weapons fire began to ping along the hillside from a few survivors of the blast, and Beckett took them down in sequence.

And then, there were the spotters. From their position on the far side of the base camp, they were responsible for detecting potential threats and warning the base command. Their failure to use binoculars with non-reflective lenses typified their stupidity. They were an easy target for Beckett. Like curious gamebirds, they popped up from their cover in response to the mayhem in the camp below them and used their binoculars to get a better look.

Beckett squeezed off the first round. The bullet darkened the glint from the first spotter's binocular lens. Unable to react with sufficient speed, the second spotter was thrown dead to the ground an instant later by Beckett's next shot.

"Gotcha!"

Boyd Fairway's voice imposed itself upon Beckett's mind. "See you next Monday?" he asked.

"Uhm… yeah; great," Beckett said, his recollection broken. "Thanks."

"Good to have you here because Jimmy Dale is a lousy partner," Fairway said with a chuckle.

Beckett laughed but, as he ambled back along Center Street toward Miss Esther's house he was struck by the dissonance in his life. His hope was seeing Cissy each day at school might help close the chasm of the past in favor of a future for them.

The apartment was empty and quiet when Beckett returned, undisturbed except for a note left in the neck of an empty champagne bottle. It bore Loretta Chesterton's handwriting.

"How could you find anything else in Destiny preferable to me?" she wrote. "But, I'm a forgiving sort. See you tomorrow… Loretta."

Beckett pondered whether to consider the note a threat or a promise. Either way, he was not inclined to satisfy Loretta's libidinous intents. He tossed the note and champagne bottle into the trash bin. Beckett smiled wistfully. Jolene would have approved.

He secured the front door and switched off the light, then, made his way into the bedroom to prepare for bed. Brushing his teeth before retiring was still a novelty to Beckett. It was a consistent practice for him as a boy but dusk in the Kandahar Valley of Afghanistan did not lend itself to good dental hygiene. He chuckled and enjoyed the minty sting of the toothpaste.

Beckett settled himself into bed and picked up from the bedside table his teaching copy of *Gone with the Wind*. He made a few notes on specific passages for the next day's classes, remembering his earlier conversation about the comfort zones of his students. Beckett pondered whether maintaining the edginess of the first day's discussion was the key to teaching the book to Cissy's generation. Beckett jotted a question at the top of the page and put aside the book and the day.

CHAPTER SEVEN
FUBAR

~~*~~

Cissy was accosted in the hallway outside of Beckett's classroom by Marilee Page, head cheerleader and girlfriend of Wade Fairway. Marilee was in an arm-waving fit as she pulled Cissy aside.

"Have you seen the question he has written on the board?" Marilee almost shouted.

"Don't shout," Cissy said. Marilee seemed to shout about everything, perhaps, because she was a cheerleader. "What question do you mean?"

"Mister Beckett…oh, go look for yourself," Marilee said. "Gawd, I'm just gonna die…"

Cissy's hopes that a good start to the first week of classes might last for her father seemed doomed. She walked into the classroom and read the question on the whiteboard at the front of the room.

"Holy moley. How does *Gone with the Wind* reflect what happened to America on September eleventh, Two-thousand-one?"

Cissy closed her eyes in disappointment. "I've… got…to save the boy this time."

She dropped her backpack onto the floor beside her desk and slid into her seat. Cissy scoured her mind for a good point Beckett might make with his question, as Devonte Washington followed him into the classroom a moment later.

"What the hey, Mister B?" Washington asked with an animated open arm throw down gesture. "You seriously gotta look at that smack. It's… in… the book. Rhett Butler is, like, old enough to be her daddy, and Scarlett is only sixteen. And, he's like all hot and bothered over her. They'd hung a Black man for that."

"No, Mister Washington," Beckett offered. "They'd hang a Black man for suggesting half of the stuff Rhett suggests to Scarlett."

"And he gets away with lopin' around with this sixteen-year-old white girl?" Devonte asked indignantly.

Cissy was taken aback, and she became concerned whether Marilee Page was right.

"You forget, Mister Washington, Scarlett married Charles Hamilton, Melanie's brother, two weeks after all the young men enlisted to war," Beckett said. "And nobody said a blessed thing about it."

The tardy bell rang and everybody settled into their seats as Beckett pulled his teaching copy of the book from his briefcase. He put a check mark beside the question on the board.

"We'll get to this in a moment," he said. "But, first, Mister Washington brings up a highly relevant point I want us to get clear. Mister Washington, you have the floor…"

Washington fidgeted in his seat for a moment. "You're okay, Mister Washington," Beckett said. "You have a legitimate point I want everyone to understand. But I want you to explain it."

"Well, it's like this," Washington began. "I was sayin' in the Civil War South, Black families got broke up a lot being slaves and being sold to different people. Sometimes, just because some white man… or woman… wanted, you know, somebody to mess around with in bed. Lot of times young girls… and boys… got sold off that way or got married to some other much older slave."

He offered air quotes to the suggestion. "And that wasn't right; not right at all," Washington said.

Agreement from other students rippled across the room. Washington took the affirmation in stride.

"But it was slavery… and nobody Black could do a thing about it," he said. "Then, I noticed in the book Scarlett, she's, like, only sixteen years old. And she's got it all bad for Ashley. But, he's gonna marry his… cousin? Man, that's all messed up. And, Rhett, he's, like old enough to be Scarlett's daddy. He hears Scarlett and Ashley talkin' and after Ashley leaves, he outright asks this sixteen-year-old girl to shack with him. She gets all triggered, but ten minutes earlier she's ready to get at it with Ashley, who is just as old as Rhett.

"These people can go around handin' out Black girls to anybody. But a Black man back then asks a sixteen-year-old white girl to shack with him gets hisself hung," Washington insisted. "But, nobody's lookin' sideways at Rhett… or Ashley… about Scarlett. It is messed up, man."

Crickets might have sounded like the French horn section of a philharmonic at that moment. Marilee Page was… aghast. Cissy was amazed at Washington's insight. She raised her hand and Beckett acknowledged her.

"So, the Civil War wasn't just about slavery; it was about the morals of Southern life?" Cissy asked. "And Margaret Mitchell exposed it."

"It was, in the North as well as the South, accepted for girls as young as sixteen to marry in Eighteen-sixty-three. But it was not proper for a white girl of sixteen to become a mistress," Beckett said. "That's what angers Scarlett about Rhett's proposition. She was born to be a Southern Belle, but she was forced to grow up outside of that ideal when the Civil War began. Which brings us to the question I have written on the board.

"I want you to think about how September Eleventh affected you and your life. How did the world around you change as a result of what happened that day? I want you to spend the remainder of the class period writing your understanding of how that event affected you… and America; and compare it with two or three points from the book about how the Civil War changed Scarlett and the South."

Marilee raised her hand. "But, Mister Beckett, we weren't born when the Nine-eleven attacks occurred," she said.

"True, Miss Page; but, the event has had an impact upon your life, nonetheless," he replied. "Try boarding an airplane with a box cutter."

"Or, a sharp pencil," Wade Fairway said.

The class broke into laughter as the point had been delivered. But, for Beckett, it was a test of comfort zones in a small Arkansas town with a similarly dramatic significance for him. The quiet which pervaded the classroom throughout the remainder of the period told him the question was taken seriously by the class. And it provoked a curiosity in him to see the results. The bell at the end of the class period produced a few groans.

"I'm not finished," Washington complained.

"No problem, people," Beckett said. "If you're satisfied with what you've got, hand it in now. If not, polish it at home tonight. We will read and discuss tomorrow."

The vividness of Beckett's recollections from Nine-eleven hung in his memory; it was the day he enlisted in the Marine Corps. Three years later, Jolene died, and Beckett did not see his baby, Cissy, until 14 years later. September 11, 2001, was the catalyst that took Beckett to the forbidden landscape of the Middle East where he changed history. But his acceptance of the point was a bitter admission.

"Are you okay?" Cissy's voice called out from the classroom doorway.

Beckett's mind clouded with memories, but he obfuscated the thought. He smiled, sending his daughter on her way content in the belief Beckett was not singularly vulnerable. He closed his eyes plagued by the televised images of the collapse of the World Trade Center South Tower which replayed across the green screen of his memory in a mental loop since the moment his sister died on Nine-eleven.

The televised close-up of his sister's expression of abject horror and realization as she stood near the shattered window in the South Tower was gut-wrenching to Beckett. Then, her legs splayed outward in a semi-split, her dress billowed open before collapsing against her face as she suddenly careened into the void toward the street some 50 stories below. Beckett's sister died of fear before her body disappeared into the rubble, smoke and dust. Penny Beckett was overtaken by the near-nuclear force of the South Tower's rush to the ground. There was nothing left for Beckett to recover, nothing over which to grieve. Penny Beckett was existentially obliterated.

"Penny...," Beckett gasped.

The moment left Beckett incensed and weakened. He trembled and clutched the side of the teacher's desk. How foolish Beckett thought were the young men of Tara, Twelve Oaks, and the other fiefdoms of the Antebellum South as they rushed headlong, whooping at the top of their lungs for the glory of war. How broken they returned. Yet, Beckett believed himself to be better invested.

Beckett slumped into the teacher's chair and buried his face in his hands. He wept quietly. He saw Jolene daily in Cissy and hoped to find the grace to be at peace for his sister and his wife as he drifted into a troubled sleep to relive the hunt for a Russian general.

"Norum al-Nahmeed filled the vacuum left in Syria when Iran's proxy, Hamas, was routed with the blessing of the Syrian elites," General Pierpont Maxwell, Beckett's operations commander explained in the mission briefing. "Al-Nahmeed is the promise of a continuing secularization of Syria which inflames the jihadists. Russia wants to build a warm water port on the Mediterranean, and ultimately to absorb Syria and Turkey into its sphere of influence in exchange for Russian dominance as a firewall against the Caliphate.

"Putin can live with Iranian impatience to destroy Israel if he gets Ukrainian ports at Mariupol and Odessa in the Black Sea," Maxwell said. "Then Russian naval power can be inserted permanently through the Aegean Sea into the Mediterranean on the Syrian coast. And that will shift the balance of pivotal force assets in the region dramatically and cast a chill across the entire underbelly of NATO and Europe. And China will look the other way."

Maxwell's voice, with its crisp, patrician pronunciation, was indelibly imprinted upon Beckett's mind at their first meeting. Beckett was a schoolteacher from South Texas; but Maxwell's family sent its sons to Annapolis. An imposing physical figure, Maxwell embodied discipline, service and military fidelity.

"You graduated the top of your group and have extensive experience on the ground in the Middle East," Maxwell said. "That is why you are here, Captain Beckett. You have been transferred to this unit to inaugurate a new chapter in the U.S. Naval Special Warfare Services. You are transferred to SEAL Team Eighteen officially in reserve status and unknown to anyone outside of this room. You will train like hell. You will be an independent, asymmetrical force operating with your unit and individually as needed. The political façade of your mission is the destabilization and destruction of the resurrected ISIS command and control structure throughout Afghanistan, northern Iraq and Syria.

"Since the George W. Bush Administration, the Russians have been heavily involved in destabilization campaigns throughout the Middle East," Maxwell said. "General Nicholai Vichinkov is the architect of those campaigns and the handler for al-Nahmeed."

Beckett studied the face on the digital whiteboard. "Vichinkov has been playing both sides against each other, supplying weapons to ISIS through Al Shuba back-channels in Somolia. And straightforward military and policy support to al-Nahmeed in Syria, and to the Turkish government on the other side," Maxwell said. "So, we take out Putin's guy and disrupt his strategy."

"That will piss off Putin," Beckett said.

"Only if you screw up and he finds out, Captain," the General replied. "So, don't screw up. Play the Three Fs with the Russian special forces operating in Syria: Find the Russian teams; Focus unanticipated combat pressure against them; and, Fix the situation by eliminating their presence."

"We make them look sufficiently FUBAR, Fouled up but army regulation, they will begin to question their own judgment and then, we put them down," Beckett said. "Each action will be unique. There is no standard plan. We assess, adapt and execute on the ground with whatever we find."

"You're a quick study, Captain," Maxwell quipped. "I'm gonna enjoy watching you work."

When the Russian team routing weapons to ISIS contacted its Al Shuba connection about a cargo ship carrying a large shipment of ammonium nitrate to be used to construct truck bombs, the Somali pirates who attacked the ship were intercepted by Beckett's team. His team was dressed in stolen Russian military uniforms and armed with stolen Russian weapons. Satellite images of the attack shown to Vichinkov confirmed the Somalis were cut down by masked men dressed as Russian special forces. Ship's crewmen interrogated by Vichinkov said the men spoke Russian. ISIS retaliated by bombing a Russian-owned oil terminal in Iran.

Beckett's take down of Vichinkov was in the fabled vampire hours around midnight when the moon shone brightest over the suburbs of Damascus, Syria. Beckett checked his watch as he nested on a rooftop some 600 yards from the rear of a luxury hotel where General Nicholai Vichinkov bedded his mistress of the evening. Beckett chuckled as he punched a telephone number into the keypad of a burner phone purchased from a room service waiter at the hotel. Beckett settled his shoulder against the stolen Russian Guryev Type P hard target sniper rifle beside him. One ring; two rings; three rings… and movement.

"Da," a gravel-tongued voice barked into Beckett's ear.

"Proshaitye," Beckett replied. The American inflected pronunciation of the formal Russian for "goodbye" drew Vichinkov bolt upright in the bed.

Beckett targeted Vichinkov's heat signature with infrared technology accounting for his height from the waist upward and calculated the drift of the shot at one to six inches. He aimed high by no more than a mil to compensate. Beckett held his breath and let his finger squeeze against the trigger of the Guryev Type P and an armor-piercing round whispered away from the barrel at approximately a thousand feet per second. The bullet sped unimpeded through the dry Middle Eastern night air, smashed the heavy stained-glass window opposite the bed in the hotel room, blew Vichinkov's chest apart, penetrated the headboard above the still sleeping prostitute, and left a hole the size of a small melon in the wall. Vichinkov did not have time to comprehend his own death.

"Fubar," Beckett murmured.

"What, Mister B?"

Beckett opened his eyes to realize his third period class was seated in front of him. "Sorry about that," he offered sheepishly. "Uhm… up late grading papers."

The remainder of the day droned by mercifully for Beckett leaving him upset with himself for his lapse into melancholy as he gathered class papers into his briefcase and switched off the classroom lights. He stopped for a moment, arrested by the activity outside as students boarded buses, piled into cars and walked home for the day.

Beckett spotted Cissy and Devonte Washington standing beside a battered pickup truck with *Washington Salvage* painted on the driver's door. Cissy seemed animated, and almost flirtatious with Washington, which took Beckett aback. The conversation was brief as Washington pointed toward the football field and Cissy nodded. She waved demurely as Washington turned and trotted away, and Beckett began to ponder a curiosity as Cissy blissfully meandered toward Center Street.

"That day in the rain. Was she waiting for Devonte?"

CHAPTER EIGHT
THIS WAS MILITARY-GRADE ORDNANCE

The buzz in the hallways at Destiny High School the following day was deer hunting talk. Boys were excited and girls were gathered in knots of quiet consolation. Beckett was bemused as he brought order to his third period class. Then all heads turned at the wail of a siren as Ouachita County Sheriff's Deputy Jimmy Dale Means' county unit raced past the school complex along Center Street and careened around the corner at North Cross Street. Students scrambled toward the windows as the cruiser barreled away from Destiny toward the Ouachita River.

"Looks like he's headed out toward your daddy's place, Cissy," Wade Fairway remarked.

Cissy tensed at her desk as she attempted to ignore the possibilities. She glanced toward Beckett at the front of the room.

"Give him a call," he said quietly.

"Thank you." Cissy rummaged about in her purse until she found her cell phone. Then, she hurried into the hallway. She returned a few moments later ashen and shaken and the buzz of classroom speculation turned quiet as everyone took their seats.

"You okay, Cissy?" Devonte Washington asked as she shuffled past his desk.

"Daddy is okay; but, they think there was a hunting accident," she said. "And one of the men who works for us was shot…"

There were immediate inquiries from around the room. Beckett held up his hands and called for quiet.

"Let her explain, people," he said firmly, as he walked to Cissy's desk. He knelt beside her. "Are you comfortable talking about it?"

She drew a deep breath and sighed; then, she nodded. "It was Frederico Mendez; he's dead," she said softly. "He taught me how to ride a horse…"

Tears swelled at the corners of her eyes and Cissy buried her face against Beckett's shoulder. Slowly, quietly, everyone in the class left their seats one by one to offer condolences.

Washington knelt beside Beckett. "I knew the dude. He was a good man; got a son who plays junior high ball. I been workin' with him some; you know, running the ball… and stuff. I'm really sorry."

Cissy sniffed and hugged Washington. "Thanks, Devonte," she whispered, then Cissy realized the reaction in the room. "His son is gonna… uhm, uh… need somebody to help him… you know…"

Washington nodded knowingly. "I got this."

The pall which descended over the classroom swept aside all discussion. "We'll call a halt for today," Beckett said. "If you've got earbuds or headphones, go ahead and quietly use them for the remainder of the period. Otherwise, if you feel like you need to talk to the school counselor, I'll cut you a hall pass."

Beckett left Cissy in the care of the other girls in the class. He returned to the teacher's desk and tapped the intercom call button on the desk telephone.

"Yes, Mister Beckett," a female voice responded.

"Miss Windemeir, we've just had a student learn there was a death related to her family. So, I may need to send some students to the counselor," Beckett said.

"Oh?" the voice replied. "That's surprising, because I've just now sent Mayor Nelson upstairs to see you."

"Roger that… uhm, I mean, thank you," Beckett said as Lloyd Nelson knocked on the classroom doorframe.

"May I interrupt?" he asked. His voice drew Cissy's attention.

"Daddy…," she mewed, and she bolted from her desk into Nelson's embrace.

The scene stung Beckett. He might have sold his soul at that moment to have her address him as "Daddy."

Nelson cradled Cissy's face in his work-worn hands. "I need to borrow your dad…uh, Mister Beckett."

Cissy blushed at the pretense. She glanced inside the classroom and offered Beckett an apologetic smile.

"I'm sorry… Daddy," she mouthed.

Beckett smiled. "No problem," he mimed.

Nelson stepped into the doorway. "Can I let Miss Windemeir take Cissy home while I borrow you, Mister Beckett?"

"Certainly," Beckett said as Cissy returned to her desk to gather her things. Beckett met her.

"Are you okay, Miss Nelson?" he asked with more formality than he preferred.

"Yes; thank you, Mister Beckett," she said.

Presently, Superintendent Bittle and Miss Windemeir mounted the top of the stairs. Cissy and Miss Windemeir disappeared downstairs as Bittle shook hands with both men. Beckett informed him of the situation.

"Don't ride herd on them too hard," Beckett said. "I don't have to tell you how things are in a small school when something like this happens."

Bittle stepped inside the classroom and closed the door, leaving Beckett in the hallway with Nelson. The Mayor heaved a frustrated sigh.

"I need to show you something," he said, "I need your… expertise."

Beckett arched an eyebrow at the tone and language of the statement. "My… expertise?" he repeated.

"You know what I mean," Nelson said gruffly.

"That's what worries me," Beckett said.

Ten minutes later, Nelson stopped his SUV in front of the supply barn and office building at the gate to the Nelson ranch road. He was remarkably silent during the drive from town, which left

Beckett modestly unsettled. Deputy Jimmy Dale Means met them on the office walkway.

"Sorry to disrupt your day, Mister Beckett," Means said almost offhandedly. "But Lloyd here don't agree with Vernon Lard's ruling this was a hunting accident."

"Who is Vernon Lard?" Beckett asked.

"The county coroner," Nelson said. "He owns a funeral home in Camden, and has been coroner since his daddy died and left him the job."

"Roger that," Beckett replied.

"The body is in the meat locker," Nelson said, pointing toward the supply barn. "Jimmy Dale, see if you can tear Vernon away from the coffee pot to join us."

"Yes, sir," Means said, turning back to the office.

Nelson unlocked the supply barn access door, chocked it and flipped on the light switch, then he strode to the meat locker door at the other end of the building. Beckett followed obligingly.

The building was as Beckett imagined at his first ranch visit; clean, orderly, squared-away. Storing a body in the meat locker went against that grain and Beckett pondered Nelson's reasoning.

Beckett began to catalogue scenarios. "You don't think this was an accident," he said. "It's not a close quarters combat killing with a knife because Cissy specifically mentioned a shooting. The shooting was initially ruled a hunting accident which means a large caliber weapon must have been involved… How am I doing?"

"Keep going," Nelson said.

Beckett crossed his arms against his chest. The set of his jaw tightened. "The only prospect left is one of 'expertise,'" he said with a frustrated sigh. "A distance shot… a sniper."

Nelson unlocked the meat locker and swung the door open, flipped on the light switch and pushed aside the opaque plastic sheeting in front of them. The body was wrapped in heavy plastic sheeting used to line packing boxes. Nelson slipped a pocket knife from his trousers and slit the duct tape holding the sheeting in place and it fell away to disclose the body of a middle-aged Hispanic man of average height and build, light complexion with a full moustache and dark, wavy hair.

"Frederico Mendez," Nelson said quietly. "He worked for me for twenty years."

Nelson turned and looked squarely into Beckett's eyes. His demeanor was bitterly somber.

"This man did not die from a hunting accident," he said. "I don't care what that excuse for a county coroner says. Frederico knew these woods. He knew who hunted and when. Hell, he knew who was poaching and where. He was as good as any game warden."

Beckett studied the wound in the middle of the man's chest. "Center mass, one shot, large caliber, judging by the damage," he said. He gingerly lifted the body to view the man's back.

"Well, what do you think?" Nelson said impatiently.

Beckett pointed to the exit wound. "You know what I think. You knew when you came to my classroom."

"I want to hear it," Nelson said testily.

"All right," Beckett said. "This wasn't a hunting rifle. This was military-grade ordnance."

"Now, I want you to tell that idiot coroner," Nelson said. "And, use small words, so he understands it."

"I'm in the room, Lloyd," a nasal, heavily Southern-accented voice called out from the meat locker doorway. Vernon Lard was five-feet-three inches and one hundred and eighty pounds of droll, parochial sarcasm. "And, I can understand big words, like conspiratorial nonsense. Those are big words."

Beckett extended his hand. "Brock Beckett," he said.

"Yeah, heard of you," Lard replied. He squared himself in front of Beckett to as much height as he could muster. "Since when does an English teacher know anything about gunshot accidents?"

"He's got the chops, Vernon. Trust me," Nelson said.

"Impress me, school teacher," the portly coroner said.

"This was a one shot kill, fired most likely, from under about three hundred yards, judging by the extent of the damage," Beckett began. "This was not a rifle shot per your typical hunting weapon. This was an ordnance round, albeit smaller variety on the level of an M14, probably using a negative lead to shoot behind his target while accounting for the target's retreat to flee."

Beckett turned to Nelson. "Has anyone heard any helicopters over the ranch property today?" he asked.

"Nobody said anything when I checked with the hands this morning," Nelson said. "But I was late getting out here today."

"Where was the body discovered?" Beckett asked.

"He was a couple hundred yards or more from the bottom of a bluff off the river about three miles upstream from here. It's a place where we typically round up strays that like to water there. So, it's away from the deer woods," Nelson explained. "There are no broken bones, so he was on grade level with the riverbank."

"And, judging by the angle of the exit wound, I'd say he was fired upon from above," Beckett said. "How high is the bluff you mentioned?"

"I'd say a good forty feet," Nelson replied.

Beckett nodded. "That's just high enough. I want to see the bluff."

"We'll need horses," Nelson said.

"You're not getting me on any damned horse," Lard barked.

Nelson looked at Deputy Means. "Tie him to the saddle, if need be, Jimmy Dale," he deadpanned.

Forty minutes later, the four men rode out of the timber canopy into the opening of a small, grassy meadow and surmounted the summit of the bluff above the Ouachita River. The slope of the bluff rose from the meadow and broadened above the riverbank below. Beckett pulled his horse up short as soon as they arrived and pointed to a large area of disturbed dirt.

"Somebody had a small chopper up here," he said.

Beckett dismounted, walked to the edge of the bluff, squatted and peered below with binoculars.

"Mendez was hit over there," Beckett said, pointing down to a blood-stained patch in the sandy riverbank upstream. He stood and surveyed the top of the bluff.

"He was shot before they landed," Beckett said.

"What the hell?" Nelson exclaimed. "Why?"

Beckett turned toward the river. He understood why the moment they arrived, but he was loathe to accept the notion. Yet, it was a singularly compelling conclusion which he kept to himself.

"Good question, Lloyd," he said almost offhandedly. "Drugs, maybe?"

Nelson scuffed at the dirt with the toe of his cowboy boot. "Damn," he muttered. "I guess they could have brought it in by chopper and taken it downriver in a small boat."

"That seems kinda complicated to me," Deputy Means said.

"Cartels have been known to hire snipers for protection," Beckett said. "Perhaps, they intended to make the exchange on the river and had their man above, and he spotted Mister Mendez."

It was an explanation that would sell Beckett's thought. But as he gazed across the Ouachita River Valley landscape through his binoculars, he was drawn to a distinct point roughly a mile away with a clear line of sight and virtually level trajectory, the second floor of the Destiny High School building.

CHAPTER NINE
WE WAIT

Beckett understood the scenario. "Once a sniper builds a nest, the kill is assured," he said after County Coroner Vernon Lard and Sheriff's Deputy Jimmy Dale Means left the Nelson ranch. "The chain of command may alter the action or abort it; but, unless and until an order is received, the target is considered dead."

"Tell me something I don't know," Nelson carped. "Jack and Jill in the first reader…"

The evidence at the ranch was clear to both men as Nelson drove them back into Destiny.

"The apparent airborne kill shot of Frederico Mendez could allow someone to build a nest," Beckett said. "The brushy cover on the river bluff, the location of the bluff itself with easy access to fresh water and a secluded locale for a campsite below are all favorable for it."

But, when Nelson later wheeled away from Miss Esther's house, Beckett was surprised the obvious question of target zones was never mentioned. The possibilities kept Beckett awake that night as he lay in bed.

"Someone was securing a nest site for a particular kill zone."

Beckett considered the high school building and grounds at one end of Center Street and the Masonic Hall at the other end of town the most reasonable target zones within a mile of the nest site on the ranch bluff. An interior shot in either case was extremely difficult, but not impossible. Beckett had done it. He rolled over in bed and sought to put the memory of Norum al-Nahmeed out of his mind, as he fell into a dream sleep.

"The death of Norum al-Nahmeed will have worldwide implications for a Middle East peace agreement and saves thousands of lives," General Maxwell said in crisp, patrician diction. "This interior shot is the most difficult ever attempted against a high-value target in a fortified kill zone. That's why it's your kill, Captain.

"The Syrian Presidential Palace in Damascus sits atop a hill carved out of the surrounding landscape and it commands a three-hundred sixty-degree view above the remainder of the city in the valley below it," Maxwell said as Beckett studied the photos. "It's located west of the Barada and Tora rivers, beyond the main city, and opposite the Beirut Road. The palace complex proper sits at the eastern end of an oval compound with open access from a main entrance roadway on the western side, which is divided into three approaches."

Maxwell highlighted the points. "The skyline to the west of the city is dominated by the palace and marked to the north by the Tomb of the Unknown Soldiers on the summit of this hill directly beyond the confluence of the Barada and Tora rivers," he said. "That's critical, because the terraced hillsides opposite the compound are covered with trees to produce a tourist panorama along both sides of the Beirut Road southeastward toward the University of Damascus main campus. That is your cover.

"The palace complex is a series of architectural deflections of lines of sight and is structurally engineered to confuse external appearances with internal usages," Maxwell explained.

Beckett nodded. "It's a box of boxes."

"Precisely," Maxwell said. "The massive complex of structures has only one open line of sight: a balconied room on the third floor of the eastern face of the complex, which can be viewed directly from the groves above the Beirut Road at the confluence of the two rivers."

There is where Beckett built his nest in a niche he dug from the side of the uppermost terrace behind the trunks of two trees growing near the precipice above the rivers. He kept a cold camp there for more than a week, tediously observing the movements which took place on the eastern side of the compound, and in the east side gardens.

"Tack, tack, tack. Tack, tack, tack." The noise penetrated Beckett's sleep.

"Tack, tack, tack."

Beckett stirred awake and sat up. "Tack, tack, tack."

Someone was knocking at Beckett's apartment door. He roused himself, pulled on a bathrobe and padded to the door. A quick glance through the curtained window beside the door disclosed Cissy fidgeting on the threshold outside.

Beckett unlocked the door and swung it partially open. "Morning," he muttered. "What are you doing here on a Saturday morning, darlin'?"

Sunlight played against Cissy's auburn hair giving it an almost liquid sheen as the chill in the air quickly enlivened Beckett's senses to notice his daughter had been crying. He pushed back the screen door and brushed his fingertips against her cheek.

"What's wrong, Cissy?" he asked.

"Can we talk?"

Beckett opened the interior door and ushered her inside the apartment. Then, thinking better of his actions, he left the interior door completely ajar.

"You're a student of mine, and you shouldn't be inside my apartment and alone with me," he explained hastily.

"Lloyd knows I'm here," Cissy said quietly. "He's the president of the school board... if anybody asks..."

Beckett took note of her address of Nelson by his given name; Cissy had never done that. He smiled. "Thanks for the heads up, Hon," he said. "Have you had breakfast? How about some scrambled eggs and toast?"

"That would be cool," Cissy said, as she unzipped her hoodie and slipped it off to reveal a U.S. Marine Corps sweatshirt beneath it. "I've always wondered what this apartment looked like. I've heard Lloyd and Miss Esther talk about it, but I've never been up here. This is nice."

Beckett nodded. "It suits me," he replied, a bit warily.

The eggs, buttered toast with honey, and fresh orange juice improved Cissy's perspective. "That was wonderful," she said. "Thanks. I do feel better."

She helped Beckett clear the table and they chatted amiably as they quickly washed the dishes, leaving the two of them standing at the kitchen sink drying their hands on a shared dish towel. Almost immediately their hands became entwined in the dish towel, binding them to each other and they stopped precipitously. They fumbled with the dish towel for an awkward moment, Cissy looked up into Beckett's eyes. She raised herself on tiptoes and hugged him gently.

"I love you, Daddy," she whispered. "I should have told you sooner."

Beckett melted. He wrapped his arms about his daughter and held her tightly against himself. "I should have found you sooner," he said. "I'm… so… sorry."

Cissy wept quietly in his embrace. Beckett sighed as though he was freed of a terrible weight.

"No, you don't understand," Cissy said. "It didn't occur to me until yesterday, when Lloyd…"

"Wait a minute," Beckett interjected. "Why are you referring to your dad by his given name?"

"That's just it. He's not my dad," Cissy replied. "You are. And it occurred to me yesterday when I got upset about Frederico Mendez and I called Lloyd *Daddy* in front of you and the whole class. I saw the look on your face… you were hurt."

"Your reaction yesterday was entirely understandable," Beckett said. "Sure, it… it reminded me I haven't been your father for a long time. Good Lord, for most of your life. So, whatever relationship we can eventually build together, I'm grateful to have."

He turned away from the sink, momentarily irritated by a bright glint of distant light which shone through the kitchen window. Cissy took his hands in her hands and tugged him away from the counter. They sat on the sofa in the living area. Cissy curled her knees up beneath her chin and studied Beckett for a long moment.

"Do you like my sweatshirt?" she asked timidly.

"Roger that," Beckett said, and he offered her a fist bump.

Cissy giggled. She bit her lower lip. "Don't misunderstand," she said, "I love Lloyd and Grace, and everything you said about them the night you came to the house for dinner is true. But it's not right that you only get to be my *father* and not my *dad*."

She offered air quotes for the distinction. "So, I came today to apologize for what happened yesterday," she added, "and, to tell you I'd like for us to hang out together some time… you know, as daughter and dad."

Beckett smiled. "I'd like that more than anything," he said. "But it may be a while longer before we can do so openly."

Cissy frowned. "Why?"

"People, hon," Beckett said. "First, your adoptive parents, Lloyd and Grace are… awesome. I don't want them to feel shut out or pushed aside. They have given you their whole lives, and we need to honor their commitment. Secondly, everybody else in Destiny is going to need to know me a great deal better for them to understand what we can and can't tell them. Do you understand?"

Cissy's mouth pursed into a tight, sardonic grimace, then slowly, she nodded. "Yeah, I get it," she said.

"Look, you think of something we can do; perhaps, at the ranch, or someplace else, and we'll give it a shot. Okay?" Beckett said.

Cissy brightened and she wrapped her arms around his neck. "Thanks… Dad," she exclaimed. "I love you."

"I love you, too… Little Red," Beckett said. He stroked Cissy's hair. "That's what I called you… Little Red. Your mother was Mama Red and you were Little Red, because you both had the prettiest red hair I'd ever seen."

The introduction to the Marine Corps Hymn suddenly began to pour from the pocket of Cissy's hoodie. She giggled. "New cell phone ring tone," she said. "Hello. Oh, yeah. Sure, uhm… Dad…"

She handed the cell phone to Beckett. "It's for you… Dad," she said.

"Hello," he said.

Nelson chuckled. "I hope you and Cissy had some quiet time together."

"We had breakfast and got to know each other a bit better," Beckett said.

"I'm glad, but I need to talk to you. Would you send Cissy home and be ready for me to pick you up in about thirty minutes?"

Beckett knew he couldn't refuse, it would not have been right or decent. But, he hated to say, "Yes."

After Cissy's four-wheeler chugged away from the driveway at Miss Esther's, Beckett showered, shaved and dressed in time to hear Nelson's pickup truck turn into the driveway. Beckett locked the apartment door behind him and ambled down the stairs. Nelson motioned him into the passenger seat.

"Where are we headed?" Beckett asked nonchalantly.

"Camden," Nelson replied. "Coroner's inquest at the courthouse. I need to be there when Vernon Lard rules Frederico Mendez's death as a hunting accident."

"I thought you had given up too easily," Beckett said. "Are you going to contest Lard's finding?"

Nelson sighed. "No," he grumbled. "A murder investigation would screw up the Social Security benefits for his family. But, I want everything documented… for later."

"That sounds a bit ominous… for later," Beckett said. "Is that where I fit in? Later? Because, frankly, I'm not comfortable…"

"Cut the crap, Captain," Nelson shot back. "You know damned well there was a sniper nest on the bluff at the ranch. What you and I have to figure out is… why?"

Beckett said nothing. He stared through the passenger window at the brilliance of the day, overtaken by the memory of a night strewn with starlight, a full moon and the sounds of street dogs barking in the distance. A chilled breeze swept through the cedar grove along the terraced hillside above the Beirut Road in Damascus. The faint strains of music drifted away from the Presidential Palace in occasional wisps to break the tedium of the night from across the valley below. The eastern gardens were decorated with colorful lights and the movement of shadows along the high walls of the palace's central complex belied the diplomatic interests on the grounds. But, Norum al-Nahmeed presided from above; from inside the balconied third floor vantage where he received guests a few at a time behind the protection of an eight-inch thick wall of glass.

Contrary to common belief, glass imperceptibly distorts images seen through it. The context of mass which the eye sees is sufficient for visual recognition of objects behind most glass. Beckett compensated for the principle with infra-red heat technology to view the human forms seated on the facing divans in the third-floor suite. He studied the heat signature of the single form on the left of the tableau, the man's habits and how he supported himself as he sat. Did he rest his palms upon his knees as he sat erect? Did he often lean against an elbow to one side, which changed his posture from the waist upward. Each component told Beckett whether he was a fidgeter, a lounger, or regally formal, critical information to Beckett's understanding how the target might naturally move at any given moment. Beckett didn't have the luxury this time of placing his target with a well-timed cell phone call. In this instance the Chinese ambassador seated opposite the target kept al-Nahmeed uncharacteristically off-balance.

"You hearing me, Captain?" Nelson's voice intruded upon the image from Beckett's memory.

"Loud and clear, Gunny," Beckett said. "Who?"

"Say, again, Captain?"

"Who is the target?" Beckett asked. "If we know the target, we know who sent the shooter."

"There's nobody in Ouachita County that valuable," Nelson said. "It makes no sense."

Beckett realized Nelson hadn't considered the obvious. He decided to let it lie.

"All we really know apart from the Mendez murder is someone has set a sniper nest," Beckett said. "If we leave it at that, then, we may not be dealing with a kill, but with a simulation."

"Makes sense," Nelson agreed. "He's practicing for someone else. But who? I mean, somebody else is going to die unless we figure this out."

"If we assume Destiny somewhat mirrors the actual kill zone, the shot is less than a mile," Beckett said. "So, what does

Destiny resemble that has a kill zone of less than a square mile with, perhaps, two high spots less than three city blocks apart?"

"A single compound of some sort?" Nelson asked. "But a compound with a forty-foot vantage that bisects the kill zone the way the bluff bisects the town."

Beckett nodded. Nelson was buying into the scenario. "He is triangulating the shot," Beckett said. Nelson nodded his agreement.

"Our shooter gets to pick his kill spot if the target is on the move," Beckett added.

Nelson became animated. "A parade or motorcade," he exclaimed. "It puts everything into place, vantage, kill zone, and triangulation. The shooter is calculating triangulated possibilities for a shot along a section of a motor route."

"No, he already has his numbers," Beckett said. "That's why there was no effort to dispose of Mister Mendez's body. The shooter has what he needs, and the murder of a witness looks like a hunting accident."

"Yeah… yeah, that's good," Nelson said. "So, where on God's green Earth does it all fit?"

"Off-hand, I can think of, maybe, a dozen places outside of Arkansas," Beckett said. "Two possibilities in Washington D.C., alone; one in London, a couple in Paris, and, about eight in the Middle East come to mind."

"You're not helping," Nelson said, and he became somber. "You realize nobody is going to believe us? I mean, I went back to the bluff and documented everything, but still, without some sort of connection to offer, nobody in law enforcement is gonna believe this."

"So… we do what we know, Gunny," Beckett said. "We wait for something or someone to tell us more."

"What if someone drops dead in the meantime?" Nelson asked.

Beckett shrugged. "The opportunity to help bring someone to justice afterward may be all we get," he said. "We wait."

Beckett turned back to the view through Nelson's truck window and his memory of Norum al-Nahmeed. He studied al-Nahmeed sufficiently to understand something vital, despite all precautions, al-Nahmeed was a man of unfailing habits. Beckett did not take his shot on that starlit night when he watched the festivities from across the valley. He waited until al-Nahmeed was alone with his thoughts on the divan in the room on the third floor of the presidential palace. After some hours as Beckett watched in the quiet near dawn, Norum al-Nahmeed settled something in his mind, and as his habit was, he slapped both hands against his knees in the moment he rose from the divan.

Then… Beckett fired the shot.

Lagniappe

CHAPTER TEN
MY RULING IS "UNDETERMINED"

The Coroner's Inquest convened at the Lard and Son Mortuary in Camden. Beckett's experience with unsettling venues aside, he disliked becoming Nelson's documenting witness. Hanging about in a mortuary on an otherwise splendid Saturday morning struck Beckett as a bit ironic. He thought for a moment how Cissy faced the recognition of death for the first time. Beckett decided to attend Frederico Mendez's funeral mass. He owed the man as much.

Ouachita County Coroner Vernon Lard's office struck Beckett as giving new meaning to the futuristic professional sterility of the Sixties, doubtless, the last time for an office remodel. The Lard and Son Mortuary building mirrored the main house at Tara in the decline of its glory. Beckett chuckled at the analogy.

"These proceedings are conducted under the auspices of the State of Arkansas, County of Ouachita, a record of which is being duly taken for transcription and filing in the County Court of the County of Ouachita…" Lard took a breath. "And, all testimony given in these proceedings will be under oath and subject to the laws of the State of Arkansas, under the penalties for perjury prescribed therein."

A somewhat mousy stenographer seated beside Lard's massive desk recorded the hearing. She seemed as put upon by the abuse of a Saturday morning as Beckett. She smiled at him demurely. He nodded politely and tried not to shudder.

"Let the record show present and attending these proceedings today are Vernon P. Lard, Coroner of the County of Ouachita; Ouachita County Sheriff's Deputy Jimmy Dale Means; Mister Lloyd Nelson, property holder and resident of Destiny, Arkansas; and…" Lard pointed at Beckett.

"Brock Beckett, resident of Destiny, Arkansas," he said. The sound of the statement hung in Beckett's mind. He had not been a resident anywhere in years.

"The witnesses will stand and be sworn," Lard intoned halfheartedly. Beckett did not stand, and Lard glanced at Nelson, who shook his head.

"All right," the portly Coroner said. "Do each and all of you solemnly swear the testimony you are about to give shall be the truth, the whole truth and nothing but the truth, so help you God?"

Vernon Lard's proceedings never adhered to the progressive pronoun-laden, affirmation hedging administration of justice. "I do will suffice," Lard directed. Each of the witnesses answered, "I do."

"All right, in the matter of the death of one Frederico Mendez, resident of Ouachita County, Arkansas, the facts as reported by Deputy Means are as follows," Lard said. "One that, on or about mid-morning of the date reported, Deputy Means drove to the offices of the River Bend Ranch to investigate the shooting death of one Frederico Mendez; and two, upon the investigation of said shooting death, a Coroner's investigation resulted. Those being the bases for these proceedings, I call Deputy Means."

Means stood, but Lard motioned for him to remain seated. "Get comfy, Jimmy Dale," he said. "All right, now it says here you investigated the call to the River Bend Ranch about mid-morning. Tell the Court what transpired thereafter."

"Well, sir, I arrived out at Mister Nelson's place, and he met me at the office and barn building; that's where they kept the body," Means began.

"So, Mister Mendez's body was moved from the scene of his death?" Lard posed.

"Uh, yes, sir," the Deputy replied.

"Were you given an explanation?"

"Well, no sir, not right off," Means said. "I asked what happened, and Mister Nelson said one of his hands, uh…" The Deputy checked his notes. "A Mister Juan Rubio brought the body to the office; said he found Mister Mendez out on the property by the river."

"Uhm, why isn't Mister Rubio here today, Lloyd?" Lard asked.

Nelson stood. "Juan is the decedent's brother-in-law, Your Honor. The funeral mass is this afternoon and, I let him go into Hope to see after things."

"Ah, okay; then, we'll pursue his testimony later, if necessary," Lard said. "Go ahead, Jimmy Dale."

"Well, sir, it seemed obvious to me, judging by the gunshot wound, that a stray hunting shot killed Mister Mendez," Means said. "I mean, it was a large caliber wound, no gunpowder residue on the body, and there have been poachers on the property previously."

"So, your immediate conclusion was death by a stray gunshot?" Lard asked. "Why not a deliberate gunshot?"

"Mister Mendez's body wasn't in the deer woods," Means said. "But it's close enough for a stray shot to be fatal."

"What about Mister Rubio? Was there any bad blood between the brothers-in-law?"

"Mister Rubio seemed pretty broken up over Mister Mendez's death," Means said. "And the other ranch hands were all surprised Mister Mendez got himself shot from a hunting accident; but nobody had a bad word to say about either man."

"What happened next?" Lard queried.

"Well, Mister Nelson knew I was gonna call you for a ruling, and he went into town and brought Mister Beckett back with him. I waited with the body at the ranch barn."

"All right what happened next, Jimmy Dale?"

"You looked at the body, and I told you what happened; then, you made a preliminary call that it was a hunting accident," Means replied. "After Mister Nelson and Mister Beckett arrived, all of us went out to the crime scene."

"Was there any evidence of suicide, such as the presence of a gun with the body, a spent shell casing in the vicinity of the body, or gunshot residue on Mister Mendez's hands?" Lard asked.

"No, sir, according to Mister Rubio," Means said.

"Did you find any evidence in your further investigation which altered your original conclusion?"

"No sir; not really, at first," Means replied. "Mister Beckett gave some ideas, but I just didn't see how they would fit a hunting accident. It just seemed sorta, well… weird… at the time…"

"All right, then; you can stand down," Lard said. "Next up, Lloyd."

Nelson stood. He recounted the events of the discovery of the body and his notification.

"Now, Lloyd, did you have an idea as to what happened to Mister Mendez?" Lard asked.

"Well, I suspected poachers," Nelson replied. "I didn't view this incident as a legitimate hunting accident because Frederico knew everyone with permission to hunt the property. He knew the deer stand locations, the type of deer rifles each hunting permit listed, and he always notified me when someone hunted on the property."

Beckett glanced away to prevent anyone from noticing his smirk. Nelson deflected the question.

"And you noted your disagreement with the Court's initial ruling, correct?"

"Yes, sir," Nelson replied.

"Did you produce any expertise to sustain your conclusion?" Lard asked.

"Well, I called on a friend with weapons expertise to offer a conclusion; yes," Nelson explained. "I was thinking poachers, but he suggested the possibility Mister Mendez might have stumbled upon a drug transaction…"

"All right, then; thank you, Mister Nelson, you may be seated," Lard interjected.

The curt conclusion to his testimony took Nelson aback, but he sat down and said nothing. He sensed Lard reached a conclusion. And the Coroner's next question confirmed the thought.

"Deputy Means…"

The lawman stood. "Yes, sir."

"Deputy Means, was there any evidence at the alleged scene of the shooting to suggest Mister Mendez might have come across a drug transaction and was shot as a result?" Lard posed.

"Well, yes, sir, there was, and I'd say it was reasonably conclusive," Means said. "You see, Mister Mendez's body was found on the riverbank upstream from a bluff above the river. I examined the area at the top of the bluff and discovered impressions in the soil to indicate a possible landing site for a helicopter. Now, up to that point, I was skeptical about a drug transaction, but them 'copter tracks, they put a different light on things."

"Thank you, Deputy," Lard said.

He leaned back against his chair and closed his eyes, the fingertips of both hands pressed into a prayerful posture as he appeared to weigh the evidence. Beckett might have laughed had he known the man any better, and it became difficult for Beckett to contain himself as Nelson turned toward him and winked. Lard cleared his throat ostentatiously, ready to announce his finding.

"After hearing the evidence and giving due consideration to the questions arising from it, I'm not prepared to say with certainty Frederico Mendez died as the result of a hunting accident," Lard said. "However, I do not preclude a hunting accident as the manner of death. I do find that Frederico Mendez died as the result of a single gunshot wound to the upper torso of his body that was not self-inflicted. As to any other manner by which the fatal wound occurred, I find inconclusive evidence to rule. Therefore, as to the accidental or intentional nature of Frederico Mendez's death, my ruling is undetermined. This hearing is adjourned."

Nelson stood and offered Lard his hand. "Frederico's family will be grateful."

"You don't get any Brownie points, Lloyd," Lard replied. "But, your friend, Mister Beckett, got me thinking about that helicopter shot business. I thought it was horse apples until I happened to see a friend from the Arkansas State Police. Turns out your Mister Beckett knows whereof he speaks."

"Oh?" Nelson seemed shocked.

Lard rocked back on his heels, his arms crossed over his chest. "That helicopter shot has been done," he said with a wry smile. "Texas Rangers got a fugitive down near the border with a shot from a helicopter a few years back."

Nelson was puzzled. "What made you change your mind, Vernon?"

"Your Mister Beckett was too confident of himself," Lard said. "He was too confident simply to be a schoolteacher. I had my ASP friend run a background on him; Arkansas schoolteachers must pass a background check. Of course, you know, you're the school board president..."

"What are you driving at, Vernon?" Nelson asked drolly.

Lard's mouth pursed into a tight, little pucker. "Mister Beckett's background came back a little bit mysterious," he said. "Had some 'not applicable' in a couple of interesting places. Of course, you'd know that, being the school board president."

"So? Beckett's not the first teacher we've had with 'not applicable' information," Nelson retorted. "What's gotten into your craw, Vernon?"

"Just saying...," Lard offered.

Nelson was perturbed. "Then, let's keep it that way, okay, Vernon?"

The old man shook his head and chuckled. "Just saying, Lloyd; just saying," he repeated.

Nelson knew the old fart was correct to surmise. But a man with Beckett's past didn't need a meddling south Arkansas hack politician like Vernon Lard poking about in his life. Still, the same question once nagged at Nelson, but he was satisfied to let it lie, if only for Cissy's sake. He glanced at his watch.

"If you'll excuse me, Vernon, I've got a funeral to attend," he said as he turned away.

"You let me know if you and Mister Beckett get anything... figured out," Lard called out as Nelson disappeared through the office doorway. The old politico smiled with a self-important satisfaction as the door slammed behind Nelson.

CHAPTER ELEVEN
THEY LIED TO ME

The concept of a Roman Catholic funeral mass without context was intimidating and confusing to Cissy as it seemed otherworldly to her. She understood it was necessary for the last rites of Frederico Mendez, who became more an "uncle" to her than a ranch employee.

Cissy remembered the games she played with the Mendez children at their home at the ranch while Lloyd and the ranch hands worked cattle or baled hay. She earned shopping money in the summers wrangling for the ranch hands alongside the Mendez brood. Cissy daubed tears from the corners of her eyes and noticed the stoicism of the Mendez children as they sat awaiting the start of the service.

Beckett was late to the service in Hope, the closest Catholic parish to Destiny, but a thirty-minute drive. He sat in the parish hall adjoining the sanctuary with the overflow crowd of ranch hands, poultry farm workers, county road crew hands, school cafeteria cooks, maids, mechanics, welders, construction laborers, and poultry plant shift workers who formed the circle of the Mendez family's life. Beckett felt awkward attending a funeral wearing a white shirt, dark tie, trousers, and a light sports coat rather than a

Marine dress uniform. Beckett hadn't been in uniform for more than two years since the simple memorial service General Pierpont Maxwell arranged for Jolene and Cissy when Beckett mustered out of military service. Beckett recalled the night he learned the truth at Maxwell's quarters.

"Are you certain about this, son? Life isn't the same out there and you don't have a family anymore."

The voice was Maxwell's; the sentiment wasn't. Maxwell was a lifer to the Corps.

"I'm done, sir," Beckett said.

"You've got a family in the Corps…"

Beckett was impatient. He studied Maxwell with stern regard.

"I had a family," Beckett said. "Jolene fought her way back from cancer and Little Red was two years old when I shipped out."

"The Pentagon said there was nothing to recover from the car wreck, Captain," Maxwell replied. "Your wife died and… Little Red is gone."

Beckett saw the hesitation in Maxwell. "Where… did Little Red go?"

"Don't push it, Captain," Maxwell insisted. "Accept it. You have no family; you have the Corps."

"What happened in that car wreck, General?"

"You know your wife relapsed; she lost control. There was nothing left, Captain. Accept it."

"You're lying, General; it's in your eyes," Beckett said. "I learned a lot about reading eyes in fourteen years and yours are lying to me. Jolene recovered from cancer the first time."

Beckett pulled the photo from his wallet he snapped in the hospital that day.

"Look at them, General; that's my family. If Jolene relapsed, then where is Little Red?"

Maxwell stared at Beckett with an imperious regard. "They didn't matter."

"Come again…" Beckett's tone was visceral.

"You matter, Captain," Maxwell said. "They call you The Ghost in the Middle East, the angel of death. You matter to the things that I say matter."

Beckett threw the first punch. It briefly stunned Maxwell. The General retaliated. The two men struck blow after blow until Beckett's grief turned into rage. He charged Maxwell and body slammed him to the floor pummeling the General until he began to spit up blood. Beckett stood over him as Maxwell lay bleeding on the floor.

"I told Jolene's family all of you were dead," Maxwell wheezed. "Your wife is somewhere in a secure cemetery in the mountains of Virginia, in a grave marked Number Three-sixty-six. Little Red went into Military Family Services custody. She was adopted by a couple somewhere in Arkansas."

Maxwell chuckled and struggled to his feet.

"Jolene's family gave all of you a nice send-off down near Sulphur Springs, Texas, beneath a sprawling oak tree on the Morgan family farm. They erected a polished granite monument to commemorate the passing of Our Children, Jolene Morgan Beckett; her husband, Brock Beckett; and daughter, Cecelia 'Cissy' Beckett. So, you see, Captain, you have no family."

Beckett smashed Maxwell's jaw and watched him slump to the floor.

"In the name of the Father, the Son and the Holy Spirit." The Hope parish priest's voice brought Beckett back to the Mendez funeral mass.

There was nothing fictitious about Frederico Mendez's death; it was too real to Cissy. She excused herself and went outside… to breathe. Grace Nelson thought to follow her, but Lloyd quietly held her back when he saw Beckett appear at the doorway to the parish hall and turn to follow Cissy.

"Let her sort some things out," Nelson said. "If she doesn't come back after a bit, I'll go see to her."

Outside, Beckett immediately spotted Cissy sitting on a bench near the parish sign. He sat beside her, but he said nothing for a long moment.

"Lloyd doesn't believe Frederico's death was an accident, does he?" Cissy asked.

The question took Beckett aback. "What makes you think that, Hon?"

"He didn't show up at school that day to get me so much as to get you," Cissy said. "I appreciated that he let me go home so I didn't bawl my eyes out in front of everybody, but I saw how he spoke to you. And, when he said he had to borrow you for a while, I figured it out later. He wanted a witness to go with him."

She looked up at Beckett and smiled weakly. "He trusts you," she said. "So…?"

Beckett nodded; she deserved some explanation. "Yes, Lloyd had questions," he said. "And he wanted me to help him, well, work through them. One theory is Mister Mendez may have stumbled onto a drug deal, which seems reasonable."

Cissy drew a pained breath and daubed at her eyes with her handkerchief. "Getting shot must hurt horribly."

"I… uhm, couldn't say," Beckett replied. He knew better. Mendez died the instant the bullet tore through his chest.

Beckett absentmindedly rubbed his right hand across his outer right thigh, which drew Cissy's attention and focused Beckett's memory of an injury. The shrapnel from a .338 round is as deadly as the bullet. The scar creased across Beckett's outer right thigh from the shrapnel fragments left by the shot snaked about eight inches downward along his leg. Beckett closed his eyes. It hurt like hell that day, but Beckett survived.

The Syrian regular army shooter who tagged Beckett took out American military advisers to the Turkish Kurd army for some time along the Syrian-Turkey border. Beckett knew the guy was too good to be a homegrown shooter; he had Russian tactical signatures. The Syrian's favorite was to cripple a soldier in the open and methodically take out anyone who tried to rescue the staked-out victim.

Beckett came to the standoff because of that tactic. But he was given bad intelligence. The shooter moved his nest to a backup location above the original site during the night. Beckett learned the hard way. His position paralleled the Syrian's original spot across the wadi and was sighted toward an empty nest. Beckett was exposed to the shrapnel shot once the two men started trading fire.

American advisers and Turkish regulars were pinned down in a wadi they controlled along a stretch of the border. ISIS insurgents used the wadi as a crossing point into Turkey. The Turkish troops opened fire on the Syrian shooter's nest in the rocks along the wall of a cliff downrange of the wadi goading him to fire and give Beckett a shot. But the Syrian's next shot came from a different position, about a hundred yards up range and higher in the rocks, which presented him a devastating view of the Turkish position.

Beckett had no choice but to fire to suppress the Syrian attack, and he left himself exposed on the lower ground. He had one alternative. As the sun stood at high noon, the shadows along the wadi disappeared, leaving any movement clearly exposed. Beckett used the time to reconfigure his nest as the shadows cast across it became deeper. Once he took a shot at the Syrian, Beckett had only a few seconds to shift his position before return fire was incoming. The impact of the Syrian's round into the rocks behind Beckett would spew shrapnel. He protected himself as best he could and waited.

The temptation was too great for the Syrian, and he began to fire into the wadi below. Beckett sighted his return shot quickly, knowing the first round would not make the kill. He squeezed the trigger, and his round smashed into the rocks immediately above the Syrian. The gambit drew the Syrian's interest when his spotter became animated and pointed toward Beckett's position. The Syrian swung about, adjusting for his spotter's instructions. Beckett rolled away, and the Syrian's round exploded into the rocks at the rear of Beckett's nest, driving a razor-sharp shard across his outer thigh and into his leg.

Beckett stiffened and gritted his teeth. He used the heightened sensory awareness of the pain to hone his shot, now eye to eye with his adversary through his rifle scope. Beckett's finger caressed the trigger, and the round sped at three hundred yards per second, shattering the Syrian's skull. The spotter screamed in fear and stood to flee, and Beckett got him, too.

Cissy's voice intruded upon Beckett. "Do you think Frederico was in a lot of pain?"

"I… don't… think he suffered, if that is what concerns you, Hon," Beckett said as he returned to the moment.

Cissy looked up at him with a rebuke and Beckett was suddenly uncomfortable. He hadn't meant to be patronizing, but it was evident from her demeanor Cissy knew better.

"I know something about guns," she said. "I know how there is a difference in combat… and, in hunting…" Her voice trailed off.

"I didn't mean to treat you like a child," Beckett replied. "I keep forgetting how much you are like your mother…" His voice trailed off.

"You never told me how she died," Cissy said. "The day we met, you said something about it, but I never knew how… or when… or where… or… anything."

Beckett drew a deep breath and sighed. "I know," he said. He stood and offered her his hand. "Let's take a walk."

Cissy let his strong hand envelop hers, and they strolled along the sidewalk and into the adjoining residential neighborhood, away from the bustle. Neither spoke for a block until they stood beneath the shade of a gnarled oak tree in front of a former elementary school. The broad front porch steps of the abandoned tan brick structure offered them privacy as they sat to talk.

"When Jolene brought you into the world, I was the happiest man on the planet," Beckett said. "But, it didn't last; your mother became ill… with cancer. By the time I took the photo I showed you, she was making a comeback, but we were all separated because I received orders for special military duty."

He looked down into Cissy's wide, hazel eyes. "I wasn't contacted when your mother died, or informed that you were adopted," he said. "For all I knew while I was gone, Jolene recovered and you two were living with your grandparents in Sulphur Springs, Texas."

"Why didn't you call… or write a letter… or go online?" Cissy asked.

"I couldn't," Beckett said. "No one was supposed to know anything about me. I spent most of the time in places accessible only by horse or on foot, halfway around the world. They wouldn't let me come home. Everything kept changing. Anyway, I finally had the opportunity to get myself home, and I took it."

He stood and kicked at the rocks in the sparse grass beneath the tree. "They lied to me," Beckett said. "They said you and your mother were killed in a car crash. For a while, I didn't bother to reconnect with the world. Then, I happened to learn Jolene's father had died. That's when I discovered everything that I believed for almost ten years was a lie."

He cradled Cissy's face in his strong, weathered hands. "It took me two years to find you," Beckett whispered. "And you don't want to know how."

"Yes… yes, I do," Cissy insisted. "How did you find me after fourteen years?"

Beckett sighed with a burdened weariness. Cissy caressed his cheek. "It's okay," she whispered.

"It was ugly," Beckett said. "Some people got hurt. I almost went to jail. I finally let them think I'd given up. And then, one night I visited a certain man and, when I left, he was still alive, barely, but I learned the truth."

Cissy looked at Beckett with a curious regard. "You were going to kidnap me that day in front of the school, weren't you?" she posed incredulously.

Beckett blushed. Then, he grimaced. "I thought about it. For about two seconds. And I decided it was unfair to you. I had to be honest with you or forfeit any chance of knowing you. I had to let you decide."

The service was over, and Beckett saw Nelson in the distance walking toward them. He waved.

"Your da…" Beckett stopped short and looked down at Cissy. "Lloyd's coming for us."

Cissy smiled sheepishly. "I'm glad you didn't kill anybody to find me," she said as a tear slipped from the corner of her eye. "I'm… just… glad you found me."

Lagniappe

CHAPTER TWELVE
YOU'RE GUESSING

The community acceptance of rumors that Frederico Mendez's death was a poacher shooting assuaged local concerns as the nights embraced the chill of Fall and the diversions of Friday night football overtook Destiny, Arkansas. Home football games also meant teacher's duty at Freemon Nelson Stadium.

Beckett never considered the unpaid responsibility an imposition upon his time. He enjoyed watching the social interactions of his students: Wade Fairway, Devonte Washington, and James Robert Bellchase steamrolled opponents as the Destiny Dragons advanced toward another championship season. Marilee Page led cheers for the crowd on the sideline and flirted with Wade at every opportunity. Cissy danced with the drill team and tumbled with an acrobatic grace through solos at halftime that would have made Jolene proud. Beckett began to allow himself a sense of a father's pride in Cissy's accomplishments.

Beckett scuffed his shoe at the gravel of the track that ringed the football field; high school was a lifetime ago for him. Beckett was thankful to witness the beginnings of Cissy's flowering. She was as gorgeous, bright, and happy a teen as he could imagine. Cissy waved to him from the sideline before the beginning of the halftime show. He smiled and reciprocated; it felt good and normal.

Cissy began to put Frederico Mendez's death into perspective, which allowed her to continue with life, and Beckett marveled at her resilience. He thought for a moment of Scarlett O'Hara and chuckled to himself; the two were nothing alike in most comparisons and exactly alike in others. Washington, whom Beckett suspected had an unrequited crush on Cissy, often brought it out in classroom discussions.

"You are jus' like Scarlett O'Hara," Washington remarked the day the class finally discussed the 9/11 essay question.

"What on Earth do you mean, Devonte Washington?" Cissy shot back. "I'm nothing like that little manipulative hussy."

The class erupted into laughter at the exchange. Beckett smiled.

"Wooo, see what I mean?" Washington posed. "Cracklin'…"

More laughter. "You'd better explain yourself, Mister Washington," Beckett chuckled.

Washington threw up his hands in mock defense.

"Naw, naw; I don't mean no disrespect," he replied. "I mean it… like, y'all know… as a compliment."

The last word came with difficulty and no little self-consciousness for one of DHS' star athletes.

"It's, uhm, how Scarlett faces up to things," Washington said. "She doesn't put on any B, except around Ashley. But, she's, like… brave."

"Isn't Scarlett forced to be brave by the circumstances, Mister Washington?" Beckett asked. "She lost everything important to her former way of life, except Tara…"

"And, except Rhett," Marilee interjected dreamily.

"Oh, please; seriously, Marilee," Cissy said.

"Naw, naw, Mister Beckett nailed it," Washington said. "Scarlett got hammered by the war stuff, just like a lot of people got hammered by the September eleven thing; and…you. You got hammered by Mister Mendez getting killed, but daaaang girl… here you are. That's brave in my book."

Applause broke out, and as Beckett called for quiet, he shot a furtive glance toward Cissy. She blushed.

The scoreboard horn sounded the end of the third quarter. Beckett smiled to himself as he recalled Cissy's blush. Washington struck a deep chord in Cissy which seemed to seal a special relationship between the two of them. Beckett assumed the inevitability of Cissy's first tangible relationship.

"She could do worse."

"Who are you talking to?" a voice beside him asked.

Beckett turned to see Nelson approaching with two cups of steaming coffee.

"You looked kinda lonesome down here by the end zone," he said.

"I like the perspective," Beckett replied. "You see everything on the field and in the stands."

He took the coffee cup offered by Nelson and swallowed a warming sip. "Oh, yeah," he said with a mild surprise. "I remember why I don't drink concession stand coffee."

Nelson chuckled. "I don't much like it either, but it's hot, and the band boosters need the money."

"They're playing pretty solid ball tonight," Beckett said.

"Shoot, I gave Freemon twenty points; they better play solid ball," Nelson quipped.

Beckett laughed. "No, seriously," Nelson said. "If they don't take Cedar Point by at least twenty points, not only am I out twenty bucks to my bookie brother, but this bunch also won't get to the state championship this year."

"Bookie?" Beckett said incredulously.

"You don't want to know," Nelson said with a shake of his head as he sipped coffee.

"Probably not," Beckett agreed, and they turned back to the game.

Cedar Point fell behind by seven points in the closing minutes of the game and the fans on both sides of the field were rowdy. Nelson stomped up and down along the five-yard line as Beckett watched with somewhat more aplomb. The two teams lined up with Cedar Point on the Destiny 10-yard line at the other end of the field, but a Destiny lineman jumped off-side on fourth down.

"Daaad…gumit," Nelson bellowed.

A quiet settled across the stadium as the two teams lined up for the first down after the penalty. As the Cedar Point center snapped the ball, a light fixture on the home grandstand side tower nearest the end zone exploded in a shower of glass shards and sparks. The disruption caused the Cedar Point quarterback to fumble the ball and Destiny recovered the fumble. Then, on the succeeding Destiny first down, another light fixture exploded. In the confusion, Cedar Point sacked Destiny's quarterback in the end zone.

"Daaad…gumit, you're giving away points," Nelson shouted.

Another lighting fixture on the same tower exploded during the kick-off, and the referees called an end to the game with time left on the clock. Fans filed out of the stadium, the Destiny faithful whooped over a narrow victory, and Cedar Point fans carped. The befuddled officiating crew huddled at the far end of the field with Nelson and Superintendent Raymond Bittle. Then, a fourth fixture on the same tower exploded.

Beckett watched the scene, somewhat confused by the situation, until the fourth light exploded. He dropped his coffee cup and stared in disbelief at the lighting tower. Three extinguished lights formed a triangle, and the fourth, a dot in its center. Beckett quickly scanned the stadium and the horizon beyond with a churlishness rising in his stomach. He recognized the configuration.

"A triangle with a crescent moon in the center," General Pierpont Maxwell explained. "It's represented on handwritten communications by a triangle with what appears to be a reversed letter 'C' in the center. It is the symbol for the Caliphate Triangle."

"The ISIS connection between Syria, Turkey and northern Iraq," Beckett said.

"Exactly, and what you've got here, Captain, is a talisman of loyalty to ISIS, much the same as the use of the name 'Allah' is automatically followed by the phrase 'Peace be to His name,'" Maxwell replied.

Beckett sighed heavily. He was frustrated. He found a cache of student essays with the symbol in an ISIS madrass, typically a Muslim religious school. Boys kidnapped from villages, and who showed promise, were trained to become ISIS martyrs. Beckett remembered the soccer ball boys he rescued with the drone strike in the mountains.

"This level of organization and indoctrination demonstrates ISIS' growth," General Maxwell said. "You've got a lot more work to do, son."

Beckett scuffed his shoe against the gravel on the football field track again. Destroying the propaganda schools was the most difficult aspect of eliminating ISIS. They were often administered and taught by kids hardened beyond their years with a chilling fanaticism.

Beckett shook his head; he didn't want to remember. The headmaster of each propaganda school wore a red sash with the Caliphate Triangle emblem on it. That made target identification simple regardless of the age of the target, Beckett recalled.

The madrass students stood in rows in front of the partially bombed-out building, which served as their propaganda school; it was the time of prayers. All of them were present and led by the school's imam, a man of about 70, and the administrator, a boy of about 17. As the prayers concluded, the boy pointed toward two students in the first row, and they broke ranks to go inside the building. Momentarily, they returned, dragging between them a bound man who appeared to be European by his hairstyle.

Dressed in an orange tee shirt and jogging pants, the man appeared severely beaten. The boys threw him to the ground in front of the imam. The old man spoke to the student administrator, who unsheathed a large knife from his belt, grabbed a handful of the prisoner's hair, and slit the man's throat, hacking through a spray of blood until the man's head pulled free from his body. The other students cheered.

Beckett relaxed his body, allowing his muscles to take on new memory as he lay stretched in the narrow confines of his nest in an attic some 600 yards up range. He rested his M40-A4 sniper rifle firmly against his shoulder, closed his eyes, and took a deep breath. Beckett opened his eyes and let his finger caress the trigger. The round threw the kid backward as it tore through his neck, dropping his body to the ground with his head dangling sideways.

The old man stiffened as though awaiting the next shot. As shock spread through the ranks of students, the imam calmly picked up an AK-47 at his feet and fired it into the air, demanding immediate submission. Silence ensued as the old man removed the red sash from the dead teen's body. Then, scanning the row in front of him, the imam pointed to a lanky boy who stepped forward and bowed as the imam draped the sash of administration across his shoulder, and the boy took his place beside the old man.

The two moments were clean and efficient, almost robotic. Beckett cursed beneath his breath, closed his eyes and exhaled. He needn't recalculate the shot. Then, he fired, again. This time, the old man died.

Beckett hated the memory, but as he looked up at the four black spots on the stadium lighting tower, he reminded himself he would never escape it. He ambled down the field toward Nelson and two referees as Bittle walked away. Beckett expected Nelson to be vocal about the officials' decision to end the game, but as he approached the group of men, he noticed they were not concerned about the football game.

"Come here, Captain," Nelson said, waving Beckett into the conversation. "We need to show you something."

"Sure," Beckett replied, shaking hands and introducing himself to the game officials. "What can I do for you?"

"Stan and Jeff served in Iraq," Nelson said. "I've been knowing these guys for years. I told them you served in the Middle East, and they think we've got a problem."

"Yeah, I was in the First Cav," Jeff, a stout man of about 40, said. "I did a lot of drone maintenance, and, once in a while, one came back shot up."

He picked up one of the damaged reflecting cones from the destroyed tower lights. The concave disk measured about 18 inches in diameter. The lighting fixture which should have been in its center was missing. He showed Beckett the damage.

"That damage isn't from an electrical explosion, Mister Beckett," Jeff explained. "That was done by military-grade ordnance."

"Yeah," Stan said. "I'm an electrician, and I know electrical explosions on these lighting towers because I work on them. I was in Iraq, too, and the insurgents sometimes set up diversions to an attack on a base camp by shooting out the perimeter lighting. I replaced those lights when they came into our shop looking exactly like this."

"Yeah, like we told Lloyd, you guys need to call the cops about this; Hell, probably, the FBI," Jeff said adamantly.

"There's no doubt we've got something to report here," Nelson said. "I'm sorta doubtful this is the result of ordnance, as much as it's just a freak thing, but it needs looking at. I appreciate your thinking, guys, and we'll give it a good look."

Nelson stood with his hands on his hips, scuffing the grass with his boot as the two referees left the field. Presently, he looked up at Beckett.

"What do you think, Captain?"

Beckett heaved a frustrated sigh. He pointed toward the lighting tower.

"Yeah, what you've got here looks... funky," Beckett quipped. "But, I'm not going to start any rumors. If you want to confirm this is ordnance damage, be my guest, but I'm not the source of your expertise this time. It's just too... funky."

Nelson turned and gazed out into the night across the expanse beyond the stadium. "Where do you think it came from?"

"You're incorrigible," Beckett said. "We only know of one spot, but *if*... and I'm being SWAG here..."

"SWAG?" Nelson asked.

"Seriously Weird-Ass Guess," Beckett said. "If this was a shot, it had to be from about a mile; otherwise, somebody would hear the report of the rifle. And I don't know anything, except a nest in a pine stand, that would be high enough from the ground to make those shots in a straight line."

"But, you've got to admit...," Nelson began.

"Nope, I don't have to admit anything," Beckett said adamantly. "Look, Gunny, we've speculated about something we believe concerning Frederico Mendez's death. We have no hard evidence other than your picture of the nest on the bluff at the ranch."

Nelson tossed the lighting fixture shield to him.

"Then, you tell me, what caused that damage, Captain?" He pointed toward the lighting tower.

"And, what caused that pattern?" Nelson asked insistently. "You can't tell me it is some sort of coincidence. It's too damned clean. Somebody took practice shots here tonight."

"For what, Gunny?" Beckett snapped.

"Not a what, Captain, but a who," Nelson retorted.

"You're guessing."

"Yeah, and we'd better start guessing right, or somebody is else gonna die, Captain," Nelson said. "This town is shaken up as it is about Frederico's death."

"What the Sam Hill do you want me to do, Gunny?" Beckett asked.

"Help me think, Captain, before someone starts asking questions I can't answer," Nelson said.

CHAPTER THIRTEEN
I'VE GOT A SECRET

Beckett scarcely slept that night, loath to admit Nelson's point. He knew the day they discovered the sniper nest at the ranch that someone was roosting for a shot; but, why in Destiny, Arkansas, remained elusive to him. The two men were no closer to producing an answer. It was frustrating to appear clueless to men like Jeff and Stan, the two football officials, when Beckett could easily explain the dynamics of the shot. He knew no one outside of Ouachita County would likely listen to Nelson's sniper theory, much less act upon it, without a definitive explanation or a specific target. Putting the problem out of his mind vexed Beckett, but a knock at the apartment door resolved the situation.

Beckett climbed out of bed, slipped into his robe, and padded to the front door. He suspected another Saturday morning visit from Cissy, which he would be happy to entertain, but that was not the case, as he grabbed his cell phone to monitor the exterior minicam on the eave above the porch.

"Oh, Lord. Loretta Chesterton."

He cracked open the door. She was stunning; her hair loose, and draped across her shoulders and framing her face, gave an equine flair to her otherwise sleek body. Loretta was, as typical for her, dressed beneath her age. What man in Destiny, Arkansas, would have cared, Beckett thought?

"Morning, Miss Chesterton," he said pleasantly.

"Hel-lo handsome," she cooed.

"I'd, uhm, ask you in, except I'm not dressed," he said.

"That's quite alright," Loretta replied. "I'm here to ask you out, in a manner of speaking."

"Oh."

"Yes, you see, I'm off to Shreveport to buy a new car," Loretta said almost matter-of-factly. "I don't know a thing about cars, and…. well, frankly, I'd appreciate it if you would come help me out. You know, so they don't take advantage of a woman."

"*Said the Spider to the Fly?*" Beckett thought. He smiled. "I'm not certain I'd be much help…"

"Oh, I'm sure you would," Loretta said. "And, afterward, we could have a lovely dinner at a quiet little place I know for your trouble, of course."

Cissy's voice screamed objections in the back of Beckett's mind, but he ignored it. He wanted the diversion despite knowing there was no challenge in it.

"I promise to behave myself," Loretta offered.

"Why not?" Beckett heard himself say. "Give me a minute to dress."

"I'll be down in my car," Loretta said.

Beckett quickly rinsed himself in the shower, dried off, and cleaned up. Ten minutes later, he ambled downstairs to find Loretta in the passenger seat of a late model Mercedes. She pointed toward the driver's seat and nodded. Beckett complied.

"This car isn't more than a couple of years old," he remarked as he cranked the engine and guided the Mercedes out of the driveway toward Center Street. "What's the rush to trade it in?"

"Oh, I'm bored with it," Loretta replied.

Beckett turned onto Center Street, drove to the Arkansas 24 intersection, and turned southward toward Camden. He set the cruise control and let it take over.

"How could you be bored with this? It drives like a dream," Beckett said.

Loretta giggled. She brushed her fingertips against his shoulder and let them slide down his right arm. She was aroused and almost giddy.

"You're clearly in a good humor, today," he said.

"I've got twenty-eight million reasons to be," Loretta squealed. "I've got a secret."

She rummaged through her purse and produced an envelope, which Beckett could see was from a Little Rock law firm. Loretta opened the envelope and handed him the enclosed letter.

"It's a letter of intent," she said. "A Chinese bank, Yashuma Bank of China, owns a manufacturing company that produces a very special fabric used in bulletproof vests and has agreed to buy the bulk of the Chesterton property. They've offered to buy the land for twenty-eight million dollars."

"Whoa," Beckett exclaimed.

Loretta rested her chin against her palm and smiled at him. "I'm gonna celebrate and buy a new car," she giggled.

"I thought all of the Chesterton property was tied up in the estate," Beckett said.

Loretta shook her head. "Not anymore," she replied. "Uncle Jimmy got a judge to say my great-great granddaddy's will was no longer in force; something called obligation of possession."

"Uncle Jimmy?" Beckett said.

"Briggs…," Loretta replied. "Briggs Law Firm and South Arkansas Bank. He's my uncle on my mother's side."

"Oh, that Uncle Jimmy."

"Yeah. Before great-great-granddaddy died, he put in his will that a Chesterton woman must teach school in Destiny, or the estate would go to the Episcopal Church," Loretta said. "Uncle Jimmy said the obligation gave possession to the original heirs. But the obligation couldn't be put upon the succeeding generations of the family because it deprived them of genuine possession of the gift of the estate from the original heirs."

"Ah," Beckett said. "So, was it a gift or a payment for services rendered?"

"Something like that," Loretta said.

"And, if it was a gift, it could not be kept back. It had to be possessed by the recipient at some point," Beckett added.

"Yep," Loretta said.

"And you are… the… recipient," he said.

"Yep," she said with a full, throaty laugh. "Twenty-eight-million-dollar recipient."

"That's a chunk of change for, what, eight hundred acres of mostly pine stands?" Beckett posed.

"I don't know," Loretta said. "I just know their check cleared the bank."

She laughed again and rested her head against Beckett's shoulder as he guided the Mercedes through Magnolia on U.S. 79 and southward toward Shreveport, Louisiana. Beckett was happy for Loretta.

"You can quit teaching school, something you never liked but only tolerated," he said. "I can't get the twenty-eight million dollars out of my mind. Why did the buyer offer that much money for Ouachita County pine timberland? Where is this patch of property?"

"It adjoins the eastern side of the Nelson place back toward Arkadelphia," Loretta replied.

"And, you said, these folks make bulletproof vests?" Beckett asked.

"Just the fabric. The vests are made in China."

Beckett worked out the math. "Twenty-eight million divided by eight hundred equals thirty-five thousand dollars an acre," he said. "I'd guess undeveloped property in northern Ouachita County typically sells for much less per acre. Unbelievable."

Beckett understood that after more than a decade in the Middle East he was behind the times. "When do they expect to start building this factory?"

"They haven't said anything," Loretta said. "It's going to require several years to develop. In the meantime, I get to be rich, rich, rich…"

"I suppose you'll move to Hot Springs or someplace bigger than Destiny?" Beckett asked.

Loretta smiled at him. "I could use some company," she purred, nipping at his earlobe.

"Uh, uh," Beckett said. He had to smile; she was hopeless. "You promised to be good."

She pouted. "It's… hard," Loretta replied, languidly resting against the passenger seat.

"So, how long is this going to remain a secret?" Beckett asked. "People will ask questions when the bulldozers move in."

"Oh, there will be a big deal announcement around Christmas," Loretta replied with a bored affectation. "The governor is supposed to show up with some U.S. senator for me to formally hand over the deed to some Chinese guy named Huang Do-Lin."

It wasn't so much the name that rattled around in Beckett's mind as the sound its pronunciation produced, something like the ricochet of a bullet. The memory of first hearing Huang's name spoken was somewhat muddled for Beckett. It came in a lucid period during several days of hanging by his wrists, naked, wet, and cold in a cave somewhere in northeastern Syria.

Beckett retreated into a deep sleep to relieve the exhaustion created by blood loss during torture, a defensive mechanism he employed to mimic death. He was captured temporarily by a stray ISIS unit when a rocket-propelled grenade exploded near his nest during a firefight to keep insurgents away from a downed helicopter. Huang, Beckett learned, was a general in the Chinese intelligence services. Beckett passed the information along to the Kurdish peshmerga fighters who helped him escape.

"Are you sure about the Chinese guy's name?" Beckett asked.

Loretta shrugged. "I don't know how to say it right," she said. "I just say it like it's spelled on the check: H...u...a...n...g, capital D...o, hyphen capital L...i...n."

Beckett recalled General Maxwell's explanation of Huang's influence.

"We've heard rumors of covert Chinese operations in the Middle East for years," Maxwell said. "The Chinese are intent on controlling Russian influence in the region, and keeping Middle Eastern oil, particularly from Iran, as a competitive force against the acquisition of hard currency by the Russians, who are selling their oil on the world markets.

"The Russians are supposedly playing the part of the good guys in Syria," he said. "But they want to contain the collapse of the

Iraqi petroleum industry in their favor by preventing ISIS from burning every oil field in northern Iraq. Russia can produce those fields and take the pressure off its domestic production. China wants to keep Russia a bit more off-balance and under its control. General Huang is the mind behind the strategy."

"So, it's still about the oil?" Beckett asked. "What about the rise of the caliphate?"

Maxwell shook his head. "The Russians give a fig about the ISIS ideology; they want the oil and the influence in the southern Mediterranean via Turkey."

"And we're trying to take Syria and Turkey out of Russia's hands," Beckett said.

"Precisely," Maxwell replied.

Beckett had not thought about General Huang Do-Lin; until now. A former high-ranking Chinese intelligence officer operating against Russia in the Middle East was now an investment banker who made bulletproof vests. Something extremely perverse in the circumstance made it all-the-more reasonable to Beckett. He pondered whether it answered the question of a potential sniper target in Destiny, Arkansas.

"I suppose Mayor Nelson and all of the county honchos are planning a big welcome?" Beckett asked.

Loretta shrugged. "Don't know whether anybody knows about it but you and me," she said offhandedly. "And you're kinda starting to suck all the fun out of it."

Beckett chuckled. "I'm sorry, Loretta," he said. "Of course, you should have fun with your newfound good fortune. And here I am asking inane questions, when I should really ask: What color car do you want?"

She brightened. "Now, you're getting it, big guy."

As Beckett wheeled Loretta's Mercedes onto the new car lot of the Shreveport dealership, James Alford Briggs, senior partner of the Briggs Law Firm and chairman of South Arkansas Bank, welcomed U.S. Senator Wilson Furman to Clearwater Lodge, the

Briggs family hunting retreat on the Mill's Ford Bend of the Ouachita River.

"The Ouachita River, near its confluence with the Reader River at the Poison Springs Wildlife Management Area, bends into an entrenched meander which forces its flow backward along a two-mile stretch creating rocky rapids at its southern bend and a smooth flowing stream northward that spreads out along a gravel beach and drops into a blue hole at its northern end before being pushed around a cliff bend to fall rapidly southward again," Briggs explained as he held forth in the great room of the lodge. "The configuration created some of the best boating rapids and game fishing in the state in my backyard."

Known as Uncle Jimmy Briggs by family, he was Mister Jimmy to friends and Mister Briggs to everyone else. The 70-year-old patron of the Briggs-Chesterton families, Mister Jimmy was the lawyer-banker with whom anyone in Destiny, a good portion of Ouachita County and southern Arkansas, dealt regarding anything substantive of property or power.

"Some people, in hushed tones of righteous indignation, call me the Silver-haired Snake," Briggs said. "Others say I'm the Silver-haired Savior of Destiny and they'd both be right."

The old man laughed. He was a bulldog in temperament and stature who kept a vigorous daily walking regimen, ate simply but well, and did not smoke. He imbibed occasionally, loathing beer or malt drinks as demeaning, and preferring the more gentlemanly Scotch or bourbon on the rocks, he drank them only in good company. Mister Jimmy married the only Chesterton daughter, who gave him one son, Edmond Alford Briggs, and she doted on Eddie for the remainder of her life. Eddie Briggs was the junior partner in the Briggs Law Firm; essentially, its day-to-day manager. He was tall, fit and good-looking; the old man wouldn't have had it any other way.

"Eddie played football for Destiny High School and was outstanding academically," Mister Jimmy said. "After college and law school, he returned to Destiny to join the family practice."

Eddie was never privy to everything in his father's life or business and was content to have it that way. He believed the less he knew, the less he could be held accountable.

"Eddie will manage most of the details concerning the Yashuma Bank project," the old man said. "So, his inclusion in the meeting is necessary."

"The General is quite impressed with how you have put this together, Mister Jimmy," Senator Furman said. "It portends to be extremely lucrative for everybody involved."

"Doubtless, Wilson," the old man replied. "But, I can take or leave the money; I'm comfortable, and my family, such as it is, remains well fixed. I'm interested in the man and what he can become in China."

"His experiences in the Middle East opened Chinese thinking to a new reality," the Senator said. "They could either wait and crush the spread of the ISIS ideology along their borders with Vietnam, Laos, Myanmar, and across the Himalayas and take the heat politically from the rest of the world for their cruelty. Or they could help kill it out cooperatively with the West. They chose Huang's course instead.

"China is no longer the isolated Middle Kingdom, that died a century ago," Furman added. "The rise of democratic thinking in economic policy from men like General Huang has fostered a great deal of opportunity for previous administrations and American business. Huang is considered an outsider by the Xi Jinping circle; but he is widely respected. A great deal changed in the Middle East after the death of Norum al-Nahmeed in Syria. Huang is significantly credited with helping to facilitate that and is well-placed to become the next Chinese president if Xi falters."

The elder Briggs chuckled. "And won't that drive the Left nuts?" he posed. "Their darling Socialism will have completely dissolved."

"It's a win-win, but only insofar as attitudes here help pave the way," Furman said.

"You let me tend to the attitude in Arkansas," Briggs said. "Just make sure their checks clear my bank."

The Senator lifted his glass of 12-year-old Scotch. "To the Yashuma Group Fabric Company," he said.

CHAPTER FOURTEEN
LAGNIAPPE

It was a deep red, more blood-red than fire engine, or candy apple red. The reason was apparent. Nobody in South Arkansas drove a blood red Mercedes convertible except Loretta Chesterton. She was giddy almost to the point of delirium as Beckett wheeled the top-down convertible out of the dealership lot in Shreveport.

He demurred in driving it first. "Oh, Lord, no," Beckett said. "It was bad enough worrying about a wreck in your trade-in. But, the new car? Uh, uh."

"Oh, please, Brock, baby," Loretta pleaded. "I'm so wired, I just know I'll wreck it right out of the lot."

"*Brock, baby?*" he thought. She was child-like. Beckett relented.

The stark red car body drank in the midday sun, giving the convertible an aura as it sliced along the streets. Beckett admitted he had more fun than he'd known in years. The car handled like a big cat waiting to be unleashed; he was completely impressed.

"This is a helluva ride, Loretta," he shouted as the autumn chill washed over them. She laughed, and cuddled herself against him.

They drove for the next hour somewhere away from Shreveport. Beckett opened up the Mercedes on a lonely stretch of

Louisiana Highway 1, and they shouted at the top of their lungs. He guided the car to a stop near a bridge over a creek surrounded by moss-laded oaks. The sound of their labored breath counterpointed to the purr of the car's engine. Loretta wrapped her arms around Beckett and kissed him hungrily.

"Brock, baby… please," she murmured. "Please…"

Beckett switched off the engine, and the quiet of the Louisiana bayou country engulfed them, broken occasionally by fevered whispers and sighs. Sometime later, as the stark shadows of the afternoon softened into lazy, dull blots along the horizon, Loretta combed back her hair, repaired her makeup and refastened her seat belt. Beckett started the Mercedes and realized Cissy's voice hadn't chided him. And, he hadn't thought of Jolene the entire time. Beckett promised himself only this one diversion.

"Loretta, I…," he began.

She pressed her fingertips against his lips, and shook her head emphatically. "Don't," Loretta said. "Please don't spoil it. Let's have a nice dinner and leave it at that."

The drive back to Shreveport was quiet; but not sullen. It was the silence of reflection that neither Beckett nor Loretta could overcome with banal conversation or enliven with bravado and was necessary for them.

Finally, Beckett spoke. "You mentioned a restaurant earlier," he offered.

"Oh, yes," Loretta said. "Up ahead, turn right."

They drove past the riverfront boardwalk and the floating casinos lining the banks of the Red River on the Bossier City side, then across the bridge into the historic section of Shreveport; through the downtown business district, which seemed sleepy rather than stoked. The Mercedes turned north along the river until it left the city behind them again. Turning onto a mossy-oak lined lane, they arrived at a restored antebellum planter's mansion with a broad front lawn that opened to the rear onto a lighted dock set with tables and chairs. A small combo played cool jazz beside a bar at the end of the dock.

Conversation and music greeted Beckett and Loretta as they left the Mercedes with a somewhat jaded valet, whose attitude disappeared when he recognized Loretta. She smiled as she handed him the Mercedes' key fob.

"Take care of my new baby, Scotty," she cooed.

"Yes, ma'am, Miss Chesterton," the valet said as he slid into the driver's seat and goosed the Mercedes forward.

A small sign at the wrought-iron gate on the walkway to the mansion announced the restaurant: *Lagniappe*. Beckett paused.

"It's pronounced 'lan-yap,'" Loretta offered. "It's French; and, it means, loosely, something given for good measure."

Beckett chuckled. "I like that," he said with a satisfied nod.

Dinner began with appetizers of grilled peppers stuffed with crab meat, served over dirty rice, followed by a lime sorbet for the palate. The main course was grilled salmon with dill sauce, accompanied by Cajun-style roasted new potatoes and grilled asparagus in season. Dessert was a hot cherry turnover with sweet cream.

"And, to honor your patronage… a lagniappe," the waiter explained as he produced two small shot glasses filled with a cloudy, white liquid. "A shot of tart flavor for good measure."

Beckett started to sip the drink. "You gotta knock it back," Loretta instructed. "If you don't, it'll take the paint off the roof of your mouth."

She covered the open shot glass with her full lips; then, throwing her head back, she swallowed the contents in one gulp. Loretta smiled as her eyes watered, and Beckett chuckled. He followed suit.

"Woo…that is about the tartest thing I've ever tasted."

"Ah, success," the waiter said. "Will there be anything more?"

"It's on me," Loretta said.

"Very good, Madam Chesterton." The waiter smiled with a short bow, and he walked away.

The evening became cloudy as they drove away from the restaurant. As the Mercedes reached the Louisiana-Arkansas border north of Haynesville, Beckett closed the roof over the car diverting the biting wind of a fall norther. Raindrops splattered against the windshield with a lazy randomness that lulled Loretta to sleep at

Beckett's shoulder. He thought it just as well. There was no point in pretending the day was not a concession to the recognition that Beckett was hiding from living his life.

The rain washed the storefronts along Center Street in Destiny with another renewal from the constant drift of pine pollen and time. Beckett gave particular attention to the lights that shone in the windows of the Briggs Law Firm. The lone vehicle in the reserved parking in front of the Briggs Building wasn't Eddie Briggs' silver Lexus; it was Mister Jimmy's olive-drab vintage Land Rover, the model that conquered the Serengeti and the Amazon Basin. Beckett half-smiled at the idea but only half. Beckett had a distinct impression from Loretta's description the changes coming to Ouachita County were an expression of the reach and power of the old man's will. He innately distrusted such power; it was too familiar.

Beckett conceded there was something almost pathologically generous in the old man's legal maneuver that made Loretta independently wealthy. He surmised that Briggs held it in his pocket to play for her at the right time to release her from the desperation of her family's legacy. Perhaps it was the only way Briggs could demonstrate his familial affection. Still, Beckett doubted the depth of the old man's sincerity because of one name: Huang Do-Lin.

Beckett guided the new Mercedes quietly to a stop in the driveway at Miss Esther's house, and Loretta awoke and stretched languidly. She smiled as she recognized the surroundings, pursed her lips provocatively, and nodded toward the apartment stairs. Beckett shook his head, then leaned across the seat and kissed her gently.

"Let's not spoil it," he whispered. "Just remember, when you're lounging on some pristine tropical beach, enjoying a cocktail as you look out across the bluest water you've ever seen, that… no man has ever said 'No' to Loretta Chesterton. You are a force of nature."

Beckett kissed her again tenderly, opened the driver's door, and climbed out as Loretta slid beneath the wheel. She smiled at him as he closed the door.

"Thank you, Brock Beckett," Loretta said. "I won't be at school Monday."

"I know."

"I won't be in Destiny on Monday," she added.

"I know," Beckett said with a nod. "But, I will be…"

Loretta shook her head as if to admonish him, but she knew better. "Quit while I'm ahead," she sighed.

Beckett chuckled. Loretta started the car, slid the transmission lever into reverse, wheeled out of the driveway, and glided away. Beckett stood for a moment in the damp chill of the darkness until moonlight broke through the dissipating storm clouds. He knew with military certainty he would be in a high school classroom in Destiny, Arkansas, on Monday. More importantly, he knew why.

In the early morning of the countryside near Wanxian, China, in the mountain lowlands along a bend of the Yangtze River, General Huang Do-Lin knelt encircled by spirals of incense smoke rising to the heavens and chanted prayers to his ancestors. Huang practiced his ancient beliefs within the security of his rural estate, essentially away from the prying eyes of Beijing, although there was the occasional military drone, which circled overhead for a few minutes and departed.

Huang stayed away from the capital for extended periods; his office on the executive floor of the Yashuma Bank of China was tended by underlings who communicated with him digitally. Huang retired from the city for the meditative peace and pace of the countryside to think, ponder, and draw near to his heart. The 57-year-old geopolitical chess master rose from his prayers and left the shrine. Huang dictated notes for a speech to the Chinese Communist Party Politburo on decisive maneuvers that appeared to change the course of Chinese trade policy toward the West as Russian hegemony grew in the Middle East and threatened the stability of southern Europe.

"An unstable Europe is disaster for Chinese business expansion, damaging the ascendancy of the Chinese Yuan and the success of the Belt and Road Initiative of President Xi," Huang said almost professorially. "China has gained acceptance in the world community much like Japan after McArthur reconstructed it from the ashes of World War II. Trump to Russia was not the success of

Nixon to China because of Ukraine. The Chinese are patient enough to let their militant Communist past appear cleansed whereas Russia under Putin longed for Soviet pretensions through brutishness in Ukraine.

"In either case, there is no substitute for the power of sheer greed." Huang smiled at the idea. "Chinese ownership in the United States is better than military conquest. And, to own the United States is to keep Russia compliant. Incremental investment in American land, resources, and business, developed over time, is the superior path. Russia's criminal oligarchs have clumsily sought to displace the Mafia, the Black street gangs, the Hispanic cartels and steal their way to success on the American mainland."

Huang stood and strolled through the gardens and into the main residence of the compound. Once inside, he ascended the stairway to the workout room of his private quarters. There, he disrobed and washed himself ritually before donning a combat gi of the Red Dragon. He strode to the center of the workout floor facing a large, plexiglass terrarium that housed a single Arkansas timber rattlesnake. The snake detected Huang's body heat and coiled itself. The General smiled, then he bowed before the solitary reptile.

Huang continued his dictation. "Alone a single serpent might merely survive in the Chinese mountains until death removed its influence. But to become truly effective, it must have a partner to reproduce and thrive. So, too, am I reminded, all the glories at the end of the path are impossible without a willing American partner. Why should I go to war with America when I can buy it?"

CHAPTER FIFTEEN
WHAT DO I DO WITH IT?

The weekly dominoes klatch at the Blue Bird Café was in session when Beckett arrived from the high school campus on Monday. Loretta Chesterton was true to her word. She resigned from her teaching position on Friday, and her absence created a buzz throughout the school and about town.

"Have a seat, Professor," Police Chief Harley Randle offered. "Jimmy Dale is out on a call, and we need a fourth."

Beckett accepted, the waitress noted his presence and sent his order to the kitchen with the others. Boyd Fairway opened the game, and the battle was engaged. Beckett enjoyed the diversion, and was thankful for Means' convenient absence.

"I heard Loretta Chesterton quit at the school," Fairway said as he arranged his dominoes.

"Apparently, so," Beckett replied nonchalantly. "At least, I didn't see her at lunch today."

The others chuckled and snickered. Beckett surmised they knew something he was supposed to know. Then he realized someone had seen the new Mercedes.

"I, uhm, understand she bought a new car," he said.

"Well, I should suppose so. Seems that she has come into quite a bit of money," retired county judge Campbell Meecham said.

Beckett dissembled. "Oh, how's that?"

"According to my courthouse sources, a substantial portion of Chesterton land benefiting her share of the estate was sold," Meecham said.

"Oh, really?" Beckett said. He tossed a domino onto the table, but quickly realized it was not his best play. He was distracted by the unfolding conversation.

"The tax stamps on the sale deed put it at better than twenty million," Meecham said.

"Dang," Fairway exclaimed.

"No kidding?" Beckett said. "Who pays that kind of money for pine timber?"

"Don't know; thought you might tell us," Meecham quipped.

"Seems like somebody was sportin' Loretta around town in a brand new, flaming red Mercedes on Saturday night," Randle said conspiratorially.

"Dang, Harley, do you check that federal grant traffic camera on Center Street daily?" Fairway asked.

Beckett hung his head. "Busted," he muttered, as the others howled with laughter.

Meecham slapped a hand against Beckett's shoulder. "That's the funniest thing to happen here in a long time," he said. "Where did y'all get the car?"

"Shreveport."

"Ooooo, Shreveport," Fairway chimed in. He leaned close. "Was she… thankful?"

Beckett struggled to prevent himself from blushing. "Uh, uhm…"

"Of course, she was thankful," Randle said authoritatively. "This is Loretta we're talkin' about."

"Gentlemen, please," Meecham interjected. "Let's give our young friend some credit for his reticence. After all, he hasn't known our Miss Chesterton as long, most certainly, in the same way as, most of us."

Beckett recalled his parting statement to Loretta. He smiled and shook his head. "I plead no contest, Your Honor."

"Dang," Fairway snorted.

"Hey, in my defense, I still ask the question: Who pays that kind of money for timberland in Ouachita County, Arkansas?" Beckett posed.

Their orders arrived, and Meecham was halfway into a bite of French fry. "A fair question, my boy," he said. "To which I can only offer that the taxes were paid through a most esteemed Little Rock law firm."

Beckett remained coy. "Any local connections to that firm?"

Meecham popped the remainder of the French fry into his mouth. "You catch on, quickly, my boy," he said. "Indeed, the money is in our dear Miss Chesterton's name, but the sale. That's a different story."

Fairway and Randle nodded their agreement and understanding. Everybody was on the same page, Beckett thought. Mister Jimmy Briggs was the connection between a Chinese bank and Loretta's twenty-eight million dollars for land the old man controlled, and that was the end of the story.

"Let's simply note dear Loretta has left Destiny with a gift which will keep on giving for many years to come," Meecham said.

Cissy was not as understanding. "You, what?" she fairly shouted when she confronted Beckett earlier that day before class about the gossip flooding the school.

"It was something like a date," he replied.

"Do you have any idea what everybody, and I mean everybody, in school is saying?" she asked. She gave him no opportunity to reply. "They're saying what everybody always says about one of Loretta's dates."

She offered air quotes. "That you two… had sex," Cissy blurted.

"Hon, Destiny is a small town," Beckett said. "That's the way people think in a small town."

Cissy scowled. "That's a bull-corn excuse, and you know it."

"Look, unless you or Lloyd have said anything, nobody knows you are my daughter," he said. "Why are you so upset?"

"Because I don't want you pushing Loretta's baby stroller," Cissy groused. "I want to be the only baby you've ever made."

Her Irish eyes were stern, with the same demand in them he knew from Jolene. Beckett realized he had endangered something precious.

"I'm sorry, Cissy," he said. "I suppose I'm fallible. I wouldn't disappoint or hurt you for the world. Apparently, I have done both."

Beckett turned away to the view outside the classroom windows. He trembled. "I haven't touched a woman… since your mother died," he whispered.

Beckett knew it had not been for lack of opportunity. He closed his eyes and sighed. The girl was another man's wife but was widowed by ISIS. Her father was grateful for her rescue by the American forces.

"She is neither a virgin nor a wife," the girl's father explained. "She may rightfully be another man's concubine by tradition."

Her eyes embraced Beckett with a genuine longing he never fully understood. The girl was gorgeous, dark-eyed, with butter-soft skin that was a true shade of cinnamon, her waist-length midnight dark hair fell smoothly across her shoulders and shimmered in the firelight.

"I… uh… am married," Beckett said.

The old man said nothing as Beckett declared his lack of intent to possess the girl. She crept to Beckett's bedside that night as he slept, and he found her there the next morning.

But she understood Beckett's English when he told her, "No." The girl kissed him with an unsettling desire, but Beckett did not respond, and she walked from the room. Her father accepted Beckett's lack of interest and presented him with three goats before Beckett left the village. Beckett sold the goats to a young farmer for the Afghan equivalent of five dollars. And the young farmer gave the three goats to the girl's father as a dowry.

Beckett turned back to face Cissy with tears in his eyes. "I get it, sweetheart," he said. "I genuinely do. It's a betrayal. And, I'm sorry."

Cissy melted into his embrace. "It's okay, Dad," she whispered. "I forgive you."

She sniffed and wiped her eyes with her fingertips before Beckett offered her a handkerchief. Cissy daubed her eyes dry then, returned his mascara-smeared handkerchief. Beckett looked at the handkerchief with a skeptical regard.

"Since when did you start wearing makeup?"

"Oh, that," she replied dismissively. "For… a while…"

The bell rang for the beginning of classes. "I gotta go," Cissy said, hurriedly gathering her purse and backpack. She turned back to Beckett as she approached the doorway.

"Bye. I love you."

"Love you, too," he said. "Oh, tell Lloyd I'd like to come by the house for a few minutes this evening."

"Cool," Cissy replied with a smile, and she disappeared into the hallway.

The dominoes klatch broke up about 8 p.m. that evening, and Beckett drove from the café to the Nelson residence. Nelson met him at the door.

"Let's walk down the street, Captain," he said.

Beckett nodded his agreement, and the two men ambled across the cul-de-sac. The evening was suited for a walk, which pleased Beckett. He enjoyed the putative backwater quiet of Destiny's streets.

"Cissy told me you wanted to talk," Nelson said. "And, I'm glad you came by this evening. You seem to have made something of a stir in town this weekend."

"Oh, that," Beckett said. "I got it squared with Cissy. Normally, I'd say that's it, but there is more to it, Gunny."

Nelson shot a questioning glance over his shoulder. "Excuse me?"

"Well… that, too," Beckett said. "But, that's not why I meant to see you."

"Don't let me hold you up from the details, Captain."

"Yeah, yeah, Loretta and I had a moment," Beckett said.

Nelson chuckled and offered him a fist-bump. Beckett stopped short and looked at his daughter's adoptive father with a raised eyebrow. "Seriously?"

"A loooong time ago," Nelson said. "In high school."

"O-kay."

The two men walked in awkward silence for a few moments. Both glanced along North Cross Street, waiting for traffic to appear and break the mood.

"I suppose you've heard about Loretta's good fortune?" Beckett asked.

"The old man sold a bunch of her land," Nelson said. "She gave me her resignation on Friday."

"She gave me the whole story," Beckett said.

"Do tell, Captain?"

"Eight hundred acres for twenty-eight million dollars," he said.

"Holy cats…."

"My thought, exactly," Beckett said. "Who pays thirty-five thousand dollars an acre for pine timber in Ouachita County, Arkansas?"

"Point taken," Nelson said. "So, did she say anything more?"

"Plenty," Beckett said. "That's why I came to see you tonight. I think Loretta's good fortune might answer our question about the shooter and Frederico Mendez's murder."

Nelson stopped and turned to Beckett. His expression was somber. "What do you mean?"

"Loretta told me the land is the planned site for a Chinese facility to manufacture fabric for bulletproof vests," Beckett explained. "She said the man behind the deal is Huang Do-Lin."

"The General?" Nelson was shocked.

Beckett nodded. "You know the name."

"Who the hell doesn't know if they've been in covert ops in the Middle East?" Nelson asked. He gave a low whistle. "The General is in the fabric manufacturing business in my town, and I don't know about it."

"That strikes me as FUBAR, Gunny," Beckett said.

"Fouled up but army regulation," Nelson complained.

"But, more importantly, Huang is supposed to be in Destiny around Christmas to announce the deal with the governor and a U.S. senator," Beckett added.

"Target rich, Captain."

"Exactly," Beckett said. "The nest on the bluff at your place and the murder of Frederico Mendez didn't make any sense until now."

Beckett stopped and leaned against a streetlamp pole. "I'm like the dog that finally catches the postman's car. What do I do with it?"

CHAPTER SIXTEEN
A SNIPER DOESN'T NEED A REASON

Classes at Destiny High School began to reflect the mood of the pending Thanksgiving and Christmas breaks, and Beckett was glad for some free time. He needed to think about how closely he should be connected to Nelson's probe of Frederico Mendez's death and the potential link to General Huang Do-Lin. Beckett never met Huang, but he saw the ugliness of the man's work. Military Intelligence connected Huang to the Syrian Army officers who fomented the sarin gas atrocities that shocked the world. Huang deftly let the Syrians twist in the wind as he agitated with the European Union through Yashuma Bank of China to quietly support the refugees the massacre created as more villagers fled the collapse of ISIS and all-out civil war.

"Satan and savior," Beckett muttered. "Rhett Butler." He chuckled at the thought; then he noted the phrase in the lesson plan for the day's discussion as the bell rang for Cissy's class.

Beckett was surprised to see Marilee Page raise her hand almost as soon as everyone was seated. He nodded toward her. "Yes, Miss Page?"

"I have a question, Mister Beckett," she said. "It's about the characters in the book."

"Okay; fire away," Beckett replied.

"Well, it all seems to be so much about Scarlett and Rhett, which I get; but what about the children?" Marilee asked almost plaintively.

Beckett's brow furrowed. He had never been asked that question. "Explain your question for us, Miss Page. You've got our attention," he said.

"Well, it just seems everything spins around Scarlett and Rhett, but Scarlett has three babies by three different men. The only one we really know much about is Eugenie Victoria, 'Bonnie Blue', Rhett's daughter," she said. "And she seems kind of put in the book so that she can die."

"Whoa," Beckett exclaimed. He was impressed. "That is a profound thought, Miss Page; please continue."

"In the book, Scarlett has three children by three different men, which I find highly surprising of Scarlett," Marilee said. "Wade Hampton Hamilton is the first child, son of Charles Hamilton, whom Scarlett married at the start of the war; then, Ella Lorena Kennedy, daughter of Frank Kennedy, whom Scarlett married to get the money to pay the taxes on Tara after Rhett refused her a loan; and, finally, Eugenie Victoria 'Bonnie Blue' Butler, Rhett's daughter by Scarlett. What do we know about the children?"

"Scarlett ain't about having kids," Devonte Washington quipped. "It's about the money."

"Explain, Mister Washington," Beckett shot back.

"Hamilton's family comes from Atlanta money, and it's tied up with Ashley's family money 'cause they're cousins," Washington said. "All the Wilkes and Hamilton folks marry cousins. So, Scarlett knocks over a Wilkes cousin to get into Ashley's family after he marries Melanie, which is seriously twisted…"

There was a smattering of laughter before Washington continued.

"Hamilton kicks off during the war, and like Marilee said, Scarlett had to come up with some money to pay taxes, but Rhett doesn't come through," Washington said. "I mean, she's always been sick on older men. Kennedy comes along, and he's got a store and some money, and she's like, 'cha-ching'…"

Laughter broke out again across the room and Beckett chuckled. "Okay, go on, Mister Washington," he said, calling for quiet.

"So, Kennedy gets shot dead doing the KKK thing. I mean, he's seriously got no sense," Washington said. "Then Rhett comes along to save the whole bunch. After Scarlett has the situation about Ashley laid out for her, she decides Rhett ain't such a bad dude. Nine months later, its jackpot, and Rhett and Scarlett are livin' large in Atlanta."

"Okay, two questions, though," Beckett retorted. "First, by this time, Scarlett is independently wealthy, and she doesn't need Rhett's money. Why does she marry him? And, secondly, why does she have another baby?"

Cissy's hand went up immediately. Beckett almost decided to overlook her, as other hands were now raised, but she persisted.

"I was first, sir."

"Okay, Miss Nelson," he said quietly.

"Scarlett didn't genuinely marry Rhett," Cissy said. "She went into business with him, including him spoiling her as if she could have been more spoiled. But he promised her that, and when Bonnie was born, it wasn't because they loved each other. It was, like in her previous marriages, that's what women did. They had babies. And, that's why we don't know much about Scarlett's children, except Bonnie. Children were part of what made life socially acceptable for their parents. We know that because Rhett tells Scarlett he intends to make Bonnie the ticket to respectability by all the rich old ladies of Atlanta society."

"Well put Miss Nelson. But let's look a little deeper," Beckett said. "Can someone describe the three children for me?"

Wade Fairway's hand went up, and Beckett acknowledged him. "Mostly wimpy," Fairway replied.

"Elaborate, Mister Fairway."

"Margaret Mitchell makes it pretty clear, Hamilton and Kennedy's kids were mostly like them, and Rhett and Scarlett's kid was mostly like her," he said. "Wade Hamilton goes all nuts when Atlanta gets blown up 'cause he's a wimp, like his daddy. And Ella Kennedy is ditzy, like her daddy, but Bonnie is all, like, beautiful, confident, sassy… kinda bitchy, like her mama."

Laughter, again. Beckett nodded. "I agree," he said. "Margaret Mitchell's reader gets a cold fact of life: We choose the things we like. And, sometimes, those choices bite us."

Washington's hand went up. "So, it's like, Rhett and Scarlett chose each other. I mean, they were hot for each other through the book. But are you saying Mitchell wants us to see, no matter what, they were never going to be happy?"

"Exactly," Beckett said. "Sometimes, we pursue bad choices into reality. We want what we believe is perfect for us. Rhett genuinely loved his daughter. Bonnie Blue's death made Rhett's life imperfect. Bonnie's death forced Scarlett to see she could not shape the world in her image.

"There is in the passage where Bonnie dies a precise parallel to the death of Scarlett's father," he added. "Bonnie drives her pony to jump a barrier it cannot clear, a metaphor for death itself. It recalls the death of her grandfather, Gerald O'Hara, who was the spirit, the passion and vitality of the family. But Scarlett's mother, Miss Ellen, was its foundation of reason. Bonnie's death is the realization of Scarlett's choices. Ultimately, her marriage to Rhett, and their lives together have neither spirit nor foundation, and cannot last.

"Rhett eventually leaves to find something of the Antebellum South he once knew. That, also, was an illusion, and, ultimately, his greatest failing," Beckett said. "The Old South could not last, whether the Civil War was fought or not because it had nothing to keep it together except the land. And, to keep the land, the South needed slaves. Scarlett returns to the land, but is not truly a child of Tara, the Gaelic word for land. The children who survived the death of the Antebellum South were not the children of the illusion that slavery did not matter. It was the merchant's children who survived."

The bell rang, and there was an immediate gathering of books and outflow toward the door. As Beckett picked up his teaching copy of *Gone with the Wind*, Cissy approached him.

"Am I a child of the merchants or the illusion?" she asked quietly.

Beckett deliberately let his hand brush her cheek. "Neither," he said. "You came from love… and don't you ever forget it."

Cissy smiled, kissed his hand, and turned away for the door. As she disappeared into the hallway, Beckett thought of Jolene. He realized that to find hope for his and Cissy's life together, he was compelled to do something because the war was coming.

Ouachita County Coroner Vernon Lard looked at the sheet of paper on his desk and shook his head. He was right to question the suspicions of Lloyd Nelson and that Beckett fellow, especially after having the schoolteacher informally investigated by a friend, a former Arkansas State Police sniper. So, Vernon engaged Freemon Nelson's services.

Freemon was an independent entrepreneur, a wide-ranging contractor for legal and questionable services. It was what he did. Freemon was skilled in using the currency of information colored outside the lines of the conventional.

"Where did you get this?" Lard growled.

"None of your damned business," Freemon said. Standing an average height with a somewhat wiry stature, Freemon Nelson struck most people as, perhaps, frail. But, he had the sensibilities and physicality of a timber rattler.

"Absent without leave? You're certain of that?" the crafty coroner asked.

"That's the word," Freemon said. "This dude damn-near beat to death a general two years ago; then, he went 'poof.' Frankly, people are interested in knowing why I asked about him. It's gonna cost you way more to keep it on the down low."

Lard tossed an envelope of cash onto the desk. "That ought to fix your habits and needs," he said.

Freemon snatched the envelope and quickly counted the take; then, he nodded. "Good enough," he said. "Watch him, old man. The dude is dangerous."

Lard chuckled. "Thank you for your concern, Freemon," he said as he slipped the military "wanted" flier into an envelope and sealed it. "I can handle things from here."

"Suit yourself," Freemon replied, as he left the old man's office.

Lard leaned back in his chair and pressed his fingertips together as he pondered the results of his inquiry. He intensely disliked Freemon Nelson, but his information was always reliable. And this was - explosive.

"If I know now, Lloyd Nelson must certainly have known earlier," Lard surmised. *"What are those boys up to?"*

He opened the Frederico Mendez file on his desk and reread his field notes. The preliminary evidence was sufficient to raise the main question on Lard's mind.

"Who uses that kind of weaponry other than the military?"

The facts appeared clear to Lard until Nelson introduced an AWOL military sniper into a case of accidental death to raise a question about homicide?

"Let's see if it bites you on the ass, Mister Mayor."

Lard pulled his "order pen" from its holder on the desk. The vintage fountain pen was a gift from a former governor; its stylus was gold-plated, and the barrel and body were ivory. The old man used it exclusively for signing official orders. Lard scanned the one-page Order of Exhumation. Satisfied with the language, he affixed his signature in a florid hand that belied his age, then Lard blotted the excess ink and folded the document.

Sheriff's deputy Jimmy Dale Means served Nelson with the order later that day. "I can't speak Spanish," he said. "And you need to know about it, Mister Nelson."

"That…old… fart," Nelson growled. "Why the hell does he want to exhume Frederico's body?"

"Beats me, Mister Mayor," Means said. "But, you gotta comply."

"'You are ordered to appear on the date and at the time herein designated in witness to the exhumation of the remains of one, Frederico Mendez, and to answer by testimony at the inquiry of the Coroner of Ouachita County, Arkansas, concerning the disposition of said remains,'" Nelson read.

"I got one here for Mister Beckett, too," Means said.

"What is the little devil up to?" Nelson asked indignantly.

The exhumation and hearing were conducted at a cemetery in Hope on a windswept afternoon which was not conducive to men with a backhoe and shovels digging away the manicured sod of the gravesite. Fine dust swirled through the air, requiring everyone to change their positions from one side of the grave to the other as the wind shifted. Nelson and Beckett were irritated at being summoned by Lard, who took up the questioning of the pair as the casket was lifted from the ground.

"Consider yourselves both sworn by your presence at these proceedings," the Coroner declared. Lard's clerk recorded the inquest from a nearby lawn chair. She squirmed as the wind constantly played with her hair.

"Now, then, gentlemen," the old politico began, "two things have brought us to these proceedings today: First, the exhumation of the remains of Frederico Mendez for submission to autopsy by the Arkansas State Crime Lab, and secondly, the necessity for your testimony regarding this man's death, upon which that submission for autopsy will be based."

"You double-crossing old man," Nelson said.

"Now, don't get your shorts in a knot, Lloyd. This is what you wanted in the first place," Lard replied. "I had to have the proper motivation to understand it. And now, I've got it…"

"Which is what, Your Honor?"

"Well, now, I get to ask the questions here, Lloyd," Lard said. "So, I might as well get started. On the day Frederico Mendez was killed, why did you bring Mister Beckett to your ranch headquarters?"

"I wasn't satisfied Mister Mendez was killed in a hunting accident."

"And how did that necessitate the presence of Mister Beckett?" Lard asked.

"He has, uhm, expertise concerning weaponry."

The portly coroner chuckled at the equivocation. "What is the nature of Mister Beckett's expertise?"

"Riflery."

"So, you consider Mister Beckett something of an expert witness, I take it?"

"Well, yes," Nelson said.

Lard turned to Beckett. "Mister Beckett, as I recall on the day of Mister Mendez's death, you offered a number of observations," he said. "Please recount those points for the Court."

Beckett shot a reproving glance at Nelson, then, he faced the old man.

"I recall making three general points," Beckett said. "First, the weaponry used to kill Mister Mendez was likely military grade ordnance, judging by the nature of the entry and exit wounds. Secondly, the shot was made from a position above Mister Mendez, which did not correlate with a shot from a deer stand. And, thirdly, the shot was likely made from a helicopter, given what we saw at the scene."

"Excellent, Mister Beckett," Lard replied. "I was hoping you wouldn't wig out on me. Now, listen carefully to my next question, and remember you are under oath. What is the exact nature of your expertise to draw those conclusions regarding the manner in which Mister Mendez was killed?"

"I have… a background…"

"What the hell are you driving at, Vernon?" Nelson snapped.

Lard pointed a slightly arthritic finger toward him. "You hush, Lloyd," he said. The old man turned to his clerk and switched off her recorder. "Irene, would you be kind enough to go get us all some coffee? It's a bit chilly out here."

Irene dutifully put away her equipment and plodded toward her car to drive into Hope. As she pulled away from the cemetery, Lard stood and stretched himself.

"Let's walk, boys," he said, striking off toward the tree line that sheltered the rear of the cemetery. Nelson and Beckett bounded from their seats and followed.

"What's going on, Vernon?" Nelson asked, as they found a patch of grass near the trees.

"We're off the record, for now, boys," Lard said somberly. "But, if I'm not satisfied with what I hear in the next five minutes, when we go back on the record both of you are gonna need lawyers. Understand me?"

Both men nodded. Lard addressed himself to Beckett, much the same as he had when they initially met in Nelson's ranch headquarters.

"I know about you," Lard said. "You're AWOL from the U.S. Marine Corps because you assaulted a general. I have a pretty good idea you're a military sniper - hush-hush stuff. So, how do you get to be a schoolteacher in Destiny, Arkansas?"

Nelson paled. "You're AWOL?"

"No," Beckett said fiercely. "That's phony. It's created by the brass to keep me quiet. If I try to go public with what Mister Lard here calls the hush-hush stuff, they'll disown me as AWOL. I told you I'm out clean. And I'm out clean. That AWOL crap is standard paranoid military operation."

"Then, who did you almost kill?"

"Brigadier General Pierpont Maxwell," Beckett said. "He's the reason it took me two years to learn the truth about Jolene and Cissy."

Lard's brow furrowed. "Who are Jolene and Cissy?"

"My deceased wife and Lloyd's adopted daughter, my daughter by birth," Beckett replied.

The old man leaned back against a tree truck. Lard seemed thunderstruck at the notion.

"Do you mean to say, son, your wife died, and this General Maxwell shipped your daughter off to be adopted, and you never knew?"

Beckett heaved a frustrated sigh. "Yes, sir," he said. "That's exactly what I mean. I stayed in the Corps for fourteen years thinking Jolene and Cissy were dead. I lived in the mountains of Iraq, Afghanistan and Syria as a one-man unit in support of a special team."

He hung his head, his steeled, toned frame quivering.

"I was angry," Beckett added. "When I found out, purely by coincidence, Cissy was alive, I beat it out of Maxwell in a fair fight. I couldn't serve under his command anymore. So, he set up the AWOL leash, but he let me go clean. It took me two years to find Cissy."

"Which brings us to Destiny and Lloyd's family," Lard said. He looked at Nelson. "Did you know?"

"No, sir. Not until after we hired him to teach school here."

Nelson chuckled. "He's got great teaching credentials," he explained. "Cissy and I were both shocked; but, he proved everything to us. The only thing I didn't know was the AWOL leash. That's FUBAR, uhm, fouled up but regulation, but it shouldn't have surprised me. I knew guys who I thought had no real reason to stay in service, but they stayed. You hear later their wife divorced them, or their parents died, some kind of story. You don't ask questions because it simply seems like life. And, some guys just go on with what they know."

Lard drew a long, worried breath. He unbuttoned his jacket to reveal a holstered .45-caliber pistol. He looked directly into Beckett's eyes.

"Deputy Means has got a bead on you with a rifle over there by the patrol car," the old man said. "So, I don't expect I'll need to use this thing, but even at my age, I can. Did you kill Frederico Mendez?"

"No, sir," Beckett said defiantly. "I had no reason."

"Naw, now, that wasn't my question," Lard said. "A sniper doesn't need a reason; just a target."

"No, sir, I did not kill Mister Mendez," Beckett insisted.

"So, then, if I sent Deputy Means to your apartment at Miss Esther's house, and he searched your apartment, he'd find a sniper rifle, but not the kind which requires the ammunition that killed Mister Mendez?"

Beckett nodded. "Affirmative, sir."

"So, what we have to find out is what kind of ammunition killed Mister Mendez," Lard said. "And, that's why I'm sending his body to Little Rock. Oh, looks like Irene is back with the coffee. We need to reconvene."

Moments later, with everyone sipping coffee, the hearing was called back into session. Lard eased himself into his lawn chair and looked down at his notes.

"Okay, before we recessed, I believe I asked Mister Beckett about his expertise," he said. "Please continue, Mister Beckett."

"I have a background in high velocity light ordnance."

"From the military?" Lard interjected.

"Yes, sir."

"Oh, really? How many years were you in the military, Mister Beckett?" the old politico asked.

"Fourteen."

"Dang proud of you son. We need more like that," Lard said. He closed the file and put away his pen. "It's my determination, based upon new evidence, the body of Frederico Mendez should be sent to Little Rock to the office of the Arkansas State Crime Lab for autopsy to resolve the questions raised by the advice of Mister Beckett's expertise. I believe we're adjourned."

The three men stood close by as the casket was loaded into a hearse for transport to Little Rock. The day turned sullen, but they ignored it, as Nelson and Beckett detailed for Lard what they knew from Mendez's death, the football game incident, and the potential connection to General Huang Do-Lin.

"Mister Mendez was unfortunate enough to be at the wrong place at the wrong time," Lard noted. "But, in death, the poor man may become a hero." Lard suddenly seemed arrested by a thought.

"Do you think you boys might be able to track down one of the bullets from that football field incident?" he asked with a wry smile.

132

CHAPTER SEVENTEEN
HAPPY HALLOWTHANKSMAS

The notion of recovering any of the four bullets fired into one of the Destiny High School football field lighting towers might have seemed ridiculously improbable to County Coroner Vernon Lard. But Beckett knew better.

"Triangulating based upon the height of the light tower and the logical angle of deflection from impact, I think we can rough out a final impact point for each of the four bullets," Beckett said as he and Nelson walked from the small Veteran's Memorial Park on Center Street toward the school campus. "You do realize this will be like an Easter egg hunt? But there are four general areas of possible final impact for the bullets fired during the football game. They are probably grouped closely."

Beckett expected all four were in the vicinity of the high school building, but he said nothing. He let Nelson assume the incident as a confirmation of his original theory.

"He's honing his shot to the area along the Center Street approach," Nelson said. "I think he wants to take the shot while Huang is at the city park."

"Seriously?" Beckett quipped. "The place is a wreck. So, you figure the shooter thinks the park will be Huang's announcement venue?"

"Line it out, Captain. You can almost see the bluff at the ranch from here on a clear day. I think the shooter is working his way down the street, starting at the campus."

"I suppose you're going to move the ceremony?" Beckett asked nonchalantly.

"Either that or call off any public announcement," Nelson said. "Folks won't like that, but it may be the only answer unless we can get somebody officially interested in our shooter."

"Or, you could take away his nest," Beckett said. "You can put a law enforcement presence on the bluff the day of the announcement."

"I can if anybody in law enforcement believes there is a need," Nelson replied. "But, for now, Vernon is the only one with any interest, and we have no conclusive evidence."

Beckett stopped short as the pair walked a search grid past an ancient oak tree between the high school and elementary school buildings. He waved Nelson to his side.

"Come over and give me a boost, Gunny. I may have something."

Nelson gave Beckett a hand step and he sprang up to one of the lower limbs. He hoisted onto the branch and reached a wye in the tree trunk. He immediately recognized damage when he leaned into the wye and saw something had blown away the tree bark, and gouged a small crater into the wood.

"Bingo," Beckett called out. "Give me your camera."

Beckett documented the damage from every angle he could attempt without falling from the tree; then, he tossed the camera down to Nelson. He began to take photos as Beckett used a mallet to pound an awl into the bark beside the crater, and work his way around the center to cut away the wood.

"I need to get up there for better shots while you work," Nelson said.

Beckett crawled back onto the tree limb and stretched along it, dangling an arm from either side. Nelson jumped upward and grasped Beckett's wrists. He began to swing forward and backward until he had momentum for Beckett to launch him upward, and

Nelson wrapped his arms around the tree limb as Beckett moved back to the wye. Momentarily, Nelson joined Beckett and resumed documenting the find.

"This wood isn't as seasoned as I thought," Beckett said as he hammered the awl into the tree.

"This tree has been here a long time," Nelson said. "It's probably diseased. Dang, that slug bored in there deep."

"High velocity, Gunny. It had enough energy after it hit the light fixture to blow away part of this tree trunk along the wye and bury itself about six inches or so inside the trunk."

Beckett sat up, holding the hammer and awl, and looked at Nelson in frustration. "Seriously, Gunny, this will take forever."

"Hey, I can't authorize taking a chainsaw to this tree without a reason, even if I am president of the school board," Nelson said plaintively. "We'll take turns."

The process required more than 40 minutes to meticulously hammer and chip away enough wood to expose a spent rifle slug. Beckett dug it out and let it fall into Nelson's open palm.

"Sniper ordnance, Captain. Different from what I've seen."

"If this hit Mister Mendez, nothing would be left of him," Beckett said. "This is the shooter's primary weapon. It's not armor-piercing, but powerful enough to do the job at less than two thousand yards. If I ventured a guess, I'd say something on the order of an SR Twenty-five, not the most brand-spanking new toy but close enough."

Nelson leaned back, resting his head against the tree trunk. "Man," he muttered in frustration.

His utterance, while reflective, proved prophetic, as well. County Coroner Vernon Lard's telephone call about the state crime lab findings in the autopsy of Frederico Mendez's body brought the result Nelson wanted.

"Arkansas State Police is sending an investigator," Lard said. "You've got your homicide."

"And, we've got your bullet from the football field incident," Nelson replied. "It's military- grade."

There was a momentary silence at the other end of the conversation, followed by a heavy sigh.

"Seems to me, we have ourselves a conspiracy," Lard said. "You let me do the talkin' when the ASP gets here, Lloyd. This has got to come from an official source for them to take it any more seriously beyond Mister Mendez's death."

"I happen to be the mayor of Destiny, Vernon," Nelson said. "But I get it. You want to be the one to fill in the blanks on the Huang project."

"Good relations with the governor, you understand?" Lard said. "From the greater county perspective."

Nelson let it lie. "Thanks for the tip."

Initiating a full-scale investigation during the pre-holiday period would not likely delay the Huang announcement. Still, it meant tighter security at the event, for which Nelson was grateful. He pocketed his cell phone.

"One murder in Destiny is enough."

Beckett was relieved by the independent confirmation of homicide in the death of Frederico Mendez. And Vernon Lard let Beckett remain undiscovered. While the point likely came with a political price for Nelson, it allowed Beckett to pursue his life with Cissy undisturbed.

Later, as Beckett washed his supper dishes, he was struck with a palpable regret over moments he missed in Cissy's life. He watched from his kitchen window while local children trooped along Nelson Street in front of Miss Esther's house dressed for Halloween night. Beckett imagined how it might have been to walk door to door with a younger Cissy in a community like Destiny on Halloween, to watch her squeal with delight as she played "trick or treat" in a costume made by Jolene.

Beckett pulled the window shade and turned away from the sink as he heard a footfall on the apartment stairway outside. Beckett frowned. He had nothing for any of the children, it was something which had never entered his mind until now. Beckett sighed, walked to the apartment door, and opened it, ready to explain himself.

"Happy Hallowthanksmas," Cissy beamed.

"Happy Hallow…what?"

"Hallowthanksmas," Cissy replied as she pulled back the screen door and stepped inside the apartment. "You know; Halloween, Thanksgiving, Christmas… Hallowthanksmas."

Beckett chuckled. He wrapped a strong arm around his daughter and hugged her. "Where did you come up with that?"

"It's a given in Destiny. I'm surprised you haven't heard it," Cissy said, discarding her jacket at the door.

Beckett smiled. "I suppose I'm just slow on the uptake," he said. "What are you doing here?"

"I'm with a bunch walkin' little kids from the Ebeneezer Baptist Church around to trick or treat," she said. "They'll pick me up on the way back down the block. Just thought I'd stop by and wish you a happy Hallowthanksmas, and let you know Mom wants you to come to our house for Thanksgiving dinner."

Cissy brightened suddenly. "The kids are gonna have a bonfire and make smores over at the Ebeneezer Baptist Church, later; wanna come?" she asked with an eagerness that told Beckett he should accept.

He smiled. "Sure, I'd love to," he said. "Where do I meet you?"

"Oh, we'll come get you," Cissy replied. "Just park yourself out front in about thirty minutes."

She grabbed her jacket and slipped it on. "Gotta go," she said. "I hear my bunch singing on the way back. Bye."

Cissy blithely disappeared through the doorway in a blur of red hair and padded back down the stairs to the revelry below. Beckett stood on the threshold, silent, amazed at the whirlwind of life his daughter had become. And, he began to consider the opportunity, the second chance he was given.

A half-hour later, as Beckett stood at the edge of the gravel driveway, he was struck by the sound of the clip, clop of hooves against the pavement. He gazed along Nelson Street toward Center Street in time to see a somewhat weathered buckboard wagon turn from the main thoroughfare. The wagon was drawn by two common-looking farm horses reined by Pastor Bellchase. Behind him, the wagon was almost overflowing with kids and a few adults. Cissy waved from the rear of the wagon.

"Whoa, whoa-up there," the minister's sonorous baritone commanded. He glanced down at Beckett and smiled. "Good evening, Mister Beckett. I understand you've agreed to join our cultural counterpoint this evening."

"An invitation from…" Beckett paused. "An invitation from one of my students in your son's class."

"Find room where you can," Bellchase replied. "Hold onto something, because the start-ups are a little shaky."

Beckett lifted himself onto the wagon's rear, his legs dangling from the wagon bed as Bellchase urged his steeds onward. The buckboard lurched forward, and the girls squealed while the boys laughed. Cissy snuggled beside Beckett against the chill of the evening and grasped his arm for balance.

"I'm gonna talk to my dad…" She paused, then quickly recovered. "I'm gonna talk to my dad, the mayor, about this street."

Beckett chuckled. "Your dad, the mayor, needs to do something. It's a bumpy ride."

The group of some two dozen merrymakers rattled down the street and made the turn onto the less-maintained, oil-topped lane where the stately old Ebeneezer Baptist Church building stood. The glow and crackle of a bonfire from a large fire pit between the church building and parsonage excited the youngsters to dismount the wagon before it halted. Cissy and Beckett let the crowd evacuate, then he stepped to the ground, deftly grasped her by the waist and lowered her from the wagon. She smiled and hurried away toward the festivities. The moment did not escape Bellchase's notice as he stepped down from the buckboard.

"Special student?" the minister quipped with a hint of sarcasm.

"Casting the first stone, Pastor?"

"Touche'. But you do seem especially close."

"I merely recognize the kindness which her family has extended to me since I relocated here."

"Yes, the affection is evident," Bellchase said with a knowing tone.

Beckett was stung. He should have said nothing; but, he did.

"Perhaps it's because in some ways I treat Cissy as though she were my daughter," he said quietly. "I had a daughter once, but then, one day, I got a message from the Pentagon informing me she had been killed in a car wreck. She would have been Cissy's age by now. She had red hair like her mother's."

Beckett turned to walk away, but he stopped short. He looked back over his shoulder at Bellchase.

"Cissy knows about my daughter and her parents know," he said. "And now you know."

Cissy waved Beckett toward the group around the bonfire. "C'mon, Dad, uh, Mister Beckett," she called out.

Bellchase heard the miscommunication. He leveled a somber gaze at Beckett's eyes, looking for deceit, but he saw none as a realization began to overtake the stoic clergyman.

"Go in peace, Mister Beckett," he said.

CHAPTER EIGHTEEN
THIS IS AN IMPORTANT TIME

Ouachita County Coroner Vernon Lard knew Mister Jimmy Briggs would fashion a legacy for his son, Edmond Alford Briggs, to manage. The sale of the Chesterton property meant Mister Jimmy was committed to something that was sure to be a money maker. So, it made sense for Lard to "pay his respects" to the younger Briggs.

The Lard family hunting lodge tucked into land along the southern stretch of the Ouachita River near Camden was a short trip to ask of Eddie Briggs. Lard laced the invitation with the incentive of female companionship. The young, leggy, sleek blonde with an almost childlike disposition, poured drinks for the two men. She served the libations, announced, "I'll be in my room," and disappeared upstairs.

Eddie took a long draught of his drink. "You have good taste, Vernon."

"I maintain a modest reputation," Lard said. Both men laughed.

"So, what's on your mind, Vernon?"

Lard shrugged. "All the cherished things," he said nonchalantly. "Money, power - you know."

The portly politico sipped his drink. "I'm not a young man anymore. You, however, are in your prime, and I might add, becoming more the man of the hour in the Briggs-Chesterton combine."

"I don't know how you figure that, Vernon, since my cousin has the twenty-eight million dollars."

"Pocket change," Lard chuckled.

"How do you say that, Vernon?"

"Simple, my boy, simple," the old man said. He rose and stepped to the picture window which commanded the rear wall of the cabin's sitting room. "You look out there and see what our forebears saw in the timberland, the river bottoms, and the plenty it produced when this place was settled not two hundred years ago. What you don't see is urban sprawl or industrial scarification."

Lard turned back to his guest. "Now, mind you, I'm no environmental prophet or preacher," he said. "But I know a bureaucratic problem when I see one. I'm amazed you have single-handedly diffused every potential environmental bureaucratic bird's nest for a project that seems to have made your cousin the big winner and left you out in the cold."

"C'mon, Vernon, get to the point," Eddie chided. "You understand how well connected we are."

"And that is exactly what I'm talking about, my boy," Lard said. "Your fingerprints are all over this project, and you have seemingly slid it through the gears of government bureaucracy with a precision which is to be congratulated."

Eddie swallowed the last of his drink, and Lard replenished his glass. He held the bottle of twelve-year old blended Scotch whiskey in his hand. The old man turned the bottle in his hand and let the light from the chandelier overhead reflect away from it against Eddie's face. Eddie flinched.

"Oh, sorry," Lard muttered with a practiced contrition. "Light in your eyes is disturbing, isn't it?"

He waved off any answer as Eddie shielded his eyes with his palm.

"No need to answer. You're young, strong and smart. You can handle the spotlight this is going to create."

"What are you talking about, Vernon?"

Lard raised himself to his full height, waving the Scotch bottle in a small circle overhead. "This is an important time. You're about to become the center of an assassination scandal that's gonna get everybody talking about how you got this all put together so quietly in the first place."

"What?" Eddie sputtered.

"The good Mayor of Destiny has uncovered an apparent plot against your General Huang," Lard said. "Seems the mayor's ranch hand, Mister Mendez, got shot by a professional sniper from a little hill on Lloyd Nelson's place. Your Mister Huang might get shot from that hill while he is being honored for bringing his project to Destiny."

"Good Lord," Eddie exclaimed.

"Now, don't get yourself worked up," Lard said. "You don't want to disappoint that little lady upstairs."

"What do you mean, Vernon?" Eddie sat still and quiet while the old man explained.

"I mean I can help you with your problem," Lard said. "The Arkansas State Police has a case file open, but I'm in control of the evidence. So, if you, the prosecuting attorney in these parts, were to stop this plot against Mister Huang, you'd be a hero. And, for my part, I'd only need a small gratuity - say, a ten percent ownership."

Eddie chuckled. "You old reprobate." He raised his glass in a salute to the diminutive politician.

The fall foliage across Arkansas reached its peak colors. Beckett appreciated it as he sat on the small stairway landing to his apartment at Miss Esther's. The second-story view, though limited, was brilliant. There was no true fall season, no transition to life, in the Middle East. Life there was tempered by a geography ancient enough to be Biblical. Beckett understood how, at the height of the year, the sweat-draining heart of the day quickly became bone-chilling cold at night without the sun's heat in the mountains of Afghanistan or the open deserts of Iraq.

Scanning the wash of autumn colors along the horizon with a Schmidt & Bender PMII3-12x rifle scope from his ordnance,

Beckett drank in the splendor across the Ouachita River Valley. He felt a sense of home settling about him. And he was quietly grateful.

Beckett leaned his chair backward against the landing railing and thought of Cissy. He enjoyed the evening they spent together at the Ebeneezer Baptist Church outing on Halloween. It gave him some insight into his daughter and who she chose to call her friends and, perhaps, boyfriend. Devonte Washington was close at hand throughout the evening. His growing relationship with Cissy was not lost on anyone at the gathering. Beckett chuckled, and it felt good to feel like a father again.

He put the rifle scope aside and turned to his notes for Monday's class. "*The concept of Bildungsroman, or the moral and psychological growth of a story's young protagonist. Coming of age,*" Beckett jotted in the margin. He paused and thought, again, of Cissy. Beckett realized he might have taught *Gone with the Wind* indifferent to the implications of the book upon a particular student had he never found Cissy. He glanced at his margin note and added: "*What does it mean to you?*"

The clarity of the day left nothing but an azure backdrop across the sky for the explosion of color from the timberlines surrounding Destiny. A stray glint of light might have seemed unimportant within the milieu. But it captured Beckett's eye in the manner of things out of place, something recognizable in a different context that should not exist here and now. Beckett snatched the sniper scope from the floor beside him and put it to his shooting eye. He calibrated the focus more quickly than he should, but as the scope responded, Beckett fully understood the image it clarified from the distance.

Beckett never saw the sniper's face, but he possessed a good sense of his adversary. Beckett immediately threw himself from the chair, crashing through the screen mesh of the outer door and into the open doorway of his apartment. He turned back toward the stairway landing to witness the anticipated impact of a high-caliber round into the staircase railing behind his chair. But there was none. With scope in hand, Beckett crawled to the kitchen counter and eased himself upward against the countertop. He slid the scope between the kitchen window curtain and the window frame for another look. The shooter was gone.

Beckett scanned the landscape around the familiar bluff where the sniper nest was located. There was no indication how or where the shooter evacuated. What remained clearly visible on the bluff were the smashed remains of a deer camera used to track the movement of wild game. Beckett pulled his cell phone from his pocket and punched Lloyd Nelson's number into the keypad.

"Gunny," he said quietly. "You're gonna need a new deer camera out at the ranch."

Forty minutes later, the two men stood on the bluff overlooking the Ouachita River, examining the destroyed camera. They were both armed with rifles.

"The video card is gone," Nelson said dejectedly.

"Ya think, Gunny? Whoever this guy is, he intends to use this site for a kill, most likely for General Huang."

"You didn't get a look at his face?" Nelson asked.

Beckett shook his head. "If I hadn't seen the glint of sunlight reflected from his scope lens, I'd have missed him altogether."

"Yeah, lucky for you. At least we know we're on the right track, and somebody wants Huang dead."

"Yeah, lucky," Beckett muttered. "An un-tinted scope; a rookie mistake."

Nelson should have figured it out, but Beckett sensed their adversary was no rookie.

The Arkansas State Police criminal investigator from El Dorado who arrived at the ranch an hour later was a rookie. Investigator Reyford Goss was four months out of the advanced academy, but Goss had been in the patrol division for 10 years. He was a rookie with instincts.

"I'm going to be honest with you, gentlemen," Goss said as soon as the introductions were completed. "I caught this case directly from my captain. Normally, assignments come from the sergeant, and they are next-in-line assignments. However, I got called into the captain's office and handed a case file on a Mister Mendez, complete with an autopsy report from an exhumation."

Goss followed Nelson and Beckett's eyes as he explained the autopsy report. "It seems the conclusions in the autopsy point to a type of military-grade ordnance. And it seems the same grade of ordnance might have been used by someone taking potshots at lighting equipment at the school football field."

He pointed at Nelson's tattoo. "You served, and I'm guessing you had an 0311 Method Of Service at the least."

"SEALs," Nelson said.

Goss nodded. "And you, Mister Beckett, look about as squared away as you can get for a civilian."

Beckett pursed his lips. "0317," he said quietly.

Goss took a reflexive step backward. "Seriously?"

"Iraq, Afghanistan and Syria."

Goss gave a low whistle. "Man. Semper fi, gentlemen. I was in Mosul."

Beckett and Nelson nodded their understanding. "We know what we are up against, here," Goss said. "What I need to know is the 'why' of it; why is this guy monkeying around here in Destiny, Arkansas?"

Nelson took the lead and explained how the discovery of the murder of Frederico Mendez brought him and Beckett into the narrative. He outlined the connection to Huang and Beckett supplied context.

"Sorta explains something that happened in Mosul," Goss said. "We were in there supporting the anti-ISIS forces, and the Iraqis were getting pounded before we got there. A couple of days before we came in, some artillery pieces we hadn't supplied showed up. Scuttlebutt was they came from China."

"Sounds about right," Beckett said.

Goss examined the destroyed "deer camera." He turned and gazed across the river valley toward Destiny.

"I've got a funky feeling we're gonna hear from the Feds before long," Goss said. "This seems ripe for them."

"As mayor of the town, I'd sleep a lot better knowing there was some sort of protection plan in place," Nelson said. "I haven't been told anything. There are no announced planning processes in the works for this thing. It's almost as though the people involved don't want to say anything, which makes me think they're nervous about what happened here."

"Your shooter is still acting as though something will happen," Goss said. "Which means he knows more than all of us."

"Point taken," Nelson replied.

Goss examined the site for the final time. "I'll bag and tag the camera and make out a report," he said. "But don't be surprised if the Feds swoop in and take over everything."

"About now, that doesn't seem like such a bad idea," Nelson said.

Lagniappe

CHAPTER NINETEEN
GOD DOESN'T CARE WHAT YOU THINK

The morning buzz at Destiny High School on Monday was decidedly abnormal. It never occurred to Beckett until then how he paid attention to such points of daily campus life. This morning the typical hum of the student scrum before classes was quieter, tentative and strained. He pulled Cissy aside.

"It's too quiet. What's up?"

"Nobody told you?" Cissy replied in a near whisper.

Beckett shook his head. "James Robert was arrested last night," Cissy said. "He and Rosalinda Mendez have been secretly dating, and she got pregnant with James Robert's baby. He was arrested for statutory rape."

"Holy cow," Beckett said. "He's a good kid. Both are good kids. She is… was… in my afternoon class. I'd wondered what became of her, and I'd meant to ask you. I thought the family moved away after her father's murder."

Cissy looked up at him; tears moistened the corners of her eyes. "The Sheriff thinks James Robert might be the one who killed Frederico," she said.

Beckett's brow furrowed. "How?"

"Pastor Bellchase does a lot of hunting," Cissy said. "The Sheriff sent Deputy Means to get a search warrant and see if, maybe, James Robert used one of his daddy's high-powered hunting rifles."

"That's nuts," Beckett blurted. "Didn't Lloyd set Means straight?"

"Lloyd told him something, but I couldn't hear because they went outside," Cissy said. "But, Lloyd came into the house shaking his head and saying something about Deputy Means getting it all wrong. I didn't know what it meant until later when he told me about James Robert's arrest."

Cissy sniffed and Beckett offered her his handkerchief. He leaned back against the building door and closed his eyes for a moment. "Surely, this wasn't Vernon Lard's play," Beckett muttered.

The first-period bell rang, and Cissy gathered her things to join the pack. Beckett gave her a gentle pat on the shoulder.

"I'll see what I can do," he said. Cissy smiled, squeezed his hand lovingly, and disappeared into the hallway.

Beckett pulled his cell phone from his briefcase and punched Nelson's number into the keypad. Presently, Nelson answered.

"Cissy just told me about the Bellchase kid," Beckett said. "What are we going to do about it?"

"I'm tied up with inventory at the store all morning," Nelson said. "But, I think we need to pay Jimmy Dale Means a visit and see where he got his information about James Robert and the Mendez girl."

"I agree," Beckett replied. "I'll swing by the store immediately after classes."

"Fine, Captain."

Classes were somewhat muted throughout the day. Beckett marked time by studying the problem at hand. James Robert did not kill Frederico Mendez, and Beckett knew how to prove it.

The day's final bell couldn't have sounded soon enough for Beckett. He hurried downstairs to his Jeep, slid behind the wheel, and guided the Jeep out of the parking lot, down Center Street to Nelson's Dollar and More Store adjacent to the Masonic Hall. He swung the Jeep into the small gravel parking lot on the far side of the lodge building and parked it.

The autumn intimations of October gave way to the chill of November. Beckett was unfazed as the rough crushed gravel of the parking lot crackled beneath his feet. He took brief notice of the odd yet seemingly congruent juxtaposition of the compass, square, and capital G in gold against the blue field of the lodge hall sign. It was a common sight across Arkansas, one which Beckett encountered in the Middle East encrusted on a ring worn by a Marine. Beckett realized the Masonic Hall was the second-tallest structure in Destiny, taller than any church house in the town. And he questioned why as he hurried along the sidewalk to Nelson's storefront.

Across Center Street in his office at the Briggs Building, Eddie Briggs made a telephone call without Mister Jimmy Briggs' knowledge. The call was made in Eddie's official capacity as deputy prosecuting attorney for Ouachita County.

"The boy admits the baby is his, and he doesn't deny he threatened the girl's father, Mister Mendez, about interfering with their lives," Eddie explained. "Of course, Pastor Bellchase maintains his son has no access to his guns, and they are locked in a gun safe at the Bellchase residence. The boy isn't saying anything; but it is our contention, Your Honor, the issuance of a search warrant and forensic testing of the guns will answer the question."

Eddie leaned back in his chair and rested his feet on his desk, a glass of Scotch in his other hand, which he sipped intermittently. He was anxious to file the murder charge against James Robert Bellchase. Eddie wanted to impress his father and General Huang with his astute resolution to the case.

"Yes, Your Honor, the boy is represented by Mickey Hathaway, from Hope," Eddie said.

Hathaway was a venerable Black attorney with a reputation for not caring about the limitations of his reputation. His family connections in Hempstead County ran deep. Hathaway rose from the roots of the Black church ministries of his grandfather and father to take the path of civil law rather than the divine. Yet there was much of the Southern Black church tradition that propelled his legal practice.

"Yes, Your Honor, Mister Hathaway was served our motion before the Court," Eddie said. "He has offered no objection."

The judge agreed and the warrant arrived in Eddie's secretary's computer email within the hour.

Eddie telephoned Sheriff's Deputy Jimmy Dale Means. "Jimmy, I've got the warrant," Eddie said through a swallow of Scotch. He wiped some excess from the corner of his mouth with a fingertip and licked his finger. "Stop by here and pick it up, then get the guns this afternoon."

"What am I supposed to do with the guns?" Means asked between bites of a donut at the Blue Bird Café.

"You tag 'em, bag 'em, and haul them up to Little Rock ASAP," Eddie ordered. "I'll have the crime lab waiting on them."

"This evening?" the Deputy posed almost plaintively.

"Yes, this evening. I want the forensics back on them yesterday, ya hear?"

"I gotta clear the mileage and motel with the sheriff."

"Charge it to my office," Eddie said. "Get yourself a sweet little honey at Charlotte's place while you're wastin' time in Little Rock and tell her it's on me."

"Yes, sir," Means said eagerly.

"Good man," Eddie said. He hung up the telephone and quaffed the remainder of his drink.

Beckett stood at the entrance to Nelson's Dollar and More Store, the autumn afternoon sun reflecting against the showcase glass on either side of the door. The place had the look and feel of a five-and-dime store of another era, a sense of general purpose pervaded its shelves along the short aisles neatly laid out inside. Beckett smiled reflexively at the feeling. Here one might purchase almost anything needed in daily life, from cloth goods to garden tools, bathroom fixtures, and bingo games. The store was a marvel to Becket.

Nelson looked up from his iPad at the sound of the door chime. He waved Beckett back to his place along the health and beauty aids aisle.

"How do you stay in business?" Beckett asked.

"What do you mean?" Nelson said. "I've got everything most folks in town need to get them through the day. I've got it cheap enough they don't drive into Camden or Hope on pricey gas, unless they're headed that way."

Beckett pursed his lips and nodded toward a Hispanic woman, two small children huddled at her side, and gave Nelson a skeptical look. Nelson scowled at him.

"It's a given in a ranching and timber town," Nelson said.

"Not judging," Beckett said. "Just sayin'."

Nelson looked at his watch and turned off the iPad. "I'll see if Jimmy Dale can meet us."

Nelson pulled his cell phone from his shirt pocket and punched a number into the keypad.

"Hey, Jimmy Dale, this is Lloyd," he said. "Captain Beckett and I would like to get a cup of coffee with you. Oh, really? When? Yeah. Well, okay, see you when you get back."

Nelson returned the phone to his shirt pocket, his expression was somber.

"What did he tell you?" Beckett asked.

"He's serving a warrant on Pastor Bellchase for his hunting rifles," Nelson said. "Eddie Briggs wants them tested by the state crime lab to see if one was used to murder Frederico."

"That's nuts," Beckett blurted. "Unless the good reverend has military-grade ordnance, they won't find anything. That's what is so FUBAR about this whole thing."

"Yeah, well, Eddie speaks, and Jimmy Dale salutes," Nelson said. "At least we know where he got the information on James Robert and Rosalinda. Eddie is the district deputy prosecutor."

"Perhaps, we should talk to Briggs," Beckett suggested.

Nelson shook his head. "Eddie and I aren't, shall we say, on the best of terms."

"Then, let's talk to Pastor Bellchase," Beckett said adamantly.

Nelson sighed and nodded. Five minutes later, Beckett steered his Jeep onto the gravel drive at the Ebeneezer Baptist Church building as Means loaded Pastor Bellchase's hunting rifles into the trunk of a squad car. Bellchase stood at the door of the parsonage, his wife at his side. She was crying as the stoic Minister held her close. A low buzz of conversation from a small crowd of parishioners on the parsonage lawn met Beckett and Nelson as they stepped from the Jeep.

Nelson strode directly to Bellchase and extended his hand. "Pastor, we're here to help."

The sturdy Black Minister offered a weak smile and shook his hand. "There is little to do but to put it into God's hands."

"I understand, Beaumont," Nelson said. "But, we think we can prove James Robert didn't kill Frederico Mendez."

Deputy Means hurriedly filled out an evidence receipt and offered it to Bellchase to sign. He took the pen from the lawman's hand and wrote his name on the bottom line with a deliberation that drew mentions of "amen" and "testify" from the onlookers.

"There is no shame in righteousness," one woman called out.

"Though I walk through the valley of the shadow of death, I shall fear no evil," a frail, familiar voice said.

Beckett smiled sardonically as he recognized Deacon James.

Means tore away a copy of the receipt and handed it to Bellchase. The Deputy turned and glared at the crowd between him and the squad car. He cinched up his service weapon belt and walked toward the car, but his anticipated pathway through the crowd did not materialize. Means stopped short.

"Pastor, please tell these folks to disperse," Means called back over his shoulder. "I don't think they understand this is the law."

Bellchase drew himself to his full stature. "God doesn't care what you think, Deputy Means," he said. "God cares about the truth."

And, with that declaration, the Minister and his wife turned and walked inside the parsonage, closing the door behind them. Means stood there, his hands on his hips, checkmated. Then, slowly, almost casually, he made his way around the crowd's edge, climbed inside the car's passenger side, and slid uncomfortably behind the wheel to drive away.

No one in the crowd spoke. They simply went home. Nelson and Beckett looked at each other.

"What just happened, Gunny?"

"They know, Captain."

"What do they know?"

Nelson sighed. "They know it's a lynching."

CHAPTER TWENTY
THE LAW IS MOSTLY WHAT A JUDGE SAYS IT IS

Visitation at the Ouachita County Detention Center was requested by inmates. Consequently, when Nelson and Beckett arrived at the jail in Camden, they were turned away in the lobby. They decided to meet with James Robert's attorney, Mickey Hathaway, in Hope.

Hathaway maintained his primary offices and residence in what once was the heart of a thriving Black business community two city blocks removed from the downtown business district. Beckett was struck by the incongruity of the small, two-storied brick building adjacent to a well-tended residence and lawn that fronted the street along an otherwise vacant block of land surrounded by more vacant blocks.

The bottom floor of the building housed Hathaway's law offices, while the upper story was given to his private office and library. Beckett and Nelson arrived as the receptionist prepared to leave for the day. Mounting the stairs by her direction, the two visitors stepped up and into the expansive second floor. Double windows dominated the wall to their left, casting the glow of twilight across Hathaway's desk into a room otherwise lit by a lamp on the desk and a low fire burning in a fireplace which commanded the right wall of the room. Shelves of books lined the wall opposite the doorway and a stretch along the wall to their right, the remainder taken by filing cabinets. A time-worn wooden plank conference table stood in the center of the room, while four wing-backed chairs and a small coffee table were situated in front of the fireplace hearth.

Mickey Hathaway was a man of lean stature, seasoned with years, yet the grip of his handshake remained strong. His eyes were aided by reading glasses, but they remained probing, inquisitive eyes. The set of his jaw was firm, though his demeanor was gracious. His was an understanding of how life was shaped historically in South Arkansas, reflected in his easy, yet prescient manner.

"Forgive a silly question, but why is the rest of your block empty?" Beckett asked after the introductions were completed.

"Urban Renewal," Hathaway said. "That blight of the social paternalism in the Seventies decimated the Black business community here and left more property vacant and worthless than it improved. I fought it, but the benevolent federal dictatorship of the times offered Black people well-regulated, low-cost housing, and many abandoned the responsibilities of home ownership and entrepreneurship for the largesse of government. I was a voice crying in the wilderness."

Hathaway smiled. "But you've not come to hear that story. You want to know what I intend to do about James Robert Bellchase. And my answer is: For the moment nothing."

"I don't understand," Beckett said. "James Robert is a good kid, an excellent student and a quiet young man."

Hathaway looked at Beckett with a quizzical regard, and chuckled.

"You're teaching *Gone with the Wind* this semester at Destiny High School, right?" Hathaway asked with a sardonic smile.

Beckett nodded. "Then, you should understand the context of this case better than most," the stalwart attorney remarked. "This isn't about character, Mister Beckett, it's about passions. The same kinds of passions that threw together Rhett Butler with Scarlett

O'Hara overwhelmed these two kids. Rhett was… twice her age? It's nothing new."

The receptionist served coffee as they settled into the worn leather-covered wing-backed chairs in front of a comfortably low-burning fireplace. She whispered something to Hathaway that neither Beckett nor Nelson understood. The attorney smiled and nodded his head, then she left the room and closed the door behind her.

"That was Gloria, my niece," he explained. "She reminds me to take my medication. And, so, I must."

He pulled a small, plastic bottle from his trouser pocket, plucked out a pill, and swallowed it with a sip of coffee. He smiled as he replaced the bottle cap.

"Child-proof, it says," Hathaway noted. "Took my great-granddaughter all of five seconds to open it. They learn quickly, it's a mark of the times, gentlemen. Too many people marvel at how quickly this generation has learned technology, but hasn't it always been the case? You knew how to operate the radio or the television in your home before your parents were comfortable with having it in the house. Children always learn before their parents because they are the future. There is nothing new under the sun."

Nelson fidgeted with his coffee cup, then set it aside. "Mister Hathaway…"

"Patience, Mister Nelson," Hathaway said. "Patience. We must all learn it, as patience is the heart of the practice of the law. Nothing gets done quickly in the courts when done properly. Time is the friend of the innocent, Mister Nelson. And, James Robert Bellchase is innocent of the murder of Frederico Mendez. He is guilty of loving Mister Mendez's daughter, and she not being of age to consent before he fathered a child by her, something that time will resolve."

"It shocked me when Frederico's family filed charges," Nelson said.

"Oh, it shouldn't be so shocking, Mister Nelson," Hathaway said. "Your good deputy prosecutor, Eddie Briggs, prevailed upon them to do so. He made it their civic duty."

"That sounds like Eddie," Nelson said. "But this idea James Robert murdered Frederico because of Rosalinda…"

His voice trailed away as the implications finally sank into his mind. Nelson glanced at Beckett with a questioning regard.

"Eddie knows."

"What does Mister Briggs know?" Hathaway asked.

"He knows James Robert could not have killed Mister Mendez," Beckett said. "James Robert is a scapegoat, and Briggs knows it."

"Old times they are not forgotten, Mister Beckett," Hathaway quipped. "Indeed, gentlemen, many of the old ways die very, very hard."

"You didn't object to the search warrant for Pastor Bellchase's rifles, did you?" Beckett asked.

Hathaway smiled presciently. "Nope."

Nelson laughed. "You've been hunting with him, haven't you?"

"I don't think the young man could hit a bull in the butt with a bass fiddle," Hathaway said, as he took a sip of coffee. "Much less with a thirty-aught-six rifle."

Nelson and Beckett laughed. "But how do you prove it?" Nelson asked.

"I don't have to prove James Robert can't do it. Eddie Briggs has to prove that he can, and did," Hathaway said.

"But, what about the forensics?" Beckett asked.

"What about them?"

"Surely, they have evidence comparable ballistics killed Mister Mendez, or they would not be looking at the rifles; right?" Beckett asked.

The question intrigued Hathaway. "Comparable to what?" he asked.

Ouachita County Coroner Vernon Lard was indignant. He hefted himself from behind his desk and lumbered into the hallway at Lard and Son Mortuary in Camden. The lobby receptionist acknowledged his presence, presenting him with a small stack of phone messages. Lard scanned through them, frowned and dropped them into the waste basket beside the desk.

"Call the crime lab, again," he barked. "I want to know what's holding them up."

Lard ambled to the lobby window where he posted notices of pending services. He peered through the glass at the clear autumn sky which overhung the Ouachita County Courthouse and the Ouachita County Detention Center at the far end of the street. Eddie Briggs stuck a 17-year-old Black kid in jail to cover the truth about the murder of Frederico Mendez, and Lard didn't like the way the narrative played out.

"Crime lab is on line one, sir," the receptionist deadpanned.

Lard heaved a sigh born of the shortness of breath that accompanied his portly stature. "I'll take it in the office," he muttered. And he steered his rotund frame back into the hallway.

A Middle-eastern-inflected voice greeted Lard when he picked up the phone. "This is Doctor Benashadi. How may I help you?"

"Doctor, this is Vernon Lard, county coroner down in Ouachita County," the old politico said. "I need the ballistics evidence from the body of Frederico Mendez I sent you several weeks ago."

Lard referred to a case number and fidgeted while his correspondent muttered over his computer. Presently, the doctor returned to the conversation.

"I am cer-tain Mister Mendez died of a single gunshot wound to the chest," Dr. Benashadi said. "What I am not cer-tain about is why you are questioning the ballistics. That is quite a question for the Federal Bureau of Investigation, you see."

"Have you referred the bullet evidence to the FBI?" Lard asked with a hint of anxiety.

"We have. And they are telling us that the projectile is not consistent with most common rifle ammunition," Dr. Benashadi said.

"So, the weapon that fired the projectile is not likely to be a hunting rifle?" Lard posed.

"No, it is not likely to be one."

"Did the FBI say anything about the weapon being military-grade?" Lard asked.

"The report which I am forwarding to you is questionable on that point," the doctor said. "But and I quote. It says, 'The metallurgy of the projectile evidence recovered suggests an uncommon type of ammunition, not at all consistent with known samples of common weapons-grade ammunition.' I am thinking that leaves only one option."

"Yes, I agree," Lard snorted. "Thank you, doctor, you've been most helpful. I look forward to receiving your written report."

Lard cradled the telephone receiver and settled back in his chair. He chuckled at the thought Eddie Briggs would need to prove James Robert Bellchase used military-grade ammunition in a common hunting rifle to kill Frederico Mendez. But that was Eddie's problem. Lard had the answer he wanted, and was happy.

The twilight gave way to the kind of star-studded night sky only autumn can bring in Arkansas, limited by the city lights in Hope. Nelson and Beckett stood at the threshold of attorney Mickey Hathaway's offices and shook hands with him.

"You gentlemen have been most helpful to young master Bellchase's cause," Hathaway said. "I appreciate your forthrightness, although I confess to being somewhat frightened by your theory. I can't say I approve or disapprove of your expertise, Mister Beckett. It is a matter of fact, and I deal with facts. They are a strange phenomenon, however, subject to interpretation."

"Which means, what, exactly, Mister Hathaway?" Beckett asked.

"It means the application of the law rests upon the interpretation of facts," the affable Black barrister replied. "Facts, in the end, only lend a rationale to a judge, as the law is mostly what a judge says it is."

The return to Destiny was somber. Beckett and Nelson knew, logically, James Robert should be freed from jail, but both men doubted it would occur anytime soon.

"I don't get what Eddie Briggs hopes to achieve out of this," Beckett said. "This whole thing is tearing at the fabric of the kids' world at school. And, nobody believes it."

"Cissy told me she talked to you," Nelson said. "She seemed to take some comfort in knowing you and I might do something. Lordy, for the life of me, I don't know what to tell her."

The thought hadn't crossed Beckett's mind until he heard it expressed by Cissy's adoptive father. It stung.

"She's strong," Beckett whispered.

The landscape across Hempstead and Ouachita counties flowed past Nelson's pickup truck window, the growing darkness lit dimly by starlight and a clouded moon. It was the kind of night that typified Beckett's world until now, the protection of darkness and the guidance of the stars always afforded him an advantage. In the Middle East, he was eminently competent, entirely in charge of the moment.

Now, half a world away from his niche, he felt - helpless. And Beckett hated the notion.

CHAPTER TWENTY-ONE
INDEED, THIS IS THE LAND OF THE BIG HUNT

The autumn vista across the Ouachita River from the outdoor deck of the hunting lodge at Clearwater was breathtaking. The trees along the cliffs were in full seasonal color above the blue hole at the northern end of the gravel beach which marked the upper boundary of the riverfront property. Brilliant with the hardwood timber canopy's gold, orange and copper tones, the late-afternoon sunlight afforded the place a mystical aura as though it were smelted from precious metals. This was also the beginning of the deer hunting season in Arkansas, an experience General Huang Do-Lin coveted.

Outfitted in custom gear from Little Rock, Huang looked quite the part as he, Mister Jimmy Briggs, U.S. Senator Wilson Furman and Eddie Briggs toasted their hunt with 12-year-old Scotch whiskey. This, too, was an experience which Huang coveted.

"I find it a most stimulating beverage," he said at his first taste, poured by the elder Briggs. "Indeed, it is more pleasant than sake but what cannot be when compared to Japanese tastes?"

Huang laughed heartily, and the others joined him. "Indeed, are we not all men here? So, let us be men," Huang exhorted. No-one disagreed.

Eddie Briggs never cherished the idea of leaving a comfortable bed or woman, at the cusp of dawn to trek into the woods and sit high above the ground in a tree for hours to shoot deer. He never thought the idea was barbarous. It was simply inconvenient. Eddie long ago fulfilled his rite of passage and was thankful to have fathered only girls. But, Mister Jimmy liked to hunt.

"Ouachita County was named from the language of the Choctaw Indians," Mister Jimmy announced over a grill of deer steaks from the day's hunt. "I call them Indians rather than Native Americans. Native American sounds too delicate for the lives these people lived. They lived from the land because it was all they had; they had no technology to advance their culture beyond its status. There is no shame in that, and people who want to confer some sort of superior appellative upon them as compensation do the peoples of the land a disservice.

"The county is named for the river, which the Indians navigated and understood," the old man said. "The Choctaw followed the bounty of the land, and it was tied to the river. The years were lean when the waters were low because the rains were sparse upriver. And, the Choctaw were driven to find other lands."

Mister Jimmy swept his arm in an arc across the scene before them.

"We have the great fortune to bring the bounty of the land to us by using the land to build technology that supports us," he said. "But we, in a certain sense, began here in the same manner as the Choctaw. This river is where a French trapper discovered the *'owa chita,'* the 'big hunt,' of the Choctaw."

"Big hunt," Huang repeated. "I like the mythos of the idea."

The insistence of Mister Jimmy's commentary upon the history of Ouachita County incited an irony upon Eddie's Scotch-dulled brain.

"Big hunt," he announced with a grandiloquent gesture to mimic his father. "And, what is the biggest hunt of all?"

Mister Jimmy's expression hardened; his son's bravado at ill-advised times wore on him. The old man stepped away from the grill hearth and rested a settling hand upon his son's shoulder. But, Eddie was having none of it.

"I'll tell you what the 'big hunt' is; it's… man," Eddie said.

"What in the hell are you talkin' about, Eddie?" Senator Furman snapped.

Furman cast a disapproving glance at Mister Jimmy, who was less put off by his son's declaration as he was curious. "I agree with Wilson," he said. "What are you talking about, Eddie?"

The rarity of holding the floor during one of his father's "men's" outings at Clearwater took Eddie aback for a moment. The silence was not as awkward as it was intuitive. Eddie put his glass aside and addressed Huang directly.

"My apologies," Eddie began. "I hadn't intended to explain this matter in so brusque and impolitic a manner."

Huang was nonplussed. "Go on, young man," he said.

"To be blunt, sir, you are in danger," Eddie said. "I have uncovered a plot against your life."

"What?" Furman fairly shouted. He turned to Huang. "I assure you, General, this must be the liquor talking…"

Huang waved him off. "Let the young man speak.".

"Yes, Eddie," Mister Jimmy said with a somber curiosity. "Tell us."

The urgency in his father's voice reflected the gravity in his gaze. Eddie leaned backward against the deck railing, his arms folded against his chest, his face down. Confronted with his own faux pas Eddie slowly settled his arms to his side and looked at Huang.

"I'm the deputy prosecuting attorney for Ouachita County," Eddie said. "In the late summer, a ranch hand on one of the local ranches was murdered with what we believe was a high-powered rifle fired from a bluff above the river, several miles from here."

Mister Jimmy's glare softened with recognition. "I recall that," he said.

"Well, I've learned the murder was apparently to cover a planned assassination attempt," Eddie said. "Originally, I met the entire concept with skepticism, until I began to piece together the potential connection between the Yashuma Group project announcement, and the clear evidence of a sniper. And I believe General Huang is the target."

"But, who…?" Furman interjected.

Huang held up his hand as if to call for silence. "The who of the matter is not relevant," he said. "I have many enemies. It is the fact of the effort which troubles me. This indicates others know about our venture."

"It's understandable. Once the Yashuma Bank purchase of the Chesterton property was made," Eddie replied. "But the murder of Mister Mendez was some weeks before. Since you are the logical target, I have taken the step to arrest a local young man for the murder, and suggested his involvement in the assassination plot, in order to stanch a couple of local busybodies."

"But, you know the boy is innocent?" Huang asked.

Eddie nodded. "There is no way a kid could make the shot this requires, in either case," he said. "This is the work of a professional. It's the only conclusion which makes sense."

Mister Jimmy was visibly shaken. "Why wasn't I told?" he demanded.

Eddie hung his head, then he looked into his father's eyes. "Because I didn't want to be wrong," he said.

Huang chuckled. He appreciated the exchange.

"Indeed, during the Maoist days, one often said nothing almost to the precipice of disaster, for fear of being wrong," Huang said. "Failure, in either case, is worse than death."

Huang laughed, again. The others attempted to follow suite, but weren't certain why.

"It is a most interesting situation," the General continued. "You have taken away the liberty of a young man whom you know to be innocent of a crime in order to silence the dissent of local cadres; not unlike my own younger days in China. But it is all past me now. So, pardon me if I find somewhat amusing your machinations in my behalf."

"I assure you, General, everything is being done to guarantee your safety when the announcement is made," Eddie said.

"Of that I have no doubt, young man," Huang said. "But, so unnecessary, as I am prepared to play my part."

"What part?" Eddie asked sheepishly.

"Yes, what part?" Mister Jimmy echoed.

"What do you mean, General?" Furman added.

Huang smiled. "They do not comprehend, young man," he said to Eddie. "So, I shall explain."

He positioned his glass at the upper right corner of the table in front of him. "General Huang is the hunter," he said.

Huang put a nearby ash tray in the center of the table. "General Huang will allow the shooter to believe the General knows nothing; that his stalking plan is succeeding."

Huang positioned Furman's glass at the lower edge of the table.

"The shooter will see a man who is supposed to be General Huang arrive at the ceremony," he explained. "But, the shooter, because he is careful, knows General Huang's face. Then, when the shooter is in place he will understand he has been discovered. And, at the moment of discovery, when the hunter becomes the hunted, General Huang will shoot him from another vantage."

Huang raised his glass. "A toast, gentlemen, to our young Mister Briggs. You have given me a great honor, young man. Indeed, this is the land of the big hunt."

CHAPTER TWENTY-TWO
I Listen Better Over a Good Burger

Friday was game day at Destiny High School, but the halls were silent and the classrooms largely empty. Students and faculty were called to the school cafetorium at mid-morning, where they were met by Nelson and the other members of the Destiny School Board, who stood grim-faced at the foot of the stage. Beckett was one of the last to arrive, and he took up a seat near the door, He felt a tap at his shoulder. It was Cissy. Beckett moved over a place, and she sat down.

"Devonte Washington called a boycott by the Black students," Cissy whispered. "They're all gathered at Pastor Bellchase's church. I want you to go with me to talk them out of it. They're all going to be suspended."

Beckett looked at his daughter with a half-shocked wonderment. "What do you think you can do?" he posed. "You need to let your dad… Lloyd… take care of this."

Cissy shook her head adamantly. "He can't," she said. "All he can do is react, and you know it… Dad."

Beckett was unsure whether to admonish Cissy for invoking their relationship in so blatant a manner, or to be proud of her demonstration of courage. He chose the latter, but with reservations.

"I appreciate your courage to appeal to your friends, but I'm not certain they're thinking straight at the moment," he said. "I'm not entirely certain you're thinking straight."

"Please," she murmured, her soft, hazel eyes imploring him. "That's why I'm asking you. You can keep them from doing something stupid. They respect you."

Cissy shook her head and sighed heavily. "Daddy Lloyd… not so much," she said. "They tolerate him because I'm friends with most of them. But he is Freemon Nelson's brother. And Freemon is… two-faced. A lot of their parents owe him money, so they can't say much."

"Good Lord," Beckett muttered. Cissy's insights seemed too adult for her years. And, yet there it lay between them like Beckett's introduction by General Pierpont Maxwell to life as a sniper so many years earlier.

"The first time you squeeze that trigger, and you see the life explode away from your target's body, you are going to grow up all over again," Maxwell said. "It has all been cops and robbers until today, gentlemen. Starting now, it is real life and real death."

The M40A1 sniper rifle mounted on the table at the head of the classroom was of a somewhat bland configuration, Beckett thought. It seemed somewhat ordinary.

"This, gentlemen, is the broadsword of individual combat ordnance. It is the definition of asymmetrical warfare," Maxwell said. "The sniper rifle is the knight crusader's trademark, much as the broadsword of the Twelfth Century. It is a misnomer of popular culture to characterize the red cross on the shield and cassock of that knight as significant of the cross of Calvary. No, gentlemen, it is the face of the weapon each knight wielded that set them apart. It is the weapon that became legendary. This weapon has an extended range of about one thousand yards with maximum ordnance accuracy of six to twelve inches. It is simple, straightforward and deadly. Like the broadsword."

General Maxwell hefted the weapon in his hand and tossed it to Beckett. He captured it with both palms, righted it, drew back the bolt and rammed it home. In combat, a round would have loaded into the chamber, rendering the weapon ready for firing.

"Make love to her, son," the old warrior said. "You're going to be married to her."

The point broke Beckett's reverie and brought Cissy's point home. He looked at Cissy and smiled knowingly.

"Okay," he said. "But we get Lloyd's blessing. Deal?"

Cissy's lips pursed into a small, tight frown. "Deal," she muttered.

The cafetorium assembly was brief; an explanation of the situation, and an assurance by Nelson the school board was working to resolve it. Cissy appreciated Nelson's aplomb in the face of an obviously divisive problem. But her confidence rested with Beckett, and she was loath to let Lloyd know it. Beckett took the lead to get his approval of their planned appeal to the Black students.

"What makes you think they will listen to the two of you?" Nelson asked.

"My point, exactly, Gunny," Beckett said. "And to be honest, it was Cissy's understanding of the situation that convinced me. I'm not saying I'm a miracle worker. Cissy seems to think the kids will listen to me because they see me day to day. They don't know you."

Nelson rubbed his jaw in a habit Cissy recognized as hopeful. "You get her out of there if you smell trouble."

"Seriously, Gunny?" Beckett asked. "I wouldn't agree to go if I thought there might be the possibility of trouble."

"Yeah, I know. Old habits…"

Beckett nodded. "Copy that."

The atmosphere that afternoon at the Ebeneezer Baptist Church was light-hearted, almost festive. But that was Bellchase's intention after most of the DHS Black student body appeared outside his office door. He was heartened by the display of young conviction on behalf of his son, and equally concerned to see the situation resolved.

"This is a matter for adults," he declared to the assembled students.

A murmur rippled across the church auditorium, His audience was not convinced. Bellchase addressed Devonte Washington as the leader of the insurrection.

"Do you understand that this will not be looked upon kindly at school or in the community?"

Washington nodded. "We all understand, Pastor," he said. "We're willing to take the consequences if the school board is willing to dish it out."

A general agreement went up from the crowd of teens.

"That's right, Pastor."

"They ain't got the guts to throw all of us out of school."

"Yeah, we here for James Robert, ain't we?"

Raucous applause rose from the assembled students.

Bellchase sought to dispel the growing animosity by showing some solidarity with the students. He offered the church building and grounds to them for the day as more of a holiday than a protest. When Beckett and Cissy arrived after the midmorning school meeting, Bellchase was grilling hamburgers and hot dogs while students were tossing footballs about, playing dominoes, and attending to the universal teen accouterment, the cell phone.

"Say, look at who come to take her daddy's place," Marcus "Doom" Robinson, a heavyset sophomore and center for the Destiny Dragons, yelled.

He strode to the gravel driveway where Beckett and Cissy parked the Jeep. Robinson was a comer for the Dragons, and scouts from Fayetteville, Tuscaloosa, and Baton Rouge had eyes on him. He was not one of Beckett's students.

"Whatcho doin' here, girl?" he snapped.

"Doom Robinson!" Washington shouted. "You stop right there, man."

Robinson turned when he heard the nickname, and rested his hands on his hips, as though he might need them at any moment. Beckett saw the kid play football, and he understood the nickname.

"We're gonna need you tonight, Doom," Beckett said with a calm admiration.

"Ain't playin'."

"That's too bad, man," Beckett said. "Pressman has got one of the best teams in the state. It'd be a shame not seein' you put the fear in them."

The youngster smiled. "I can do it, too," he said with an emphatic nod.

"You can't play if you're suspended from school," Beckett said quietly.

Washington stepped between the two of them. "They suspended us, Mister B?" he asked, disappointed at the prospect.

"No, not yet. And you have Cissy to thank," Beckett said.

Washington gave her a grateful smile. She bit at her lip but said nothing. Bellchase joined them and directed everyone to a picnic table set with hamburgers and trimmings.

"I believe we would all be better served if we broke bread. Don't you agree, Mister Beckett?"

Beckett smiled. "I listen better over a good burger."

The students gathered at the picnic tables and Bellchase called for quiet. "Let us pray," he said.

As everyone bowed their heads, Cissy grasped Beckett's left hand. She extended her other hand to Washington, an unspoken plea passing to him in her eyes. He reached and gently clasped her petite hand in his linebacker's maw.

"Lord," Bellchase began, "we are gathered here to partake of this food, prepared for…"

His voice began to break. Tears settled along the respected minister's cheeks as he thought of his son. A strained silence stilled the crowd. Bellchase drew a deep breath struggling to continue. But he could not.

Then, a small, feminine voice rose through the quiet of the fall day.

"We are gathered here to partake of this food, prepared for mutual understanding and forgiveness," Cissy said. "Please, Lord, temper our thoughts and guide our actions, so we can remain of one heart, as we have always been here in Destiny. And bless James Robert and deliver him home, again, in safety. Amen."

"Amen," Bellchase whispered. He smiled at Cissy. "Thank you, young lady."

"So, Mister Beckett, you know we're not gonna bail on James Robert," Washington asserted.

Beckett pointed to Cissy. "Talk to the mediator," he said. "But I'd suggest before you go past a point of no return you consider a couple of things: One, we can prove James Robert is innocent."

A cheer went up across the tables. Washington called for quiet. "How are you gonna do that, Mister Beckett?" he asked.

"I got a look at Pastor Bellchase's rifles the day Deputy Means confiscated them," Beckett said. "None of them use the kind of ammunition that killed Mister Mendez."

"Yeah, but they'll just say James Robert stole a gun from somewhere. You know how it is, all them Blacks steal things," Robinson said angrily.

Cissy shook her head. "No, you're wrong," she said. "The school board is on James Robert's side. That's what my… the board… said this morning at school. They agreed to let us come tell you."

"What's the other thing, Mister B?" Robinson asked.

"Yea, right," Beckett said, gathering his thoughts. "When Mister Mendez's body was found, the county coroner made a report which estimated the time of death. If his report is anywhere near accurate, James Robert couldn't have shot Mister Mendez because he was at early morning football practice with you guys when the shooting occurred."

Bellchase gave him a stunned look. "Really, you can prove that?"

"I was there, Pastor," Beckett said. "I heard Vernon Lard make the determination on time of death. It didn't occur to me that point might be important. Then I thought about the type of shot required to kill Mister Mendez. I began to go over the whole scenario as it related to what we know. I asked Coach Cleveland before we came here if James Robert was at football practice that morning. He confirmed it. And I'm certain the rest of the players saw him at practice."

"Heck, yeah, he was there," Washington said. "There's no way James Robert killed Mister Mendez."

"That was one of the things we learned at the assembly in school this morning," Cissy said. "Everybody was upset about James Robert being arrested. So, when you guys didn't come to school, Mister Bittle called the board members. We had an assembly this morning and the board said they were behind James Robert because they knew he was at football practice."

"Mister Nelson asked if anyone had any information which might help clear James Robert," Beckett added. "It didn't hit me until I saw Mayor Nelson talking to Coach Cleveland in the cafetorium."

"Soooo, we kinda messed up?" Washington asked sheepishly.

"No, not entirely," Beckett replied. "It took guts to stand for your convictions like this. But you needed to have all of the facts first."

"Everybody else was kinda, you know, mad that the starters blew off tonight's game," Cissy said. "But almost everybody understands."

"So, what do we gotta do, Mister B?" Robinson asked.

"You all have an unexcused absence from school for the morning, but you can make it up in detention," Beckett said. "Just show up for the rest of the day and be ready to serve detention. And you football players, be ready to run a bunch of wind sprints at football practice on Monday."

"That's it?" Robinson asked.

He hung his head. The remainder of the student contingent fidgeted in their seats amid a low buzz of shocked realization.

"You students have acquitted yourselves well on behalf of James Robert," Bellchase said. "I thank you for that. And I thank Mister Beckett for being the instrument of the Lord's hand that will free my son. And now, to you all, I say: Go in peace."

A few students splintered away from the tables, and soon only Washington, Beckett, Cissy and Bellchase remained. Everyone involved in the student revolt returned to campus before the end of the day. Nelson appeared at Beckett's classroom door after the final bell.

"I want to thank you for handling the boycott response," Nelson said, offering his hand. Beckett clasped it and remembered how firm Nelson's grip felt. He smiled.

"I genuinely felt useful," Beckett said. "And I've never been prouder of Cissy."

"She's something else, isn't she?" Nelson said, chuckling. "You know, you're getting pretty good at this dad stuff."

Beckett laughed. "Hardest thing I've ever done. But, I'm getting there."

CHAPTER TWENTY-THREE
WE NEED TO KNOW MORE ABOUT MISTER BECKETT

The office of the Ouachita County Deputy Prosecutor was housed in the Briggs Building on Center Street, in the rear of the building where Eddie Briggs' legal practice was located, a matter of economics for Ouachita County. But, Monday morning, Beckett, Nelson, Bellchase and Hope attorney Mickey Hathaway sat in the spacious, well-lighted and curtained front office of Mister Jimmy Briggs which fronted on Center Street. Mister Jimmy sometimes watched the daily comings and goings of Destiny through the tinted one-way glass in the broad window behind his desk.

"Mickey, it's good to see you," Mister Jimmy said as he stepped from his private washroom and sat at a massive oaken desk dominating the window view.

"Likewise, James A.," Hathaway replied. He was, perhaps, the only person in south Arkansas who dared address the old man as directly. Neither man offered the other his hand from either side of the desk.

The center of the room was commanded by an oblong, teakwood table, where the remainder of the group sat, including

Eddie. Two walls of the room were covered with shelves of legal reference books, while the third, nearest the door, was filled with honorariums and memorabilia reflecting Mister Jimmy's acquaintance with the great and powerful. The table was set with pens and pads for each participant, an assortment of pastries, a tray with a carafe of coffee, and cups, sugar, milk and spoons. The stiff, formal leather wing-backed chairs on either side of the table and in front of the desk were reminiscent of a different era. No-one, except Mister Jimmy and Hathaway, seemed comfortable sitting in them.

The elderly Black lawyer was the only one in the room to avail himself of the coffee and pastry. He munched contentedly on a pastry, sipping coffee heavy with sugar and cream between bites. As Hathaway finished his pastry, he leaned back in his chair and checked his pocket watch, then he nodded as though confirming a thought to himself.

"You're not going to produce James Robert, are you?" he said, directing his query to Mister Jimmy rather than Eddie.

"You know it's not possible without a sworn statement from the coach," the elder Briggs replied.

"You mean, *unless* there is a sworn statement from the coach," Hathaway remarked. "Never mind the dozen or so players who were with him at the time."

A small, crooked smile creased Mister Jimmy's face. The old man chuckled, and drew a heavy breath.

"Still a smart-ass," he said off-handedly.

"But, a smart-ass who knows how things work," Hathaway retorted.

Hathaway turned and rested an elbow against the arm of his chair. This time, he directed a droll glare toward Eddie. The younger Briggs fidgeted with his necktie.

"I can't act unilaterally," Eddie said. "You know very well, Mister Hathaway, a judge has to sign-off on the release of the boy."

"I'm listening," Hathaway said.

"Well, we are not prepared to ask the judge to authorize bail."

Hathaway's brow furrowed. "Bail?" he asked. "I thought we were talking about dismissal of charges."

He turned back to face Mister Jimmy, his arms crossed against his chest. "Your son isn't making sense, James A.," he deadpanned.

"Oh, but it's eminently sensible," Mister Jimmy replied. "The boy is being handed over to federal jurisdiction."

"Federal jurisdiction," Nelson exclaimed. "You know damned well we can prove James Robert didn't kill Frederico Mendez."

"Yes, I'm well aware Mis-ter Mayor," Mister Jimmy said calmly. "But, the boy is a key witness, now, in a federal investigation."

Hathaway shook his head. "How in the hell do you figure that, James A.?" he asked with a coy smile. "If you're thinking this was a hate crime, you know James Robert was nowhere near the scene of the crime when it was committed."

"Oh, the boy isn't being held in the death of Mendez," Mister Jimmy said. "He's being held in the investigation of Mendez for violating federal immigration law."

Nelson shot to his feet. "That... is... the most dumb-ass thing I've ever heard," he shouted. "Frederico was a citizen, for cryin' out loud."

"That may be so, Mis-ter Mayor," Mister Jimmy said. "But, the boy admitted knowledge of Mendez's violations of federal law to federal agents."

"Seriously, James A.?" Hathaway posed drolly. "James Robert was interviewed by federal agents without representation?"

"Oh, he was represented, Mickey," Mister Jimmy said. "He was represented by me."

The Black lawyer turned to Bellchase, who shook his head. Hathaway turned to Eddie.

"I can take you to the judicial commission over this, Eddie," Hathaway said.

The younger Briggs shook his head. "I'm sorry, Mickey," he said. "The larger point is out of my hands. It no longer involves the state case. Those charges have been superseded by the boy's relationship to the federal case."

"His name is James Robert Bellchase," Bellchase interjected. "And, I'd appreciate it if you would stop referring to him as *boy*, as though he was some yard slave, and you were deciding what to do with him."

Beckett's estimation of Bellchase hadn't completely solidified, at least not until the boycott the previous week. Beckett gave him credit for showing an appreciation to his son's contemporaries for their support. And, for recognizing the need to have them listen to reason. Now, he was completely impressed by the man.

"You're ruse makes no sense," Beckett said.

"Oh, but it makes all the sense in the world," Eddie replied. "I shouldn't call it a ruse, but more a pre-emptive legal strategy."

"How so?" Hathaway asked.

"Your client isn't the problem, but his father can be," Eddie said. "We want assurances he won't be a problem, and from the Mayor and Mister Beckett. We want assurances their pursuit of a wild-eyed theory about grand conspiracies stops – now. That being understood, the boy might be home by, say, Christmas."

Hathaway laughed. "You're an uptight, anal-retentive little bastard," he said with a satisfied smile. "Send James Robert home by Thanksgiving, and you've got a deal."

Eddie shot a glance toward his father. The old man shook his head.

"Not before December First," Eddie said.

Hathaway rose. "Send me the paperwork. It's been as nasty as always doing business with you James A. I think I'll go home and take a shower, now. A – long – hot – shower."

Hathaway turned away from the desk and nodded toward Bellchase. The meeting was over. Beckett and Nelson rose, and the four of them left, quickly and quietly. Mister Jimmy turned his chair from his desk to view their exit from the building.

"I'd lie if anyone asked," he said, "Mickey Hathaway is still a smart ass, but he's a formidable smart ass. Hathaway will keep Bellchase quiet, and Mis-ter Mayor Nelson won't spoil anything."

Mister Jimmy turned back to Eddie. "We need to know more about Mister Beckett."

The rear booths nearest the kitchen and the back doorway at The Blue Bird Café were the traditional seats for Black customers, an orthodoxy which Mickey Hathaway was typically not willing to honor. Today, however, was different. The Black booths were integrated.

"We're getting the hairy eyeball from some of the patrons, gentlemen," he observed. "I declare, old habits die damned hard."

"This is the first time I've been in this establishment," Bellchase said.

"No sin, Pastor. Just letting the good folks of Destiny know James Robert will be coming home," Hathaway explained.

"How's that?" Beckett asked.

Nelson smiled and chuckled. "You've got a lot to learn, Captain."

"Obviously."

A slightly befuddled Black waitress brought water glasses to the table and distributed menus. Then, she beat a hasty retreat to the kitchen. The white waitresses remained bunched near the cash register beneath the flat screen television mounted to the wall at the front of the café.

"Let's get down to business, gentlemen, before we wear out our welcome," Hathaway said. "It is obvious neither Eddie Briggs nor his venerable father want the two of you to pursue what seems to be a strange theory of conspiracy about the death of Mister Mendez. Which makes me think they believe it. And, if they believe it, they must have information upon which to base their belief. So, the potential assassination of this General Huang is a reality."

"Vernon Lard," Nelson muttered.

"Excuse me?" Hathaway asked, perplexed by the name. "How does your county coroner figure into this, Mister Mayor?"

"The old fart knows the story," Nelson said. "He's the reason for the exhumation of Frederico's body and the ballistics report on the type of weapon used in the crime. I'd be willing to bet my last dime Vernon has cut himself in on the development deal for Huang's project. He's the only one besides Captain Beckett and me who knows the full extent of the evidence in the murder."

Hathaway nodded. "Makes sense," he said. "I've dealt with the old boy, and it sounds about right for him."

"So, what are we going to do?" Nelson asked.

"Keep quiet," Hathaway replied. "And stay under the radar. If the feds suddenly decide James Robert needs to go into witness protection, there is precious little any of us can do to stop them from whisking him away to Lord knows where."

"Surely, they can't do so without his parents knowing or approving?" Beckett asked.

"They can and will. If little Eddie's father pushes the right buttons," Hathaway said.

"So, we are intimidated into doing nothing; remaining silent in the face of the will of the great James A. Briggs?" Bellchase asked indignantly.

"No, that's not what I said," Hathaway replied. "There is a difference between remaining quiet and doing nothing. I'll keep the feds at bay by filing the necessary paperwork. It's Mister Nelson and Mister Beckett the venerable James A. Briggs intends to bottle up.

"You fellas must have really rattled the old reprobate," Hathaway said, turning to Nelson and Beckett. "You will need to convince him you're docile enough for him to continue his plan, which, I assume, is intended to impress General Huang of his safety and the safety of his pet project. So, gentlemen, I don't care what you unearth. Simply do it without James A. knowing it."

Hathaway rose and gestured for Bellchase to follow.

"Don't contact me, again, until after December First. That's the old man's sacred date when the deal goes down with Huang," Hathaway instructed.

"How do you figure?" Bellchase asked.

"It's the date Eddie offered," Hathaway said. He glanced toward Nelson. "And, that, Mister Mayor, is your deadline, so to speak."

The evening dinner crowd paid little attention to the two Black men as they left the café. When she returned to take orders, the young, Black waitress seemed somewhat perplexed. But, she jotted Nelson and Beckett's meal orders on her pad and hurried away.

"I hate to admit he's right, but we can't afford to antagonize Mister Jimmy," Nelson said.

"Then, make peace with him," Beckett said.

"What do you mean, Captain?"

"The old man likes to be in control; so, let him control things," Beckett said. "Suggest the state police lock down the sniper site during the December First announcement. If the shooter doesn't have a nest, he can't make a shot."

Nelson heaved a frustrated sigh. "He may have moved, for all we know."

"Then, let's check out the possibilities, and show the state police all of the possible nest sites for the shot," Beckett said. "It puts you, particularly, in Briggs' good graces."

"I don't know," Nelson said. "It was an intense meeting, and I'm not sure the old man will listen."

"Then, let Eddie take the suggestion to him," Beckett said. "It makes him look good, too."

"Not a bad idea, Captain," Nelson said, as their orders arrived. "Not bad at all."

CHAPTER TWENTY-FOUR
WE ARE MEN OF INTEGRITY, SOJOURNERS

There were few places in Destiny, Ouachita County, or south Arkansas, where the Briggs name was not respected. The New Moon Masonic Lodge, Prince Hall No. 33, was one of those places; it was merely tolerated there. The Black Masonic chapter predated its white counterpart to the days of Reconstruction, and like Black churches, were intended to provide a haven for the flowering of Black ideals.

The New Moon Lodge derived its name from the practice of meeting at the new moon, where natural light was traditionally used in the rituals of the lodge hall. And it was in this circumstance that Beckett found himself standing beside Nelson in the antechamber of the Black lodge meeting hall on the Thursday evening before Thanksgiving. The invitation to the solemn assembly came from the Worshipful Master of the lodge, John Charles Washington, Devonte Washington's father.

"We have leaders in the Black community who want to talk with the two of you about what happened to James Robert Bellchase," John Charles explained. "We feel Mayor Nelson, as past master of the Destiny lodge, can vouch for you, Mister Beckett; and, in this venue, both you and we can speak openly."

"I don't know what I could offer that hasn't been put forward to the authorities," Beckett said.

"Trust me, Captain; it's important to these folks," Nelson said. "This kind of invitation is extremely rare."

They were met on the first-floor lobby of the lodge hall by a man neither of them knew, who was wearing the lodge's white apron regalia.

"Where are you from?" the Black Mason inquired immediately.

"I'm Brock…."

Nelson cut him off with a shake of his head. "We are men of integrity, sojourners, come by the light of the new moon from a lodge of the Holy Saints John of Jerusalem," he said.

The Black Mason extended his right hand, Nelson gripped it in oddly, and then the two men stepped away from Beckett a few paces and conversed in low tones for a moment. Presently, Nelson returned to Beckett's side as the Black Mason ascended the stairway to the meeting hall.

"I've vouched for us to the appointed committeeman. He will announce our presence to the Tiler of the lodge," Nelson explained.

"Understood," Beckett said.

A few minutes later, the Black Mason appeared at the doorway at the head of the stairs. "You may pass this way," he announced.

Nelson and Beckett ascended the single flight of stairs and stepped into what appeared to be a well-lighted banquet room with two doors at the far end of the room. They followed the man to the right-hand door, where he knocked three times and was answered by three knocks from the inside. The door opened and a Mason bearing a Crusader's sword replica stepped into the banquet room, acknowledged the committeeman in a short exchange and admitted the three men into an anteroom. The Tiler blindfolded Beckett and took Nelson aside.

"Where are you from?" the Tiler asked solemnly.

"We are men of integrity, sojourners, come by the light of the new moon from a lodge of the Holy Saints John of Jerusalem," Nelson replied.

The near singsong of a dialogue between the two men ensued for a few moments outside Beckett's hearing. Beckett and Nelson were escorted from the anteroom to the center of the lodge room and the blindfold was removed from Beckett's eyes. The light of a full harvest moon shone into the lodge room through three tall, arched windows behind John Charles Washington as he rose from an ornately carved chair at the center of an elevated stage at the far end of the room. He wore a business suit with a white top hat and white gloves, a chain of office, and a colorfully embroidered Masonic apron. Washington rapped a pedestal at his side three times with a short, stone cylinder, and everyone in the room stood. Nelson and Becket were introduced, and a short prayer was offered by the lodge chaplain. Washington rapped the gavel once and everyone was seated. Two chairs were brought to the center of the room for the visitors.

"We thank you for your attendance in our communication this evening," Washington said. "Although informal, I assure you, our discussion is taken most seriously, Brother Nelson and Mister Beckett. Nothing said here this evening will leave this room. You are trusted men in this community who have taken the side of truth against an injustice which we all in this room recognize. You have acted on the side of truth. For that, we all thank you."

He began to applaud them and was joined by the lodge members. Washington rapped the gavel once and the applause died away.

"Honored visitors, and brothers, I will be blunt," he said. "There is still fear in our community over the events of the arrest and detainment of young James Robert Bellchase. He remains in jail in Camden, and while we are hopeful of his release, we are worried."

A low buzz of agreement drifted across the lodge hall. Nelson raised his hand and Washington recognized him.

"May I speak to that, Worshipful Master?"

"Stand on the level, brother," Washington replied.

"Thank you, Worshipful Master," Nelson said as he stood. "I've brought with me this evening a man many of you know because he teaches some of your children and grandchildren in our local schools. He is a man of integrity. Truly, he is a sojourner who has come our way, perhaps, for a time such as this."

Beckett was taken aback by Nelson's prose; the man had a literary side he hadn't displayed. Beckett smiled at the thought.

"It is through Mister Beckett's dogged understanding of the events that we know James Robert Bellchase to be innocent of the charge of murder," Nelson said. "He has made it clear to the authorities and has secured the young man's release on December First."

Excited reactions spilled across the room, and Washington rapped his gavel. "That is good news, brother," he said. "It will go a long way toward settling the community's temperature. But, the larger question is this: Why did it come to this point when there has been so much harmony in Destiny?"

Nelson turned to Beckett and cocked his head with a questioning regard. "You want to tell them, Captain?" he asked.

Beckett shook his head. "You're doing fine," he said quietly. But, Washington took notice of the moment.

"Can you enlighten us, Mister Beckett?" he asked with a gravitas that challenged Beckett to respond.

He scowled at Nelson and stood. "Uh, Mister…"

"Worshipful Master," Nelson whispered.

"Worshipful Master," Beckett began. "I came to this community simply… to teach literature. I've found myself in the middle of a murder mystery, and I don't entirely understand why. But here I stand. I have no historical family roots in Destiny, as do most, if not all of you. But I appreciate the demands of such roots. They go back, in many cases, to the Civil War and indeed to the latter struggles of the Civil Rights Movement. Let's be blunt, as you have suggested. There are still cells of racism within this community, and many others like it, which can only be overcome generationally, one community at a time. And I believe there is now in Destiny a generation to resolve it, if we let it do so.

"James Robert is a good kid. He's no murderer," Beckett said. "Has he been made a scapegoat? Yes, I believe he has been wrongly accused. And once he is freed on December First, please… do as the symbols of your brotherhood imply, even to the uninitiated eye, that you are circumscribed and made true by God. The truth will become more completely known in its good time. That much I can promise."

Whether the similarity was intentional Beckett could not discern, but the murmur among the members punctuated by intermittent calls of "That's right" and "Uh, huh" reminded him of the voices he overheard at the Ebeneezer Baptist Church service. He decided to sit down.

"The man speaks wisdom," Washington said as though to announce the thought. "Can we follow its promise, brothers?"

He rapped the gavel against the pedestal three times and everyone stood. Then Washington sounded the gavel once and the Masons sat down. He smiled as he addressed the two visitors.

"You are men of integrity, sojourners, come to bring light, and our brotherhood has been enlightened," Washington said. "Go in peace."

He rapped the gavel three times and, as the members responded, Nelson and Beckett were escorted from the room to applause. Once outside the lodge room, Beckett turned to Nelson with a perplexed regard.

"What just happened?" he asked.

"You convinced some important folks to do the right thing," Nelson said.

CHAPTER TWENTY-FIVE
ANYWAY, I DON'T LIKE TURKEY

Unlike most teens, Cissy never begged for anything. But this was different. It was important, and Nelson recognized that in her eyes before she said a word.

"Please, Dad," she implored. "If you and Daddy Brock ask, I know they will let us do it."

They were the Ouachita County Sheriff's Department, specifically Ouachita County Sheriff Randolph "Buster" Jones. Sheriff Buster was noted for arresting the last of the madams of the Chesterton brothel which became Esther Franklin's residence. The closure of the place was the theme for his first campaign as sheriff.

"I'm going to bust her out of business," Jones declared, and the nickname was born.

Buster Jones' tenure survived change principally because he was allied with Mister Jimmy Briggs. James Robert Bellchase was afforded the protection which minors were given while in custody, but none of the privileges which youthful white offenders received for good behavior, or parental influence.

"You know Sheriff Buster won't let James Robert have visitors because he is Black," Cissy said indignantly. "That's just plain wrong. It's wrong for him to spend Thanksgiving in jail without anybody."

Nelson understood; he agreed. But he was wary for the sake of the deal which Mickey Hathaway, he and Beckett made with Mister Jimmy; something Nelson could not bring himself to explain to Cissy at the time.

"Listen, Hon," he said. "I know this is important to you but how well have you thought it through? There is a lot to consider in making a request like this, and we don't know whether your friends support the idea…"

She cut him off with a sheet of notebook paper in her hand, a petition with the signatures of almost every student at Destiny High School affixed to it. Nelson looked at the petition and shook his head.

"This is a request for Thanksgiving Day," he said. "The Sheriff will never allow it."

"How do you know, if you don't ask?" Cissy retorted. "At least, give me permission to go ask him if you won't."

"I didn't say I wouldn't," Nelson said. "But I can't speak for Captain Beckett. You have to get him on board, first."

Cissy was certain Beckett would agree; she wouldn't have asked Nelson otherwise. She snatched the petition away, gave her adoptive father a hug and kissed his cheek, and telephoned Devonte Washington.

"It's all set for us to go ask my da… uhm, Mister Beckett," Cissy said.

"Cool," Devonte replied. "Pick you up in ten minutes. There are some others are coming with us."

"Cool, see ya," Cissy chirped.

Beckett used his Sunday afternoons to read a bit, watch a little television and nap; three things which he had no luxury to enjoy for years. He was not disposed to answer the knock at the apartment door until he heard Cissy's voice.

"Mister Beckett, it's Cissy," she called out. "It's important."

Her persistence and subsequent admonition were enough to rouse Beckett from the bed. He slipped his feet into a pair of house shoes, a comfort which he now afforded himself, and padded into the living room to unlock the door. His expectation of a quiet visit from Cissy was immediately shattered upon opening the door and finding the landing and staircase to the apartment filled with high school students.

"What the Sam Hill is going on?" Beckett blurted. "Did they hold classes today, and I missed it?"

The teens laughed, and Cissy stepped forward from the small klatch on the landing. Beckett took note of the hopeful plea in her hazel eyes.

"What's wrong? What's happened?" he asked.

"We've come to ask for your help," Cissy said. "We want you and my… uhm, uh… dad to help us get permission to visit James Robert Bellchase in jail on Thanksgiving Day."

"We got together a petition," Washington said. "Nearly everybody in the school signed it."

He handed the notebook page to Beckett, who quickly perused the text.

"This is very noble of all of you," he said. "Assuming I could be of any value, how do you all plan to get to Camden to present this petition?"

"We got it covered, Mister B," Washington said.

"I don't know," Beckett said warily. "This is something I need to know has your parents' approval."

"Indeed, Mister Beckett and, so it does," John Charles Washington's voice boomed from below the staircase.

Beckett leaned over the staircase railing to see Devonte's father standing with, perhaps, two dozen other parents of students. "Holy cow," he muttered.

Beckett turned back to the student delegation. "Everybody down stairs," he said. "This is too crowded up here."

The teens clambered down the staircase and made a path for Beckett at the bottom. He followed Cissy and Devonte and was met at the foot of the stairs by John Charles. Beckett extended his hand and Washington's father grasped it firmly.

"As you can see, Mister Beckett, our children have faith in you," John Charles said.

Beckett scanned the small crowd, but Nelson wasn't there. "It was all my idea," Cissy said. "Dad said he would agree if you agreed."

Beckett smiled. "No pressure there."

Cissy returned his smile. "No; no pressure," she said. Then, her expression turned melancholy. "No pressure; just love."

"Folks, I'm no miracle worker," Beckett said. "I'm just a school teacher."

"You know how to speak truth to power, Mister Beckett," John Charles offered. "That is important to this community. We'd appreciate anything you can do for our children."

The caravan to Camden on Thanksgiving morning was impressive by Destiny standards. As Beckett guided his Jeep along Highway 24, with Nelson in the front passenger seat, he was struck by the thought of Cissy asking to ride with the Washington family.

"She's growing up, Gunny," he said.

"She has had a couple of little boyfriends. Nobody you would know. But, yeah, this seems… different."

"They're good people, Gunny," Beckett said quietly.

"Oh, hell, I know, Captain. It's just that, something like this makes you see how she has grown."

Beckett chuckled. "No pressure."

"Yeah, right," Nelson agreed with a sardonic smile.

A respectful silence ensued over the next few miles of the trip as both men considered the possibilities which Cissy represented to them. Nelson was the first to speak.

"So, I guess we'd better have a plan, if we're going to pull this off," he said.

"It'd be a good idea," Beckett said. "What do we know about Sheriff Jones that might give us an appeal that will reach him?"

"He has got to be eighty years old, if he's a day," Nelson said. "He has been sheriff as long as I can remember. One thing in our favor is he lets Jimmy Dale Means handle most of the difficult stuff and most people believe he will make Jimmy Dale his successor."

"He sounds a lot like the esteemed County Coroner Vernon Lard," Beckett noted.

"You're not far off the mark; they're brothers-in-law."

"Seriously?"

"I kid you not," Nelson said. "Some things never change in South Arkansas, Captain."

The Ouachita County Detention Center was not imposing; it was a squat, square, brown brick, federally funded institutionally ugly structure tucked away on a corner along Southwest Alley Street off downtown Camden, a few blocks from the Ouachita River. Inmates who successfully walked away from transport to court or trusty duty invariably ran into the wooded area between the jail and the business district. They found themselves confronted with swimming the river to complete their escape. Not many made it to the far side.

James Robert Bellchase was housed in the newer "juvenile unit" at the jail, which was nothing more than a couple of secure dormitory-style rooms, one for males and another for females. Juveniles were allowed visitors in a juvenile day room located between the two dormitories.

"The old buzzard wouldn't take my telephone call," Nelson said as the Destiny caravan arrived at the jail. "He told Jimmy Dale he would consider meeting with us if we drove over on Thanksgiving Day. It was because I've never officially supported Jones. We only tolerate each other."

"Perhaps, we can use it in our favor," Beckett replied.

Nelson seemed perplexed by the remark. "How are we going to do that?"

"I'm working on it, Gunny."

The buzz of animated conversation met the two men as they climbed from Beckett's Jeep and saw the students and parents bunched together in the parking lot. Nelson called for quiet.

"Now, a couple of ground rules," he said. "First, Mister Beckett and I do the talking; nobody yells out from the crowd. Secondly, Cissy and Devonte act as student representatives; third, everybody follows the jail rules. No matter how silly any rule may seem, or how uncomfortable it may make you feel, follow it now and complain about it later."

Nelson deferred to Beckett. The tension in the crowd was palpable to him.

"The Mayor is right," Beckett said. "We have no assurance anyone will be allowed to see James Robert. We don't know what the rules may be if we are allowed to see him. This will take some time to sort out, and everyone may leave disappointed. At the least, you will have shown Sheriff Jones the respect for his office it deserves."

A calm settled over the group, which Beckett and Nelson took as a sign of acceptance. Together with Cissy and Devonte, the two men walked across the parking lot to the jail lobby doors, and the quartet disappeared inside. They were met by Deputy Means, a second deputy, and a jail matron.

"Ya'll are gonna meet with the Sheriff in his office," Means said. "But, first, we've gotta search you for contraband or weapons."

Nelson glared at Means. "Seriously, Jimmy Dale?"

"That's my orders," Means replied. "The young lady can go into the ladies' bathroom, and the matron will accompany her."

Beckett and Nelson both shot a reproving glance toward the matron. Devonte took a step forward as the matron approached Cissy.

"No, Devonte," Cissy whispered. "It's the rule."

Cissy had no concept of what was about to occur. Beckett quickly slipped off his belt, kicked off his shoes, and dropped his trousers to the floor with his hands atop his head, and fingers interlaced.

"You served?" the deputy doing the male searches asked almost timidly.

"Iran, Afghanistan, Syria," Beckett said dryly. "I know the drill."

Inside the women's restroom, Cissy fought through her embarrassment. "Can I go inside the stall and hand you my clothes from there?"

The matron nodded, and Cissy hurried inside the stall, leaving the door ajar. Momentarily, Cissy handed her clothes over the top of the partially open stall door.

"I have to see whether you've hidden anything internally," the matron said.

Tears slid away from Cissy's eyes. She pulled open the stall door, turned to face the wall and closed her eyes. And, then it was over.

"Get dressed," the matron muttered as she dropped Cissy's clothing onto the floor.

Cissy immediately reached for Beckett when she rejoined the delegation in the lobby. She trembled as he consoled her.

Devonte's notice recalled Cissy's sometimes careless references to Beckett as "dad," which the glares of steeled indignation from Beckett and Nelson toward the matron seemed to explain.

"It's cool; we've got your back," Devonte said, as Cissy slipped her hand into his.

Cissy's first impression of Sheriff Buster Jones was of a shriveled old man. Jones sat with an almost regal bearing about him in an oversized executive chair behind an expansive, almost empty desk, in an office filled with memorabilia of a younger, stouter man. He wore an expensive Stetson that looked too large for his head and clenched an unlit cigar between slightly brown teeth.

"He looks like the Devil," Devonte whispered into Cissy's ear. She bit her lip to stifle a giggle.

Beckett glanced at Nelson. The set of his friend's jaw was more defiant than needed for the task. But the old man spoke first.

"Good morning, folks," Jones said almost cheerfully. "So, you are the delegation to visit with our little murderin' boy."

His distinct pronunciation of the epithet might have escaped Devonte's understanding were it not for Beckett's literature class. Devonte stiffened at the term, but Cissy squeezed his hand as hard as she dared. He bit his lip and looked into her deep hazel eyes, which now seemed strong and wise.

"I trust my deputies were thorough," Jones said.

"Duly, sir," Beckett replied with a military bearing which took the old man aback.

"You're the Beckett fella my brother-in-law was tellin' me about, aren't you?" Jones asked.

"Yes, sir."

"Said you served in the military; some kinda expert with a rifle, I believe," the old man added.

"Yes, sir." Beckett stood at attention.

The old man smiled. "You kill a lot of A-rabs, son?" he asked with a fanboy eagerness.

"I did my duty, sir."

Jones laughed, though it was not so much a laugh as a cackle one might expect from a scarecrow come to life on Halloween. He leaned back in his chair and pressed his fingertips together in somewhat the same prayerful pose Beckett had seen from Vernon Lard. Then, Beckett formulated his strategy.

"Sir, if I may?" he posed in his best military manner.

"Go ahead," Jones said.

"What you see by this demonstration of the efficiency of your office is only part of the reason for your success," Beckett said. "No one gets past your sense of duty to the office, which then, imparts no particular favors. Am I correct, sir?"

The old man nodded. He was enjoying it.

"Guided by that principle, may I suggest, sir, you take a look out of the window, and you will see a contingent of people from Destiny," Beckett said.

Jones pushed up two or three slats of the Venetian blind covering the exterior window beside his desk. He nodded. "See what you mean. So?"

"Sir, I suggest the contingent outside represents two things: the past and the future," Beckett said. "The past is the adults who have voted in Ouachita County, and the future is the young people who will vote in Ouachita County. Sir, I suggest that whatever may have been lost in the past can be gained in the future with one tactic, which granting the request of this group can help achieve."

Beckett turned to Nelson and looked him straight in the eyes. "Am I correct, Gunny?"

Until that question, Nelson pondered whether Beckett had lost his mind. Now, he understood.

"That is correct, Captain Beckett," Nelson said. "It is the chain of command principle, sir. The younger generation learns from its elders what is best for Destiny and Ouachita County and acts on its knowledge."

The little military sketch the two men played out was lost on Cissy and Devonte, but they remained quiet. Whatever Cissy's two fathers were doing appeared to be working. Cissy squeezed Devonte's hand, and he reciprocated.

Sheriff Randolph "Buster" Jones leaned back in his oversized chair behind his oversized desk, wearing his oversized Stetson, and again assumed his prayerful posture. Slowly, he came to a decision.

"You make a compelling point, Mister Beckett," Jones said. "So, here is what I will do with it: You four get to see the boy; nobody else. You admit you have been properly inspected, so you're ready to go. But, I don't have the time or inclination on

Thanksgiving Day to take care of the rest of your bunch. So, that's the deal, just the four of you. But, in the end, the credit goes to this office. Understood?"

"Roger that, sir," Beckett said crisply.

It was a poor deal, but more than Beckett believed possible. So, with their wallets, watches, belts, shoes and other personal effects held at the book-in desk, the four visitors were admitted to the juvenile day room to wait for James Robert.

The room was spare, with a table and two benches in the center, a television monitor mounted to the wall in one corner near the ceiling, and a small bookstand with magazines and a few books strewn on it below. A single rectangular window ran the length of the exterior side of the room near the ceiling, providing a source of natural lighting during the day. The room was otherwise lit by a single fluorescent electrical fixture mounted in the center of the ceiling. Beckett immediately noticed there were no cameras in the room.

He motioned to Nelson and Devonte. "Get those benches and put them under the window," he said. "We can at least let everyone get a look at James Robert."

Devonte laughed and grabbed one bench, while Nelson positioned the other one. Beckett climbed onto one bench and Nelson onto the other.

"Good, we have enough height to get him to the window," Beckett said.

"But, how will anyone outside know?" Cissy asked.

"Trust me, girl, they'll know," Devonte replied.

When he saw the four visitors, James Robert's hangdog expression brightened into a full laugh, and he rushed to give Devonte a bear hug and lifted Cissy from the floor.

"Oh, man, it's good to see you guys," he exclaimed. "I thought nobody was ever gonna see me, again."

"Hey, man, you got my lady here and Mister Beckett to thank for that," Devonte said.

"Your lady? You two?" James Robert asked. "Oooohh, man."

Then, he saw Nelson. "Sorry, sir," he muttered.

Nelson laughed; then, they all laughed.

The visit was too brief, but it was long enough to get James Robert to the window where he saw his parents and friends for the first time since September. He wiped tears from his eyes as they waved and applauded before he finally stepped back onto the floor.

"Thank you, Mister B."

"Hang in there, young man," Beckett said. "Your lawyer has got a deal to get you out of here by next week."

James Robert's eyes became wide with realization. "No lie?"

"No lie," Beckett said. "None of us believes that you killed Mister Mendez; so, you hang in there. Stay on your best behavior; follow the rules. We will all come to get you."

"I know it's a horrible way to spend Thanksgiving," Cissy said. "And, we couldn't bring you anything; but, happy Thanksgiving, James Robert."

"Hey, girl, it's my best Thanksgiving ever," he said. "Anyway, I don't like turkey."

CHAPTER TWENTY-SIX
NO ECHO. REPEAT, NO ECHO

The release of James Robert Bellchase on December 1st was low-key; something which Beckett and Nelson had not expected, knowing Eddie Briggs' penchant for theatrics. The damage done to the Bellchase family's lives was a matter to be settled at another time and another place. The urgency of the moment lay with the young man's freedom and Beckett and Nelson's agreement to say nothing. And it was to that end Eddie met with the two men a final time.

The venue in the offices of Coroner Vernon Lard confirmed Beckett and Nelson's suspicions of Lard's ability to worm his way into the Huang development. And it made taking the meeting with Eddie disgusting to Beckett, but he was determined to have Eddie believe the Briggs were in control.

"Noon, CST; the boy is out," Eddie said as he looked at his watch.

Lard chuckled. "You're too dramatic, Eddie. These gentlemen understand that without word from you otherwise, the boy was to go free at noon."

"Oh, was I being dramatic?" Eddie posed. "Forgive me."

Beckett briefly considered different scenarios to take out the little creep with a shot Eddie would never hear coming. But he quelled his sense of outrage, secure in understanding the danger in Eddie's vanity. Beckett smiled, a static, satisfied expression, turning it deliberately toward Nelson, who reciprocated.

"We appreciate your efforts," Nelson said. "And, we'd like to offer our support in securing the success of your announcement on the Twelfth."

"How so?" Eddie asked.

"I'm prepared to lockdown my ranch; put state troopers and county sheriff's deputies all over the place to ensure nothing happens to mar your announcement of the biggest thing to come to Destiny since its founding," Nelson said. "Your project will put Destiny on the map."

"Admirable of you, Mayor Nelson, but quite unnecessary. We have our own security arrangements for the announcement," Eddie replied.

"But it's obvious the threat comes from…"

"Don't push it, Lloyd. It's out of your hands," Eddie said.

"I'm only thinking of what is best for the people of our town," Nelson said as affably as he could stomach.

"All very admirable of you, Mister Mayor, but entirely unnecessary," Eddie retorted. "Now, I believe you have someone you need to collect at the county jail."

"Seems as though that's our cue to leave," Beckett said.

Outside, in the parking lot of Lard and Son Mortuary, a cell phone call to Cissy confirmed the release of James Robert and the start of a caravan of supporters on the way back to Destiny. Beckett wheeled his Jeep away from the mortuary, and Nelson pointed toward the parking lot of the City Diner down the street.

"I'll buy your lunch," he said. "We need to talk; and I'm too steamed to go to the house."

"Roger that," Beckett said, as he parked the Jeep at the cafe.

The two men found a booth near the rear of the restaurant. They said little until the food arrived, and they were reasonably certain of being undisturbed. Nelson dug into his chicken fried steak and gravy with gusto as he marshaled his thoughts. Beckett let him fume. Finally, between bites, Nelson came around.

"You have any idea what that little piss ant Eddie is going to do?" he asked.

"I'd hate to venture a guess," Beckett said. "Something monumentally stupid, I suspect."

"That's the problem, Captain," Nelson said. "Whatever he does, Huang has to sign off on it."

Beckett mulled the thought for a moment. "Huang has always loved a challenge. That's his reputation; so, you're saying whatever Eddie does to secure Huang's presence for the announcement will be off the wall and will appeal to Huang?"

"He could give a flip about the reputation of Destiny," Nelson said. "But, I'm the mayor; people depend upon me to keep our community's reputation clean. It hasn't been easy lately, for obvious reasons, but I've got a bad feeling this will be absolutely FUBAR."

"You offered the best you could ensure," Beckett argued. "The promise of a lockdown of your property was more than most people would consider, not to mention the idea of having a heavy law enforcement presence on the property."

"But it bothers me how readily the little cow muffin turned it down. Whatever he calls his security arrangements, I can assure you, are not in our best interests," Nelson carped. "We've got to do… something."

"Like what?" Beckett asked. He munched on a tasty final morsel of steak. "You don't need his permission to follow through. Talk to Investigator Goss and get some people on your property if it will help your sense of civic duty. Just know while you're standing there and giving Huang the key to the town, or whatever the mayor does, somebody else will have eyes on the sniper nest."

"Or, we could echo back on him," Nelson said quietly.

Beckett almost choked on his steak. "Wha…? Are you nuts? Look, just call the ASP and leave it alone, okay?"

"No, think about it, Captain," Nelson insisted. "If Eddie thinks we've given up, we can do this. He looks stupid to Huang if we've already taken the guy down."

Beckett leaned into Nelson's face. "You're thinking about an echo shot, and you are not the one being suggested to make it. That's murder."

"No, it's defense of another," Nelson said. "It'd make you a freakin' hero."

"Like hell it would," Beckett muttered. "Look, Goss seemed squared away about the situation, let him handle it. Besides, the feds may have people in place and we'd only screw things up."

"But, what if they don't have anything in place, Captain?" Nelson complained. "Listen for a second: Goss clearly didn't like what he was hearing, but what if nobody believes it? He called the shot at the stadium, 'monkeying around.' What if nobody really believes the connection that we believe? Eddie included."

Beckett shook his head. "You and I both know…"

"That's right, Captain; you and I know," Nelson said. "But, nobody else around here has the expertise."

"That's where you're wrong, Gunny. Remember what Goss said about the shooter being ahead of the game." Beckett insisted.

"He was fanboying you," Nelson replied testily. "All he did was bag and tag and make out a report. Have we heard anything from him? Has there been any follow-up?"

Nelson tossed his napkin onto his unfinished steak; his appetite was gone. "We've got to do something."

"You want me to bead down on this guy while he's beading down on Huang and do what?" Beckett asked, the set of his jaw telegraphing his disdain for Nelson's idea.

"Just… put him off the shot. That's all we need, isn't it?" Nelson said quietly.

Beckett leaned back in his seat and sighed. "Yeah, I can do that."

The weekend prior to the announcement left Beckett and Nelson ample time to coordinate the shot. Beckett decided to take the shot from the kitchen window of his apartment.

"This shot requires practice," Beckett said. "Most shots I've taken in the past fourteen years were made in combat to protect troop movements or support asset extractions. A few required practice, either because of special circumstances or special terrain. This shot is both."

He pulled back Miss Esther's kitchen curtains. Beckett was fond of the apple blossom pattern, faded as it was, and he took precautions to tie the curtains away from the window to prevent collateral damage.

"We have a ten to twelve-degree variation, and the apartment interior will absorb most of the recoil noise," Beckett said. "Sniper ordnance is not completely silent. I need to outfit the area around the kitchen window and the countertop below with sound suppressant material."

"The ceremony will begin at noon at Veteran's Park after a parade along Center Street," Nelson said. "We've got the works, the high school marching band, and a contingent from the local veterans' organizations to present the colors and open the ceremony with the Pledge of Allegiance. Pastor Bellchase will give a prayer, and I'll make introductions. General Huang will make the announcement, and the whole thing will take less than half an hour."

Beckett sighed. "Plenty of time for more than one shot if our boy misses the first time," he said. "Easier for me, but tougher for you."

The kitchen window was an excellent shooting space; it opened directly above the sink and countertop immediately to the right of the sink, allowing the use of the countertop to fix the rifle.

"An *echo shot* has to resemble as closely as possible an echo of the shot another sniper intends to make," Beckett explained. "The other sniper becomes the *echo target*. So, you keep an eye out downstairs for me to get the sequence right without any interruptions."

Nelson watched the street and sidewalk below from the bedroom window while Beckett worked out the sequence for opening the window, assembling his rifle station, positioning himself prone on the small dining table shoved against the counter, setting the rifle, and sighting the scope. The entire process lasted less than a minute; but it required practice.

"It needs to feel as natural as possible," Beckett muttered as he sighted the shot. "As natural as possible…"

"Hey, this is as natural as it gets for you, Captain," Nelson called out from the bedroom.

"Gimme a break, Gunny," Beckett said. "A shot with a window of opportunity less than five seconds in length is anything but natural. Lee Harvey Oswald's window was much longer; it was a shot which is still studied in sniper schools worldwide because it was anything but natural."

"Dumb luck," Nelson quipped.

"Oswald's single shot in the window of opportunity reflected in the Zapruder footage was theoretically impossible," Beckett said as he studied his scope settings. "Yet Oswald is the one credited with successfully making it. Perhaps, that was the case because his shot was anything but natural."

"What's the saying, Captain, once made and twice done?" Nelson asked.

Beckett closed his eyes and remembered explaining the notion to four generals assembled on a narrow, barren stretch of beach at the Laguna Atascosa National Wildlife Refuge south of Port Mansfield, Texas.

"It's the point about monkeys, typewriters, and the works of Shakespeare, gentlemen. The odds become better as the attempts grow. The impossible is the only thing which is impossible; the improbable can be achieved."

The target was marked inside the bridge of a derelict battlecruiser towed parallel to the shoreline two miles offshore at top speed for such an operation. The window of opportunity for the shot on the target was clear for approximately five seconds. Beckett settled into his nest atop a hand-assembled PVC pipe tower on the crest of the dunes, and sighted the bridge of the ship the moment it broke the horizon. The ability to sight the shot grew exponentially with the passage of the cruiser, creating the shot window.

The rifle was one-of-a-kind; produced especially for the mission, combining the best elements of modern ordnance at the time. The shot was anything but natural, accounting for wind velocity, the ship's pitch and roll stability, targeted angle, daylight, and vectoring for the right-left movement of the vessel on the horizon. The first 15 attempts were low, high or wide; the 16th grazed the target.

"It's a crap shoot at best," the ranking general groused. "But, it's the only opportunity we have. The woman hasn't been outside of North Korea in more than a decade."

The improbable crossed paths with the optimum ten days later when the North Korean Navy conducted maneuvers in the straits off a small cluster of islands near Wonsan. The flag ship sailed into position some two miles offshore as the accompanying fleet began a barrage toward positions inland on the largest of the islands. Beckett's nest was positioned in the canopy of a palm grove almost immediately off the beach. Shells from the barrage roared overhead and exploded inland as he sighted the movement of the flag ship and drew the bridge into view. Were it not for the concussion wash from the barrage, the wind velocity would have been zero; the skies were clear and daylight high. Beckett drew a deep breath for the shot and rested his finger against the trigger.

Beckett blinked and shook the memory away. He sighted the shot against the sniper nest on the bluff at the ranch, again.

"Just enough to put him off the shot," he whispered. "Where do I place it?"

Beckett's target was not the shooter himself, but a pinpoint somewhere beside or above the shooter's head, close enough to make him flinch, but far enough to be certain he was not fatally injured by shrapnel. Beckett chose the wye between two limbs in the bushes immediately to the right of the shooter's nest. He practiced placement with laser guidance until he was satisfied with the shot.

Beckett built his sniper platform in the kitchen early the day of the Huang announcement. He sighted the shot a final time at midmorning and waited. Beckett checked his watch; ten minutes until parade time. He telephoned Nelson.

Less than four blocks away at the Masonic Hall parking lot, Nelson checked his watch as his cell phone dweedled.

"Yeah, Captain?"

"I'm ready," Beckett said.

"Good, because I'm being kept out of the loop with Eddie's people," Nelson said. "All I know is I meet the big guy here at the lodge hall; get in the car, and we ride to the park."

"FUBAR," Beckett said.

"Copy that, Captain," Nelson said. "Have you got eyes on the echo?"

Beckett put his cell phone aside and settled onto the dining table. He lifted his rifle and nestled the scope against his shooting eye. He sighed and opened his eye letting it focus naturally. The sniper nest on the bluff was empty. Beckett grabbed his ranging binoculars from the countertop beside him and scanned the timber canopy along the horizon. There was no movement of birds in the trees to reflect movement on the ground. Beckett turned back to the sniper nest; it was undisturbed.

"What the…?"

Nelson never heard the exclamation. He stood in the middle of Center Street in front of the Masonic Hall, shaking hands with a small, slightly portly Oriental man who was introduced to him as General Huang Do-Lin. But something about the small man's grip told Nelson his guest was not the military-political legend from China.

"I'm pleased to meet you, General," Nelson said quietly.

The little man smiled and nodded. Nelson realized then what Beckett discovered moments earlier. Beckett set the rifle aside, snatched his cell phone from the countertop and switched to text messaging.

"No echo. Repeat, No echo," he typed.

Nelson's cell phone chimed. He looked down at the screen.

"No echo. Repeat, No echo."

"Something's FUBAR here, too," Nelson replied.

"Explain?" Beckett sent back.

"Little guy here ain't the man."

"What?"

"Trust me."

Beckett heaved a frustrated sigh and rolled onto his back. His fear was confirmed. There was no attempt against Huang. But Frederico Mendez was killed by a sniper. Beckett turned back onto his stomach and sighted the scope, again, with the same result. The sniper nest was empty.

CHAPTER TWENTY-SEVEN
WHERE IS MY QUARRY?

General Huang rose before dawn that morning. His hunting platform was secured against two large limbs of a 40-foot tall pine tree growing along the same bluff line about a quarter mile from the sniper nest. He honored the day in a quiet prayer as he faced the rising of the sun before leaving the hunting lodge.

"My plan is simple. Wait until the sniper is assured of his target, then the moment the shooter determines to make the shot on the man he believes to be me, I deliberately place my first shot above the head of my quarry," Huang explained. "By that means, I engage my adversary."

Eddie Briggs was intrigued and appalled.

"I am no mere executioner," Huang said. "I am a hunter of worthy quarry, thus I leave him an opportunity to return fire at least one time. That will make his death more worthy."

"We can equip you with an ear bud and have a security team standing by," Eddie said.

"Absolutely not, young man," the General replied. "This is not an Englishman's hunt, with beaters and nets. This must be the true hunt of venerable opponents."

"At least take a cell phone and text me… when you're done," Eddie pleaded.

Huang sighed. "Very well, I shall do that, but no more," he said with growing irritation. "I am most interested to learn how my adversary prepares and who among my enemies he represents."

"Uhm, who might that be?" Eddie asked a bit sheepishly.

"The Russians would certainly send a Mongolian sniper, as they are the most skilled across the Russian military," Huang explained. "Chinese adversaries would likely send a North Korean sniper. The Syrians might rely upon a Russian contractor; someone employed by the oligarchs."

"Surely, not," Eddie said.

"Perhaps, not the Russian oligarchs since I have made them a great deal of money to further corrupt Putin. Still, for the right price, the right deal for anything is possible," Huang mused. "I have many enemies."

Now, in the chilled stillness of the early December morning, Huang scanned the bluff in the distance, eager for the arrival of his opponent. A growing drift of Cirrus clouds across the sky left Huang somewhat disappointed in his hope for clearer weather, but it made little difference. He checked his watch: 6:05 a.m. Huang was, perhaps, too anxious.

Abrupt movement beyond the trees near the bluff broke the monotony of the scene. Huang focused his binoculars in the general direction of the sound. He held his breath in anticipation of discovering his nemesis, but was offered, instead, the emergence from the timberline of a magnificent buck deer. The buck's rack spread was a solid twenty inches from tip to tip, sporting no less than twelve points.

"Exquisite," Huang murmured.

The buck sniffed the air and took the measure of the small meadow between the timber along the bluff and the forest canopy. Satisfied with the absence of activity, he snorted once; and, a young doe made her way, tentatively, into the opening, followed by a slightly wobbly fawn. She guided the fawn between her and the buck, and they began to graze under the vigilance of the big male. Presently, two more does and a fawn walked from the timber and began to graze. Then, a young buck, perhaps, six points, and another doe arrived. The small herd grazed uninterrupted for about a half hour before the big buck snorted and they began to move back into the timber.

"Go in peace, magnificent one," Huang whispered. "Today, I seek another game."

He checked his watch: 8:18 a.m. Life in the countryside, and Destiny beyond it, began to awaken, and Huang was perplexed. The shooter should have been in place by now. He considered whether young Mister Briggs had done something foolish, after all, and spoiled the day. Huang secured his rifle and turned himself on the platform to get a better look at the ranch road beyond the trees. There was no activity and no signs of any human presence.

Soon, time became torturous to Huang's patience. He was a man accustomed to patience; waiting was a skill he believed most men never appreciated. He re-checked his watch: 9:22 a.m.

"*Perhaps,*" Huang thought, "*he is watching me. Indeed, that would be worthy.*"

The hardwoods along the timberline were spare of leaves to provide cover, offering only dead branches and evergreen foliage from the pines. Huang's position was such that discovering him in the pine timber from the sniper nest on the bluff would be difficult, but a different vantage point for his adversary might prove helpful. Huang considered the lines of sight to other points in each direction. After more than an hour of scrutinizing his surroundings, he decided his position was safe, and looked at his watch, again: 10:45 a.m.

The parade was to begin in forty-five minutes. Where was the shooter?

Huang chuckled involuntarily. "*A game of nerves?*"

The possibility had not occurred to Huang the shooter might not arrive until the final few minutes before the window of opportunity closed. However foolish it seemed, Huang was impressed by the prospect of such confidence.

"*Is he being coy?*" Huang smiled at the idea. "*Worthy, indeed.*"

He looked at his watch: 11:15 a.m. What should have been obvious never occurred to Huang.

As the ceremony in Destiny Veterans' Park concluded the little man who played the part of The General accepted the honorary key to the town from Mayor Lloyd Nelson, and Huang began to realize the truth. He unzipped his hunting vest and retrieved the cell phone provided by Eddie.

Tapping furiously against the virtual keyboard, he pounded a text message: "Where is my quarry?"

Approximately a mile away in the park, Eddie Briggs felt his cell phone vibrate in his coat pocket. He applauded with the remainder of the crowd as the ceremony concluded, uncertain of the message he received.

"Where is my quarry?"

Eddie's brow furrowed at the inquiry. "What do you mean?" he typed in reply.

"Have been in this tree for hours; no quarry."

Eddie burst into laughter. He paid no attention to the looks of other ceremony attendees as he laughed with nervous relief at the realization there was no sniper. He pulled Nelson aside.

"I just found out your bogeyman didn't show up," Eddie said through an almost girlish giggle.

"What are you babbling about, Eddie?" Nelson asked indignantly.

"Nobody showed up to shoot the general," Eddie repeated gleefully.

"I guess your security measures scared him off," Nelson said sheepishly. "Congratulations."

The point galled Nelson as he and Beckett sat down in a booth later at the Blue Bird Cafe.

"You were wrong, Captain… FUBAR wrong," Nelson growled.

"You called me, remember? I didn't invent Frederico Mendez's murder," Beckett said.

"But you could have committed it," Nelson said stonily.

Beckett was stunned. "You think I…? Screw you, Gunny," he blurted as he stood to leave.

Nelson stood and blocked his path. "Sit down, Captain," he said through clenched teeth.

"I've got nothing to say, Gunny; get out of my way," Beckett replied.

Nelson did not back down. "You're going to hear me out," he said. "I know you didn't kill Mendez; but, somebody did."

"You just accused me," Beckett said.

"I said you could have; but, we both know you didn't because you were fifty yards down the sideline from me at the ball field when somebody took the shots at the stadium lights," Nelson said. "And, the bullet we pulled out of the tree at the back of the school building doesn't fit anything you own. So, cool your jets, Captain. Sit down. We need to talk."

Beckett found it maddening to admit what happened. And more-so after the incident of the rookie scope glare at his apartment.

"He has gotten our attention," Nelson said.

"Not our attention. He has my attention," Beckett said.

"What do you mean, Captain?"

Beckett sighed.

"I'm not certain," he said. "But I know two things: One, he knows who I am, because he had me cold one day at my apartment when I saw his scope glare. And, two, he wants me to know that he is exceptionally good."

"Some kind of challenge?" Nelson posed.

"I don't know," Beckett said.

Nelson took a sip of his coffee. "You knew he wasn't after Huang," he said quietly.

"I suspected," Beckett said. "But I couldn't take the chance, so I played along with the idea. I honestly had to see whether he would show up today."

"You know, when I first met you, something you said struck me," Nelson offered. "You said you weren't here for anybody, but it never occurred to me somebody might be here for you."

"Seriously, I can't say," Beckett replied. "It has bugged me since the moment I saw the nest on the bluff, but yeah, whether it's me, or somebody else… he's here for someone in Destiny."

"We've got to take this to…" Nelson began.

"To whom?" Beckett asked. "Nobody will believe us now since we've been so spectacularly wrong."

Nelson slumped back in his seat. "And Eddie Briggs will be certain everyone knows," he groaned.

Eddie quickly informed his father, who was on his way to Clearwater Lodge with Senator Wilson Furman. Clearwater Lodge was less than two miles from the blufftop sniper nest at the Nelson ranch, which placed it less than one mile from Huang's vantage in the pine trees. The early afternoon sunlight was awash across the lodge's outdoor deck fronting the river, where Eddie, Mister Jimmy, and Senator Furman later enjoyed a celebratory Scotch. The Huang doppelganger was appropriately dismissed with payment in hand, and the party awaited the General's arrival.

"He's probably pissed he wasn't allowed to murder someone today," Eddie reminded the others.

Furman sputtered through his drink and Mister Jimmy chuckled. "I wouldn't waste too much concern on that detail."

The glint of brilliant sunlight against the broad picture window at the rear of the deck turned everyone away from the cabin to sit facing the river in the sturdy Adirondack-style chairs provided for guests. Fresh from the day's success, the scene might have been typical of any alcohol-oiled male celebration, except for a singular difference. As Mister Jimmy rose to turn the steaks on the outdoor grill, a brush of air grazed his cheek A sound resembling a crack of lightning shattered the tranquility as it echoed back and forth along the bluffs on either side of the river as the cabin's picture window exploded, showering the revelers with shards of glass.

"What...?" Eddie shouted as he dove for cover.

He cowered beside the grill in the ensuing silence, while Mister Jimmy awkwardly recovered from the floor of the deck and Senator Furman shook glass from his hair and clothing. Presently, the stillness yielded to the irritating dweedle of Eddie's cell phone. The three men stared at the device on the arm of Eddie's chair as it continued to sound off.

Eddie crawled to the chair and reached for the phone. "Hello," he said almost plaintively.

A low chuckle from a recognizable Asian voice was the only response, and then, nothing. Eddie drew the phone away from his ear and looked at it as though it were some unfaithful lover. He threw the cell phone into the gaping void of the destroyed picture window and rolled onto his back.

"Who was it?" Mister Jimmy demanded.

"Yes, my boy, who was it?" Furman echoed.

Eddie laughed. "It was Huang," he blurted. "I told you he'd be pissed."

CHAPTER TWENTY-EIGHT
POLITICS WASN'T MY COLLEGE MAJOR

"All Texas was flying to Jett Rink's party," Beckett read aloud as he scanned Edna Ferber's novel, *Giant* between classes the following morning.

Beckett enjoyed re-reading Ferber's classic about the often-misplaced opulence of the nascent era of big oil in Texas. He anticipated the class discussions the clash between cattleman Jordan "Bick" Benedict, Jr. and wildcatter oilman Jett Rink might generate about the legend of Texas as it was changed by "black gold." Beckett sighed as he prepared to teach the book, again after 14 years.

Jett's party scene was climactic to the conflict in *Giant*. General Huang's party, by contrast, was anticlimactic. Beckett was keenly aware what that distinction meant for his new hometown. The Yashuma Project announcement struck a nerve in the small town of Destiny that seemed to displace the uproar over Frederico Mendez's murder. Beckett felt a particular relief to let the remaining questions lie muddied.

Now, the point of Beckett's personal concern was open to address, and he could no longer treat it casually. He was a potential target.

The bell rang for the start of the next class period, which meant James Robert Bellchase's return to class. Cissy organized a "hero walk" for him earlier in the day. The entire student body lined the sidewalk outside of the building and cheered as James Robert got out of his father's car. Beckett was proud of Cissy for creating the moment. It was another unifying event for Destiny High School and the town of Destiny.

"Ready to tackle finals?" Beckett asked as James Robert settled into his seat.

"Had nothing better to do but study for the last two months, Mister B," James Robert said. "I can just about recite *Gone with the Wind*."

Beckett laughed. "Just in time for the change to *Giant*."

"Aw, maaan," James Robert moaned.

Beckett walked to his desk at the head of the room.

"Okay, people, let's settle down. Finals week begins Monday; you have study guides, and if you follow them, you should have no trouble with the essay question."

Momentarily, Beckett realized he was clearly visible through the classroom window at the head of the room. He glanced to his side to note the sight lines; the head of the room seemed less optimal for a shot than the center of the room. Beckett changed his lecture pacing from forward to rear to a side-to-side pattern and put himself away from the windows to keep students out of any shot scenario. Now, Beckett's daily life assumed a new perspective.

Despite enjoying the chilled morning air, Beckett drove to the campus on Monday rather than walk from Miss Esther's house as was his custom. Superintendent Bittle was stunned to see him claim his parking space.

"Given up walking, Mister Beckett?" Bittle asked blithely.

Beckett hedged. "Well, it becomes a bit inconvenient to walk back to Miss Esther's if I have errands to run or if something unexpected arises."

Cissy's voice called to him from the far side of the parking lot. "What's up with that?"

"Ah, I'm just getting lazy in my old age," Beckett said.

"Bull," Cissy retorted. She caught up with him at the door.

Beckett hugged the perimeter of the building, putting a bit of distance between himself and Cissy. He turned the corner to the central doorway sharply; almost too sharply. Cissy blanched.

"Hey, wait up," she said. "Are you okay?"

"Fine," Beckett said crisply.

"Oookay," Cissy replied as he held the door for her. "Does this weirdness have anything to do with our final today?"

"Uh, yeah, yeah; that's it," Beckett said. "You know, just a little, uhm, first finals concern."

"What? Are you gonna get obscure on us, or something?"

"Oh, no. Nothing like that," he said. "It's, well, I haven't given a final in, you know, sixteen years."

Beckett hated hedging with Cissy, but he had no choice. He began to feel - hunted. And he could not escape ruminating about the possibilities and the nagging question: Why? Through 14 years of assignments across Afghanistan, Iraq, Syria, and elsewhere, Beckett was never spotted; he was never completely exposed, although he had been wounded. That memory was vivid.

"The Russians call you 'The Ghost,'" General Pierpont Maxwell said. "Their intelligence has a unit assigned specifically to find you. They've shaken down every brothel and bar from Kabul to Baghdad to get information on you."

Maxwell laughed; the raucous, knowing laugh of a rounder with a secret. "Never occurred to them you were such a do-gooder. Let's just hope nobody told the goats for the girl story."

Beckett was not amused; not then, not now as he attempted to live up to his nickname.

"You sure you're okay, Dad?" Cissy asked.

Cissy stood at the foot of the staircase to the second-floor classroom wing, her hands resting on her hips, a puzzled expression on her previously cheerful face. She disliked Beckett's disquiet.

"Hey," she said sharply, snapping her fingers. "Earth to Dad..."

"Uhm, uh, what?"

"Class, final exam, school," Cissy said sarcastically.

"Yeah, sure, honey," Beckett said. "I… was… distracted by a memory."

Beckett was experienced against the Spetsnaz, or Special Purpose Forces, Soviet Russian tactical warfare units skilled in rapid insertion/extraction combat. Beckett knew the history from the 1979-1989 Soviet campaign in Afghanistan, from the 1979 Operation Storm-333 to forcibly remove the Afghan government in a raid on the Tajbeg Palace to the support of regular Syrian forces in the Battle of Palmyra in 2015.

The presence of a full unit near Destiny, Arkansas, seemed preposterous to Beckett. But a single former Spetsnaz sniper was a different matter altogether.

The noise of the classroom brought Beckett back to the moment. He picked up a dry-erase marker and wrote a single question on the whiteboard: "Explain two important lessons *Gone with the Wind* teaches in your generation."

"This is open book and notes," Beckett said. "You may incorporate arguments in comparison between the book and the movie. Consider thematic points as well as characters in your answer. When you are finished, turn in your test booklet, and I will see you after the holidays."

Beckett was bemused by the speed with which Cissy addressed the question. She jotted notes and page numbers on passages from the book on the inside cover of her test booklet, then she began writing. And she did not stop until almost the end of the period. Beckett was equally stunned to see most of the class doing the same; they were completely engaged in the question. Beckett reached for his copy of *Giant*.

Giant followed the arc of ranch hand turned wildcatter Jett Rink against the creeping stagnation of the sprawling Reata ranch and cattleman Bick Benedict to an inevitable intersection. As he read Edna Ferber's anxious prose, Beckett recalled the limited similarities in his life. Much like Bick Benedict, Beckett was a man almost hard-wired to a philosophy which was consistently tempted by change. Beckett recalled how General Pierpont Maxwell made the argument.

"You would be worth a mint in politics, kid," Maxwell said.

"Please, General, there is no need to be crude with Captain Beckett," the older, more erudite Senator Wilson Furman remarked.

Furman was in his element. He fancied himself a king-maker. The question at hand was a familiar one.

"What will the next generation of leadership in this country look like, Captain Beckett?" Furman asked.

"I don't know, sir. Politics wasn't my college major."

Furman chuckled. "Precisely, my boy," he said. "This country has, indeed, grown tired of politicians, i.e. the ubiquitously slick model or the pre-packaged ideological model on the one hand, the patrician entitlement model, and the egotists on the either side of the aisle. And then, there were the COVID years… egad. No, the new face of politics must appear apolitical at the least. That seems assured."

"So, how does that involve me?" Beckett deadpanned.

"It's time for a hero," Furman offered. "The country craves heroes, and it is the heroes who will lead the next generation of politics."

"Trust me, Senator, I'm no hero," Beckett said. He chuckled to hear himself utter the cliche.

"Aw, hell, son," Maxwell insisted. "You are exactly what a hero looks like these days."

"Heroes don't kill from hiding," Beckett said. "…Sir."

"You merely have done what you were trained to do and ordered to accomplish," the General said, drawing a long draught on a sleek, firmly rolled Cuban cigar. "Details, son; just details."

"Yes," Furman agreed. "It is commendable that you have served your country with conscience, but General Maxwell is correct. What you have done simply reflects your attitude toward service. And, I would say heroic service, at that."

Maxwell handed the Senator a dossier, which the older man perused with a delighted interest. Furman began to read aloud.

"Two Bronze Stars, with oak cluster, two Silver Stars with cluster, four Purple Hearts, and the Navy Cross," he said. "I would say you have found yourself in the way of some serious combat."

Furman smiled. "I'd recommend you for the Medal of Honor but for the fact I'd have to explain your existence," he said almost nonchalantly. "But, you go back to teaching school somewhere, someday. I can find you. And, if you are interested then I'll get you a seat in the House. After that, who knows?"

"With all due respect, Senator," Beckett said quietly. "I'm not so inclined."

Furman laughed. "What is the saying?" he posed. "Never say never."

The end-of-period bell brought Beckett back to his classroom. He looked up to see the sobriety of final exams melt into the light-hearted chatter of holiday conversation. Beckett smiled, glad now he was not seduced by Furman.

James Robert appeared out of the scrum. He was smiling.

"I actually enjoyed writing this, Mister B," James Robert said. He extended his hand. "Thank you, sir."

Beckett stood and grasped the young man's hand firmly, resolutely. "No… thank you, James Robert. You are a hero to a town in need of one."

James Robert shrugged. "It's cool. You have a good Christmas, Mister B."

He turned to leave, but paused, a thought fresh on his expression. "You're welcome to Christmas at our house," James Robert said. "You know, if you want a place to go."

Beckett smiled. "Give your folks my thanks. I've already accepted an invitation from the Nelsons."

James Robert nodded. "It's cool, but anytime, you know..."

"I get it," Beckett said with a smile. "And, I appreciate it."

He gathered the test booklets from the desk and deposited them into his briefcase. Without consideration, Beckett scanned the room for late papers and noticed Devonte Washington engaging Cissy near the classroom doorway. The husky ball player seemed almost cowed as the two teens talked. Presently, he reached into the pocket of his letterman's jacket and produced a small, wrapped gift.

Devonte hung his head and offered the gift to Cissy with the shyness of a grade schooler addressing himself to a girl for the first time.

Cissy was taken aback. She reflexively glanced toward Beckett with an almost plaintive regard. He chuckled, smiled at her, and nodded his approval. She gave Beckett a wry, quick smile, took a deep breath and opened the gift.

"O…M…G" she murmured, plucking from the box a football cleat suspended from a delicately wrought silver chain. "Devonte…"

"You like it?" he asked, half-anxiously.

"I… love it," Cissy whispered. "But, I didn't get you anything."

"I know," Devonte said. "Wasn't supposed to. I just did this because… well… you're a good person, and, well… you know…"

Cissy leaned closer toward him. "What, Devonte?" she murmured. "What do I know?"

"That… that, I want you to be my lady," he said quietly.

Cissy slipped the necklace over her head and let the metal cleat settle against her turtleneck sweater. "Yes," she whispered.

Cissy extended her hand, and Devonte clasped his about it gently as they walked from the room. Cissy glanced back across her shoulder toward Beckett, smiled giddily, and shrugged. He could not help himself; Beckett guffawed.

CHAPTER TWENTY-NINE
MERRY CHRISTMAS, BROCK BECKETT

Rosa Linda Mendez was five months pregnant, living in Camden with her aunt and uncle, and home-schooled. She had not seen or spoken with James Robert Bellchase. Rosa Linda's family was displaced when her mother found new work to support the Mendez children despite Nelson's protests. Rosa Linda was denied any opportunity to build a relationship with James Robert, despite his vindication in her father's death. But she kept James Robert's cell phone number. James Robert responded immediately when her ID appeared in his text message queue.

"Super glad to hear from u," he wrote.

"Miss u soooo much." She punctuated the message with heart emoticons.

"How r u doing?"

"Me and baby fine." Stork emoticons followed.

"Wait; baby. Already? When?"

"Due in April."

"I want to be there…" James Robert replied.

"I'm ok. ok?" Smiley face emoticons. "Had to talk to you."

"Glad."

"Something upsetting me… about Papa."

"What?"

"Day we found out about baby. Strange car at our house. Heard man argue w/Papa in front room."

"What did they say?" James Robert asked.

"Something about money, Mr. Nelson's ranch."

"What did they say? Rosa Linda? You there?"

"Sorry, gotta go bye."

"Hey…"

James Robert's cell phone screen remained blank, but his mind was churning. He climbed out of bed, quickly dressed and headed for the front door.

"Where are you going, young man?" his mother called after him as James Robert bolted through the kitchen.

"Gotta see Mister B. I'll be back by lunch."

James Robert kissed his mother's cheek, disappeared into the front room and out of the door. The walk to Miss Esther's house was five blocks, but James Robert cut across country, climbing fences and slipping through the brushy latticework of back paths which overlaid the neighborhood. His breath frosted in the sharp December air as he emerged from an alleyway across from the former Chesterton brothel house.

James Robert cleared the stairway to the apartment landing in four bounds, creating a distinct noise that alerted Beckett. He set a sheaf of final exam papers aside and tapped the mousepad of his laptop to see James Robert on the screen standing at his front door. Beckett roused himself from the comfortable clutter of exam papers on the sofa and opened the apartment door.

"You must have second sight," he said as James Robert recovered his breath.

"'Scuse me?"

"I just finished grading your final exam paper," Beckett said. "But, I didn't think you were overly anxious about it."

"Naw…uhm. No, sir," James Robert said.

"You had me with the first sentence," Beckett replied. "*Gone with the Wind* taught me that, lame as it sounds, 'tomorrow is another day.' That's an 'A' any day."

"No kidding?" James Robert said. "That's cool, sir. But, it's not the reason I'm here. It's about Rosa Linda Mendez, sir."

Beckett swung the screen door open. "Come inside; it's too cold for you out there."

James Robert hung back for a moment, then he stepped inside the apartment. He glanced about to take in the room, familiar with the history.

"It doesn't look like a… uhm. It looks nice."

"Thanks… I think," Beckett said. "I was sure you were about to say it doesn't look like a brothel."

Beckett grinned.

"Naw, naw, Mister B. It's not like that," James Robert hedged. "This is the first time I've ever been up here."

Beckett laughed and offered a seat on the sofa. "You said something about Rosa Linda Mendez. How is she doing?"

"Best I know, she is okay," James Robert said nervously. "I haven't seen her or talked with her since I was arrested. But here's the thing, Mister B; she got me on a text message this morning and wrote something weird."

Beckett settled onto the other end of the sofa. "Weird? How so?"

"She didn't tell me everything," James Robert said. "She had to get off her phone for some reason."

"What, exactly, did she say that was weird?"

James Robert was typically a more focused student. His sudden randomness struck Beckett as significant.

"Slow down and try to remember exactly what she said," he directed.

"I can show you," James Robert said eagerly. He scrolled to the conversation on his phone. "Here."

Beckett took the cell phone and read the exchange carefully. The intimacy of the two teens' concern for each other reminded him of Jolene and their last trip to the beach at the Santa Monica Pier.

It was one of those Sundays in December when the California sky was lifeless, dulled by clouds that hung heavy against the horizon; when the Santa Monica Pier was almost empty, the Ferris wheel was out of commission, and the bay was flat. The seagulls did not seem to care that there was little trash along the beach for them to scavenge, or there was no one to pester with their constant squawking. Beckett did not care particularly, even though he and Jolene drove some distance for the outing.

He looked down into Jolene's bright, hazel eyes and pondered what made him this lucky. She was everything he ever wanted, and when they met Beckett was still pained over his sister's death on 9/11.

"I graduate from command school this month," Beckett said. "I ship out to the Middle East ASAP. When we met while I was at Corpus Christi, I had no idea how much I could love you, until now."

Jolene giggled and shook back her mane of Irish auburn hair. Her eyes danced with happiness.

"You swept in like a hurricane, and my folks didn't have much time to catch their breaths," she replied. "They liked the idea of their daughter marrying a schoolteacher; stability and all that. But I fell in love with you because you enlisted. I saw what you saw on television that day."

"The world was changed," Beckett said. "All of that remained clear to me until I met you."

During their three years together, Beckett took Jolene from one end of the country to the other. The depth with which his journey through special operations training affected the remainder of his life, and the end of Jolene's was intentionally never written into Beckett's understanding.

"It's only a two-year tour of duty," Beckett said. "Then, I come home to teach at command school, and after that I teach everybody's kids how to appreciate Dickens."

Jolene giggled. "'Tis a far, far better thing I do, than I have ever done,'" she whispered.

"Close enough," Beckett said as he kissed her.

Jolene smiled. She left Sulpher Springs, Texas, to study marine biology. She was a naturist through and through. Now, as she delighted in collecting brightly colored seashells, she did so with a new perspective.

"It makes you wonder," Jolene said as she examined a specimen. "Had this little guy remained whole, undisturbed on the bed of the bay, who knows how large it might have become; they grow at an almost glacial pace. That's why you see so many of them along the beaches in the United States; the breeding beds are constantly disturbed by commercial fishing, coastal development or petroleum production.

"Don't get me wrong," she added. "I'm not anti-progress, but the growth of these little guys within the larger ecology has a purpose. I'd simply like to find a way for us to recognize it, beyond using these shells to produce lime and make cement."

Beckett smiled. "Environmentalist whacko," he quipped. He didn't care about Jolene's point. Beckett simply liked the lilt of her voice.

"Militarist," she shot back with the cute little smirk which always melted him.

Beckett reached for Jolene and pulled her to him, kissing her firmly, with a longing as playful as it was sincere. She responded eagerly. Jolene had a talent for maintaining the moment well beyond it. Such was her gift to him that Christmas Eve as they lay in the shelter of the dunes near a pleasant fire and far away from the commercial side of the beach.

"Merry Christmas, Brock Beckett," she murmured.

The soft wash of the moonlight gave her skin an inviting glow. Jolene smiled up at Beckett and pulled him closer, nipping at the nape of his neck and giggling with the sexy little titter that told him she was aroused. He pressed himself against her and she moaned with a satisfaction which invited his growing intensity.

That was the night Cissy was conceived. Christmas Eve.

James Robert's voice invaded Beckett's reverie, bringing him back to the Destiny apartment. "What do you think, Mister B?"

Beckett looked at the text conversation again.

"When she mentions 'Day we found out about baby,' did Rosa Linda's father know she was pregnant when he had the argument she overheard?" Beckett asked.

"I guess not," James Robert said. "But what does it mean, Mister B?"

Beckett heaved a worried sigh. "I don't know, for certain," he said quietly. "But Rosa Linda clearly has a story to tell which no one has heard."

"Maybe, she will tell you."

"I'm not convinced, James Robert," Beckett said. "I'm not certain she would appreciate that I know about this conversation. This sounds like something she wants to share with you, but she can't now. She is reaching out to you, not to me. And I think we should respect her point."

"So, what do I do, Mister B?"

"As much as it troubles me to say, I think you wait," Beckett said. "Allow Rosa Linda to come to you with the rest of the story."

James Robert seemed mollified but unconvinced by Beckett's advice, and Beckett understood. Deep down, he, too, wanted to know what Rosa Linda overheard about money and the Nelson ranch.

CHAPTER THIRTY
NOBODY MESSES WITH LA NINA

Beckett stood in the middle of an aisle in Lloyd Nelson's variety store the day before Christmas Eve feeling perplexed. He had no idea of a suitable Christmas gift for Cissy. His helpless expression compelled a store clerk to pity him.

"Can I help you, sir?' the young woman asked quietly.

Beckett scuffed his shoe heel against the floor. "I honestly don't know," he muttered.

The floor clerk appeared no older than Cissy but the small, plain wedding band on her left hand offered Beckett some context. She wasn't one of his students, and Beckett could only surmise why she married.

"Are you shopping for someone special?" the girl asked politely. "Female?"

Beckett hesitated. "Yes, someone special," he said. "Female."

"We have some nice perfume and make-up sets," the girl offered.

But nothing suited Beckett's purpose, though he assumed it might fit Cissy's tastes. Still, he felt uncomfortable leaving without allowing the young girl to make a sale. Beckett bought a boxed bath set. He paid for the gift and left the girl smiling. Beckett walked to the door and pushed out into the cold of the holiday evening. Center Street was remarkably active with last-minute gift shoppers and Christmas season cooks. The typically spare main street in Destiny was veritably brilliant, strung from side to side along the business district with colorful strands of Christmas lights. Beckett smiled. Mayor Lloyd Nelson apparently enjoyed Christmas. The only window front along the street not decorated for the season was the Briggs and Briggs law firm. Beckett thought it unremarkable and entirely in character. He chuckled.

Beckett found the attitude which he met in most people genuinely charming. Destiny was small enough to afford Beckett some recognition, particularly by the parents of his students. He took a distinct pride from the fact, something Jolene characterized as the "feel at home factor" in a community. Beckett stopped almost mid-stride, struck by the paradox of his loneliness without Jolene and the growing satisfaction in his relationship with Cissy. He supposed the problem was normal for active-duty veterans who lost a wife. But Cissy was a different story altogether. The deliberate removal of Beckett's daughter from his life to extend his useful service verged on the immoral to Beckett. He put the point out of his mind and concentrated on his good fortune in finding Cissy. Finding a gift to convey the idea to her on their first Christmas together in some 14 years was frustrating for him.

Beckett ambled across the street and casually glanced at the storefront window of Briggs' Pharmacy and noticed something he hadn't expected: jewelry. He was met by Marilee Paige almost as soon as he walked through the doorway.

"Welcome to the Briggs Pharmacy, Mister Beckett," Marilee chirped. "How can I help you?"

Beckett smiled. "I didn't know you worked here, Marilee."

"Pretty much since I started high school," she said. "Saving up for college. I work after school most days when I don't have cheer practice and on Saturdays. 'Course, during the Christmas break, too."

"I noticed in your window you stock jewelry," Beckett said.

"Oh, yeah, Mister Beckett," Marilee said brightly. "We have some nice things, of course we're the only place in town with fashionable jewelry. Are you buying for someone special?"

She smiled, the sort of smile intended to elicit information without being obvious. Beckett struggled to suppress a chuckle.

"I'd like to buy a nice silver neck chain, nothing fancy but something pretty," he said.

"Ooooh, that's nice, Mister Beckett," Marilee offered. "I know what you mean, you don't want to be too showy, but you want to wear good quality jewelry."

Marilee fairly pranced to a display counter in the center aisle of the store. Beckett shook his head. He thought for a moment of abandoning his purchase but the idea he had in mind was too perfect. He decided to endure Marilee Paige.

"Here is our best selection," she said, presenting Beckett with a display shadow box.

He perused the offerings, impressed with the variety and quality, but not struck with the right concept. Until, along the second row of the display, he saw a silver chain with a Celtic weave. He slipped his finger around the strands and rubbed his thumb across the surface of the interlaced links. Jolene would have liked it.

"I'll take this one," Beckett said.

"Wow," Marilee gasped. "Must be someone really special. This one is one hundred-twenty-nine dollars."

Beckett smiled. "Yeah, special," he said.

He paid cash for the necklace, leaving Marilee with her curiosity aflame. Beckett stepped back into the growing chill of the evening. He was anxious to return to the apartment to complete the gift. He crossed the street, climbed into his Jeep, and quickly wheeled away from the curb, the three block drive heightening an anticipation he had not felt in years. Beckett guided the Jeep into the garage at Miss Esther's then, he hustled up the stairs to the apartment.

Once inside, he dropped his jacket onto the sofa and fumbled beneath his shirt collar, producing a standard military-issue neck chain and "dog tags" from beneath his shirt. One of the two small aluminum rectangles was plain gray. The other was red. Beckett unclasped the chain, and slid the gray tag away from it. He clasped the chain and put it back beneath his shirt.

Beckett opened the gift box from Briggs Pharmacy and pulled the gleaming silver Celtic chain from it into his substantial palm. He smiled, unclasped the chain and slid the plain, gray "dog tag" onto it and let it slip to the full length of the necklace loop. Carefully, Beckett closed the necklace clasp, folded the necklace and placed it with the "dog tag" into the gift box. He smiled, again. Jolene would have approved.

Cissy left the Nelson's store before Beckett arrived. She normally worked the holiday break until about 5 p.m. each day, but today she left early to go to the ranch with Lloyd and prepare for the family Christmas at the cabin. She loved the Christmas holidays; it was the one time of the year when the family closed the house in Destiny in favor of the semi-rustic riverside lodge.

"Please, don't let Daddy Beckett sleep on the deck," she pleaded as she and Lloyd rolled up to the cabin in the family truck. "I couldn't take that in this weather, and I don't, for the life of me, see how he does it."

"He does have his ways," Lloyd said. "I don't think he will do anything to freak out your mother."

Cissy nodded. "Good," she said resolutely. "I've got too much to do to have him freak her."

She hadn't listened to the perturbed familiarity in her tone. But Lloyd was listening, and it puzzled him.

"Are you okay, Hon?" he asked.

"Sure," Cissy replied. "Why?"

"You sound almost as fussy as a housemaid," he said. "Is something about Beckett worrying you?"

Cissy seemed taken aback, until she realized his point. "I just… I want him to like… to like what I got him for Christmas," she murmured.

"Oh, Hon, I'm sure he will," Lloyd replied. "He'd like anything from you. Trust me."

Cissy seemed to take comfort in Lloyd's assessment. She climbed out of the truck and headed toward the rear of the cabin.

"I'm gonna check the firewood," she called back to Lloyd. "I hope the hands remembered to stock it."

Lloyd unlocked the front door and stepped inside with one of the several bags of food Grace sent for the holiday stay. He opened the foyer closet and found the breaker box, flipped the main breaker and the cabin was awash in light. Most of the first floor was open throughout, with a vaulted ceiling and a central stone fireplace and chimney extending from floor to ceiling and open on two sides. A broad hardwood mantle ran across the face of the hearth at shoulder height on all four sides. The front half of the room was furnished for entertaining near the fireplace, while beyond it was the dining area and kitchen. The master bedroom was to the immediate left from the foyer, with a family bathroom between it and Cissy's room to the rear opposite the kitchen. Guest quarters were upstairs from the staircase on the right side exterior wall beyond the dining table. The cabin was large enough to be comfortable, but small enough to feel cozy - Cissy's concept when she convinced Lloyd to build it.

Cissy stomped laden with firewood into the kitchen through the rear doorway. "You're gonna need to talk to the hands, Dad," she said testily. "It looks like they've been drinking around the fire pit, again."

Lloyd nodded and grunted as he helped stock the firewood box beside the hearth. He never admitted to Cissy he did not oppose the ranch hands having a few beers at the end of the day on a Saturday evening. Frederico Mendez always ensured they behaved themselves.

"It lets them work off a little steam at the end of the week, Senior Nelson," Mendez had offered. "Makes them a little happier to go home to their wives with a whole paycheck; and, not spend it all at Senior Freemon's place."

Lloyd missed Frederico, the good foreman and good man. "I'll talk to them, Hon," Lloyd told Cissy.

Frederico's murder continued to rankle Lloyd, but without any connection to a motive, even County Coroner Vernon Lard's investigation had gone stone cold. And Vernon was never one to let a good murder go to waste if there was political advantage in resolving it to the detriment of his enemies. Lloyd sighed.

"Build us a good fire, Hon," he said. "Don't want our guests to get chilled."

Despite the installation of independently-regulated propane heaters in each bedroom, they were rarely lit until the evening was concluded and everyone was ready for bed. The fireplace was the principal source of heat for the cabin during entertainment hours and through the day.

An overlay of clouds across the horizon told Lloyd there might be snow for Christmas. Cissy's hopes for a perfect holiday seemed to be falling into place. And Lloyd was quietly grateful. No matter the special nature of their memories together as a family, Lloyd and Grace were not Cissy's parents. He felt a momentary melancholy at the thought as he watched his adopted daughter skillfully build a toasty, glowing fire.

"Looks like it might snow tonight," Lloyd said.

Cissy smiled brightly. "Yeah, that would be super cool."

The Nelson Christmas Eve party at the cabin was a tradition which grew from a sleepover for Cissy's friends the first year until it became a community destination during the holidays. Ranch hands ferried guests from the ranch headquarters to the cabin and back during the evening. The afternoon ranch Christmas party at the headquarters barn was usually concluded before the first guests arrived at the cabin. Lloyd looked at his watch.

"Got to get a move on, Hon," he called out as he put the extension leaves in the bird's eye maple dining table. "We don't want Santa to be late at the barn party."

"OMG, that's right," Cissy blurted.

It was a tradition Cissy started after wheedling away at Lloyd for him to agree to play Santa Claus the first year. Now, he wouldn't miss the opportunity for any reason, not only for Cissy's sake but also because tonight Frederico Mendez and his family were absent.

The festivities were in full swing when Lloyd and Cissy arrived at the headquarters complex. She delighted in the sound of "Jingle Bells" played mariachi style by a group of ranch hands. The thumping polka-style beat which emanated from the equipment barn adjacent to the headquarters office filled the air already redolent with the aroma of freshly cooked tamales.

Two long sawhorse tables were set to one side of the building, one filled with platters of tamales, pots of rice and beans, fajita meats, guacamole, chicken and beef enchiladas, and mounds of Mexican wedding cookies covered in achingly sweet confectioner's sugar, as well as baskets of hot, fresh sopapillas with honey, and fruit-filled empanadas. The other table was covered with brightly colored tablecloths and decorated with Mexican luminaries.

Lloyd stood to give his annual Christmas speech after the meal. He spoke almost haltingly.

"We… all miss Senior Mendez; and, we remember him and his family to the blessed Christ child," Lloyd said quietly. "He was a good man. But let us also remember we each take the lessons Senior Mendez has taught us, each day and not just on special days. Let us live with his memory as a blessing to all. And I raise my glass and a toast of Felice Navidad to his name. Senior Mendez…"

"Felice Navidad Senior Mendez…," the crowd responded.

Cissy wiped back a tear from her cheek. She leaned across the corner of the table and hugged Lloyd.

"That was beautiful, Dad," she whispered.

Grace smiled from the opposite side of the table and gave Lloyd's weathered hand a gentle squeeze. She rose and joined the other wives clearing the table, Lloyd's cue to quietly disappear for Santa to appear. Cissy stood to help, but turning at the press of a hand against her shoulder, she saw standing behind her a tall, slender man in his early 20s, with strong classic Spanish features and dark, riveting eyes.

"May I have this dance, Senorita Nelson?" he asked with perfectly inflected English.

The music in the background was a Mexican folk waltz. Cissy thought to politely decline, but was given no opportunity, as the man slipped an arm about her waist and pulled her onto the dance floor. He looked down into her hazel eyes and drew her to himself firmly. Cissy gasped, but she said nothing.

"My name is Joaquin de la Rosa," he said. "And, I have admired your beauty all evening; torturing me to hold you in my arms and, make you dance… like a woman."

He pressed himself against her more aggressively. Cissy flinched; and Joaquin smiled.

"Ah," he whispered. "You do understand."

"Where? Who?" Cissy muttered. "I don't know you."

"Ah, yes; of course, you don't," De la Rosa replied. "I only this year, have come to your father's ranch."

"When?" Cissy asked breathlessly.

"In the summer," De la Rosa said flippantly. "I am from Mexico City; where I studied architecture at the university."

"What the heck are you doing working on a ranch in Destiny, Arkansas?" Cissy asked.

"Living, my dear," De la Rosa said through a careless chuckle.

"And…" He swung Cissy outward and gazed at her with an impudent smile. "Lusting."

The scene played out on the dance floor did not go unnoticed. A group of Destiny football players were abuzz in the corner of the room beyond the serving table.

"Who is that guy?"

"That's De la Rosa; the college guy from Mexico City."

"Man, why don't we go get him off her?"

Vincente Vega, an all-conference defensive lineman for the Destiny Dragons, started across the floor. But Cissy tore herself away from De la Rosa's grasp and fled from the building. He turned to pursue her but was intercepted by Vincente and the others.

"Hey, man, back off," Vincente ordered.

"Sayyy what you talkin' about, big man?" De la Rosa replied. "I don't see no brand on her; least not till I put mine there."

Vincente scowled into De la Rosa's eyes. "Nobody messes with La Nina," he growled.

"La Nina?" De la Rosa asked incredulously. "She ain't no child. She's ready to be a woman."

"I'n tellin' you man…"

"No, we tellin' you," a second voice interjected as the group closed in around De la Rosa.

Vincente nodded. "Yeah, man, we tellin' you. We got a good life here and La Nina is a big reason for it. She's got a good heart, and everybody trusts her; so, don't you do nothing to bring El Patron down on us, man."

"Take your machismo somewhere else, cousin," De la Rosa shot back. "I'm here legally; how about you?"

"Don't think you can lay crap on us, man; just because you went to college and you work in the office and not in the pastures," Vincente said testily. "We gonna be watchin' you, bookkeeper man."

"I don't have to stand here and take this from you… peones."

Vincente raised himself to his full playing height. "Maybe, you better leave… now," he said.

De la Rosa took the measure of the hefty ball players. "Felice Navidad, companeros," he said and hastily made for the door.

The band struck up a rendition of "Santa Claus is Coming to Town," Lloyd's cue to enter as Jolly Old Saint Nick and distribute gifts to the children and bonuses to the ranch hands. As he burst into the room with a full volleyed "Ho, Ho, Ho," Lloyd noticed Cissy was nowhere in sight.

Lagniappe

CHAPTER THIRTY-ONE
IT'S AN IMPORTANT PART OF ME

Beckett arrived at the Nelson cabin shortly after the party began, uncertain what to expect but glad for the invitation for the evening and the holiday overnight. Somehow, the cabin seemed different from the early fall outing, perhaps because it was stirring with life and laughter. Beckett's note of the guests told him this was a premier event of the holiday season in Destiny. He was introduced to the Destiny City Board members, Destiny School Board members, local businessmen, sales representatives, cattle buyers, area ranchers and a few county officials. Beckett recognized members of the Blue Bird Cafe dominoes klatch, school administrators and athletics staff. Noticeable among the guests was Lloyd's brother, Freemon.

"You must be the super teacher I've heard so much about," Freemon said as he extended his hand to Beckett over a plate of food. "Freemon Nelson."

"I don't know about the super part, but I am the literature teacher at Destiny High School," Beckett said, giving Freemon's hand an assertively firm squeeze. "Brock Beckett."

Beckett deliberately let the small talk die. He was not anxious to spend more of the evening with Freemon, regardless of his relationship with Lloyd. Yet, Freemon kept the hook inserted.

"No, I know for a fact my niece thinks you're pretty super," Freemon said almost offhandedly. "Almost think she has a crush on you the way she goes on about you."

"Well, uh, Cissy is one of my best students."

It was the only thing Beckett could think to say. He felt lame, knowing there was decidedly more to his daughter than Freemon needed not know.

"Yeah, she gets real dreamy about you, sometimes," Freemon offered. "Course a teacher has gotta be careful about things like that these days. It's not like back when I was in school, and you could take the teacher into the coat closet… if you know what I mean?"

Freemon chuckled. Beckett did not. "I treat my students with respect," he said through a growing impatience.

"Uhmm, yeah, Cissy is a little honey, though; it'd take a lot to keep your hands off that package," Freemon said with a flippancy which disgusted Beckett.

Beckett turned and glared at Freemon with the bearing of a Marine top kick. "And, how would you know, Mister Nelson? Have you… unwrapped the package?"

"Me? Oh, Lord, no," Freemon replied with a nervous laugh. "Hell, my brother would castrate me in the middle of main street at high noon if I tickled her fancy. He used to be a Navy Seal you know. Lord knows I wouldn't want him on my case. Those Navy Seal guys, they say those guys never forget how to kill. It stays in their blood."

Freemon pestered a piece of ham on his plate. "You serve?" he asked offhandedly.

Beckett was wearied with a sense of being interrogated. He glanced at Freemon's plate of food. Beckett snatched an olive from it with a single, smooth motion, sliding the small morsel into his mouth from the toothpick that held it and drew the sharpened toothpick end across Freemon's throat with a deft flick of his wrist. Freemon flinched at the brush of the toothpick point against his skin and Beckett's eyes punctuated the gesture.

"Yeah, I served," Beckett said.

Freemon cleared his throat and nodded. "Uhm, well, nice talking to you, Brock Beckett, super teacher. I'll wave from across the street next time I see you."

"You do that, Mister Nelson. You do that," Beckett said.

Despite the tenor of Freemon's remarks about Cissy, Beckett was perplexed by her absence. He sought out Lloyd for an explanation.

"I have a gift I want to give Cissy, but she's not here," Beckett said. "Is she okay?"

Nelson snorted in the manner all fathers do when their daughters have been upset by a new facet of life. "She's okay," he replied. "Something happened earlier this evening at the ranch party, and frankly, I've kinda expected it for a while now, but not exactly this way."

"Make sense, Lloyd," Beckett said testily.

"Well, it seems one of the ranch employees, who is several years older than she - hit on her pretty aggressively," Nelson explained. "Scared the bejeebers out of her."

Beckett's face reddened. "Anybody I know?" he asked indignantly.

"Naw, he is our bookkeeper; college boy from Mexico City," Nelson said dismissively. "Got him through an agency back in the summer; just before the Frederico Mendez thing. He came with good references."

"Apparently, they weren't good enough," Beckett said.

"Don't get your skivvies in a knot, Captain." Nelson chuckled. "The young man got a clue from some of Cissy's friends; and he came to me and apologized to her. Like I said, this was something I've halfway been expecting for a while now. I mean, good Lord, man, have you taken a look at our… your daughter? She's a knockout."

Untrained by more than 14 years for the intricacies of parenting, Beckett was at a loss to respond. But momentarily, Cissy glided into the room from the kitchen, carrying a small box wrapped in bright Christmas paper. She was dressed in a simple hunter green velvet Christmas dress, her auburn hair falling almost carelessly across her bare shoulders. Her lips were a smooth smear of muted red which gathered Beckett's gaze to her almost auricular facial lines and wide, hazel doe eyes.

"Holy Christmas," he muttered.

"Yeah, Captain. That's your daughter," Nelson said.

Cissy's face lit up at the sight of Beckett. "Merry Christmas…," she called out as she approached his side. She hugged him lovingly.

Beckett took her hands and pushed her back at arm's length. "Look at you, all grown up," he said quietly.

"Yeah, go figure," she said sheepishly.

Nelson glanced at Beckett with a knowing regard. "I'm going for more eggnog," he said nonchalantly. "See you two later."

Beckett looked up and called after him, "Don't get lost. I've got something to ask you," he said. "About Frederico Mendez."

Nelson smiled. "I'll be circling the eggnog," he replied, disappearing into the party milieu.

Cissy presented Beckett with the gift she held. "I hope you like it," she murmured.

He fingered the brightly wrapped package for a moment. "I've got something for you, too," he said. "Is there someplace we can find a little privacy?"

The question puzzled Cissy, but she almost instinctively pointed toward the rear of the cabin. "The fire pit is lit," she said. "If there's nobody outside, we can sit there."

"Perfect," Beckett said.

Cissy retrieved a coat from her room and met him at the back door. She looked at Beckett with a questioning regard. "What is it about you and being out in the cold?" she posed.

He chuckled. "Attitude," he said. "Remember, it's all about attitude."

She shook her head. "I'll never understand it," she muttered as they stepped onto the deck.

The fire pit was in full blaze, the benches encircling it unoccupied. They sat on the nearest bench, and Beckett reached into his jacket pocket for the gift box from the Briggs' Pharmacy. He handed it to Cissy.

"Merry Christmas," he said a bit nervously.

Together, they opened the two gifts. Together, they were both struck in a moment of silence.

Beckett opened the small photo album titled "My Life," and began to peruse the photographs from birthdays, summers,

Christmases, grade school, and junior high graduations, which filled Cissy's life in Destiny. He struggled against the urge to cry.

"It's beautiful, Little Red," he whispered. "You couldn't have given me anything better."

Cissy's fingers trembled as she opened her gift, and she gasped. She lifted the necklace from the box, the plain, gray dog tag dangling from the chain.

"What is it?" she asked, incredulous.

Beckett took the necklace, opened the clasp, and slipped the Celtic chain about Cissy's neck, and fastened it. The dog tag drew a counterpoint against the silver chain.

"It's an important part of me," Beckett said. "It's my original military identification tag. It's as much of that part of me as I can give you. But I want you to know the rest of me is here to stay. And whatever you want me to be for you, I'm prepared to become."

Cissy lifted the "dog tag" and read from it: "Beckett, Brockton; USMC Res. Capt.; 10/12/79; 08796620317."

She looked up at Beckett, tears crowding the corners of her eyes. "What does it mean?" she whispered.

"Name, service, rank, date of birth, and serial number," Beckett replied. "That's the whole story when you enlist in the military."

It wasn't the whole story, but Beckett let that explanation slide. He hoped his outline was enough for Cissy.

Cissy slipped the chain and tag beneath the neckline of her dress. "It's your story," she said quietly. "And it will always stay next to my heart."

She smiled and rested her head on his shoulder. "Merry Christmas, Daddy," Cissy whispered.

"Merry Christmas, Little Red," Beckett replied, as he held her tightly against his side.

The scene, though played out privately, did not escape Freemon's notice, as he followed the two of them as far as the back door and observed through the kitchen window after they left the cabin. The super teacher, AWOL Marine with the dark dossier, and the school board president's daughter. Freemon was right. But now, how to use it was his dilemma?

Freemon rubbed a fingertip against the small, red mark on his throat. "Very carefully."

The evening sped by for Beckett; it was too short by a great deal. But, as the guests said their goodbyes, and he quietly lent a hand in the cleanup, Nelson sought him out.

"You're bunking upstairs; take your pick," he said. "How did you and Cissy get along?"

"It was a moment I want to thank you for allowing me," Beckett said. "We learned a little more about each other. I am simply in awe at how she turned out, Lloyd. I credit you and Grace with all of it. I'll always be grateful to you."

Nelson snorted, again, the way a father snorts when he is proud of his children.

"She's been a joy, Captain," he whispered. "My Lord, I'd be as much worth shooting as Freemon were it not for her. I remember a time when I was mad as hell at Frederico; ready to fire him off the place on the spot. She was all of eight years old and she saw us arguing and about to go at each other, and she just broke out bawling her little eyes out."

Beckett chuckled. "What did you do?"

"Oh, hell, we both quit arguing and ran over to see what was wrong with her," Nelson said. "Know what she said to us?"

Beckett shook his head obligingly.

"She said, 'I thought you were friends, and friends don't curse at each other and hit each other,'" Nelson said. "We both realized how silly we must have looked. She gave us a chance to look at ourselves and each other honestly. She prevented me from making a drastic mistake that day."

"Was Frederico pretty quick-tempered?" Beckett asked.

"Yeah, he could be, but, shoot, so was I back then," Nelson said. "We grew to be good friends."

"The reason I ask," Beckett said, "has to do with something James Robert Bellchase told me about a week ago. It seems he got a text message from Rosa Linda Mendez about an argument she witnessed between her father and another man. Did Frederico ever come to you about something like that?"

Nelson shook his head. "No, why?"

"According to James Robert, the argument involved money and your ranch," Beckett said.

"He never mentioned anything about it and, we talked reasonably freely about almost everything," Nelson said. "He was intimately involved in everything in running the ranch which left me free to concentrate on the store."

Nelson turned the thought over in his mind. "When was this argument?"

"Rosa Linda told James Robert it occurred on the day she found out she was pregnant," Beckett said. "She saw the two men arguing in the living room of their home when she returned from the clinic in Camden."

"Who was the other guy?" Nelson asked.

"I don't know," Beckett said. "James Robert's conversation was cut off before he could learn anything more. Do you still have any contact with the Mendez family?"

"Of course," Nelson said. "Grace and I set them up with Missus Mendez's brother's family in Camden and helped her find a job. I had accidental death insurance on Frederico as a key employee and she wanted Rosa Linda near a hospital when the baby is born."

"So, you knew she was pregnant by James Robert?" Beckett posed.

"Only after Frederico's murder," Nelson said.

"It might be helpful to talk to Missus Mendez about the argument. Frederico may have said something to her," Beckett suggested. "We need to find out who was on the other end of that argument and why."

Nelson looked into Beckett's eyes. "You're going to stick with this; after everything went south on us?"

"I suppose I have to, Gunny," Beckett said. "It keeps coming back to my door."

"Roger that," Nelson said. "Okay, let's get Christmas out of the way, and then go over to Camden and see what Missus Mendez has to say."

Lagniappe

CHAPTER THIRTY-TWO
HE WAS VERY POLISHED

A semi-technical manufacturing economy dominated Camden, not a Silicon Valley type hub, but a place where a high school education had limitations. The town was old and historical in the annals of Southwest Arkansas. Consequently, there was work in domestic service Anna Maria Mendez obtained through references from Lloyd and Grace Nelson. It was a modest position, but it was work that allowed Anna Maria to be home in the evenings at her daughter's side as the time for the birth of Rosa Linda's baby grew closer.

The arrival of Nelson, Cissy, and Beckett at the home of Anna Maria's brother, Carlos Vasquez, was timed after the Christmas Day dinner. Nelson, Beckett, and Cissy left Destiny after a stop at the Nelson store for gifts for the two families. Most of the day celebrating the Nelson family Christmas was quiet, and Beckett's inclusion puzzled Grace.

"You understand, Lloyd, I do not mind; it's that I'm… well, at a loss about this friendship," Grace said quietly over their Christmas morning coffee. "And its effects upon Cissy. She seems almost… smitten with him."

"What do you mean, Hon?" Nelson said.

She sighed, frustrated by the situation. "Last night… oh, how do I put it?" she said. "Well, Freemon pointed out something I found - disturbing."

"Freemon?" Nelson shot back. "What's my rat brain brother up to, now?"

"He may have done us a service, Lloyd," Grace said a bit testily.

"I couldn't think how he might," Nelson said.

"Lloyd Ray, this is serious," she insisted.

Grace's use of Nelson's full given name was a red flag. He put his coffee cup aside, fully intent upon her.

"What did he tell you?" Nelson asked.

"Cissy and Mister Beckett went outside to the fire pit, where they exchanged Christmas gifts," Grace said. "And then, she put her head on his shoulder, and he held her to himself… firmly."

Nelson digested the point carefully. Then he understood how County Coroner Vernon Lard knew so much about Beckett since the beginnings of the Frederico Mendez investigation. He took Grace's hand in his and patted it lovingly.

"I think it's time you know the truth," Nelson said.

Bucolic wasn't a word Beckett used often; he thought of it rarely. But, standing at the window of the upstairs guest room in the Nelson cabin, the view across the Ouachita River toward Destiny was genuinely *bucolic* to his mind.

A light snow fell during the night, covering the landscape with a Norman Rockwell brush stroke. Beckett smiled. He stretched himself, urging muscles which had spent too many Christmases huddling against cliff niches and in field tents to acclimate to a comfortable bed. It felt good to begin to feel normal.

Noise emanating from downstairs stirred him to shower and dress quickly. Beckett did not want to miss a minute of the day with Cissy. When Nelson knocked at his door, Beckett was squared away.

"Morning, Gunny," he said cheerfully. "Merry Christmas."

Nelson hung his head and scuffed at the floor with the heel of his house shoes. "I, uh, need a minute, Captain," he said quietly.

"Sure, come on in," Beckett offered.

Nelson rested his hand firmly against Beckett's shoulder. He nodded toward the staircase.

"We need to give Grace and Cissy a little time, right now," he said. "She saw you two outside last night, and I had to tell her the truth."

Beckett was stunned, yet somehow, he felt a sense of relief at hearing the statement. He nodded.

"How did she take it?" Beckett asked.

Nelson chuckled. "A damn sight better than I thought she might," he said. "You know, Captain, somehow, I think, deep down, she knew. She probably knew the first day we had you over for dinner. Anyway, she and Cissy are… well, sorting through it right now."

"I hope Grace understands I don't intend to disrupt your lives, Gunny," Beckett said.

"Yeah, I think she got the impression," Nelson replied. "Not so much from anything you've done, I guess, as from what you haven't done; if that makes sense."

"Absolutely," Beckett said. "I've tried to be careful with Cissy's emotions… and mine."

Nelson sighed. "Guess we'd better go face the music, Captain," he said.

Beckett stepped into the upstairs gallery and walked to the staircase landing. Cissy and Grace were seated at the fireplace beside the Christmas tree below and they were laughing and hugging each other. Beckett almost stumbled on the staircase landing and steadied himself.

"Combat was easier than this," he muttered as he descended the stairs.

"You ain't tellin' me anything, Captain," Nelson said.

Christmas was different in Camden for Rosa Linda Mendez; she had no father. She listened from the small pantry her uncle converted into a bedroom for her. Her younger siblings were delighted by the diversion of Santa Claus on Christmas morning, limited as it was. Still, Rosa Linda was grateful. She softly stroked her growing midriff.

"Felice Navidad, mi amo poquito," Rosa Linda murmured.

Rosa Linda pulled her cell phone from beneath her pillow; it was a singular concession by her mother to the change in their lives, allowing Rosa Linda to remain connected with friends. She sent a text message to James Robert Bellchase.

"Felice Navidad, my love."

He answered almost instantly: "Merry Christmas."

"Miss u so bad," she replied.

"R u ok?"

She sighed. "Yes… just want to…"

"What's wrong?" he asked.

"Nothing. So lonely."

"I can try to come c u."

Rosa Linda smiled and sniffed back a tear. "After baby born."

"OK. Hard to wait…"

"I know."

Rosa Linda sat for a moment, anticipating James Robert's response, but nothing appeared in her chat box. She checked her battery; it was still full.

"R u there?" she typed.

A long moment lapsed as Rosa Linda began to despair of something wrong. Then, she heard the familiar "boop" which preceded a message, and James Robert was back. But his tone was different.

"U left me worried about u," he wrote. "Never explained man arguing with ur father."

"I know. Sorry. Don't be upset. Please. It's ok, now."

"Got to trust me to help u. I talked to Mr. Beckett."

"Ohhh, Mister B.," she replied. "Maybe, he could help. I don't know."

"What happened… or I can give u Mr. B's address, if will help," James Robert wrote. "Just want to help u, babe."

The text message from James Robert came during a quiet, but confessional, Christmas luncheon at the Nelson cabin. But it would remain unanswered for the better part of the day while Beckett's cell phone lay on the night table beside the bed in the guest room. Cissy paved the way for Beckett to approach Grace by placing much of the reason for the secrecy upon herself. Beckett immediately rectified the notion.

"Just shows you how well you have raised her, Missus Nelson," he said quietly.

"Grace," she replied. "Surely, we can drop the formalities."

"Okay, Grace," Beckett said. "Cissy has learned how to be self-sacrificing, among other wonderful character traits you and Lloyd have taught her. And I'm grateful. Now that you know my story, I trust you understand how important Cissy is to me. And I understand how important your life together has become.

"I've been affected by her absence from my life," Beckett added. "I'd be lying if I said I weren't at least a bit jealous of your years together. But I don't begrudge them to you. There are others who owe me that debt. Sitting with her now, and last night, in the moment we shared, I've found such… joy that I can only be thankful rather than vengeful."

"I can't say I'd blame you at all, were I in your position, Brock," Grace said. "It was a ghastly business played out upon you. Cissy's adoption is certainly understood within our contemporary circle in Destiny, and she has been aware of her adoption since she turned sixteen."

Beckett smiled. "I wondered why she took the notion I was her father so calmly when we first met," he said.

Cissy blushed. "That day in the rain, when you called my name, I ran across the street and told Daddy Lloyd. You remember I stopped and looked back at you?"

Beckett nodded. "I was deciding," Cissy said. "I was deciding whether I wanted you to be my father, whether I wanted to know everything. You had a kind look in your eyes that made me want to take the chance."

"So, how do you propose we address the situation, Brock?" Grace asked.

"I don't think we need to do anything at the moment," he replied.

"Nonsense," Grace said. "Your relationship to Cissy deserves some form of recognition; that's only civil. Leave it to us girls. We'll think of something."

Beckett thought to respond, but Nelson cut him short with a shake of his head. "Don't go there, Captain," he said. "You're out numbered."

James Robert's text message to Beckett gave the Christmas Day trip to Camden significance beyond its original purpose after Beckett informed Nelson of the development. He shook his head as he read the text message.

"Rosa Linda wants 2 talk 2 u about what she heard," James Robert wrote. *"Please help her, Mister B."*

"I wish all our teachers were as trusted by their students," Nelson said quietly. "I'm not certain whether Missus Mendez is willing to let Rosa Linda talk to us, given the circumstances."

"Can I help?" Cissy asked.

Nelson looked at Beckett as he drove them away from the variety store. "What do you think, Captain?" he posed. "It might sit better with both of them."

"I agree," Beckett said. "We can talk to the mother and Cissy to the daughter. We might get better information more comfortably."

Beckett turned to the back seat of the SUV to address Cissy.

"I appreciate you wanting to help," he said. "But remember, whatever Rosa Linda tells you may have to be repeated in court someday. So, I want you to be completely certain about doing this."

"I understand," Cissy said quietly. "We've been good friends. She sent me a Christmas text so, I think she will be comfortable talking to me. But I won't push it if she is not ready."

The evening crept upon the SUV as the sun slipped below the horizon to offer a brilliant full moon, the only light along the lonely stretch of Highway 24. Cissy called up a musical playlist on her cell phone and plugged a pair of earbuds into her ears for the ride to Camden.

The festive lights at the Vasquez house were muted, as was the neighborhood. Yet there was holiday activity inside and warm greetings of the season to meet the guests. The gifts brought by Senor Nelson were received with delight by the children, as both Anna Maria Mendez and her sister-in-law sought to offer their guests some form of holiday meal after their travels. The women brought out tamales, refried beans, rice, and holiday dishes as they insisted the three visitors share their table.

"Muchas gracias, Senora Mendez," Nelson said. He glanced at Beckett. "Dig in, Captain, you're gonna love it."

The smells transcended Beckett's description as they mingled with the spicy flavor of the tamales, the buttered warmth of fresh tortillas, and the rich texture of the beans. He ate as much as he thought polite, but Beckett craved more.

"We prayed today to the Blessed Mother for your family," Mrs. Mendez offered. "You have been a blessing to us, and we are thankful."

The house, a Victorian relic, was remodeled to accommodate multiple families. Children played between rooms, and older siblings and cousins watched television in the main sitting room of the antique manse. Cissy and Rosa Linda sat and talked quietly in a corner by the vintage fireplace.

"You've got a lot of family around you. It must be nice," Cissy said.

"It helps," Rosa Linda said. "But I miss the ranch and you and your parents; and my friends."

"We miss you, too," Cissy said. She bit at her lip, wanting to be careful of her friend's sensibilities. "I, uhm, guess you've been in touch with James Robert?"

Rosa Linda nodded. "It's okay, Cissy," she said. "I saw Mister Beckett with you and Mister Nelson; and I'm glad you came. Do you know what James Robert and I texted about?"

"I don't want you to feel like you have to tell me anything," Cissy said. "But I want to help."

"Truthfully," Rosa Linda said, "I feel more comfortable talking to you."

"What's it about?" Cissy asked.

"The day I came back to the ranch from the clinic, when I learned I was pregnant, I was feeling confused and frightened," Rosa Linda explained. "I didn't want to talk to anyone or see anyone, so, I hurried from the van to the back of the house and went inside. I just wanted to go to my bed and cry."

Cissy took Rosa Linda's hand in hers. "I can't imagine how you felt," she whispered.

"I had a million things going around in my head, but the worst thing was what my father was going to say," Rosa Linda said. "And, when I heard his voice in the front room, he sounded angry. I thought, 'OMG, he is going to send me away somewhere.'

"But then, I heard another man's voice," Rosa Linda added. "The other man, he was very polished, you know, his English was clear and good. So, I got up and went into the kitchen, where I could hear better."

"What were they angry about Rosa Linda?" Cissy asked.

"I'm not sure what it meant, but my father said something about hunting on the ranch," she said. "He said nobody hunted without Senor Nelson's permission, no matter how much money they paid."

Cissy mulled the thought. "So, the man asked your father to ask my father's permission to hunt on our ranch," she surmised.

"No, I don't think that was why they argued," Rosa Linda answered. "It sounded like the man wanted to pay my father money to let him hunt and your father wasn't supposed to know."

"Did you get a look at the man arguing with your father?" Cissy asked.

Rosa Linda shook her head. "He had his back to me, and I was trying to stay out of sight," she said. "But he was tall, and slender, and his English was very good."

"What do you mean; his English was very good?" Cissy asked.

"He was Hispanic," Rosa Linda said.

"Did the man seem to be someone your father knew?" Cissy asked. "Did you recognize his voice?"

"No, I don't know who he was," Rosa Linda said. "I have never heard him."

"Did he say how your father was supposed to keep Dad from knowing he was hunting on the ranch?" Cissy asked with a hint of incredulity. "I mean, Dad knows every inch of the place; if someone put up a deer stand, he'd find it. Was your father supposed to hide it?"

"I don't know," Rosa Linda said. "I had to go back to my room because my mother came into the front door at that time."

"Oh?" Cissy said. "Did she say anything, or did she recognize the man?"

"I don't know," Rosa Linda said. "I couldn't hear clearly."

Cissy patted Rosa Linda's shoulder. "Thanks for talking with me," she said. "I know it was hard for you."

Rosa Linda whimpered and settled her head against Cissy's shoulder. Cissy let her cry. The moment attracted Beckett's attention. He was certain whatever was said between the two girls concluded the conversation. He stepped back from the dining room doorway and nodded discreetly toward Nelson, who was finishing a second plate of tamales.

"Muy bueno," he announced. "Senora Mendez, I do so much miss your cooking. Is there no way I can bring you and your family back to the ranch?"

Anna Maria smiled, then she shook her head. "No, Senor Nelson, we must be near the hospital for Rosa Linda," she said solemnly.

"What about after the baby is born?" Nelson asked. "Will you come back and cook for the ranch. There is no one living in your house, and I can install a commercial kitchen. You can cook breakfast and lunch for the ranch hands and I will buy everything for you."

"Aye, Dios mio, you are so kind," Anna Maria exclaimed. "I think about it."

"Bueno," Nelson said. "I know life has taken many hard turns for your family, and Senor Mendez, God rest him, was a man who provided and lived with integrity."

"Si, es verdad; so true," Mrs. Mendez said with a nod.

"I only wish there were some way we could bring justice for him," Nelson added. "I wonder, Senora, was there anything that happened in the days before he was taken, anything unusual he spoke about, or you have held in your heart? Anything at all?"

"Aye, it is all so how to say… confused," Mrs. Mendez said.

"What do you mean?"

"As you say, Senor Nelson, my Frederico, he was a good man. He provided," Mrs. Mendez explained. "He was honest; and he did not like when someone ask him to do a wrong thing."

"Who asked Frederico to do wrong?" Nelson asked.

"It was the man who I saw with him on the day we come back from the clinic with Rosa Linda," Mrs. Mendez said. "I don't know him; but he was a how you say… smooth man. He talked smooth with me as soon as I come in the house. He say, 'Senora Mendez, you look lovely today, you have a nice house and family. How you like to have a better house, nicer things?' He was smooth. I say, 'I don't know what you talking about;' and he say, 'Talk to your husband; convince him.'"

"Convince him of what?" Nelson asked.

"I don't know, because Frederico, he gets mad, and he shoves the man out the door," Mrs. Mendez said. "I ask him, 'What makes you so mad?' And he say, 'I don't want to talk about it.'"

She became quiet, pensive. Nelson feared he would learn nothing more, but Rosa Linda and Cissy walked into the dining room, arm in arm like good friends, and they disappeared toward the girl's room beyond the kitchen. Mrs. Mendez sighed and nodded, as though she had reached a decision.

Beckett settled himself in a chair beside Nelson. The woman looked up at both men, tears in her eyes.

"Early the day Frederico is killed, I see him on the telephone; he is angry," Mrs. Mendez said. "He has a big envelope in his hand, and he is waving it around, talking angry, saying, he is not a crook."

"What was in the envelope?" Nelson asked quietly.

Mrs. Mendez shook her head. "I don't know, but I think it was a lot of money."

"What makes you think so, Senora?" Beckett asked.

"Frederico, he says he wants to meet who is on the telephone, that he never said he would help," Mrs. Mendez said. "He says, 'I meet you out there and you go away, or I take this and tell Senor Nelson what you try to buy.'"

Mrs. Mendez shook her head dejectedly. "After that, Frederico goes out on the ranch, and I don't see him anymore until one of the hands comes and tells me to go to the ranch office because Frederico has been shot."

"About what time did Frederico have the telephone conversation?" Beckett asked.

"About six o'clock that morning," Mrs. Mendez said.

Nelson glanced at Beckett. "He was found about ten o'clock," he said. "And no envelope, nothing was found with him."

"Senora Mendez," Beckett said. "Did you tell any of this to the county sheriff's deputy, or Mister Lard, the county coroner?"

Mrs. Mendez shook her head. "I didn't talk to nobody at the ranch office," she replied. "Senor Means, he don't let nobody inside, so I go home, like he tell me. And I wait there but nobody comes to talk to me."

Beckett and Nelson looked at each other incredulously. "Nobody talked to the wife," they said in near unison.

The two men listened quietly on the return trip to Destiny as Cissy recounted her conversation with Rosa Linda. Beckett and Nelson were intrigued.

"The two accounts of mother and daughter fit into a general narrative which put Frederico Mendez at odds with someone who supposedly wanted to hunt illegally on the Nelson ranch," Beckett said. "Now we have a plausible motive for Frederico's death."

"The shooter wanted to pay to use the nest on the bluff above the river," Nelson surmised.

"He characterized it as a simple hunting lease, but when Frederico balked, and met him to return the bribe package, the shooter killed him and took the money, assuming you and everyone else would call it a hunting accident," Beckett said.

"The man Rosa Linda saw arguing with her father is probably the killer," Cissy said.

"Possibly," Beckett said. "He might also be a middleman for the shooter."

Cissy plugged in her earbuds and leaned back against the SUV seat. "He is Hispanic, tall and slender, and well-spoken," she whispered.

Cissy immediately thought of a name: Joaquin de la Rosa. But she said nothing.

CHAPTER THIRTY-THREE
YOU'RE A BAD MAN

Suspicion created a growing carelessness within Cissy which seemed reasonable as she was drawn to her questions about Joaquin de la Rosa. The start of classes after the New Year left her with little time to develop answers, but she persisted. Cissy's distraction, however, did not go unnoticed by Beckett.

"Okay, people, today we shift gears and centuries in content, but not necessarily in perspectives," Beckett announced to Cissy's American literature class. "*Giant* is not so different, in many ways, from *Gone with the Wind*, especially its treatment of racial inequality. The point is much the same, while the ethnic and cultural distinctions involved are worlds apart."

Beckett pointed toward Devonte Washington. "Mister Washington, what is your opinion of Hispanics?" he asked.

"Say what, sir?" Washington asked.

"What is your opinion of Hispanics, as a whole?" Beckett repeated.

"Uhm, I don't know..."

"Exactly," Beckett said. "Which is part of the point. In our community and across Arkansas, the integration of Hispanics into daily life has occurred much more quickly than anyone anticipated. It is not akin to the issue noticed in Edna Ferber's Nineteen-fifty-two novel *Giant,* in much the same way Black Americans have become more widely integrated into society today than in Margaret Mitchell's Nineteen-thirty-six novel *Gone with the Wind.*"

"Isn't that kinda obvious, sir?" James Robert Bellchase asked. "After all, slavery was right in the middle of *Gone with the Wind.* Hispanics didn't have that to deal with in Nineteen-fifty-two."

"True, and why was it the case?" Beckett asked. "It is a matter of a significant difference in the history. Texas was historically Hispanic until the latter half of the Nineteenth Century. After the Alamo and the Texas Revolution, when Texas became a nation, much of what had been historically Hispanic in its society began to become more 'gringo,' or white. And, while Black culture has affected the historic Old South, it never ruled the Old South. Hispanic culture ruled in Texas for almost a hundred years before Stephen F. Austin and the other 'empresario' colonists settled white culture in Texas.

"*Giant* is as much a story about the transformation of Texas by oil money in a way that historic Hispanic influences could not immediately counteract as it is about racial inequality," Beckett said.

Beckett pointed toward Cissy. "So, Miss Nelson, which author hits racial inequality harder: Margaret Mitchell or Edna Ferber?"

Cissy remained quiet for a long moment, almost as though she had not heard the question. Marilee Paige reached across the aisle and nudged her.

"Cissy," she whispered and pointed at Beckett.

"Uhm, uh, what was the question, sir?" Cissy asked.

Beckett gave her a surprised glance. "Welcome back, Miss Nelson," he said. "I asked which author hits racial inequality harder: Margaret Mitchell or Edna Ferber?"

"I'd say Margaret Mitchell, sir," Cissy offered. "The point never leaves the main characters because you always have Mammy and Prissy, two slaves, with Scarlett and Melanie, their owners, even after the war…"

"But, aren't the Hispanic ranch hands, especially Old Polo, and his family, with Bick and Leslie Benedict almost in the same fashion?" Beckett retorted. "The fact the Benedicts become wealthier after the oil money rolls in doesn't noticeably change the Hispanic hands' lives."

Cissy became flushed, an embarrassment and anger rising in her face.

"We treat our ranch hands respectably, and pay them better than anybody else," she shot back. "Some ranch employees even have a college education, like Joaquin de la Rosa, the bookkeeper."

The comment created a ripple across the classroom, and Beckett called for quiet. "I'm not arguing anything personal, Miss Nelson," he said. "Please, don't take it that way, although you make an excellent point."

"Oh," Cissy said sheepishly.

Marilee Paige leaned across the aisle. "Nice save," she whispered.

But the plan which began to crystalize in Cissy's mind had little bearing on circumspection about her father's business. Cissy's opportunity to put her gambit into play presented itself on Friday when she accompanied Nelson to the ranch.

The ranch office was Spartan to some degree, a two-room, one bathroom metal building with a stonework wainscot across the front. The immediate interior was De la Rosa's office where the general business records were kept, and employee business was conducted. A coat vestibule from the front entrance opened into the room, with two comfortable cushioned chairs along the immediate right exterior wall and an overstuffed sofa against the left exterior wall in front of De la Rosa's desk. The remainder of the room was taken up with filing cabinets, a floor-to-ceiling bookcase and a coffee nook. A doorway midway along the right interior wall opened to a short hall with a bathroom immediately to the right and the door to Nelson's office on the left.

Nelson's office reflected the man. The floor was partially covered with large rawhide rugs, two large sofas against the right and left walls immediately inside the doorway, and the rear wall dominated by a large window with Nelson's desk in front of it. A built-in display case against the right wall was filled with memorabilia and awards.

Cissy planted herself on the sofa adjacent to De la Rosa's desk as Nelson walked into his office and closed the door. Cissy gave De la Rosa a quizzical glance, then she tossed back her hair and smiled demurely. De la Rosa was immediately drawn to her hazel-doe eyes.

"About what happened at the party," Cissy said. "I got terribly angry, and you apologized. But I've had a lot of time to think about it."

She breathed a small, coquettish sigh, then she bit her moist, candy-apple-red lower lip with a schoolgirl's frustration. De la Rosa took notice.

"Anyway, I want you to know…" She popped her lips open from a tight pout. "I get it."

"Excuse me?" De la Rosa replied.

"I get it," Cissy said in a conspiratorial whisper.

Cissy stood, letting her jacket fall to the sofa to disclose tight-fitting denim jeans fashionably ripped in strategic places and a black leather crop top that strained against her cleavage. She leaned across the desk with the neckline of the crop top open and smiled at De la Rosa.

"Here's my number," Cissy cooed, and she nestled a slip of paper into his hand. "Call me."

Cissy smiled, pressed her lips against his lightly, and drew away quickly. She picked up her jacket and sauntered toward the bathroom. De la Rosa smiled at the sway of Cissy's hips as she disappeared into the hallway.

"So naïve, so easy," De la Rosa muttered.

Cissy shut the bathroom door and closed her eyes. She drew a deep breath to calm herself, shuddered and wanted a hot, cleansing shower.

"Eww… that's step one."

De la Rosa's call came later that evening in the form of a chat message. Cissy retrieved her cell phone from its bedside charger and looked at the chat tag: El Matador.

"Really?" she muttered disdainfully, as she opened the chat.
El Matador: "I am glad u understand."
Ranch Girl: "Completely."
El Matador: "So, what do you propose we do about it?"
Cissy quivered. "Eww, eww, eww, eww."

Ranch Girl: "Get 2 know u better."
El Matador: "What's to know? U r more interesting."
Ranch Girl: "Haven't been to college; traveled, got a job; or... wonderful dancer."

Cissy included emoticons with each point. De la Rosa looked at the response and chuckled.

El Matador: "I can take you places you've never been."
Ranch Girl: "Where?"
El Matador: "Mexico City, Cancun, Rio during Carnival... so amazing."
Ranch Girl: "OMG..."

An image of Rhett Butler propositioning Scarlett O'Hara popped into Cissy's mind. She shook her head.

"How typical."

El Matador: "Can you slip away tonight? I have a car."
Ranch Girl: "To go where?"
El Matador: "The Hot Spot in Destiny?"
Ranch Girl: "Lord, no! My uncle owns it."
El Matador: "Break off the shackles..."

Cissy was loath to type her response, but she maintained the charade.

Ranch Girl: "ok"
El Matador: "Ten minutes, at end of the block."
Ranch Girl: "ok"

Cissy trembled, but she was compelled to know. Fifteen minutes later, she was seated in a sporty convertible driven by De la Rosa to the one place in Destiny she was absolutely forbidden to go.

"I knew you would come around, Chiquita," De la Rosa said. "You understand, it is all about life now."

He pulled Cissy close to him and kissed her. Cissy had never been fully kissed, and the impassioned press of his mouth against her inappropriately luscious lips warmed Cissy as much as it frightened her. She urged herself to maintain perspective, to remember... this was dangerous.

The Hot Spot was the sort of place where the patrons who entered alone often left accompanied. Couples who arrived earlier in the evening invariably returned to the cars and extended cab trucks in the parking lot at intervals. The sound of an R&B band beyond the oversized wooden sliding door at the entrance filtered through the corrugated metal roofing and spilled into the parking lot, where several of the car windows were fogged from the inside. The parking lot gravel crunched beneath Cissy's calf-high, form-fitted leather boots. She wore the same pairings she showed De la Rosa at the ranch office that day, and the frigid evening cut through the fashionably ripped denim jeans and leather crop top.

The thunder of the house band immediately filled everything, enveloping the noisy drunkenness that was The Hot Spot as they stepped inside the building. Cissy steeled herself against the environment. She shook back her hair, smiled demurely, and slipped her arm beneath De la Rosa's. He was her only protection from everything but himself. He looked down into her eyes and smiled.

"Life, Chiquita," De la Rosa shouted into the din.

Cissy nodded, and they followed a waitress to a table in the far corner away from the dance floor. The waitress took food and setup orders, the rest was left to the patrons. But she gave Cissy a second look.

"Am I gonna have to card you, honey?" she asked.

De la Rosa slipped a $20 bill into the woman's hand. "No," he said.

The waitress glanced down at the money and smiled. "Right," she replied. "What'll you have?"

"Two colas," De la Rosa said. The waitress nodded and slouched away.

Whether Cissy was recognizable was questionable. She went to lengths to ensure her appearance was as different from her daily life as possible. Now, in the dim cacophony of The Hot Spot, her gambit was in full play, and Cissy was unsure how long she could deflect De la Rosa's intentions. The waitress returned to the table with two bottles of cola and plastic cups. De la Rosa poured half of one bottle of soda into each cup, then he pulled a pint of bourbon from his coat pocket and laced both cups generously with it.

"La Vida," he said, raising his cup.

Cissy smiled sheepishly. She lifted her cup. "La Vida," she said.

De la Rosa took a stiff drink from his cup. Cissy put her cup against her lips. She used a technique learned in a drama class at school. Timing the press of the cup against her lips and tilting her head backward while raising the cup from the bottom gave the impression of drinking. The bourbon soda wet Cissy's lips but she never swallowed it. Still, the smell of the laced soda irritated her nose, and she coughed.

"Ah, too strong, Chiquita?" De la Rosa posed. "It is an acquired taste, much like you."

He slid his hand beneath the table and grasped Cissy's upper thigh. She flinched, and he leaned closer to her.

"You feel… firm, warm, tense," De la Rosa said. "Let's dance."

De la Rosa stood and pulled Cissy up with him, and they found a spot in the dance scrum. He held her against himself and pushed between her legs, forcing her into a grinding motion leaving Cissy embarrassed and confused. She became frightened and tried to break away, but the crowded dance floor afforded her no escape. Cissy felt De la Rosa's breath heavy against the nape of her neck and she trembled.

"Feel the fire, Chiquita," De la Rosa said. "Feel the fire."

A fight broke out on the dance floor, and Cissy fairly raced back to the table after the music stopped. She sat down, crossed her legs, and scooted her chair away from De la Rosa's. He arrived a moment later, downed the remainder of his drink and opened the second soda bottle. After lacing his drink heavily, De la Rosa reached for Cissy's cup, but she snatched it away loosely enough that it slipped from her hand and fell to the floor.

"Ooops," she said.

"No problem, Chiquita," De la Rosa said. He handed her his cup. "Take a drink."

Cissy demurred but De la Rosa persisted. He pressed the cup to her mouth and slipped his hand beneath her chin. He pressed his thumb and middle finger against both sides of her lower jaw. Cissy gasped, and as she opened her mouth, and De la Rosa poured the laced soda into it, she swallowed. The bourbon in the cup was cut only slightly by the soda and Cissy coughed.

"You want to be a woman, you drink like a woman," De la Rosa insisted.

He put the open bourbon bottle to Cissy's lips and squeezed beneath her chin, again. She struggled to push him away, but as slender and polished as he seemed, De la Rosa was strong. The bourbon splashed down Cissy's throat. It tasted harsh and stung. She coughed and De la Rosa relented to take a drink.

"Life, Chiquita," he said with a snarl.

The undiluted alcohol affected Cissy almost immediately, her ears became dull against the driving music, her eyes lazy in the dimness. De la Rosa pushed Cissy's arms into her jacket and helped her to her feet. She felt herself weaving as she walked toward the door supported by his grip. Cissy stepped into the chill of the night but felt no sting, only the warm rush of heated air inside De la Rosa's sportster as they drove away from The Hot Spot.

Cissy turned, flaccid against the seat belt, and smiled at De la Rosa. "I know who you are," she said.

"Oh, who am I, Chiquita?" he replied.

"You are…" Cissy struggled to marshal her thoughts. "You are… hot, no, no, you are him…"

"Him? Who?" De la Rosa teased.

"You're a bad man," Cissy muttered.

"Bad because I make you want to live, Chiquita?"

"Yeesss, bad man… sooo hot," Cissy said dreamily.

De la Rosa laughed. "Why am I a bad man, Chiquita?"

"Rosa Linda's father," Cissy replied. "You… killed him."

De la Rosa stopped the car. He turned to Cissy, his expression no longer flippant, and De la Rosa studied Cissy with a somber regard for a long moment.

"So beautiful, Chiquita," he whispered. "But you should not play with fire."

Cissy struggled to comprehend his intent, then she passed out.

CHAPTER THIRTY-FOUR
HE'S HERE FOR ME, GUNNY

An irritatingly brilliant ray of sunlight beamed between the curtains of Cissy's bedroom window striking her eyes at a most inconvenient time – morning, or more precisely, late morning. She groaned and turned away from the light, certain her head would explode at any moment. Then, she awoke with a start at the realization she was in her room, in her bed, in a warm, fuzzy bunny onesie.

She sat bolt upright. "Oooh myyy Lord," she moaned.

The question that screamed in Cissy's mind was not how she got home, into her room, into a onesie and into bed, it was substantially more personal. She crawled from bed, pulled down the window shade, and in the ensuing dimness made her way carefully into the bathroom. Moments later, in pain and bleeding when she urinated, Cissy froze. Then, she became frightened by understanding.

Cissy decided to confront the possibility directly. She used the callback function on her cell phone to open a text chat with Joaquin de la Rosa's number. There was no answer. There was no number. The account was closed.

"I should have known," Cissy groaned.

A single unanswered chat message remained in her inbox. Cissy opened it.

El Matador: "Ole, Chiquita."

There was a photo attachment. Cissy opened it, and her fears exploded into reality as she saw herself unconscious in De la Rosa's car, semi-nude with an almost empty bourbon bottle in her hand. Tears rolled down Cissy's cheeks.

"Noooo," she whimpered.

Downstairs, Nelson was perturbed as he sat down for breakfast. Grace noticed his disquiet.

"You were restless last night," she remarked, sipping her coffee.

"I could have sworn I heard the sound of a car engine starting, then leaving from the driveway about six," Nelson said. "I looked out at the window and saw a pair of taillights at the end of the block."

"Cissy doesn't have a car. Did it sound like her ATV?" Grace asked nonchalantly.

"Oh, no, I peeked in on her, and she was dressed in a bunny onesie and snoring like a lumberjack," Nelson said. "Nothing seemed out of place. Has she come down for breakfast?"

Grace shook her head. "Haven't heard a peep."

Nelson finished his eggs and toast. "Tell Cissy, I've gone out to the ranch without her. She can ride her ATV out if she wants."

He gave Grace a peck on the cheek, drained his coffee cup, and headed for the door. As he settled into the driver's seat of his truck, Nelson pulled his cell phone from his pocket and punched Beckett's number in the favorites. He fastened his seat belt, started the engine, and waited for Beckett to pick up.

"Morning, Gunny," Beckett said.

"Good mornin', Captain," Nelson replied cheerfully. "I'm headed out to the ranch to catch up on some things, want to come with me?"

"Heck, yeah," Beckett said. "Give me five minutes."

"Be there in three."

Cissy's absence surprised Beckett. "Where's Little Red?"

Nelson shrugged. "Teenagers, go figure," he said, as Beckett climbed into the passenger seat. "Anyway, I wanted to talk to you about something Anna Mendez told us that has been bugging me."

Nelson wheeled the pickup truck out of Miss Esther's driveway. Beckett sensed an anxiousness in Nelson's voice.

"It struck me whoever Frederico Mendez was dealing with already knew about the bluff by the river," Nelson said. "Either he or someone he represents researched the possibilities along the river. I've got a hunch about something, but first we should talk to my ranch bookkeeper."

"Your people work a six-day schedule?" Beckett asked.

"Saturdays are reserved for maintenance and catching up on business for Monday," Nelson said. "Joaquin comes in about nine o'clock"

But when Nelson and Beckett arrived, they found the office building locked. Nelson was perturbed as he unlocked the office door.

"That's strange," Nelson said. "Joaquin usually calls if he is going to be out, and there is nothing he needs to do in town today."

A quick check with the line hands making equipment repairs at the main barn confirmed De la Rosa's absence. Nelson was visibly upset.

"Joaquin lives in Camden, so I'll try his cell phone before we have to drive over to Camden for me to fire his sorry butt," Nelson said. "He's supposed to have his phone with him on workdays."

There was no answer from De la Rosa, only a message which sent Nelson to voice mail. He punched in the Global Positioning Satellite application for the phone, asking for the location of De la Rosa's unit. The small map on the screen showed the phone to be at the ranch office.

"What the…?" Nelson blurted.

The two men walked from the main barn to the office. Nelson pulled his master keys from his pocket and unlocked the front door. He immediately saw De la Rosa's phone on the desk in front of them.

"This makes no sense, Captain," Nelson groused. "Why can't I find my bookkeeper?"

"What did you want to ask him?" Beckett posed.

"Well, I keep a pretty tight rein on the use of cell phones for the ranch," Nelson said. "And I got to thinking about what Missus Mendez and Rosa Linda both said. Frederico talked to the same man on the phone on two occasions. They didn't have a landline, Captain. The only phone Frederico used was his ranch phone. And we keep close records of phone usage, with a breakdown on the bill every month."

"And the number of the phone call to Frederico on the day he was killed should be listed at least twice," Beckett interjected. "It gives us an identity."

"Precisely," Nelson said.

Several minutes of searching through file cabinets finally produced the files for cell phone usage. Nelson retrieved the bulky file and laid it on the desk. He began sifting back through the monthly records.

"Yeah… got the month," he said.

The call log recorded the date and time of each incoming and outgoing call and other usage of cell phones issued to ranch personnel. Nelson ran his finger down the list of entries.

"Frederico was a hands-on sort of foreman, so he did not use his cell phone extensively," he said.

"Most of the calls to and from his number are fairly brief," Beckett said. "Except these two from the same number, one just after the first of the month, and this one… at five-forty-eight in the morning on the day he died. That is almost spot-on for the time Missus Mendez said she heard him arguing about the payoff envelope."

Nelson turned to Beckett, a troubling realization on his face. "Those two numbers are from Joaquin's phone," he said.

He dropped the phone log onto the desk and settled into the chair. Beckett picked up the file and began to examine it, again.

"Why was Joaquin calling the Mexican Consulate in Little Rock?" he said quietly.

Nelson glanced at the list. "We had some immigration issues with a couple of hands, relatives of his," he said. "No big deal."

"So, that explains the calls to Mexico City?" Beckett posed.

"I suppose," Nelson replied. "Anyway, he was handling it."

He stood and began to pace. "This is not good," Nelson said. "Joaquin has to be the man Rosa Linda and Missus Mendez saw, but neither of them seemed familiar with him. He hadn't been working here long enough. But it's still an incomplete picture. Was Joaquin the shooter or just a middleman?"

"I'd say Joaquin isn't the shooter," Beckett replied.

"What do you mean?"

"Every kill is on a schedule for a shooter," Beckett said. "If Joaquin is the shooter, he wouldn't disappear before he made the kill, it raises too many flags and screws up the schedule. No, I think Joaquin is a middleman. He was supposed to arrange for the nest, and he tried to bribe Frederico to secure the site and the time."

"But that went south on him, so the shooter killed Frederico and stuck to the plan," Nelson said.

Beckett heaved a frustrated sigh. "And, with Joaquin in the wind, we don't know what the schedule is, or..." He cut himself short.

"Or, what?" Nelson asked.

"I was about to say, or the identity of the target," Beckett said. "But, I'm just fooling myself. He's here for me, Gunny."

"What?"

"I figured it out the day Frederico Mendez was murdered, as soon as I got to the top of the bluff on the river," Beckett said. "It's a straight shot into my classroom at the high school."

Nelson shook his head. "No, Captain. That's FUBAR."

"Think about it, Gunny," Beckett said. "Joaquin acts after I've gotten here, which means he has put the schedule into motion for someone. Things go south, but he stays with the schedule, as we said. Those are his orders. Then, there are the shots at the football stadium. The shooter was testing his range. He assumed nobody knew the specialized nature of what was occurring… except me.

"But, we come along with the Huang scenario and screw things up for him," Beckett added. "That delays his schedule but does not put it out of reach, somehow; that part I haven't figured out, yet. And, I haven't because of what happened on my apartment porch. You remember that?"

"Someone had you cold that day," Nelson said. "But he didn't take the shot."

"Instead, he gave me a glimpse of him by using a rookie mistake to draw my attention," Beckett said. "That confirmed it for me, but I let the Huang scenario ride, hoping to learn more in the interim. I assumed you would eventually figure out I'm the target."

"It never crossed my mind," Nelson muttered. "There is no motive."

"I'd suggest we take what we know to the ASP investigator. That Goss fellow," Beckett said. "He is the only one who hasn't blown us off yet over the Huang scenario. And, he can get access to information we need to know about Joaquin de la Rosa; and who he represents."

Arkansas State Police Investigator Reyford Goss had not dismissed the death of Frederico Mendez as a hunting accident overblown by local "snoops." He was one step ahead of Nelson and Beckett.

"I researched your military records," Goss said, as he sat on the sofa in Nelson's ranch office two days later. "Both of you were credited with SEAL service, but your commendation records told me the story. That information led me to look at the expertise both of you, and particularly Mister Beckett, represented relative to your explanations. What nailed it for me was some old-fashioned footwork. The routine list of ranch employees Mister Nelson furnished was the key. Why did you hire Joaquin de la Rosa, Mister Nelson?"

Nelson shrugged. "He's Hispanic, had a good resume, a college degree in business administration, and good references, which checked out," he said. "He made a good impression in the interview."

Goss unzipped his briefcase and retrieved a photo from it, which he handed to Nelson. "Is this the man you know as Joaquin de la Rosa?" he asked.

Nelson glanced at the photograph almost nonchalantly, then he looked again. "No," he said quietly. "That's not Joaquin."

"Unfortunately, it is the *late* Joaquin de la Rosa," Goss said. "This is the man from Mexico City who corresponded with you and arranged to interview for the job."

Beckett rose and stepped behind Nelson's chair to look at the photo. "You said, 'the late Joaquin de la Rosa,'" he said. "What happened?"

"He was murdered not long before someone stole his identity and that person began working for Mister Nelson," Goss replied. "I ran him down through the Mexican Consulate in Little Rock. They told me an investigation was ongoing with the belief his killer had assumed De La Rosa's identity and was in the United States."

"The consulate phone calls, Gunny," Beckett said. "He wasn't checking on an immigration issue for one of the hands, he must have been monitoring the investigation."

"What phone calls?" Goss asked.

Nelson retrieved a folder from the filing cabinet and handed Goss the cell phone bill file.

"There are several calls to the Mexican Consulate and to a number in Mexico City," Nelson said. "We became interested when we learned Frederico Mendez argued with someone during a telephone call on the day he was murdered. The call is on the list, and the number comes back to the ranch cell phone which was issued to Joaquin. Or whoever I hired."

"De la Rosa, or whoever this man is, attempted to bribe Mendez, the ranch foreman, to allow access to the ranch property for someone under the guise of setting up an illegal hunting site," Beckett said. "Mendez refused, and he arranged a meeting to return the bribe money delivered to his home. The fake De la Rosa murdered him."

Goss set the file aside. "Why?"

"He needed a site for a sniper nest," Beckett said. "We thought the Huang scenario answered that question, but we were wrong. Whoever this man is, he still intends to kill someone."

"I thought you said De la Rosa wasn't the shooter, Captain," Nelson said.

"That was before I learned De la Rosa isn't De la Rosa," Beckett replied. "The man is our shooter, he has a schedule, and I believe he has a target… me."

Goss leaned forward, his gaze fixed on Beckett. "What makes you think you are the target, Captain Beckett?"

"You've seen my public military record," Beckett said. "What did you read between the lines?"

"You mean in the gaps?" Goss asked.

Beckett nodded. "I might think you've pissed off some heavy-duty people," Goss said.

"And, you'd be right," Beckett replied.

CHAPTER THIRTY-FIVE
THEY CALLED HIM EL BORRACHO, "THE DRUNKARD"

Cissy's depression over her disastrous ploy at The Hot Spot with Joaquin de la Rosa, and subsequent rape by him, gave her nightmares which she lied to hide from Lloyd and Grace. Her feeble efforts drew Grace's suspicions.

"You haven't felt well for a week," she said. "Perhaps, we should take you to the doctor."

Cissy hedged. "No, Mom, no, I'm good. Busy at school and getting ready for Roundup Festival, you know."

She wanted desperately to believe, somehow what she had done was essential to resolving Frederico Mendez's murder. But, still, she could not bring herself to rationalize how that might be the case. Finally, on Friday afternoon the anguish became too crushing for Cissy, and she tearfully offered her story to her two fathers as they left the ranch after regular rounds.

"I did something… really… stupid," she said as they climbed into Nelson's pickup truck.

Nelson put the truck into gear. "Oh, Hon, I'm sure it's not that bad," he said nonchalantly. "Wait until we get to the house, and we'll talk about it, then."

"I can't," Cissy said. "Both of you need to know. It's about Frederico's murder."

"What do you mean, Little Red?" Beckett asked.

Cissy drew a deep breath and sighed. "I… I snuck out of the house last weekend and went to The Hot Spot with Joaquin de la Rosa," she said quickly, quietly, contritely.

Nelson crushed the brakes and brought the truck to an abrupt halt. "You, what?" he shouted.

He threw the truck out of gear, killed the engine, and ripped off his seat belt. Beckett jerked off his own seat belt as Nelson turned angrily toward Cissy in the rear seat.

"Cool your jets, Gunny," Beckett demanded, ramming his open palm against Nelson's shoulder to stop him. "She is confessing, let her confess."

Cissy had never seen this visceral side of Nelson and she shrank back.

"Don't hit me," she pleaded.

Nelson melted into his seat, his eyes wide with realization. "Hit you?" he said. "Oh, baby, no. I'd never hit you."

Nelson sat shocked by the moment and Beckett stared blankly at his daughter. The chill of the day began to seep into the pickup truck, and no one stirred against it. The quiet was palpable.

Cissy's eyes filled with tears that streamed across her cheeks. "I'm sooo sorry," she whimpered.

"Does your mother know?" Nelson asked quietly, steeling his anger beneath his tone.

Cissy shook her head. "Really?" Nelson said.

"She wouldn't understand. She doesn't know everything about Frederico's murder," Cissy said. "I… thought you might help me explain it to her."

"Well, right now, I want to find that lyin' sonofabitch, Joaquin," Nelson said. "But, yeah, we'll talk to your mother… later. At the hospital. It's time she should know everything."

Nelson glanced at Beckett, and both men nodded in silent agreement. Beckett stroked his fingers through Cissy's full auburn tresses, and remembered the silky softness of Jolene's hair.

"It's okay, Little Red. We've got you."

Cissy smiled weakly. "I... I... I..." She had no words and sobbed uncontrollably.

"It's okay, baby. Let it out," Nelson said. "Can you tell us what happened?"

Cissy composed herself, leaned against the seat, and wiped her eyes with the sleeve of her coat. She shook back her hair and sniffed. "It's cold in here."

Nelson started the truck's engine, and the cabin began to warm. Cissy crossed her arms against her lap.

"I started thinking when we left Camden on Christmas Day," Cissy began. "It seemed like Rosa Linda and her mom were talking about the same man: someone who was Hispanic, tall and slender, and well-educated. That fit Joaquin de la Rosa... and he worked at the ranch."

Beckett and Nelson glanced at each other. "Right in front of us," Nelson said. "Go on, baby."

Cissy caught her breath. "Well, after what happened at the ranch hands' Christmas party..."

"He was grooming you," Beckett said.

"Huh?" Cissy said with a confused regard.

"He was setting you up for something to happen," Nelson said. "Go, on."

"Last week in class we were discussing *Giant*, and it occurred to me I might represent for Joaquin what Jett Rink wanted from Leslie Benedict," Cissy explained timidly. "I'm the boss' daughter: the prize. I thought if Joaquin saw me that way, he might get arrogant and slip and say something."

She sighed and glanced toward Nelson, then Beckett, her lips pursed tightly, and her eyes turned down. Then, she whispered, "I came on to him."

Nelson was incredulous. "You what? When? How?"

"Last Friday, when we came to the ranch," Cissy said. "I changed clothes in the restroom at the store and put on a long overcoat, but what I was wearing under it was the same outfit I wore later to The Hot Spot only, I made a couple of adjustments that night."

Nelson rubbed his forehead in quiet frustration. "Holy cow, baby. What were you thinking?"

"I wanted to shake him up," Cissy said. "I wanted him anxious, so I gave him my cell phone number and told him to call me. He did, late that night. And I snuck out of the house, and we drove to The Hot Spot."

"He got you drunk?" Nelson asked. She frowned and hung her head. "Figures," he said. "Just how were you going to trap him if he got you drunk?"

"I'm sorry," Cissy muttered. "Everything happened so fast."

"Did you learn anything from him?" Nelson posed sarcastically.

"No," Cissy said. Then she became indignant. "I woke up Saturday morning in my bed, dressed in a bunny onesie, and I have no idea how that happened."

"I can tell you how it happened, young lady," Nelson said.

"Cut her some slack, Gunny," Beckett said. "She messed up. She's hurting."

He turned to Cissy. "I'm not happy with what you did, either," Beckett said. "But, I think both of us understand it. We need you to understand whatever happened, the man you know as Joaquin de la Rosa is extremely clever and dangerous."

"Wait," Cissy said. "You said 'the man you know as Joaquin de la Rosa'? He's not Joaquin?"

"No," both men said.

Cissy fell backward against the seat. "Who is he?" she asked, her eyes wide with fear.

"We don't know," Beckett said. "The Arkansas State Police are trying to locate him. He murdered the real Joaquin de la Rosa and stole his identity, most likely as part of a larger plan involving other people."

Cissy paled. "O... M... G."

Nelson looked into her hazel eyes with pained expectation. "Did... he... rape you?" he whispered.

Tears swelled again, in Cissy's eyes. "Yes," she sobbed. "There was blood in the morning..."

Nelson stormed out of the truck cab and cursed at the top of his lungs. He grabbed a loose fence post lying on the ground and pounded it against a nearby tree trunk until the post cracked and split apart. Beckett pulled Cissy into his arms. He trembled with anger but quelled it for her sake as he looked into Cissy's eyes.

"Were you unconscious when he raped you?"

Cissy bit her lower lip. "Yes… I think so, I don't really remember."

The two men climbed into the rear of the cab on either side of Cissy. She instinctively rested her head against Nelson's shoulder, but grasped Beckett's hand and held it tightly. Beckett looked at Nelson with stern resolve in his eyes.

"I know what you're thinking, Captain," Nelson said.

"Can you blame me, Gunny?"

"No."

Cissy took the measure of their indignation, and said, "There is something more."

She slipped her cell phone from her jacket pocket and retrieved the photo attachment to Joaquin's last chat message. Cissy handed Nelson the cell phone, and Beckett leaned across the seat to look at it.

Nelson's face became beet red. He looked at Beckett. "You know what I'm gonna do to that bastard…"

It was not a question; Beckett understood. "It would be easy, Gunny. He would never see it coming."

Nelson looked at Cissy, his breath labored as he thought. "No, Captain. We do this right," he said.

"I'm so sorry," Cissy said. "I've messed up everything; and didn't do anything right. I'm sorry."

But, as she began to cry and Nelson sought to console her, Beckett took closer notice of the photo, and lifted the cell phone from Nelson's hand, studied it momentarily, then handed the phone back to Cissy.

"Is there a way to enlarge a portion of the photo?" he asked.

"What do you want to see?" Cissy asked.

"The bottle," Beckett replied. "It was bourbon, right?"

Cissy nodded, and she manipulated the photo to enlarge the image of the bottle. She handed the phone to Beckett. He saw the label clearly.

"Damn," he muttered. "I think I know our man's identity."

"Huh?" Cissy blurted.

"What do you mean, Captain?" Nelson asked.

"I know the name of the man posing as Joaquin de la Rosa," Beckett said. "He is, or was, a former shooter with a highly specialized team."

Cissy was befuddled. "How do you know this guy?"

"The bottle," Beckett said. "I recognized the general shape of the bottle and the color scheme of the label immediately. A closer look confirmed it."

"What's so special about it, Captain?" Nelson asked.

Beckett turned back to Nelson. "You know how shooters often carry talismans, good luck charms?" he asked. Nelson nodded.

"This brand of bourbon is expensive and rare; you can't simply walk into any liquor store and buy it," Beckett explained. "This is his talisman, and he never let the bottle out of sight. He carried it with him everywhere. He took one sip, just a sip, before each shot; he said it cleared his mind."

Cissy clasped Beckett's face in her palms and turned his gaze toward her. "Who the hell is he?" she shouted.

"His name is, or was, Ramon Pena y Reyna," Beckett said. "They called him 'El Borracho: the drunkard."

"You said his name was Ramon Pena y Reyna," Nelson said.

"He is supposed to be dead," Beckett said. "I saw a building collapse beneath his nest. The team that went in to get his body never found it. Son… of… a… General Maxwell told us later the guy was dead."

"So, what do we do now, Captain?" Nelson asked.

"We take Cissy to the hospital and screw up Pena y Reyna's schedule by reporting him to Reyford Goss at ASP for the sexual assault of … our daughter."

"Oh, Lord," Cissy moaned.

"Don't fret, Little Red," Beckett said. "You might have beaten him, after all."

"How?" Cissy groused. "By having everyone think I'm a slut? Oh, joy…"

Beckett smiled. "No, baby, by having him arrested before he can kill anyone."

Cissy looked at her two fathers through tear-wearied eyes. "I hadn't thought of that," she said.

She settled back and closed her eyes. She fell asleep almost immediately as the pickup truck pulled away from the ranch later. Nelson glanced back across his shoulder, then he turned to Beckett.

"You realize, Captain, this will only make Pena y Reyna move up his schedule?" he asked.

"Perhaps, if we rush him, he'll become careless. And the ASP can get to him before he takes the shot."

"That's a big maybe," Nelson said.

"Roger that. But it's the only thing we've got," Beckett said.

Lagniappe

CHAPTER THIRTY-SIX
HE'S DONE PLAYING WITH HIS FOOD

Cissy reluctantly recounted to Arkansas State Police Investigator Reyford Goss in El Dorado on Monday her story of the night at The Hot Spot and the rape by Pena y Reyna. Beckett explained the connection of the bourbon bottle from the cell phone photo, and Goss was immediately intrigued.

"That's a helluva story from you and your daughter, Captain Beckett," he said after taking Cissy's full statement and sending her to the break room with a female trooper. "It puts what we already know in an entirely different light. I called in a couple of favors to get to know your military background a little closer; and, you were right, Captain. You pissed off some heavy hitters."

Beckett studied Goss for a moment. "You were in military intelligence," he remarked.

Goss smiled. "Like I said, I called in a couple of favors."

He opened a folder on his desk and began to read from it.

"General Sakem Akmenon, Egyptian, Syrian base commander for ISIS; taken out on a live internet feed about to execute two missionaries. Everyone was talking about that a few years back," Goss said with a chuckle. "Sheikh Khalid al-Ruhwani, a caliphate overlord who ran a kidnapping network to provide boys for ISIS and girls for prostitution. His camp was destroyed by a drone-directed missile strike, and his son was killed by a sniper. General Nicholai Vichinkov, Russian military policy director for the Middle East, killed by a sniper shot while in bed with a prostitute. And, a big one… Norum al-Nahmeed, president of Syria; killed by a sniper shot through an eight-inch-thick window of the presidential palace."

Nelson was agog. "Seriously, Captain?"

"It was a long time back, Gunny," Beckett deadpanned.

"It's a motive," Goss said. "You've got two governments and ISIS involved in the four years before you mustered out. Any of these players could have put Pena y Reyna on to you."

"Yeah, but wasn't Pena y Reyna working for the good guys?" Nelson asked.

"You would be surprised how many former shooters go to work for private contractors after they're out," Beckett said.

"But, Frederico Mendez was not military contract work, Captain," Nelson said. "That was murder."

"That's true," Goss noted. "But, Captain Beckett is another issue altogether. Legally, he is a civilian, but this probably has little to do with civilian status if Captain Beckett is the intended target."

"How could it be otherwise?" Beckett said in frustration.

"I'm simply keeping every option open, Captain," Goss said.

"It all points to me," Beckett said. "How Frederico Mendez was killed, the ease with which the sniper's nest was discovered, the ranging shots at the football field, and a purposeful rookie mistake with a scope lens reflection are all related things I would recognize. El Borracho knew about me in Afghanistan. No, it can't be anyone else. The only question is: Why?"

Goss held up the dossier. "And we have that pretty well covered."

"Okay. So, we say Captain Beckett is the target and Pena y Reyna is the shooter," Nelson said. "If we figure out the why, then we know who gave the order, and perhaps, that helps stop this thing."

Goss tossed the dossier onto his desk. "This is waaay higher than my pay grade, and I'm out of favors."

"But I'm not," Beckett said. He turned to Nelson. "There is one person who can give us the answers we need. I'll be back in a couple of days, Gunny."

"Whoa," Nelson interjected. "Where do you think you're going without me, Captain?"

"Can't take you this time, Gunny," Beckett said. "I'm the only face that needs to show up at that door."

A cliff in the hills above the northern fingers of Lake Travis near Austin, Texas, formed the southernmost boundary of 1,000 acres of prime real estate ostensibly owned by a development company based in Maryland. The property belonged to Brigadier General (Retired) Pierpont Maxwell. Beckett knew the address and remembered his introduction to Maxwell's Spanish-style hacienda years earlier.

"My family was one of the early developers of Lake Travis," Maxwell said as they stepped through the front door of the residence that day. "My grandfather built this place as a hunting lodge. The plan was to have two brothers out of Victoria, Texas, who were big in cattle and oil, buy the property next door on the eastern side. They wanted to combine the acreage into a game preserve, but then World War II intervened."

"Does your family go way back down here, Sir?" Beckett asked.

"Not so much," Maxwell replied. "We come from Maryland; Annapolis roots."

"You gonna retire here, General?"

Maxwell smiled. "That's the idea, Captain," he said.

Beckett never gave the moment much thought in the years since. But his understanding of Maxwell's lair was explicit. And, as Beckett drove his Jeep from Arkansas, into East Texas and south through the hill country of Central Texas, he pondered how much, if any, Maxwell had changed since the day Beckett beat the truth about Jolene and Cissy out of his commanding officer. His anticipation, however, was met with disappointment when he arrived at the gated entrance to the property.

"Captain Brock Beckett to see General Maxwell," he said clearly into the intercom. Beckett waited for the security camera to confirm his identity; but he was addressed by a disembodied voice from the intercom.

"I'm sorry, sir, but General Maxwell no longer receives visitors," a somewhat rarified Australian accent replied.

"Excuse me? Since when?" Beckett asked.

"The General has received no visitors since he was diagnosed some months ago with Alzheimer's disease," the voice said. "It is doubtful he would remember ya, sir."

Beckett rested against his seat in shock. He poured through his mind to recall whether there might have been some clue to the onset of the illness he missed. Beckett hit upon a thought and depressed the intercom call button.

"Would you please tell the General that Texas found Little Red?" he asked.

"Pardon, sir?"

"Tell General Maxwell that Texas found Little Red," Beckett said.

A few minutes later, the massive double doors to a library in the hacienda opened into an expanse of volumes from the classic works of literature, philosophy, and politics. Valuable works of art marshaled the mind toward other places and times, and an array of the memorabilia of war, collected from the points of the compass, were exhibited and shelved along three walls and upward into a second story, creating a cavernous effect upon the eye. Sunlight filtered into the room through the opaque dome of its turreted roof and scattered across specks of dust floating aimlessly in the air from the nearby open balcony doors. A stocky, middle-aged man entered quietly and approached a lone figure in a wheelchair on the library balcony. The exchange was awkward, but as the message was delivered, the man in the wheelchair thought for a moment and smiled.

Presently, Beckett walked into the sprawling library and addressed himself to the man in the wheelchair. Beckett was taken aback by the withered, broken shell before him.

"General Maxwell?"

Maxwell did not readily respond to Beckett's voice. He spoke, again, but with a different address.

"Texas to Lone Ranger, over," he said.

The older man looked about to find the voice. "Lone Ranger," he muttered. "That was my old call sign in the Marines. And... Texas. Are you Texas?"

"Roger that, sir," Beckett said crisply.

"Texas had a daughter; called her Little Red," Maxwell muttered.

"Roger that, sir. Texas has found Little Red, sir."

"Her mother… died," Maxwell said haltingly. "Buried her… but, never got the little girl, Little Red. Found her in Arkansas."

Maxwell looked up at Beckett blankly. "And, you say, Texas has found Little Red?"

"Roger that, sir," Beckett repeated.

The process was slow, at times infuriatingly so. But, over the course of the next hour, Beckett managed to bring Maxwell to a fundamental understanding of Beckett's identity. And, as Maxwell began to show flashes of prescience about the past, Beckett struggled to stitch them together into a narrative to address the identity of Ramon Pena y Reyna.

"El Borracho," Maxwell said with a laugh. "Damn fine shooter. I busted his ass out over a thing with an Afghani diplomat's daughter. She claimed he raped her. We parked him down in Mexico."

"You kept El Borracho tethered, like Texas," Beckett said. "But you let El Borracho game the system to become Joaquin de la Rosa."

"Never did like him much," Maxwell said with an addled frown. "He had a bad habit of playing with his food."

"Borracho played with his food, he had a relationship with his target?" Beckett asked the old man. "Wasn't that a no, no?"

Maxwell grinned; he was in the light of the moment. "They are usually bat crap crazy when they're like him. He had a thing for teenage girls, he liked them fresh. Made himself out as a ladies' man."

"After he was busted out, did El Borracho ever come up for air?" Beckett asked.

Maxwell shook his head and shrugged. "Don't know…"

The old man's expression became empty. He looked up at Beckett.

"Who'd you say you are?" Maxwell asked.

"I'm Texas and Texas found Little Red."

"Oh, yeah. I knew a kid by that handle," Maxwell said. "Made a helluva shot off Wonsan. We buried his wife… he never knew. But Little Red, he called the girl Little Red. She's somewhere in Arkansas, now."

The old man grew quiet as the blank stare overtook his face. Beckett lost him to the ether of the past. He sighed, frustrated by learning too little. Beckett gently rested his hand against Maxwell's shoulder, but the old man did not stir.

"Goodbye, General," he whispered.

As he turned away to leave, Maxwell's assistant entered the library. He acknowledged Beckett immediately.

"The old rounder doesn't easily take to anyone these days," he said quietly. "Ya musta put somethin' in his mind with that Texas and Little Red business."

The Australian aide turned aside to an ornately decorative liquor cabinet, unlocked the main cabinet and opened the doors to disclose an array of fine liquors. He removed two shot glasses from the cabinet.

"He takes a sip about this time each day," the Australian said. "Might I pour ya one?"

Beckett shook his head. "No, thanks. I need to get on the road."

But, as Beckett stepped away, something made him stop, an impression of shape and color. He turned back to the liquor cabinet as the Australian aide poured a shot of Bourbon whiskey from a distinctively shaped bottle with a uniquely colorful label.

Beckett reached across the liquor cabinet and grasped the bottle. "Where did you get this?" he asked insistently.

"Uhm, well, sir, if ya're to know. It was a gift to the General," the Australian replied. "Bloke came to call just before the General began to go down."

"A Hispanic man, tall, slender, and well-spoken?" Beckett asked. The aide nodded.

"What did they discuss?"

"Just stories about old times, as best I know, sir," the Australian said.

Beckett turned toward Maxwell, and his mind raced to consider a possibility, an incredible but distinct, possibility. But he was foreclosed to act as Maxwell's head was thrown backward by the force of the shot that tore away most of his skull. His lifeless body remained upright in the wheelchair on the balcony.

"Down," Beckett shouted.

They dove to the floor with the expectation of another shot which did not come. Beckett crawled to the balcony doorway and scanned the landscape through the wrought iron balcony railing.

"See anything, mate?" the Australian asked anxiously.

"Follow the line along the direction opposite Maxwell's head," Beckett said.

He waited for a long moment until the answer appeared in the distance.

"There…"

Beckett pointed toward a small ridge along the south boundary of the property where a sharp glint of sunlight burst into view, and it appeared to move from right to left and back again.

The Australian pulled himself beside Beckett on the balcony floor. "Crickey, that's up about a mile," he said.

The reflection in the distance bobbed up and down twice, as if to mimic a goodbye wave. Then, it disappeared. Beckett rolled onto his back and stood, and the Australian followed hesitantly.

"He's gone," Beckett said quietly. "He's done playing with his food."

CHAPTER THIRTY-SEVEN
YOU ARE GONNA SUFFER

The stillness in the library of the late General Pierpont Maxwell seemed otherworldly to Beckett, broken gently through the open balcony doorway by the call of wild mourning doves in the distance. Within moments of Maxwell's murder, his Australian retainer initiated a telephone call, which explained to Beckett an intimate understanding of the General's significance to someone else.

"Ya'd best not be here, mate," he warned Beckett as the Australian pocketed his cell phone.

Beckett nodded. "I'll find the shooter," he said with a cold determination.

"Give 'im one for me when ya do," the Australian said.

"Roger that," Beckett said.

Five minutes later, Beckett was in his Jeep and on the road out of Travis County, Texas. He drove until he turned onto Interstate 30 near Dallas. At a burger joint in Rockwall, he telephoned Nelson and told him the story.

"Holy Moses," Nelson said quietly. He spoke in a low, almost conspiratorial tone. "Does anybody know you were there?"

"Only the Aussie," Beckett replied. "And he made it clear, not only should I leave immediately, but also I was never there."

"This sounds like spook stuff," Nelson said.

"I expect the same forces were in play when my wife, Jolene, died," Beckett said. "As far as anyone will know, General Maxwell died of Alzheimer's in his sleep at his home. This is a deep food chain, Gunny."

"So, the shot on General Maxwell, you're sure it was Pena y Reyna?" Nelson asked.

"He knew I was there, Gunny. He waved goodbye to me with a scope reflection. Yeah, I'm next."

"That's why he hasn't shown up here in Destiny to take his shot," Nelson said. "General Maxwell was first on the schedule. Watch your six on the way into town, Captain."

"He's not a back shooter. That's not Borracho's style," Beckett said. "He has too much invested in the sniper nest at your ranch."

"Yeah, but he is certain to know we're onto him by now," Nelson replied. "Surely, he's changed his tactics."

"I don't think so, Gunny," Beckett said. "I think he wants to make a point, whether we know about him or not, he intends to use the nest on the bluff. I have to force his hand on my terms."

"So, how do you go about that?" Nelson asked.

"Frankly, I don't know," Beckett said. "I've got to figure it out before I get to Destiny."

"Stay gone for a couple of days, and let's see if anything looks hinky before you show up," Nelson said.

"That's no good," Beckett said. "I've got to be in class tomorrow..."

"Hey, I'm the school board president," Nelson insisted. "I can give you the time off. Besides, there is no school Friday because of the Winter Roundup this weekend."

Beckett chuckled. "Pulling rank on me, Gunny?"

"Dang straight."

Beckett turned the thought over in his mind, and it made sense. "Okay. Two days and I come back."

"Good deal."

Beckett pocketed his cell phone and stared at his burger and French fries. He had two days to figure out a man he had known briefly and by reputation for 14 years. Nelson, on the other hand, went into action as soon as he clicked off his cell phone. He grabbed his office phone and punched in a number.

"Yeah, hello, Wanda, darling; this is Lloyd Nelson over in Destiny," he said. "Is Frank in the office? I need a heavy-duty bulldozer and a couple of dump trucks."

Cissy took notice of Beckett's absence after their return from Investigator Goss' office in El Dorado. She intended to approach Nelson about it that morning but was pre-empted by his early departure for the store to take in merchandise for the upcoming Winter Roundup over the weekend. Cissy decided to ask about Beckett that afternoon when she reported to work at the store. Today, however, was taken up with important social responsibilities connected with Winter Roundup, the highlight of the post-Christmas commercial season in Destiny.

"It goes back to the pioneer days of Destiny, when lumber, cotton and cattle were shipped from the old port on the Ouachita River up where the Briggs' Clearwater Lodge is now," she explained to Beckett during the drive to El Dorado. It gave her a respite from thinking about the rape.

"Is there anything around Destiny without a Briggs connection?" Beckett asked.

Cissy laughed. "Hardly," she said. "Winter Roundup actually began with the Chesterton family rounding up all of its cattle and herding them through town up the road to the other side of the bridge at the far end of Center Street, and cross country up to the river."

"So, it's become more of a community event since then?" Beckett asked.

"It's our big festival," Cissy said. "There is a parade through town on Saturday that ends with a small herd driven through town just like the old trail drive. I usually ride with some of the ranch hands on the trail drive, but this year…"

"What?" Beckett asked.

Cissy blushed. "I'm the Winter Roundup Queen," she squealed. "So, I get to ride on the Winter Roundup float."

"Well, congratulations," Beckett said. "We have royalty in the family."

"You'll be there to see it, won't you?" Cissy asked anxiously.

Beckett smiled. "Nothing could keep me away."

Cissy reached over the front seat of the ranch pickup truck and wrapped her arms around his neck. "Cool," she murmured.

The conversation almost slipped Beckett's memory, and as he picked at his French fries, he recommitted himself to his promise. His mood turned sullen as Beckett remembered something Investigator Goss said.

"You stirred some big pots in the Middle East, Captain."

Beckett tinkered with a French fry. Each possibility Goss outlined led Beckett back to the same question: "Who turned El Borracho against the Maxwell team?"

"My favors told me the Russians had the most to gain back then," Goss offered. "ISIS wouldn't have sent a shooter; they'd have blown up your house. This feels personal, Captain Beckett."

Sleep escaped Beckett that night. He turned over in his motel room bed and stared into the suburban white noise lighting the night sky. And, for the briefest moment, Beckett longed desperately for the mountains of Afghanistan.

The landscape above the Ouachita River changed the following morning. The bluff nest was gone. The bluff was gone. Ramon Pena y Reyna was infuriated.

"So, he wants to play it that way," he muttered, surveying through his rifle scope the leveled ground where the bluff and his sniper's nest, once stood.

Pena y Reyna was forced to reconfigure the shot, a basic to the skill. But, El Borracho took such inconveniences as a personal affront.

"No head shot for you," he groused. "You are gonna suffer."

He scanned the timberline to the rear of the former bluff nest, the best line of sight to the original kill zone. The change added, perhaps, a hundred yards to the shot.

"Chingaua," Pena y Reyna spat. "I did you a favor and taught your chiquita to be a woman; and this is how you respect me?"

He retrieved a cell phone from his jacket and opened an internet application to find the main telephone number to the Travis

County, Texas, Sheriff's Department. He punched in the number and waited for a moment.

"Hello, es these the Travis County Sheriff's Department?" he said in a thickly rural Hispanic accent.

"Yes, sir. What is your complaint?"

"I don been workin' out en de road crew where at the big hacienda a man was killed," Pena y Reyna replied. He recited the address.

"Please explain, sir."

"I seen a man drive out from there in a kinda red lookin' Jeep about half a hour before a ambulance come and they take a man's body away," Pena y Reyna said. "De man en de Jeep, he driven out like a bat outta hell."

"Can you describe the man, sir?"

Pena y Reyna gave a meticulous description of Beckett. "And, your name, sir?" the dispatcher asked.

"Joaquin de la Rosa."

He gave a false address, thanked the dispatcher for her interest, and ended the call. Then, he dropped the cell phone to ground and pumped four rounds into it with a pistol. Pena y Reyna assumed Beckett would explain himself to the authorities once he was located. But Beckett would be tethered for a couple of days; enough time for Pena y Reyna to adapt.

Beckett felt the pressure soon enough when he stopped for gas in Sulphur Springs, Texas; his cell phone buzzed. He took the call; it was Goss.

"Where the hell are you, Beckett?" Goss asked.

"I'm at a gas station in Sulphur Springs, Texas," he replied. "Why do you ask?"

"Travis County, Texas, Sheriff's Department has a BOLO out for a Jeep that fits your vehicle and a suspect that fits your description," Goss said testily.

"A BOLO, why?"

"The complaint of a murder," Goss said.

Beckett sighed. "This is getting weirder by the day. You remember I told you I knew someone who might give us a lead on El Borracho?"

"Yeah; you said to give you a couple of days…"

"Well, I found him, and so did Pena y Reyna," Beckett said. "General Pierpont Maxwell, my former commanding officer, retired to a place off Lake Travis near Austin, Texas. I went to see him because I figured he was Pena y Reyna's former commander, as well as mine. And, I was right. Too much so. Borracho took him out with a shot from about a mile away while I was standing near the General."

"Seriously?" Goss blurted. "Well, did you learn anything before it happened?"

"Not much. The old man had Alzheimer's," Beckett said. "Look, Goss, this is all way above our pay grade, like you said, but it's something I have to deal with in my own way. I need you to give me that much time."

"Well, this BOLO isn't an arrest or detain; it's simply stop and question," Goss replied. "And I'm thinking it's because the Travis County people are about as confused as I am. You witnessed a murder, but didn't report it, and that is serious."

"But, I'm telling you, Goss, there won't be a body," Beckett said. "It's that kind of spooky, if you catch my meaning."

"Covert stuff?"

"Extremely so," Beckett said. "Goss, the man was a retired brigadier general, but nobody will ever know where he is buried, much less that he is dead. Do you understand?"

"Roger that, Captain," Goss said warily. "Roger that, but keep in touch."

"Will do," Beckett said, and he clicked off. He paid for his gas and wheeled out onto the street with a decision to make: turn back onto the interstate or travel cross country. He opted for the latter.

Beckett drove through Sulphur Springs headed north, then turned west at the far end of town. He eventually came to a crossroads at the rural community of Mahoney, where he turned back northward again for several miles before coming upon the hamlet of Dike. As the Jeep rolled past the small Church of Christ building, Beckett noticed an abandoned country store in the arc of the curve that bisected the little burg, and he let his Jeep glide into the gravel drive behind the building.

The weather turned wet, and Beckett decided the abandoned store was perfect for his needs. He retrieved a sleeping bag from the back seat, got out of the Jeep, and climbed a bank of steep concrete steps to the rear door of the building. The building's heyday was the Fifties or Sixties, closed for more than half a century, yet the sturdy construction and thick concrete foundation rendered the building surprisingly tight and comfortable against the cold of the encroaching nightfall.

Beckett surveyed the interior of the building for stray animals or rats, the metal merchandise shelving, long emptied, reflecting dull and gray against the beam of his flashlight. He found a suitable spot along the front of what had been the checkout counter and unrolled his sleeping bag out onto the wooden tongue and groove floor. Errant moonlight filtered into the room through the patina of time covering the windowpanes on both sides of the building, providing sufficient illumination for Beckett's purposes. He had bedded down in less commodious places. Beckett unzipped the sleeping bag and slid into it. There was little to do until morning except sleep.

CHAPTER THIRTY-EIGHT
SOMETHING FOR GOOD MEASURE

Raindrops from leaden clouds draping the interstate like parade bunting splattered against the windshield of the Jeep and reminded Beckett he drove into Destiny in the middle of a late summer thunderstorm a brief six months earlier. On that morning, he had notions of an idea. Now, he knew everything.

Sunlight broke across the landscape of South Arkansas as Beckett turned away from Interstate 30 at Hope and headed toward Ouachita County. He looked at the digital clock on the dash of the Jeep: 11:30 a.m. Beckett had half an hour before the start of the Winter Roundup parade.

"Man, Cissy's gonna be upset if I'm late."

Beckett felt the vibration of his cell phone in his jacket pocket. He retrieved it and looked at the screen; it was Nelson.

"Hey, Gunny," Beckett said. "What's the report?"

"Where are you, Captain?" Nelson asked. "I was expecting to see you by now."

"Detoured," Beckett said. "After El Borracho took out General Maxwell, I had to camp out in an abandoned country store near Sulphur Springs last night because someone called the cops on me after I left the General's place."

"Come again?"

Beckett retraced the events at Maxwell's hacienda in light of Goss' BOLO information. He attempted to put them into a context, as he explained it to Nelson, but pieces kept falling off the puzzle.

"It makes no sense, except in the larger picture of retaliation, taking out Maxwell and everyone associated with him," Beckett said. "But, it doesn't explain who put Borracho into play to do it, although my money is on the Russians."

"Did you get anything from Maxwell that might confirm it was the Russians?" Nelson asked.

"Negative," Beckett said. "He kept rambling about Jolene and Cissy; called her Little Red."

A question began to rise to the fore of Beckett's mind.

"How did you and Grace come to adopt Cissy?"

"Military family services," Nelson said. "Why?"

"I've often wondered how she wound up in Destiny," Beckett said.

"Yeah. And I've wondered how you came to Destiny, Captain," Nelson said.

"General Maxwell was a cagey cuss," Beckett said quietly. "Perhaps, he was too cagey. I think he might have led me to Destiny and Cissy."

Nelson snorted in disbelief. "What makes you think that?"

"Something Maxwell told me has bothered me," Beckett said. "I've always wondered whether he let me win that fight with him. It seemed in some ways too easy, and I'm beginning to think it's true."

"You're rambling, Captain," Nelson said with a clipped, military precision that brought Beckett back.

"Sorry, Gunny, but Maxwell referred more than once to burying Jolene, but when he spoke about Cissy, it was as though…"

"What, Captain?" Nelson asked testily. "It was as though… what? Exactly, what did Maxwell say about Cissy?"

Beckett's face flushed with understanding. "He said they never got her but found her in Arkansas. Lord…have…mercy; that's it. He led me to Cissy because they never got her. Gunny, Cissy is the target…"

"No… why? It makes no sense, Captain," Nelson said.

"It makes perfect sense, Gunny," Beckett shouted. "Maxwell wasn't killed because the Russians were retaliating. Maxwell was cleaning house. He found Cissy before I did. But, when I originally showed up and confronted him, he simply let me win the argument and put me together with Cissy to make the clean-up easier."

"But, Pena y Reyna took out Maxwell, Captain, that makes no sense," Nelson said.

"Yes, it does, Gunny," Beckett said. "The old man had Alzheimer's. He didn't want to go out that way. A quick shot to the head from a mile away was much easier for him. He never saw it coming, but knew it was coming… he committed suicide."

"No, no, no, no," Nelson growled. "Then, why didn't Borracho take you out at the same time?"

"Because he likes to play with his food, Gunny. It's the one thing which never made sense, but it does now. That's why he raped Cissy, why he made the ranging shot at the football field, and why he made the rookie reflection mistake when he had me cold on my front porch. Maxwell said Pena y Reyna is nuts that way. He plays with his food."

"Well, he can't make any shot now," Nelson said with a hint of satisfaction. "Problem solved, Captain."

"What did you do, Gunny?" Beckett asked anxiously.

"I called a contractor and had the bluff at the ranch bulldozed. El Borracho, or whoever he is, ain't got a nest anymore."

Beckett almost lost the wheel of the Jeep. "You did, what?" Then, he began to laugh, a low near-giggle that swelled into a full, breathless belly laugh.

"I gotta give you credit, Gunny," Beckett said. "It was a helluva idea; but it won't stop this guy. He's completely nuts."

"Damn," Nelson spat. "Cissy is supposed to ride in the Winter Roundup Parade in less than an hour. Where are you?"

"I'm turning off Highway 24. I'll be in town in five minutes," Beckett said. "You've got to get Cissy off that parade float."

"She has already left the house, and I'm on the other side of town," Nelson said anxiously. "We've got ten thousand people in town today."

"Call her cell phone, get your police chief, Harley Randle, to her. Just get her off that float."

"What are you gonna do, Captain?" Nelson asked.

"The only thing I can do," Beckett said somberly. "I'm going to make myself a moving target, and then, I'm gonna make an echo shot."

A long silence ensued from the other end of the conversation. "Good hunting, Captain," Nelson said resolutely.

"Thanks, Gunny…"

Beckett floored the gas pedal, and the Jeep careened ahead. Destiny was in view, but as he drew closer to town, Beckett realized the significance of Nelson's crowd estimate. There were people everywhere in the carnival-like atmosphere choking the view along Center Street. Beckett had no opportunity to get to Cissy in time to stop the parade. As he wheeled the Jeep away from the main street, Beckett prayed Nelson contacted her.

Cissy did what any teenager did when staying in contact was important. She turned off her cell phone.

"I don't want any distractions today," she told Marilee Paige as the two girls prepared for the parade. "I want to pick my dad out of the crowd and throw him a great big kiss."

The piercing wail of sirens from the west end of Center Street filled the air, as Nelson wheeled his pickup truck into the driveway at City Hall at the east end. He glanced at his watch: 11:58 a.m. Police Chief Harley Randle started the parade early. Nelson climbed out of the pickup and began to elbow his way through the crowd at the Nelson Street intersection. He tapped Randle's cell phone number into the keypad of his phone. There was no answer.

Nelson walked into the middle of the street and began waving his arms to stop the oncoming parade. But, three blocks away, Randle and his officers, along with the Destiny Volunteer Fire Department were tossing candy to the children along the parade route. Nelson broke into a trot down the middle of the street, his arms flailing frantically in the air. He was suddenly showered in shards of asphalt pavement exploding upward not six feet in front of him as he approached the Veterans' Memorial Park.

Nelson froze.

As thousands of eyes were turned westward toward the far end of Center Street, Nelson turned north. His eyes strained to peer into the distance across the park toward the timberline beyond the Ouachita River. He stood still, almost at attention, offering himself in his adopted daughter's place.

But there was no second shot.

Beckett's Jeep flew into Destiny behind the parade but with no time to stop it, he went cross country behind Fairway Lumber, plowing across back lawn fences, flower beds and driveways, jumping North Cross Street beyond the parking lot of the South Arkansas Bank, and barreling ahead across alleyways toward the Freemon Nelson Stadium parking lot behind Destiny High School. He almost ignored the ringtone of his cell phone, but he recognized Nelson's number and answered the call.

"I'm a little busy, now, Gunny," he shouted.

"He's here, Captain," Nelson said in a tense stage whisper.

Beckett glanced away from the Jeep's carnage briefly to see his friend standing in the middle of Center Street at the city park, with the parade flotilla slowly bearing down upon him. He floored the gas pedal and the Jeep raced ahead.

"Where is he, Gunny?"

"Somewhere in the timber on our side of the river, I think," Nelson said. "He stopped me with a ranging shot into the pavement. He has his range, so he has to be somewhere in the line of sight with the city park where I'm standing."

Beckett cursed as the middle of the Jeep's roof tore away and the glass in the passenger door shattered. He shook his head to clear away the effects of the concussion.

"What's wrong, Captain?" Nelson asked.

"He's after me, Gunny," Beckett laughed. "It was always a parade, like we said: Occum's Razor."

"Say, again, Captain…"

"William of Occum, Fourteenth Century philosopher, said, 'Among all the possibilities the simplest is most likely true,'" Beckett said. "We thought this was a parade shot. Now, we know. So, I'll give him a parade to shoot at."

He swung the Jeep around the corner of the elementary school building and barreled through the closed bus yard gate at the stadium as another round smashed into the Jeep's engine. Beckett bore down on the brakes to bring the vehicle to a long, skidding stop behind the east end of the home football grandstand. He grimaced from the pain inflicted by the small shards of metal and glass embedded into his scalp and arms. Beckett recovered himself and reached behind the driver's seat, depressed a switch beneath the rear seat and the seat cushion popped up to disclose a storage unit with a rectangular gun case inside. He retrieved the gun case, closed the seat cushion and put the case atop it. Inside the case was a disassembled XM107 Long Range Sniper Rifle and three ammunition magazines.

Beckett's hands moved as though they had second-sight, and within moments, the rifle was assembled, loaded and mounted to a collapsible tripod. He secured the scope to the rifle, clambered out of the Jeep, and began to stalk along the rear of the stadium. He stayed low once he reached the east end of the grandstand. Beckett studied the sky for a moment. The district championship pennants hanging on the playing field flagpole were rippling toward the north on a mild breeze.

"He's shooting against the wind…"

The sounds of the festival parade drew closer from the west, pushing Beckett toward a decision. He crept back to the Jeep and retrieved a tire iron from beneath the driver's seat. Beckett slid the tire iron beneath his belt, pirate style, and returned to the east end of the grandstand. He waited for a moment, as a cloud drifted across the sun, and he used the shadow to scurry up the steps and into the home side stands, darting up the steps to the top of the stadium, and across the top row to the door of the home side press box.

Beckett pulled the tire iron from his belt, inserted the flat end against the door latch, pried open the door with a single motion and dove inside. He stayed low as the top of each of the press chairs in front of him blew apart in succession while he made his way to the rooftop filming deck stairs. Beckett climbed the stairs, slid the filming deck door open, and peered northward. Crouching on the landing, he slid his rifle onto the deck and crawled out onto the filming deck. The safety rail footing across the front of the filming deck made a suitable rest for the front of his rifle tripod. Beckett settled himself against the deck floor, to reconnoiter his shot.

He retrieved his cell phone from his pants pocket, and tapped in Nelson's number. "Where are you, Captain?" Nelson asked.

"Rooftop of the press box at the stadium," Beckett said. "Start walking and stop the parade."

"That first shot was within six feet, Captain. I'd say he has his range."

"He's not after you, Gunny, but the further Cissy is from your position…"

"Roger that," Nelson interjected. "Make him change his shot,"

"He's been lighting me up so, I can triangulate back to him," Beckett said.

"Good hunting," Nelson said. He put away his cell phone and turned back to the oncoming parade.

Cissy saw Nelson standing in the middle of the street, waving his arms. She rolled her eyes in embarrassment. She stood to make a perfunctory wave back when Chief Randle noticed Nelson standing in the middle of the street, waving frantically, and the lawman brought the parade to a halt.

Nelson ran to Randle's car. "Keep the parade stopped while I get Cissy off that float," he ordered.

"What's going on, Mayor?"

"Just, do it, Harley," Nelson shouted as he turned away from the car.

Randle got out of the car and stood there, as the fire chief dismounted the city's ladder truck, and other drivers called out about the delay. "Mayor's orders," Randle shouted.

Beckett studied the timberline beyond the site of the original sniper nest for more than five minutes without any success. He was becoming worried. He never sweated before taking a shot; but now the palms of his hands felt faintly moist, and the back of his neck was chilled by the breeze. Beckett waited.

The pigeons which normally roosted atop the arched façade at the vacant Dolly's Antiques and Notions scattered as the body of one of the flock blew apart. A few seconds later, one of the Nelson Ranch bulls leading the Roundup herd was thrown to the ground in a bloodied heap. The crowd along the parade route realized something was terribly wrong, and the parade began to collapse into chaos.

Nelson stood powerless as he saw the terror spread. People stampeded into the nearby stores for cover as he forced his way through the flow and bounded onto the pickup truck tethered to the queen's float.

"You girls get into the truck and stay low," he shouted.

"What's happening?" Cissy cried out.

Nelson looked across the float and into her eyes with a knowing regard. She gasped.

"He's here, isn't he?" Cissy shrieked.

Nelson nodded. He clambered across the float, grabbed her arm, and pulled her to the side of the platform. They jumped to the ground and Cissy herded Roundup princesses into the rear of the four-seater as Nelson kicked the truck's trailer hitch free, and the float nosed to the asphalt noisily. Nelson ordered the driver into the front passenger seat, as Nelson slid behind the wheel. Terrified festivalgoers fled in every direction around them as Nelson guided the pickup truck backward to Fairway Lumber Co., where they drove into the bulk lumber shed, surrounding the truck with stacks of lumber.

Nelson turned to Cissy. "You're in charge of keeping everybody together. I've got to try to restore some order."

"Be careful, Dad," Cissy said. She reached for him as he opened the pickup door. "Where is Daddy Brock?"

Nelson grimaced. He looked into her eyes and gave Cissy's hand an assuring squeeze.

"Your father is taking care of business."

Three blocks away atop the stadium press box, Beckett focused his scope high into the trees on the near side of the Ouachita River timberline. His moving target gambit gave Pena y Reyna too tempting a target. Becket quickly calculated the trajectory of his adversary's shots into the press box.

"Nice nest for a vulture."

Beckett drew a deep breath, then rolled away toward the press box door, rifle in hand. A chunk of the press box safety rail footing flew apart. Beckett shook his head, and pulled a wooden splinter from his cheek.

"Come on, hombre, one more time," he growled.

Beckett rolled back onto his stomach, positioned his rifle at the damaged section of footing, and put his shooting eye to the rifle scope. Pena y Reyna sipped from a bottle of his signature bourbon, then positioned for a second shot.

"Cocky SOB, aren't you?" Beckett muttered.

Beckett locked into his adversary's position. A thought more akin to a definition than an action flashed through Beckett's mind. Something Loretta Chesterton said. Beckett drew a deep breath and held it, then he squeezed away a round.

The question of response resting upon Pena y Reyna's mind was fully realized at the same time as excruciating pain invaded his left arm. He looked down to see his hand, and the bourbon bottle it held, both gone. Driven by an arrogant anger that numbed shock, Pena y Reyna nestled his shooting eye against his rifle scope, and rested his finger beside the trigger. El Borracho never fired. He saw the muted flash of Beckett's rifle muzzle, but not the bullet that shattered his rifle scope, his eye, his skull… and his life.

Beckett rolled onto his back and closed his eyes against the brilliance of the sunlight above him.

"Lagniappe," he whispered. "Something for good measure."

The ensuing months were chaotic as explanations were manufactured. Beckett was exonerated by a court martial and the Ouachita County Grand Jury for acting in defense of civilian lives against a terrorist threat. Beckett's AWOL status was removed, and he was honorably discharged from the U. S. Naval Reserve. Jolene was given a family burial provided by Lloyd and Grace Nelson. And General (ret.) Pierpont Maxwell's military record was sealed in exchange for a lifetime annuity for Cissy from the Maxwell Family Trust. Construction of the Yashuma Fabric Company project started at the first of the year, and the tendrils of a nascent evil began to grow quietly in Destiny, Arkansas.

The rains which greeted the day at the start of the new school term in August had not abated all day. Beckett drove his new Jeep Cherokee from the faculty parking lot onto Center Street, where he stopped and waited. Presently, a girl pushed open one of the double doors at the high school building's main entrance. She could not have been more than seventeen, but she was gorgeous, the right kind of gorgeous.

Beckett switched off the engine and sat silently, watching as the girl looked out into the rain. He opened the passenger door and honked the Jeep's horn. The girl jerked about with a start and immediately saw the Jeep with the passenger door ajar. Beckett waved and smiled.

"Come on," he shouted. "I'll take you home."

"Maybe, I don't know you from Adam," the girl said. "You might be a pervert."

"I might be your father," Beckett called back.

Cissy bolted through the rain and into the Jeep. She shook back her mane of auburn hair and laughed.

"I might be your daughter," Cissy murmured as she hugged Beckett.

"Yeah, now wouldn't that be something special?" Beckett said. "Just you and me, kiddo."

Beckett put the Jeep into reverse and drove away from the school campus. The Jeep rolled out of town on North Cross Street and a few minutes later glided through the main gate at the Nelson Ranch. The Jeep swung away onto the lane toward the cabin on the bank of the Ouachita River and stopped at a mailbox that read: *Lagniappe*.

THE END

Acknowledgements

Producing a novel is not a hermitic exercise, it requires help. And I appreciate the help I've received, including the patient shepherding of publisher Shannon Christensen of CS Publications. The careful editing of Pam Kumpe, an experienced author who knows her way around a sentence, shaped the narrative and kept it within the lines of genuine expectations. And the design talents of cover artist Randi Gammons have created a mood and atmosphere that are arresting to the eye and compelling to the mind. Finally, there is the Golden Quill Writers Guild, a dedicated group of authors learning to improve their skills and providing resources for one another to bring concepts to reality without which I would only stare at a blank computer screen.

About the Author

K. D. McLemore retired from a 30-year career in newspaper journalism in 2022 but never retired from writing. Capping an award-winning tenure as editor of the *Hope Star* with investigative work that mattered and extensive courts and trial coverage, McLemore lives in Hope, Ar., with his wife of 50 years, Carolyn, an avid mystery reader. A native of Texas, graduate of Baylor University, and dedicated "classic rock and roll" fan, McLemore is known for his attention to detail in work that reflects life as people live it and its sometimes -fantastic consequences. *Lagniappe* is McLemore's debut novel, which introduces The Destiny Arkansas Series of eight works that arise from the response of Destiny's residents to a corrupting evil that threatens the soul of the small, rural Arkansas community.

Author's Note

Popular fiction often derives plot lines and characters from current events. It is not the author's intent to knowingly represent any similarities in story lines or character development as true in fact or person beyond the reasonably acceptable norms of literary fiction concerning persons living or dead and known events. No character in this work is knowingly based in fact or person upon any person living or dead beyond what is known generally of public figures living or dead.

About the Artist

Randi Gammons is a freelance graphic designer from Northeast Texas. She has a passion for layout, typography, branding, and all things print. She specializes in book cover design and loves working with selfpublished authors, bringing their works to life.

Since graduating in 2019 from Southern Arkansas University with a bachelor's degree in graphic design and starting her freelance business, Randi has worked with a variety of clients from all over the world and has designed over 120 book covers. Some of her works include the Mountain Man's Substitute Bride multiauthor collection, The Underground Book Readers series, and The Journeys Of Braven series.

As a designer, she is very self-driven, and strives to do everything to the best of her abilities, even in small tasks. One of the things she loves most about design is there is always something new to learn whether it's in the design field or doing research for a project. When not creating, Randi enjoys spending time with her family, watching T.V., or curling up with a good book.

Referenced Works

Published works in this novel referenced, mentioned by title, or used by limited quotation include the following:
The Bible, King James Version.

Giant, Copyright 1952, by Edna Ferber, Doubleday and Company, Publisher, Garden City, New York.

Giant (film), from the novel by Edna Ferber, Warner Brothers, Produced by George Stevens and Henry Ginsberg, Screenplay by Fred Guiol and Ivan Moffat, Distributed by Warner Brothers, Released October 10, 1956, New York City.

Gone with the Wind, Copyright 1936, The Macmillan Company, New York, Author Margaret Mitchell. Renewed Copyright 1964, Stephens Mitchell and Trust Company of Georgia as Executors of Margaret Mitchell Marsh, Copyright renewed 1964 by Stephens Mitchell. Currently held in partnership through the Eugene Mitchell Trust with the Roman Catholic Archdiocese of Atlanta, Atlanta, Ga., William Morris Entertainment as Agents.

Gone with the Wind (film), from the novel by Margaret Mitchell, Selznick International Pictures/Metro-Goldwyn-Meyer, Produced by David O. Selznick, Screenplay by Sidney Howard, Distributed by Lowe's Incorporated, Released December 15, 1939, Atlanta, Ga.

Roots, Copyright 1976, Alex Haley, Doubleday and Company, Publisher.
Texas, Copyright 1985, James A. Michener, Random House, Publisher.

To Kill a Mockingbird, Copyright 1960, Harper Lee, J.B. Lippincott Company, Philadelphia and New York Publishers.